ALSO BY WALT GRAGG

The Red Line
The Chosen One

"A superb political as well as military thriller, *The Red Line* stitches an all-too-plausible doomsday scenario that pulls no punches in scoring a literary knockout. Terrifyingly prescient in its premise and scarily spot-on in its execution, Walt Gragg's debut novel channels both Tom Clancy and W.E.B. Griffin."

—Jon Land, *USA Today* bestselling author
of *Strong Cold Dead*

THE
LONG
NOVEMBER

WALT GRAGG

BERKLEY

NEW YORK

BERKLEY
An imprint of Penguin Random House LLC
penguinrandomhouse.com

Library of Congress Cataloging-in-Publication Data

Names: Gragg, Walt, author.
Title: The long November / Walt Gragg.
Description: First edition. | New York: Berkley, 2024.
Identifiers: LCCN 2023031473 (print) | LCCN 2023031474 (ebook) |
ISBN 9781984806352 (trade paperback) | ISBN 9781984806369 (ebook)
Subjects: LCGFT: Thrillers (Fiction) | Novels. Classification:
LCC PS3607.R3326 L66 2024 (print) | LCC PS3607.R3326 (ebook) |
DDC 813/.6—dc23/eng/20230717
LC record available at https://lccn.loc.gov/2023031473
LC ebook record available at https://lccn.loc.gov/2023031474

First Edition: May 2024

Printed in the United States of America
1st Printing

Book design by George Towne

To my wonderful grandchildren, Adan, Alan,
Ethan, Ava, Alison, and Grayson.

May a fulfilling life find each of you.

Man has no need to fear any future hell.
For by his actions he has created his own in the here and now.

WALT GRAGG

Marine captain Samuel Erickson stood watching as the loading of the King Stallions began in earnest. In the swirling dust and consuming darkness of a nearly moonless night, the company commander observed the expanding activity around the six widely spaced CH-53K cargo helicopters. At India's insistence, before arriving, any identifying information on the King Stallions had been painted over, masking what they were and to whom they belonged.

Groups of recently roused men rushed in every direction. For many, a fitful sleep still clung to their eyes. Each was gathering weapons of war and depositing them near the noisy craft. Anxious directives from their platoon and squad leaders filled the air. All understood that if they were going to prevail in their desperate attempt, little time remained. An hour at most before the Marine Company's incursion inside Pakistan had to begin.

They'd arrived on the previous night and been secreted away in a desolate portion of the Indian air base. They weren't supposed to be here. And India's government strongly desired to keep the Americans' presence secret. Nonetheless, given the severity of the situation, they'd reluctantly agreed to allow them onto their country's soil. Even if only briefly.

Erickson had been told his men were to be the backup portion of the American rescue plan. In all likelihood they wouldn't be needed. The situation called for them to remain sequestered at the air base for no more than a couple of days prior to being airlifted out of the country. They were to sit on their packs and wait for word to come. Only if things went unforeseeably wrong would they be called into action. They were to be ready but could anticipate doing nothing more than sweating beneath an unrelenting Indian sun before being withdrawn.

Yet, to their surprise, things in Islamabad had, in fact, gone awry. And Erickson had received the frantic call to action. With little notice, he was readying his men to rush headlong into the middle of a vicious civil war that already had claimed millions of lives. While they prepared to depart, the secrecy of the operation was of paramount importance. They couldn't risk the rampaging jihadists across the border being warned of their activities.

The first of the company's lethal up-armored Humvees eased up the rear ramp and disappeared into the belly of the foremost helicopter. Under the King Stallion senior crew chief's direction, it edged forward to the front of the hold and settled into place. Before its driver could turn off the engine, the aircraft's pair of crew chiefs began securing the combat-ready vehicle in preparation for the coming flight. Soon a trio of Humvees would be nestled inside each of the six large helicopters. The company's men would then bring on board the heavy machine guns, mortars, Javelin and TOW antitank missiles, ammunition, medical supplies, rations, and materials needed to support the company's men for up to a week of intense combat. The list was nearly endless. When filled, each heavily laden transport would contain three Humvees, stacks of boxes and equipment, and up to thirty men.

As the pace quickened, the company's executive officer, Scott Tomlin, approached Erickson's position. The first lieutenant's somber face carried the uneasiness each of the Marines felt.

Erickson had to shout to be heard over the helicopters' droning engines and the frenetic activity around them. "Scott, I know we've had little time to prepare for whatever it is we're walking into, but have you been able to brief the platoon leaders and platoon sergeants?"

"Yes, sir," Tomlin replied. "I've gone over the situation and laid out each platoon's role. As soon as we're airborne, they'll brief their squad leaders and men. With things evolving so quickly, even with the embassy's Marine security detachment doing their best to establish a semblance of control over the landing zone, when we get to Islamabad, I've directed our men to treat this as a hot landing and to be prepared for any eventuality."

"Good. I don't want any slipups. We need to be ready for whatever it is we're about to face."

"I've made your expectations clear. Once we're on the ground, 1st and 2nd Platoon will form on the roadway south of the embassy. At the same time, a squad from 3rd Platoon will establish a perimeter while the remainder of the company empties the King Stallions. As each helicopter's unloaded, we'll fill it with the first of the waiting civilians and get them headed back here."

"That should work," the dark-haired Marine commander replied. "I've spoken with the King Stallion flight leader. He said on each round trip his six CH-53s can handle four hundred or so of those we're evacuating."

"When we arrive I'll make sure the embassy folks are briefed on that, sir," Tomlin said.

"The King Stallion flight leader's confident that after the four hundred evacuees are unloaded, there'll be adequate time remaining for his crews to fill each CH-53 with all the food and water each can carry. Once they have, they'll head back to Islamabad, dump their loads, and pick up a second four hundred of those fleeing Pakistan. So if all goes well, we should be able to get eight hundred out of harm's way before the sun rises."

"If we can pull it off, freeing eight hundred from this mess in the first few hours is a pretty good start, sir."

"Yeah, but that'll be it for tonight. Given the circumstances, there'll be no possibility of evacuating more until tomorrow evening. With what we're going to be facing, attempting daylight excursions would be suicidal. So it'll be up to us to hold off the crazies while waiting for night to arrive once more. Even with darkness masking our actions, each rescue attempt's going to be iffy."

"How many flights do the pilots estimate we can get in each night, sir?" Tomlin asked.

"Given the distance, along with the loading and unloading at both locations, we're estimating four hours for each round-trip. That means if things go perfectly, the helicopters will be able to complete three rescues before each night ends."

"So we're looking at twelve hundred escaping this nightmare prior to every sunrise. That doesn't sound too bad. Have we received a count on how many people are waiting in Islamabad?"

"Not an accurate one. When I spoke to the embassy security detachment's gunny, he said they didn't know exactly what we'll be facing numbers-wise. So we're going to have to play it by ear until we've gathered everyone and can make an actual determination. We know we're going to have to evacuate the staffs and families from multiple embassies along with the four thousand civilians waiting at the Islamabad Marriott."

"So maybe five or six thousand, sir?" The concern in Tomlin's voice was unmistakable.

"Sounds about right. But even that number might be a bit low."

For the first time, the company's executive officer began to comprehend the enormity of the situation. "Six thousand people butchered in the most hideous of ways if Salim Basra and his fanatics get their hands on them."

"That's not going to happen, Scott. Not if we have anything to say about it. Until the final person's on these King Stallions, it'll be up to us to make sure those people are safe. Is that understood?"

"Absolutely, sir."

"You need to make sure our men realize what we're up against. We're going to save as many of those people as we can, but there's no way this is going to be easy. Even if things go off without a hitch, we're looking at at least five days of intense combat against thousands upon thousands of hell-bent assassins before the last of us reboards these helicopters and gets the hell out of Pakistan. And you know as well as I do that in these situations things rarely go as planned. So don't be surprised if this ends up taking a week, possibly longer."

The rock-hard Tomlin's jaw clenched. He took a look around. There was determination in his response. "This company contains some of the finest Marines I've ever been associated with, sir. I don't care what the enemy throws at us, we'll handle it. And we'll save those people."

"For that to happen, while I'm leading 1st and 2nd Platoons to the Marriott, it's imperative you get the embassy's defenses laid out and our preparations underway."

"I'll start on them the moment we touch down, sir. Any chance of reinforcements arriving?"

"Not anytime soon. With the limits India has placed upon us, we're all there is. And these six are all of the King Stallions they allowed us to bring. So this is on us. We've got to take advantage of every break to have any chance of succeeding. With the enemy closing in, you can anticipate being under attack long before the helicopters return tomorrow evening to pick up further evacuees."

"What about air support, sir?"

"For now, we have none. The president has decided that unless the Pakistani leadership fully commits to us joining their efforts, he wants to do everything he can to stay out of this war. The only involvement he's willing to risk is the rescue of all non-Pakistanis trapped in Islamabad. Beyond that, the United States is officially neutral in what he's calling the Pakistani people's 'internal struggles.'"

"Understood, sir."

"But tomorrow, who knows? This really is an evolving situation. Worse come to worst, that directive might change if those we're protecting are in extreme peril or our government finds itself with little choice but to get further involved. That's a call higher-ups tell me he'll make if and when he needs to."

"Yes, sir."

"Then let's make this happen, Scott."

The fleeting minutes rushed past as the company's scrambling efforts continued without pause. Finally, all was ready. With the Humvees and equipment in place, the battle-tested Marines shuffled on board.

First Sergeant Claude Vickers stood watching as the last of the 175 men, all in full combat gear, silently headed up the rear ramps. "We're all set, sir," he relayed to the company commander.

As Erickson walked toward the lead King Stallion, he took a final look around. He'd done his best in the brief interval he'd been given. He had what appeared to be a viable rescue plan. Yet, given his unfamiliarity with the terrain and the exceptionally volatile situation in Islamabad, he realized in the coming hours that even the best of approaches couldn't anticipate what his stoic force might encounter. There were bound to be surprises and split-second, life-defining decisions to be made. For all he knew, by the time they arrived in the Pakistani capital, hordes of jihadists could be swarming over both the hotel and the United States embassy. Each compound could be fully engulfed in flames, with no chance of escape at either location.

As he took his spot in the windowless hold, the ramp began to close.

The company commander's mind was racing. He'd been in tough spots before, but this mission was one that could challenge him beyond even his immense limits. He had to wonder what horrors might be waiting. He had to question whether his unit would arrive in time to change a horrific destiny for thousands upon thousands of anxious people. Little did he know that the woman he'd fallen in love with three years earlier during another desperate struggle was among those waiting. If he had, his growing concern might have overwhelmed him.

One by one, the helicopters rose into the blackness and roared toward the west.

They'd hug the broad valleys and wide plateaus. They'd skim the rugged, snow-encrusted mountain passes to evade detection by both the surging terrorists and any rogue elements of the Pakistani military. From this moment on, their lives would be on the line.

It was 12:01 a.m.

For the onrushing Marines, the first fateful moments of November had arrived.

2

As Sam Erickson's men started loading the King Stallions, in Islamabad the United States embassy's regional diplomatic security officer, Steven Gray, and Marine Gunnery Sergeant Eric Joyce, walked into the ambassador's office.

Alan Ingram was waiting. After his wife's recent death from lymphatic cancer, he'd used the immense requirements of his position to hide from his all-consuming sorrow. With three decades of experience in some of the most dangerous places in the world, the stately American, his dark hair turning gray, was every inch the consummate professional needed for this critical posting. As Pakistan devolved into madness, his country had the right man in the right place with the distinguished Ingram. He could be counted on for a cool head and keen judgment no matter how difficult the situation became.

"Well? Are the rumors true?" he asked the moment the pair entered the room.

Gray and Joyce glanced at each other. The disturbing

developments they were about to convey were written across their features.

"It's confirmed, Mr. Ambassador," Gray replied. "The Marine Security Augmentation Force, along with the armada of commercial airliners they were escorting, turned around and headed back to Germany an hour ago. The Pakistani forces guarding the Islamabad airport have been overwhelmed in a massive attack by the insurgents. The jihadists are in firm control of every inch of the place. Once they seized it, they blew huge craters in the runways. There's no longer a possibility of even a single plane reaching us, sir. Any attempt to do so would be suicidal."

The ambassador couldn't mistake the significance of what he was being told. Their well-planned escape route had fallen into enemy hands. Until this moment, he'd thought their efforts to evacuate all non-Pakistanis in the next few hours would be accomplished with little or no loss of life. In an instant that belief had changed. An exceptionally difficult situation was becoming an impossible one.

Gray could see the recognition in the ambassador's eyes. Without pausing, he continued to brief the embassy's leader. The sooner Ingram understood the gravity of the situation, the sooner they could get his approval for what they had in mind. "Many of the explosions you hear are those half-crazed idiots blowing up everything they found waiting on the tarmac," Gray added. "Our sources tell us they've already destroyed the control tower, all of the landing lights, and every plane they found sitting on the ground. The passenger terminal's little more than smoldering rubble."

"Our original plan's gone, Mr. Ambassador," Joyce added. "And the alternative idea we discussed about escaping overland is out of the question. Even if we had enough vehicles to pull it off, all roads south are cut off—or will be shortly."

Ingram hesitated. Still, he did everything he could to remain calm and businesslike, masking the panic welling within him. "What're our alternatives?"

"To be honest, sir, with the sudden turn of events," Gray said, "we're kind of making things up as we go. But the pieces of a makeshift rescue are starting to come together. Understand, however, that what we're going to attempt isn't perfect. Yet, given the likelihood that the embassy will be surrounded by thousands upon thousands of enraged zealots well before morning, it appears to be our best chance."

"We've notified the Marine infantry company waiting in India," Joyce added. "They're getting organized and preparing to load onto six transport helicopters. So there should be an entire company of combat-experienced Americans headed our way shortly. They have a decent understanding of what they're going to find here and are attempting to load as much firepower onto their King Stallions as they possibly can."

As Joyce finished speaking, like the paralyzing tremors that follow a massive earthquake, another huge explosion, its distance and direction indeterminable, rattled the stout compound's thick walls and reinforced windows. Another of Islamabad's modern office buildings had been destroyed. A reactive fear flashed in each man's eyes. With this latest blast, there could be no denying how desperate things were becoming.

The terrifying explosion finally fading, the ambassador asked, "Any word on when they're taking off?"

"They're planning on leaving Spinager Air Base within the hour," Joyce said. "That should put their CH-53Ks on the ground here around one thirty. I've been in contact with the company commander and briefed him on the tactical situation. He was my platoon leader in North Africa during the Pan-Arab War, so I know him quite well. His men will be exceptionally well trained and ready for any eventuality."

"Glad to hear it, Sergeant Joyce. Until we find a way out of this mess, hopefully they'll be able to defend the embassy no matter what the lunatics throw at us."

"I've little doubt they'll sure as hell try, sir."

"Okay. With the change of plans, my next question has got to be what're we doing about rescuing those waiting at the Marriott?"

"Plan's still the same, Mr. Ambassador," Joyce replied. "The only difference is that, with the augmentation force headed back to Germany, Captain Erickson's men will be taking over that role. The moment they land and get organized, he'll take two of his platoons and the majority of his Humvees and head for the hotel. The remainder will stay here and begin setting up defensive positions around the embassy. Because of how massive this place is, there's going to be a great deal of ground to cover."

"With the Fedayeen Islam moving so quickly, are you positive those at the hotel will be safe until we can reach them?" Ingram asked.

"Given how things are evolving, we can't be sure of anything, sir. But at least for the moment they should be," Joyce answered. "Should things deteriorate faster than we anticipate, we may have to adjust our plans. For now, we believe the thirty soldiers the British sent over there this afternoon should be able to defend the hotel against any scattered jihadist units wandering into their path. Should a large-scale force appear, however, that'll be another story. Just be aware we can't be certain the British will be able to hold off significant attacks from hundreds or even thousands of Basra's diehards. Still, both the British embassy and Captain Erickson are in agreement that four thousand unarmed civilians stumbling around in the fog in the middle of this is a risk we'd rather not take."

"All right, then. If you're comfortable with waiting to evacuate the hotel until the reinforcements reach us, I'll defer to your judgment. Hopefully, it won't take too long after the Marines touch down to undertake the rescue mission. The last thing I want is to idly stand by while so many innocent people are slaughtered."

"Yes, sir."

The ambassador let out a deep sigh. "I'll be a whole lot happier when I see the folks from the Marriott walking through our gates."

"So will we, sir," Gray responded.

"Our embassy staff and their families and the four thousand non-Pakistanis gathered at the hotel shouldn't even be here now," Ingram replied. "The president should've listened and let us evacuate all nonessential personnel the moment the war between Pakistan and India began. I warned him there was no way this would end well, but he didn't want us to appear to be taking India's side and abandoning our mission in Pakistan."

"Yes, sir," Gray said. "You really can't blame him much. No one foresaw such a rapid turn of events. Who would've thought we'd find ourselves in such a predicament in little more than a handful of weeks? And none of the other embassies reacted in time, either. They're all in the same predicament we are."

"I know, but that only makes matters worse. Do you realize what the Fedayeen will do when they capture what remains of the city? There's no chance they'll show even a moment's mercy. Every foreigner they get their hands on, whether they be man, woman, or child, will be put to the sword."

"No doubt, sir," Gray answered. "That's why we've already reached out to the nearby embassies' security folks and informed them of the situation. When they learned the original escape plan was no longer viable, they were eager to accept our invitation to withdraw from their compounds and consolidate their efforts here."

"All but the Chinese and Russians, that is," Joyce added. "Each refused the invitation to join us. Tried to reason with them, but both were convinced the Fedayeen will consider them friendly countries and take no action against them."

"Given what our intelligence folks know about Salim Basra, there's not a chance that's going to happen," Ingram said.

"We know, sir," Gray said. "We did our best to make that clear, but it was no use."

"If it would do any good, I'd try to change their ambassadors' minds. But it'd just be a waste of time and we have far greater things to worry about. Have any of the folks from the other embassies arrived yet?" the ambassador asked.

"No, sir," Joyce replied. "The first should be headed our way shortly."

"So tell me more about this new evacuation plan of yours."

"Our idea's certainly not perfect, Mr. Ambassador," Gray said. "Yet, given the circumstances, it's going to have to do. Even with as large as our compound is, with all the buildings spread out across it, there's not nearly enough open space to bring in six huge helicopters," Gray said. "We'd be lucky to find an adequate location to land even one. So we're going to have the King Stallions land on the roadway south of the embassy grounds and the parking lot outside the western wall. Sergeant Joyce's detachment will secure the area once word arrives they're near. After the Marines have unloaded their equipment, we'll begin filling the helicopters with as many of the families of our embassy staffers and those of the neighboring embassies as we can. They'll race back to India. After a quick refueling and a refilling of their holds, the helicopters are going to return once more to drop off further supplies and take on a second load of women and children. So if all goes as planned, we should be able to evacuate a significant number of people by morning. That, however, will probably be the extent of it for tonight. We'll have to wait for tomorrow's nightfall before beginning the process anew."

"We'll keep going, bringing in the helicopters each night loaded with whatever we need to sustain ourselves and taking people out until the last of us leaves this place," Joyce explained. "With a bit of determination and luck, maybe we'll be able to hold off the bastards long enough for most to escape unharmed."

"With Basra's uncountable legions heading this way, it's going to take far more than that, I'm afraid," the ambassador replied. "Even so, let's hope for a successful escape for all of us."

"For that to happen, even with a company of Marines to support us, we're going to need to create the stoutest defenses possible around the embassy grounds," Gray pointed out.

"Steven, have you identified how many of the embassy's staff and the CIA's folks have military or weapons training?"

"Yes, sir," the recently divorced, retired Army officer said. "There are fifty or so. They're presently filling sandbags and taking them out to create a network of bunkers in the trees outside our walls. As soon as we've finished here, I'm going to begin handing out M4s and assigning defensive positions. Once the jihadists get close, I plan on leaving my force to guard the area closest to the embassy while the Marines take up forward positions around the compound. Any forces the other embassies show up with will be integrated into those defenses."

"That'll help, Mr. Ambassador," Joyce noted, "but it won't solve all of our problems, unfortunately. Even as big as our embassy grounds are, there's no way we can shelter everyone inside these walls. Still, if we put our heads together, we should be able to come up with something viable. We've emptied the diplomatic enclave in preparation for leaving for the airport, sending everyone to their embassies late this afternoon. If we're going to fit all these people in, we'll have to fill its apartment buildings again. That'll greatly increase the area we'll need to defend. But it's probably the only way we can find space for everyone."

"So, after the evacuation of the hotel and the nearby embassies, how many people do you estimate we'll need to shelter?" the ambassador asked.

There was a lull in the conversation as Gray and Joyce went over the numbers in their heads.

"Rough guess . . . maybe six thousand," Gray said. "But if we use both our buildings and the enclave next door, we should be able to squeeze everybody in."

"Six thousand . . . Have either of you thought about what we're going to do for food for so many people?" Ingram asked. "There's not enough in our kitchen to feed that many even a single meal, let alone for the days that follow."

"We discussed that with Captain Erickson, Mr. Ambassador," Gray said. "That's no doubt an area of concern. But we've come up with an idea that'll hopefully be adequate to meet our needs even with all those additional mouths to feed."

"What've you got in mind?" Ingram asked.

"When the rescue party reaches the Marriott, we've asked him to empty the hotel's food lockers and bring every morsel with them," the tall, sandy-blond-haired Gray said. "Although the Indian government is limiting our activities, they've agreed to allow us to fly in and stockpile food and water at Spinager. The first Air Force C-130 should be touching down with MREs and hundreds of five-gallon containers of potable water shortly. As long as it doesn't get too out of hand, they've also agreed to allow a reasonable amount of fuel and additional weapons to pass through the air base."

"What about more troops to reinforce our position?" Ingram asked.

"That request, I'm afraid, has been met with a resounding no," Gray said. "They feel they've risked enough already. They don't want to chance the response they're going to receive if the Chinese find out they're allowing American soldiers to use their country as a jumping-off point. China and India are on the verge of going to war over what has happened. Any little thing could trigger it. Our leadership is applying a great deal of pressure on India in the hopes of getting them to change their minds, but so far they won't budge. So unless something unforeseen happens, the Marines that're on the way are the only support we're likely to see for the foreseeable future."

"But at least India's allowing us to use Spinager to provide needed supplies and as a conduit for getting those the King Stallions rescue out of here," said Joyce. "And if the C-130 arrives at Spinager on time, the helicopters should be loaded with MREs and water when they return later tonight. We anticipate that the hotel's stores, along with what the helicopters bring, will buy us at least a couple of days. The King Stallions will then continue to supply us with food and water for the rest of the time we're here. That and fuel to run the embassy's generators will be our top priorities. And remember, the number of people we'll need to feed will be steadily dropping as more leave. So the need for additional food should lessen each night."

"It's going to be close, but if our plan works, there should be adequate food and water, sir," Gray reasoned. "In fact, as the demand falls, we should be in a position where instead of food the helicopters can bring in weapons and ammunition to replace whatever we've expended in battling the insurgents."

"And if we have to, we can try to arrange C-130 airdrops to supplement both our food and defenses," Joyce said.

"That sounds pretty good, I guess," a less-than-certain Ingram agreed. "Such an approach should hopefully give us a fighting chance."

"And to aid what we're doing," Joyce said, "we've asked each embassy to bring any food they have along with all their weapons and ammunition. That should help even more."

"All right. It certainly isn't ideal, but given what we face, it'll have to do," Ingram acknowledged. "Let's just hope those Marines reach us in time."

"Yes, sir," Gray said.

The duo turned and left the ambassador's office. As they did, the clock reached 12:01.

At the American embassy, the first day of November also had arrived.

3

While Sam Erickson prepared to rush into the evolving furor, Lauren Wells stood holding a microphone a few feet to the right of the Marriott's shimmering main entryway. A heavy fog, thick and menacing, continued to roll in. Its smothering image overwhelmed her world.

As her cameraman, Chuck Mendes, made the final adjustments to his equipment, she prepared to record an interview to be aired on her network's highly popular *Seven Days* program. It was scheduled to run in eight hours during the show's prime-time viewing.

Behind Wells, frazzled individuals and fleeing families could be seen entering the mist-shrouded structure, the assembly point for their planned evacuation from a deteriorating northeastern Pakistan. The unspeakable carnage throughout the countryside was spurring them all. Near the doorway, a pair of soldiers, part of the small British contingent defending the hotel, showed their anxiousness as they examined each worried face.

In the background, the incessant small-arms fire of the

house-to-house fighting occurring throughout the western and northern portions of the city was growing with each passing minute. The frightful sounds of the raging struggle, accompanied by unpredictable flashes of brilliant light and soul-shaking explosions, were unmistakable. A significant portion of the sprawling city was on fire. The Fedayeen Islam's lead elements were drawing near. Even if the few remaining Pakistani army units held on, it was a matter of hours at the utmost before the bearded dogmatists reached this portion of the capital.

Hopefully, the Marines would arrive at the hotel first. If not, the British contingent of thirty soldiers, armed with little more than automatic rifles, hand grenades, and one light machine gun, would be on their own in their defense of the inviting target and its frightened occupants. Each would do his best to stem the onslaught. Still, given the reality of the situation, the soldiers understood that, should a massive attack appear, there'd be little hope of prevailing.

"We about ready, Chuck?" she asked.

"All set, Miss Wells. Tony Watson should be on the line momentarily."

As if on cue, the *Seven Days* anchor's voice reached them. "Are you there, Lauren?" he asked.

"I'm here, Tony."

"Ready to roll tape?"

"Absolutely," she replied.

"With the gunfire I can hear, it sounds like we've no time to lose."

From behind the camera in New York, the countdown began: "Five . . . four . . . three . . . two . . ."

Tony Watson appeared in his familiar position behind the anchor desk. The program's rousing theme music began to play. As it ended, Watson looked up at the camera.

"Good evening and welcome to *Seven Days*, America's first choice for the week's latest in news and entertainment. Tonight, as the ruthless Fedayeen Islam continues their blood-soaked march across Pakistan, we're going to begin our show with a report from Lauren Wells, who's on special assignment covering the unprecedented events unfolding there." The screen split to show both Watson and the highly attractive, auburn-haired Wells. "Good evening, Lauren."

"Good evening, Tony. Tonight I'm coming to you from outside the main entrance to the Marriott Hotel in Islamabad. From my vantage point, I'm barely a mile from the abandoned Pakistani government's capital complex. As your viewers can no doubt hear from the sounds of the fearsome fighting, the swift advance into the heart of Pakistan—and the capital itself—by elements of the Fedayeen Islam terrorist group is well beyond anything anyone could've imagined. The immense populist army's spreading far and wide across vast portions of this battered country. In six weeks, this relatively unknown band of extremists has swollen from a few hundred obscure individuals to up to four million fighters. Thousands more are joining their ranks with each passing hour. This ragtag assembly of disillusioned peasants and ruthless Islamic zealots have roared across northern Pakistan at incredible speed, vanquishing all who dare to stand in their way. Behind them, the trail of atrocities flows like an endless stream."

"Lauren, is there any possibility of the Pakistani military rallying and putting down the rebellion?" Watson asked.

"None whatsoever, Tony. The entire country's in disarray. The Pakistani military's essentially defeated. In the northern part of the country, only a few scattered units are still fighting. And while some of the most loyal continue to provide a vigorous defense, the majority of those facing the insurgents are offering little more than token resistance. The remainder are in full retreat. Many have deserted. Entire units have surrendered en masse. Countless soldiers have stripped off their uniforms and joined the militants without giving it a second thought."

"That doesn't sound the least bit encouraging. Certainly, the sudden turn of events can't be pleasing to the president or the Pentagon."

"Of that, I've no doubt. Radical Islam taking control of this uneasy nation of more than two hundred million is something no one wanted to see. This turbulent portion of the planet has always been cause for worry. Given what's happened in a matter of a few short weeks, those grave concerns were obviously justified. Now the world faces the reality of a country with a stockpile of two hundred nuclear weapons being seized by a force of enraged zealots bent on lashing out in every direction to inflict death and destruction on anyone falling beneath their twisted shadow. If those weapons fall into their hands, the result could be catastrophic. There's a real possibility that a significant portion of this planet may soon face an unspeakable end beneath rising mushroom clouds. And that doesn't even take into account the conventional weapons the advancing militants are seizing with each victorious attack."

"Isn't there anyone who can put a stop to this before things are completely out of hand?" Watson asked.

"Like who, Tony?"

"Can't America and its NATO allies step in and bring an end to the chaos?"

"Step in how? No one was prepared for what happened. It caught the entire world by surprise. With as rapidly as things are unfolding, we're well beyond the point where it might be possible for anyone or anything to affect the outcome. Unless there's an unforeseeable miracle, in at least the northern half of the country the terrorists are going to prevail. And for so many reasons, both politically and militarily, our becoming entangled in an all-out war on such a massive scale is fraught with potential issues. This is a highly devout Islamic country with a huge population. For years, surveys have shown that the Pakistani people fear the United States more than they fear the extremists."

"So there's nothing we can do? We're going to stand by and give free reign to these incensed killers?"

"Honestly, Tony, at this moment it's impossible to say what our response will be. There's always the possibility of something forcing our hand. And even without that, we may decide there are no options left. If our leadership concludes we've no choice but to become involved militarily, who knows where that'll lead? Or how it might end?"

"If the Pakistani military can't stop this, isn't there anything their government can do to rally the people and stem the tide?"

"Government? What government? There is no government. The Pakistani leadership fled days ago. The streets of the capital are empty. Other than the thousands of non-Pakistanis gathered at this hotel, this part of Islamabad's little more than a ghost town. Those in power are running for their lives . . . first from India's attack and now from the Fedayeen. You've got to remember what the reason is for all this. This falls entirely on those in the Pakistani government who were behind the ill-conceived plot to destroy the Indian Parliament. They've no one to blame but themselves for what has occurred because of their misguided actions. Their unleashing of that horrific suicide bombing six weeks ago against the Indian legislature is the direct cause of what's happening here."

"Are we certain Pakistan was behind the attack in New Delhi? There've been those in this country and around the world who've questioned that conclusion."

"Not anyone in a position of authority. Despite those who've tried to come up with some fanciful answer for who was behind the attack, there's no doubt. I've spoken with multiple intelligence sources. Each told me the evidence is irrefutable. Pakistan not only condoned this action; they supported and helped plan it. When India identified the source of the slaughter that killed over four hundred in their parliament, they saw no option but to launch a full-scale attack in response.

"How do you think we'd have reacted, Tony, if our enemies had blown up our capitol and killed half of Congress in such a way? We'd have demanded retribution. So India's actions should've surprised no one. Quite honestly, the decision to stop once they'd seized all of the disputed Kashmir territory showed incredible self-control on their part. I've no doubt if they hadn't, both countries would've unleashed their nuclear arsenals weeks ago. The entire subcontinent would've been wiped out with hundreds of millions dying if India hadn't shown the restraint it did. Still, India has to be watching what's happening with a great deal of anxiousness. Even with the Chinese assembling a massive army on their border and threatening war over any further incursions into Pakistani, the Indian government may be unable to hold itself back much longer.

"Once the militants get their hands on this country's nuclear arsenals, all bets are off. India might have no choice but to launch a preemptive nuclear attack before the dogmatists have the opportunity to do the same. If India sees no option but to do so, most of the two hundred million in this country are going to die. If that happens, there's little doubt what the rest of the fanatics will do. They'll rise up in an anger that knows no bounds. They'll lash out. The entire world, while also facing a monumental nuclear catastrophe, could be engulfed in a spreading religious war of unimaginable intensity."

From the surprised look on Watson's face, there was no doubt he was shocked. Like most Americans, he'd no clue about the dire threat present events were creating.

"I had no idea where this was leading," he said.

"Few people did, Tony."

He did his best to recover. "I guess if things are as bad as you say they are, it really doesn't matter what the cause was. Given what you've told us, there might be no way to stop this."

"None that I can see, Tony. Unless something totally unanticipated happens, the Fedayeen Islam terrorist group is going to seize control of the majority of this country. And they may eventually take it all. When they do, they've every intention of using Pakistan's nuclear weapons to drag the planet back to the Stone Age. Salim Basra has said as much. Just look at what they're doing. Along with their indiscriminate slaughter of those unfortunate enough to cross their path, they're destroying everything that reminds those they've conquered of the modern world. They've smashed every television, computer, and modern convenience they find. They've destroyed nearly every cell phone tower. They've blown up every building. Wherever they march, power and running water are disappearing. Basra's unimaginable vision is an unspeakably dark one. This brutal man from the wild tribal territories plans to apply his bizarre views across as much of the planet as he possibly can. The backwards existence his followers are creating is as primitive and sick as they can possibly make it."

"How long before the capital falls?"

"Most of it already has. The northern and western portions of the city are on fire. The attack the Fedayeen launched against the Pakistani capital a week ago when they poured out of the Margalla Hills and the snowcapped mountains beyond will soon be complete. Conservative estimates are that nearly three hundred thousand Fedayeen fighters are in or near Islamabad. And absolutely nothing is slowing them down."

"So how much time do we have before they overrun all of the northern portion of the country?"

"A few days . . . a week, maybe . . . When that occurs, the threat we'll face will be far too real."

His director indicated that the time for Lauren Wells's grave report was at its end.

"With that sobering thought, I see we're out of time," Watson said. "Thank you, Lauren, for your insights. Do your best to stay safe."

"Thank you, Tony. We'll do what we can."

The picture in America's homes returned to showing an obviously stunned Watson. "We'll be back after these messages," he said.

At the Islamabad Marriott, Chuck signaled they were clear.

"What do we do now, Miss Wells?"

"At the moment, there's not much we can do. Go ahead and break down the mobile satellite and gather your equipment. Let's get inside. I feel more than a bit vulnerable standing out in the open like this with all that's going on."

"Yes, ma'am."

"When we're in the lobby, maybe we should interview some of the people gathered there," she said. "Might make for some nice background stories on what's going on."

A few minutes after she finished her interviews, the British sergeant, commander of the small detachment, walked into the expansive lobby filled with agitated people. Each of those present was growing more troubled as the endless minutes passed. Given no other choice, they'd complied with what their governments had directed and found shelter within the hotel. The gathered thousands, spread from top to bottom throughout the building, were as varied in nationality, age, and description as they could possibly be. Families with children, couples of every sort, and those who were on their own had found their way to this location. With every arriving evacuee, the rumors of what was happening beyond the hotel grew. The sudden disappearance of the Marriott's staff two days earlier had added to the mounting confusion and growing fears within the five-star hotel's resplendent walls.

The noise in the high-ceilinged room was deafening as countless voices, competing to be heard, echoed throughout the space. The sergeant did his best to get their attention so he could relay the information he'd received from the British embassy. His every effort to hush the fearful gathering failed. He reached for the whistle dangling from his uniform and brought it to his lips. A long, shrill blast pierced the man-made discord. Standing little more than five feet from the shrieking sound, Wells was certain she'd lost an eardrum. The clamorous crowd went silent. Each curious face turned and looked the sergeant's way.

"May I have your attention, please?" he said. "I've received word from the British legation that the decision's been made to conduct an orderly evacuation of all of you from the hotel. An American Marine company will be headed our way shortly. They'll be escorting everyone, no matter your nationality, to their embassy. Once there, we'll begin the orderly evacuation of each of you."

"When will the Marines arrive?" Wells asked.

"Not too much longer, ma'am. They're hoping to be here around two," the sergeant said.

His answer was one none wanted to hear. They were far too aware of the harsh reality of their approaching destiny. Many had been in the hotel for days, waiting for salvation to find them. With each passing moment, their worry had grown. The spreading rumors of the unspeakable barbarism headed in their direction had turned their fear into a raging inferno. The last thing those present were anxious to accept was remaining in this increasingly vulnerable place for another two hours.

The sergeant's response was met with outrage. In an instant, the cavernous room erupted with the furor of an untold number of voices. Scores shouted questions and expressed their displeasure at the same moment. There was no way for the harried soldier to either understand or respond to the riotous acrimony. The struggling sergeant motioned for the crowd to calm. Despite his every attempt, the uproar continued. The whistle returned to his lips. He paused, hoping the gesture would quiet the onlookers. Yet even the threat of the piercing refrain had no effect. He had to gain control of those within the massive lobby. It was that or face the possibility of many in the gathering ignoring his orders and striking out on their own from the hotel. If he didn't act, the mounting mutiny would be impossible to constrain.

He was out of options. He took a deep breath and blew the whistle with all his might. Ten . . . fifteen . . . twenty seconds, the echoing sound worked to drown out everything within the magnificent space. He didn't stop until he'd expelled every ounce of air from his lungs. The grumbling crowd grew silent once again. Even so, the unhappiness on their faces couldn't be denied.

"Listen to me, all of you," the gasping sergeant said. "I know you want to reach safety as rapidly as you can. But your best option is to stay here and wait for help. The last thing any of you should do is panic and attempt something rash. With the heavy fog outside and our present circumstances, we need to go about this as smartly as possible. The danger in the streets is unmistakable. Heading out on your own is the worst possible thing any of you can do. We've no idea what's out there. For the moment, there are thirty rifles protecting this hotel. They're being held by some of the finest soldiers the British military has to offer. I promise you, my men will keep you safe until help arrives."

He knew what he'd told them was far from the truth. Given the situation, however, it was a commitment he needed to make. "So let's do what we need to do to stay alive," he said. "In another two hours, significant assistance will reach this place. We'll then escort you in an orderly fashion to the United States embassy so we can begin the process of getting you home. If you haven't already done so, please gather your belongings in preparation for our departure. The Marines will be here before you know it."

"Why don't you and your men lead us out of here rather than waiting for the Americans?" someone near the back of the room yelled.

"We've given that some thought, sir. Unfortunately, there aren't enough of us to protect you while on the move. With at least four thousand of you, our column could easily stretch two kilometers. With only thirty of us, that would mean, at best, I could place each of my soldiers a hundred meters from the next. Should a significant enemy force appear, as lightly armed as we are, we'd be much too scattered to stop them. So our best hope is to wait for the Americans and the firepower they're bringing. So please show some patience and do your best to remain calm while we do so."

He looked at the disturbed forms. It was apparent that many, if not most, were quite unsettled. Even so, he had no more time for those inside the lobby. His soldiers needed him to return to his position and direct their defensive actions. Should the enemy appear, his place would be with his men. He turned and walked away.

As the sergeant pushed through the hotel's expansive front doors, Wells looked at the tense scene inside the space. She looked at her cameraman. "Chuck, let's hope those Marines get here real soon."

As she spoke, the clock reached 12:01.

At the Marriott, the first minute of the first day of November had arrived.

4

Only the slightest sliver of a waning moon's faltering autumn light shone down upon the wind-swept plateaus and towering mountains of northeastern Pakistan. The first of the interminable evening's burgeoning fog was rolling in on the high mesas. Blood-tinged fear dripped upon its moist edges.

In the enveloping darkness and expanding mist, a heavily shaded, black-clothed figure, the leader of a lethal force, moved through the thinning forest of spruce, juniper, and mulberry. He headed toward the thick rows of razor-honed concertina upon the wide plain. After a quick look around, he motioned to his followers. Others, identical in dress, began appearing behind him. Their numbers continued to swell. Each carried an assault rifle, satchel charge, and menacing sword. Each was ready to fight to the death for their consecrated cause.

In all, the determined aggressors measured more than two hundred. They outnumbered their adversary four to one. The imposing force split up. Within minutes they were ready. On all sides of the mobile nuclear weapons launch facility the toxic attackers moved toward their target. Their pitiless onslaught would be swift and brutal. No quarter would be given. No mercy shown.

Throughout Pakistan, scores of similar groupings from the fanatical Fedayeen Islam were doing the same. Their missions were identical: seize the nuclear weapons and control them until their sources obtained the launch codes.

Along with many others, Mishira was now perilously close to the retreating Pakistani army's crumbling front lines. Scores of nuclear launch facilities should have been moved hours, even days, earlier. The orders to withdraw the launchers from their vulnerable locations and move them to safety in the south had been prepared three days prior. Yet, in the chaos, there'd been a monumental mistake. The directives had never been issued. And the nuclear armaments were there for the taking.

The weapons were no direct threat to the United States or Europe. The missiles didn't have the range to strike such targets. Yet the powerful rockets' slaying contents could reach to every corner of India. The trio of nuclear weapons on the Mishira plateau were programmed to strike and annihilate the same city: Mumbai, India's largest, with its twenty million dwellers.

Outside the menacing wire, a dozen Pakistani soldiers patrolled the quarter-mile perimeter. In the hilltop's center, the three Shaheen-III missiles, each rising from its sixteen-wheel transporter-erector-launcher, pointed skyward. The deadly missiles towered over the handfuls of billowing tents and the dozen or so stationary military vehicles that surrounded them.

The apprehensive sentries outside the barbed wire, like the majority of the country's crumbling military and confused citizenry, were dispirited and disillusioned. After their defeat by the reviled Indian forces and India's seizure of the Kashmir territory, the people's faith in the Islamic nation's civilian leadership and its military had all but dissipated. The collapse of the central government and the resulting turmoil had left an immense void that the Fedayeen rushed to exploit. Despite the cruelty of their tactics, a significant portion of the populace, with nowhere to turn, had joined the zealots' ranks. With lightning speed they were seizing control of wide swaths of the country. The Pakistani military, the seventh largest in the world, with its modern weaponry, was powerless when faced with the popular uprising. Like their government, they, too, were in disarray.

No one could have predicted such a dire turn of events. Pakistan's civilian leadership had always been questionable. But their armed forces had been a source of tremendous pride and stability in this chaotic corner of the planet. Now even they'd lost the support of most of their countrymen.

Sheltered by the night, the determined two hundred edged closer to their prize. Inside the makeshift facility's grounds, elite Strategic Arms Division soldiers prowled. These were the best of the best within the Pakistani forces. Each had been thoroughly vetted and was exceptionally well trained. Each believed in their critical mission with absolute certainty, even in the perplexing events of the past weeks.

Since their initial nuclear test firing in 1998, the Pakistani government had assured an uneasy world that their policies guaranteed the apocalyptic devices were safe from unwelcome hands. They'd endlessly proclaimed that their measures to safeguard the fearful armaments were more than adequate. Normal policy was for the nuclear warheads and their trigger mechanisms to be separated, rendering their cataclysmic payloads harmless. Yet, as soon as the war with India had begun, the Pakistani nuclear arsenal was assembled and prepared for possible launch. All two hundred fatal armaments were armed and ready. The only thing missing were the launch codes.

The hushed assailants reached the end of the sheltering forest. They were scarcely thirty yards from the stretching wire. A stealthy black figure, his heavily bearded face covered by a matching cloth, slowly unsheathed his glistening, curved sword. The remnants of dried blood clung to the blade's edges. The moment the guard nearest his position passed, the assassin rushed from the cloaking trees. His lethal weapon was raised high.

The young private heard the approaching footsteps much too late to have any chance. He had little time to turn and none whatsoever to protect himself from the murderous weapon's blow.

His gruesome task completed, the cold-blooded killer signaled. From every side, the attacking force rushed forward. The fearsome howls of a horrific death for all who opposed them shattered the eerie scene's uneasy silence. The lethal two hundred raced across the broad mesa. The harrowing force was everywhere the startled defenders looked.

The Pakistani troops scrambled toward their defensive positions. An initial crackle of automatic-rifle fire pierced the ominous darkness. Others soon followed. The hilltop exploded in a riotous calliope of deafening noise and desperate battle.

One of the attackers went down, his death rattle soon upon him. More soon followed. Their fading life's essence seeped into the plateau's damp grasses. Yet the illiterate peasants didn't falter. They raced to seize the immense treasure. No matter how severe their losses, they wouldn't be dissuaded. Allah's hand would guide them to a glorious victory. Of that, all were certain.

The ill-prepared regular soldiers outside the wire were soon engaged. Each attempted to fight back. And they most certainly took a toll upon the intense raiders. Even so, the swarming cultists came on. Their overwhelming numbers were far too great for the staggering guards to stop. They roared toward the compound like an irresistible avalanche.

Outside the wire, it was going to be no contest. The surging enemy was far too strong and determined. Their numbers were much too great. In little more than a frenetic minute, the slaughter was complete. All twelve soldiers lay dead.

The deranged mayhem outside the nuclear enclosure now over, the twisted ones turned toward the more daunting task. They had to defeat their deft foes within the menacing concertina. They realized this wasn't going to be easy. They understood that the forty highly skilled defenders protecting the tantalizing bounty would fight until their dying breath.

From their fortified positions surrounding the missiles, the resolute guardians opened fire. Lethal tracers spewing from the ends of their automatic rifles lit up the night as they went forth in search of venomous prey.

Still, the insatiable insurrectionists remained certain that conquest would be theirs. On each of the compound's four sides, handfuls of cloaked figures rushed forward. They tossed satchel charges at the sharp-edged rows of concertina that blocked their entry into the isolated outpost. Fierce, smoke-filled explosions rocked the trembling night. Huge holes appeared in the disintegrating barriers. Many more scurried forward to press their advantage. They were soon inside the besieged facility. Running shadows were everywhere.

In the north, the main force, nearly half of the interlopers, moved toward the primary entranceway into the compound. The outmanned Strategic Arms Division fighters were waiting. The severe numbers and long odds weren't going to deter them in the slightest. They'd defend their institution and its invaluable weaponry with immense talent and unyielding determination. Inside the compound, a duo of strategically placed machine guns opened fire on the raging miscreants headed toward the opening. In seconds, the first of the extremists attempting to breach the makeshift roadway lay dead, his chest ripped open by the chattering guns. Additional black figures went down. Rifle fire consumed the night. Exploding hand grenades sent hot metal racing across the battlefield. Disorder reigned. The death toll rose for attacker and defender alike. With exacting accuracy, another satchel charge was hurled by a fury-filled invader. Inside the assailed enclosure, a ten-ton truck exploded. Its consuming blaze erupted, lighting up the horrific scene. Additional explosions quickly followed. The first of the outer tents began to burn. The unyielding intensity of the terrifying firefight consumed the blighted hilltop. It menacingly echoed from the not-so-distant mountaintops. Unrelenting screams of august agony pierced the blighted vista. The dead and dying were everywhere the eye surveyed. The unspeakable savagery of the relentless attack went on unabated. At far distances or at arm's length, the horror-edged fray consumed them. Five . . . ten . . . fifteen minutes passed, with neither of the contestants gaining an advantage.

The embattled protectors fought with incredible bravery. The country they loved might have been falling apart, but that mattered not to any of them. They understood what the consequences would be should the frenzied aggressors seize victory.

Still, the howling rabble were equally fixed. And their numbers were great. Despite their losses, they came on with voracious fervor. They were God's chosen, and with his immeasurable might they'd annihilate and prevail.

The desperate struggle raged past the half-hour point. Two attackers were succumbing for every plateau soldier who fell. The odds, however, were just too great for the defenders to overcome. Through sheer numbers and unceasing will, the merciless ones began pushing them back. The Strategic Arms Division's despairing soldiers were pressed into an ever-tightening circle around the fearsome missiles in the center of the compound. The hideous battle continued without pause. With each sordid engagement, with every passing minute, the downcast protectors dwindled until only a fitful few remained.

Another succumbed. And yet another. One by one their numbers dropped until there were no more of those wishing to keep the unspeakable weapons out of the dire assailants' hands.

As the last soldier fell, the victorious attackers ran into the center of the enclosure, intent on claiming their prize. Their anger unfettered, they soon reached the towering missiles. They'd lost more than half their number, but it was of no importance. Those who'd survived the perverse conflict began to celebrate in earnest, firing long bursts into the air and screaming in rapturous victory. They'd done it. The all-devouring weapons were in their hands.

At their leader's direction, the triumphant throng began stripping everything of significance from the defeated dead and cannibalizing all of the equipment that remained on the fiery hilltop.

Meter by meter, tent by tent, the grinning victors began a systematic search of their imposing conquest. As the clock neared midnight, the exploration of the crippled compound continued. In a nondescript tent near what had been the complex commander's headquarters waited an unanticipated bounty. To the elated conquerors' surprise, the fluttering structure contained twelve crates. As his triumphant fighters gathered around, the Fedayeen's assault leader pried opened the first of the containers. It only took a moment for him to recognize the enormous secret hidden within. A perverse smile came to his grime-streaked face at his momentous discovery. Inside was a modest-sized tactical nuclear weapon. Each of the remaining eleven crates held a similar treasure. The nasty little weapons were intended for use on the front lines to address short-range targets. Fired from artillery pieces, they were designed to create a nuclear explosion encompassing more than a square mile. They'd instantly destroy everything within that space. The resulting blast and malignant radiation would kill even farther out.

The smiling leader looked toward his second-in-command, the pleasure in his words unmistakable. "Our great leader, Salim Basra, will be quite pleased with what we've found hidden in these crates."

"An immense prize indeed."

"Now we wait for the launch codes to arrive. Once they're in our hands, we'll fire the Shaheen missiles and, along with our comrades, level every city in India."

"And Allah's glory will be ours."

"After our men finish searching the camp, send messengers to locate any of our units nearby. They're to insist each join us in our sainted mission to protect this plateau. Tell them such orders come directly from Basra. We need at least two hundred more warriors if we're going to succeed. Three hundred would be even better."

"It will be done."

Throughout northern Pakistan, the invaders' conquests were nearly all successful. Along with the tactical nuclear arms discovered at Mishira, the attackers had seized the vast majority of the two hundred nuclear weapons and their accompanying launchers. They were more than adequate to destroy India and kill a significant portion of the neighboring country's 1.3 billion people. Once fired, they were enough to create an ever-expanding nuclear winter that would lead to the starvation deaths of untold millions across the planet. No corner of the globe would be unaffected.

Until the launch codes arrived, the nuclear missiles were no threat. After the terrorists obtained the firing sequences, however, the horror that an unsuspecting world would face was unmistakable. It would be hours, days at most, before the threat would reach its climax and the world face an undeniable peril. Once the heinous missiles rose from their launch platforms there'd be nothing mankind could do to stop the end result.

With the Pakistani forces in disarray, the immeasurable task of keeping that from happening would fall upon the yet-unaware Americans. And the time remaining to stop incalculable numbers of people from dying was fading.

The clock had reached 12:01.

At the bloodied nuclear sites, the first day of November had arrived.

5

In the middle of the surreal scene, Sam Erickson stood in the center of the queuing relief column. Despite his best efforts, the company commander's uneasiness showed. With so many innocent lives at stake, he recognized there wasn't a moment to lose. To have any chance, it was now or never for his Marines. With all haste, they needed to begin the perilous journey.

Erickson turned to look at his gathering force. Without the aid of his night vision equipment he wouldn't have been able to see more than a few feet in any direction. The sticky fog, as thick and unyielding as any he'd ever witnessed, made sure of that. Yet the enveloping malaise was far from his only worry. For this sinister night held even greater concerns. Within the spanning metropolis, immense fires rose high into the clinging clouds. In every direction, the shattering thunder of the relentless explosions, one after the next, assailed them all. With each passing instant, the flames consuming the city were growing more intense. The horrendous sounds of the nearing battles ebbed and flowed.

What exactly was occurring, Erickson had no way of knowing. Nevertheless, there was no doubt the once-sparkling Pakistani capital was being torn apart. The Fedayeen Islam's fighters were determined to ensure that not a single structure still stood.

With twelve idling Humvees, 1st and 2nd Platoons were forming on the narrow roadway south of the embassy. Erickson's eighty-eight-person rescue party would soon be ready. If all went as planned, in no more than half an hour, the lengthy line of well-armed Marines would reach the Marriott.

Swathed in a consuming world of smothering smoke and morose gray, forty-eight Marines would ride to the hotel in the fierce combat vehicles. The remainder of the wary force would be on foot as they rushed to reach those praying for their appearance.

Second Lieutenant Jeffrey Ambrose, 1st Platoon leader, was at the head of the formation. Standing near the thick tree line west of the American compound, he was little more than twenty yards from the Italian embassy. While they marched, Erickson would be positioned one hundred yards behind the column's leading edge. When the last of his men were ready, Second Lieutenant Zack Marshall, in charge of 2nd Platoon, would take his place at the rear of the relief force.

Behind the forming line, Alpha Company's final two platoons continued their determined efforts to empty their recently arriving King Stallions and set up a makeshift perimeter. Ghostly figures worked to clear the holds while their comrades went forth to locate solid defensive positions. Cutting through the heavy fog, many rushed about, gathering and carrying the piles of critical supplies toward the huge American complex's main gate.

At the same moment, inside the embassy grounds, the first four hundred women and children scheduled to leave on the cargo helicopters were being readied for the flight to India. The evacuees represented more than a dozen nationalities.

The opening foray in what would hopefully be thousands of fraught people's journeys home was minutes away. From each of the area's retreating embassies, the mothers with the youngest children would be in this initial grouping. Standing inside the American embassy's protective walls, the apprehensive gathering prepared to leave the harboring complex and cross the parking area to their assigned craft. Steven Gray and a dozen of his men would lead them out and cover their departure.

With a toddler in hand, the troubled face of the first woman in the tense gathering was right inside the main gate. The young mother peered at the confusing world in front of her, unable to make out much. Finally, all was ready. With the last of the combat equipment in each helicopter removed, the order was given. Infants cradled in their arms or small children and their older siblings in tow, the struggling assembly started walking in single file along the outside of the staid facility's high western facade. With the exception of a dozen or so crying infants, silence was the order of the day. Each moved as rapidly as the conditions would allow. One by one, the furtive figures headed for the King Stallions. Gray's heavily armed team took up strategic positions around the hurrying women and children. As each helicopter's engines roared to life, the hundreds of departing evacuees rushed through the threatening world and scurried up the rear ramps. With a mixture of absolute relief and lingering concern, they settled in for the dismaying ride across the fearful landscape.

Freedom awaited. If all went as planned, in little more than a day, even those from the most distant of countries would be back on their native soil. Hopefully, in scarcely more than a handful of worrisome dawns, the husbands and fathers they'd left behind would join them.

Four hours from now, with the oppressive darkness and unrelenting gray still seizing the early morning, all six whirling aircraft would return with their holds filled with thousands of pounds of food and water. Every helicopter's second load of critical cargo frantically emptied, they would grab another four hundred and roar away. The first eight hundred would be gone by the time the initial hours of November's gloom disappeared.

As they ended their second scrambling run, the primal hints of the coming dawn would be upon the lumbering helicopters.

It would be far too late for another restive sprint into Pakistan's life-consuming strife before the sun's betraying rays fully appeared. While the impatient King Stallion crews waited at Spinager for night to fall again, the CH-53Ks would be filled with more supplies for those remaining in Islamabad. When the faltering day's light finally relinquished its grip, the Americans would begin the rescue process anew. They wouldn't stop as long as darkness masked their efforts.

Even with a nearly moonless world in a twinkling black sky to conceal them, the helicopters' swift flights would be filled with risk as they roared into a vicious whirlwind. None could foretell what fates awaited their brash missions to swoop in and save thousands from the heartless extremists' swords. Yet, if all went as planned, in days—a week on the outside—the last of the trapped evacuees would abandon the beset city. Their mission complete, Erickson's surviving Marines, the final Americans remaining in Islamabad, would make their escape on the same King Stallions that had ferried them into harm's way on this foreboding night.

The loading of the women and children complete, the lead helicopter, filled with grateful beings, slowly rose into the air. Five others soon followed.

In seconds, they disappeared.

6

While the earnest six rushed away, Erickson took a final look at the last of his gathered men. Satisfied that everything was ready, he spoke into his headset. "All right, 1st and 2nd Platoons, move out."

Ever alert, Ambrose's most trusted four-man fire team, the company's lead scouts, started west down the constricted roadway south of the embassy. The fearsome team consisted of two Marines holding M4 assault rifles, a third with an M4 equipped with a grenade launcher, and a final member cradling a .30-caliber light machine gun.

The entire formation would head in this direction for half a mile. The trudging Americans would then turn right onto Constitution Avenue, the primary boulevard in the northeast portion of Islamabad. They'd remain there for the bulk of the harrowing pilgrimage. On the broad roadway they'd be out in the open for over twenty minutes of the quest.

On their right, for the initial portion of the northern march, they'd be passing the deserted embassies of those retreating to the protection of the American defenses. To their left, a few hundred yards distant, would be a line of ghostly government buildings of various shapes and sizes. There could be no denying the threat those structures posed. Under normal circumstances, each would have been a perfect ambush spot. The potential for a fierce attack on this spanning section of the roadway was unmistakable. Still, it couldn't be helped. This was the most direct route to the Marines' destination. Even if highly hazardous, there wasn't time for anything but a bold advance down the swiftest passage to the hotel. They'd be risking their lives every step of the northern journey. Nonetheless, it was a gamble Erickson had to take.

Despite the company commander's concerns, they'd received a significant stroke of good fortune. Even with the betraying sounds from the Humvees' engines, the ground-hugging clouds that swallowed whole the world around them would help to conceal their size and location. While the Marines' night vision equipment would aid their efforts, their far less sophisticated opponent would have no such advantage. The struggling insurgents would only be able to see for the scant distances the crippling conditions would allow. In order to engage the Americans in the flickering, fire-shaded darkness the fanatics would have little choice but to brave the open areas closer to the imposing roadway. The fight, should it come, would be up close and personal if the dogmatists hoped to prevail. With the oncoming platoons' superior equipment and advanced technology, any such attempt would be identified and negated long before the jihadists got within a few hundred yards of the convoy.

Even so, the vaunted rescue party had every right to be apprehensive. What the platoons would encounter, they hadn't a clue. The entire length of their fitful venture could be quiet and uneventful. Or multitudes of swarming insurgents could be waiting.

If Erickson's unit was successful in traversing the open boulevard, as they neared their journey's end they'd turn left onto Aga Kahn Road and head west once again. In one thousand feet, they'd reach the entrance to the hotel.

Satisfied that the point element was far enough away, Ambrose signaled for the remainder of his platoon to follow. With the lead fire team thirty yards ahead of them, the spreading procession started to move. Six on each side, evenly spaced throughout the formation, the Humvees crept forward. All but two of the small combat vehicles were armed with powerful .50-caliber machine guns. The remaining Humvee pair carried TOW antitank weapons.

They didn't anticipate a significant armored threat appearing. Yet it was better to be safe than sorry. The Fedayeen Islam's conquests had included seizing over one hundred top-of-the-line Al-Khalid tanks and a generous number of armored personnel carriers. Where those armored forces might be, the Americans were unaware. In case the absolute worst were to happen, the Marines would need the protection of the tank-killing TOWs.

At a highly aggressive pace, Erickson's remaining men began walking down the narrow street. Every Marine was on edge. All knew the next halting breath, the next stilted movement, could be his last. The fearful sounds of gunfire were much too near. The disconcerting, fog-hewn blazes raging throughout the city provided an ominous backdrop none of the rescuers could ignore.

They had to hurry. They also needed to make no mistakes. Step by furious step, the Marines undertook the steadfast mission. Thirty inches at a time, the sodden pavement passed beneath their feet. In minutes, still unchallenged, the vigilant Americans turned right onto Constitution Avenue. So far, things were proceeding exactly as planned. Even so, their bile rose as they entered the wide boulevard. Rifles and machine guns at the ready, they continued on, steadily eclipsing the abandoned embassies' ghostly images. So far, they'd encountered no one.

Forward, ever forward, the slow-moving vehicles and persistent boots moved. Ten endless minutes passed for the wary assembly. The lead elements were one-third of the way to the Marriott. Not a single Marine could deny that things were going far better than any had anticipated. Yet suddenly, to no one's surprise, the grievous stakes were about to be raised.

Corporal Genovese, the company radio operator, rushed up to walk next to Erickson. "Sir, we just got word. The hotel's under attack."

Erickson stopped dead in his tracks, the words sinking in. "How bad is it?"

"Bad enough. The British are fully engaged with a significant number of insurgents hitting them on both the northern and western ends of the facility. The hostiles are presently attempting a flanking movement to encircle the defenders and break through to the Marriott's main entrance. There's complete chaos both inside and outside the hotel. The moment the fighting began, a number of evacuees panicked and tried to escape. Those who elected to run were gunned down by the attackers. The sergeant in charge of the British forces believes at least fifty men, women, and children are dead or severely wounded. There's flowing blood and dead bodies everywhere he looks."

"Did he give any indication of what they're up against?"

"He estimated the attacking force his thirty men are facing numbers at least three hundred and could easily be twice that. More are arriving every minute. So far the Fedayeen assault has involved only small-arms fire, but that could change at any moment. The British detachment has three dead and twice as many wounded. Every second things are growing more desperate. They're uncertain how much longer they can hold on against such overwhelming odds. They're requesting immediate assistance."

Erickson responded without giving it a second thought: "Relay to the British that we're on our way."

7

Erickson would have to risk it all to reinforce the British detachment. There was only one way to do so. Even on the run, weighed down by their weapons and equipment, it would take the Marines on foot too long to arrive on the scene.

He'd scant minutes to change the outcome of the assailed hotel's one-sided battle. He knew he couldn't wait for those on the ground. He'd have to split his force. The Marine captain keyed his headset. "Change of plans," he said, trying to sound as calm as possible. "The Marriott's under attack. Without immediate action, we're going to be too late. Humvees are to leave the formation, rush to the hotel, and reinforce the British. I'll lead the assault. We need to be there in three minutes, no more. Two would be even better. The rest of you are to begin double-timing toward the hotel. Lieutenant Ambrose, take charge of those on foot."

"Aye, aye, sir," was Ambrose's response. "First and 2nd Platoons double time," the lieutenant ordered. The men on the ground, all in magnificent shape, began running through the tortured landscape.

Erickson turned toward the nearest Humvee, identifying which fire team it carried. "Sergeant Zepeda, have one of your men exit the vehicle to make room for me."

"Yes, sir."

In seconds, Erickson was inside the Humvee and racing toward the front of the formation. The five vehicles behind his rushed to join them. Those ahead picked up speed. All twelve quickly reached the front of the extended force.

The moment they were free of those on foot, the company commander was back on his headset. "Humvees forward," he ordered.

A dozen well-armed vehicles raced away, disappearing into the swirling haze.

"Sergeant Mayfield," Erickson said. "You're team's got point. I want you to take a position fifty meters in front of the rest."

"We're on it," Mayfield responded as his driver pulled farther ahead of the trailing convoy. "How fast do you want us to proceed, sir?"

Erickson knew their counterattack would need to be undertaken on a murderous razor's edge. In the middle of the fiery city's disarray, they'd have to maintain an accelerated pace, bordering on suicidal, if their frantic efforts were to stand any chance. It was a huge gamble in so tenuous an environment. But there were far too many lives at stake to consider any other alternative. "Take her up to forty and leave her there." A pedestrian speed under normal circumstances, but—given the blanketing fog and possibility of a waiting enemy force—it was an exceptionally precarious one.

"Will do, sir."

The lead Humvee surged forward. The rest of the desperate procession did the same.

The furious twelve plunged deeper into the leaden world. They soared down the broad boulevard. In little time they were charging past the first of the Pakistani government buildings. The damp asphalt spun beneath their wheels. Yet to those in the surging vehicles it felt as if they were standing still as they sprinted through the engulfing night. In the suffocating conditions, each yard of passing pavement was identical to the one prior and the next to come. Every languishing cloud bank was the same as the ones they'd previously endured.

The initial minute elapsed without incident for the speeding Humvees. It felt much, much longer. Every tick of the clock was a tortured eternity in their riotous attempt to reach those in need of their assistance. One kilometer remained. As the Marines hurried forward, chewing up the distance, Erickson's confidence grew. Little could he anticipate that their peril-filled venture was about to take another turn.

"Sir, we've got extensive movement ahead!" Mayfield suddenly cried out. "I'm picking up a number of images headed this direction. They definitely appear to be armed."

"In vehicles or on foot?"

"On foot. No sign of any vehicles."

"Where?"

"Ten o'clock, right past the final government building on the left. They're about thirty yards from that scattering of trees next to the roadway. I'd estimate they're no more than about three hundred meters from my Humvee. They've got to be hostiles."

The relentless invaders' forward elements had chosen this moment to find their way into this portion of the city. At their present speed, in twenty seconds the Humvees would reach the oncoming enemy. Through his night vision, Erickson scanned the morbid landscape in the direction Mayfield had indicated.

"Roger, I've got them," the Marine leader said. "Got to be at least fifty, maybe more. Everyone cut your speed to ten miles an hour while we get organized."

The Humvees slowed to a crawl. Erickson knew doing so would chew up painful seconds on an exceptionally critical clock. Nonetheless, it couldn't be helped if the Marines were going to survive to reach the struggling British. Even though he recognized the delay could cost additional suffering at the besieged Marriott, it was far better for his Humvees to be a minute late than to not arrive at all.

"We've spotted another group, even larger, moving through the open field beyond the first formation," Mayfield added. "What're your orders, sir?"

"Can you identify if any are carrying RPGs?"

Erickson understood the biggest threat to his nimble teams' swift vehicles would be the existence of shoulder-fired rocket-propelled grenades. The ability of an RPG to destroy a Humvee and kill all inside had been documented far too often in the decades of war in the Middle East.

"Can't tell for sure, sir," Mayfield said. "None of my guys have spotted anything but automatic rifles in either group. But in the darkness and fog, our observations are not much more than a guess."

The danger to his force was unmistakable. If the enemy had a significant number of RPGs, the entire formation could be destroyed. They might all die in the coming moments without ever coming near the hotel. Under normal circumstances, prudence and restraint would've been the correct approach. They'd have fallen back and identified precisely what they faced before deciding upon the appropriate action.

But their commander never gave such an approach the slightest consideration. Once more, he had little choice. The consequences of a further delay were beyond anything he wished to contemplate. Four thousand lives were going to be lost if his Marines didn't soon appear on Aga Khan Road. They needed to intercede in the assault on the Marriott. They needed to do so now.

There'd be no hesitation. His Marines would attack with blinding speed. Their maniacal response would, by necessity, be filled with bravado and a great deal of on-the-spot ingenuity. Exactly the kind of thing Marines throughout history had been exceptional at executing.

To succeed, he'd have to split his force further. Erickson knew there'd be no opportunity for the entire formation of Humvees to confront and destroy the oncoming jihadists if they were going to make it to the hotel in the brief moments remaining. With an ever-increasing, depraved force nearing the roadway, even if they prevailed in the impending conflict, it would take far too long to eliminate the threat. It was possible they'd get pinned down in a protracted struggle from which they couldn't extricate themselves as the horrifying minutes passed. An hour from now, the unrelenting fray might still be underway. If that happened, they'd be much too late in reaching those in desperate need of assistance.

When they arrived at the hotel, an unutterable scene would welcome them. Their delayed appearance would be greeted by the haunting silence of uncountable corpses. All four thousand would have perished in the most hideous of manners. A surging sea of fresh blood would wash over the Marines, drowning them in its essence. The hotel's vast fires would be roaring. The lingering imprint of death's gnarled hand would be everywhere.

He had to find a way out. He had to reach the hotel. He needed to be bold and beyond aggressive. He had to somehow address the heartless killers blocking his path while also reaching the waiting four thousand.

He understood there was no way Salim Basra's unmerciful

force wouldn't hear his Humvees as they drew near. Twelve rumbling engines would see to that. Even so, he didn't believe the enemy's knowledge of the approaching vehicles would necessarily prove fatal. He could still take the perverse peasants by surprise. He could still rule the night.

There was an excellent chance on the evolving battlefield that each band of jihadists was essentially independent of the others. And it was highly probable there was little communication between the disjointed elements as they advanced. They were most likely acting on their own, without guidance from anyone and rare interaction with those around them.

Unaware of the Marines' arrival, the surging jihadists would likely assume the oncoming column belonged to mobile Fedayeen forces attacking in the same area. They wouldn't risk opening fire until it was clear who was headed in their direction.

While the Humvees continued their slow advance, he keyed his headset. "Okay. Let's hope you aren't wrong about those RPGs, Mayfield. . . . We're facing two problems. We've got to get to the hotel while also addressing the elements in front of us. So here's what we're going to do. We'll leave a third of our force to engage the immediate threat. Hopefully, that'll be enough firepower to hold 'em until help arrives. Sergeant Sosa and Corporals Blithe and Connors, bring your vehicles alongside Mayfield's team. Once you have, pick up speed. The four of you are to head up the roadway on the far left and engage the enemy without delay. Mayfield, you'll command the attack. You'll destroy the enemy without hesitation. Is that clear?"

"Yes, sir."

"At one hundred meters, stop, discharge your teams, and engage whatever it is you face. They won't be expecting you to be who you are. And at that range, without night vision equipment, they've no chance of seeing you through the dense fog. With any luck, you'll be able to eliminate a sizable portion before they react and counterattack. Strike as hard as you can with everything you've got. Hold nothing back. I want a suppressing stream of rifle and machine-gun fire and a shower of grenades raining down upon them so fierce that little in the targeted area will survive the initial onslaught. Given what's going on, even if you handle the first wave, you can expect a continual stream of lunatics to appear behind them. Hold your positions and take them out. Is that clear? Don't stop until you've finished off every last one. Your fire teams are to keep the pressure on until those on foot reach you. Once the rest of us arrive at the hotel and identify what we're up against, we'll let you know whether you're to stay here to cover our return or rush to join us. Do all of you understand what's expected from you?"

A chorus of voices replied, "Yes, sir."

"Then let's take it to the sorry bastards. While you begin your attack, we'll hang back. As you put the pressure on, the remaining Humvees will form a single line and swing to the far right. The noise of your actions and the covering conditions should mask our sudden appearance. Hopefully, with the intensity of the fire-fight they won't hear us coming until we're right on top of them. We'll hit them with our .50-calibers as we rush past. That should cripple them even more. Before the opposition realizes what's happened, we'll have skirted their position and be gone. You've got your orders: Undertake them without delay."

"We're on it, sir," Mayfield said. "My force, head for the left edge of the pavement."

The deadly quartet responded with lightning speed. In a passing moment, they were roaring side by side up the wide pavement. In frenetic seconds, they'd reach the one-hundred-meter point.

The remaining Humvees dove to the right. They lagged behind the initial grouping, waiting for the fierce encounter to commence. Once that occurred, they'd attempt to maneuver past the mortal conflict, firing as they went.

"Place the two Humvees with TOWs in the middle of the formation," Erickson directed his remaining force. "We need to make sure they're protected until we really need them."

The eight arranged themselves and prepared for the moment when they'd rush forward and break through the fierce fight.

Erickson keyed his headset once again. He knew the Marines on foot would have heard everything those in the Humvees had been discussing. "Lieutenant Ambrose, get your men up here without delay," he directed. "Assist Mayfield's teams in taking out the opposition. When you're through, join us at the hotel."

"Got it, sir. We're on our way," was the response.

The running Marines picked up the pace.

8

"One hundred meters! Halt your vehicles and engage the enemy!" Mayfield screamed. "Don't hold anything back."

All four Humvees slammed to a stop, skidding on the glistening pavement. Three Marines leaped from each. In an instant, twelve expert marksmen spread out across the open thoroughfare. Each dropped to a prone position on the dank ground and prepared to open fire. They had the enemy in their sights.

In unison, the Americans standing behind the powerful .50-caliber machine gun mounted in the center of each Humvee unleashed their weapons. A steady stream of devastating five-shot bursts spewed defiance and death at the ill-prepared forms caught in the rapidly exploding maelstrom. From behind the protective metal barrier shielding them from harm, all four machine gunners laid down a destructive curtain. The heavy machine guns overwhelmed the startled jihadists. The passing rounds, tearing through their flailing bodies, crushed them all. In ones and twos or muddled clumps, they dropped to the ground. Caught in the open, waves of stunned combatants went down. Yet the interlopers' agony scarcely had begun.

Near the stilled Humvees, a quartet of .30-caliber light machine guns joined their powerful brothers. Each spewed death toward the startled invaders. The quartet of marksmen armed with M4s squeezed off the first of many rounds from the highly accurate rifles, their night vision easily identifying each inviting target in the faltering queues. At this distance, there was no chance even a single bullet from the talented Americans would miss. With absolute precision, figure after distorted figure fell.

Most moved no more. For the bewildered horde, the furtive journey to a beckoning next world had begun. They were followed by another . . . and another . . . and another . . . without pause.

At the same instant, each of the fire team gunners armed with grenade launchers began inserting a crippling 40mm canister into the stubby launcher beneath his rifle's barrel. All four readied their murderous munitions. Before the dazed swarm could react, an initial launcher trigger was pulled. Others soon followed. Cutting through the hovering mist, each headed straight for the startled throngs clustered in the wide grasses. A fraction later, an initial spirit-seizing detonation arrived. Three more soon followed. Four devastating explosions rocked the lurid night. Absolute violence and certain extinction filled the tumultuous scene.

Without conscious thought, the Americans mowed them down. The unanswerable horror that reached out for their stunned victims was beyond description. The lethal poison that struck the faltering cultists was absolute. The mighty strike, certain and precise, swallowed them whole.

Each of the four gunners reached for a second grenade. At a rate of seven or eight per minute, the relentless Americans tore their adversary's world apart. Caught in the open, the initial Fedayeen force was ripped to shreds. In little more than the blink of an anguished eye, ten . . . twenty . . . thirty . . . forty were felled. Most never knew what hit them. In seconds, only a faltering handful of the first fifty survived. The rest lay dead or dying upon the dew-clutched soil at the edge of the significant avenue.

The survivors dove for elusive cover that was nowhere to be found upon the well-manicured lawns. Each blindly attempted to return fire at an antagonist they could neither see nor identify. From one hundred meters distant, the Americans' muzzle flashes were swallowed whole by the elements, masking their positions.

Behind the ill-fated marauders, the far more significant force reacted. Each threw himself onto the ground close to the nearest building and opened fire. Still others appeared from the rear of the imposing structure. In a steady buildup, unyielding numbers joined in on the intensifying clash. Erickson's men spotted each distant invader hurrying toward the scene. An immense gathering of dissidents was in progress. Their numbers, reaching into the hundreds, were rapidly evolving.

The Americans had the element of surprise and the superior weapons. The grappling jihadists had the significantly larger force. In the beginning, surprise was winning. The slaughter was hideously brutal. Still the Marines' struggling opponent soon regrouped, got to their feet, and began edging forward. No matter the cost, they refused to disengage and withdraw. As the vicious battle mounted, they continued their dogged efforts, moving inch by inch, foot by foot, toward Mayfield's modest force. The gathering rabble knew only one way to fight and it didn't involve retreating even when the situation called for such an action.

Every arriving zealot quickly joined in the erupting fray. With only the echoing battle sounds to guide their wild efforts, they opened fire on the unseen assailants. An immense barrage began stinging the ground around the idling American vehicles. Ricocheting bullets struck the Humvee's motionless frames over and again. Death's unrelenting image surrounded each of the compelling Marines.

"God, they're everywhere!" Mayfield yelled into his headset. "My team's got those on the extreme left. Connors, your Humvee will take any force appearing on or near the roadway. Sosa and Blithe, your men will handle the center."

The moment the life-crushing contest began, the trailing Humvees roared forward. One hundred meters behind Mayfield's group, with Erickson in the lead vehicle, they raced toward the furious encounter.

"The moment you're past our guys, open fire with your .50-caliber," the company commander directed his force. "Select your targets on your own initiative and let them have it. Get off as many bursts as you can as we rush by. After that, it'll be up to Mayfield to hold them until Ambrose's force arrives. Drivers, don't slow no matter what. Just keep going. We've got to reach the hotel." With rounds stinging the ground around them, the first of the racing combatants roared past their own defenses. "Now!" Erickson screamed.

Above him, his crew's machine gunner opened fire. Even at a full sprint, the malignant shells tore into the encroaching enemy. The crushing .50-caliber armaments, adding to the swirling turmoil, ripped the unfortunate apart. Scores of mangled bodies fell once more. A fraction later, the second Humvee in the tightly bunched line opened up, stinging the exposed mob. Like the first, the adept gunner's efforts staggered their unending opponent. The passing line and Mayfield's Marines had them in a cross fire. The shocking assault appeared to be hitting the confused peasants from every direction. Who was inflicting it, and where they'd come from, they hadn't a clue.

The third American crew in the speeding line joined the raging storm. As it did, Erickson's team, free of the skirmish, ceased fire and headed toward the turnoff for the hotel. Seven more would soon follow. Machine guns two and three also went silent as both crews escaped the spider's web of death and destruction. For the briefest of moments, the firing from the eastern side of the roadway paused as the two Humvees carrying TOW missiles rushed past. But the lull was swiftly shattered as the final three in the speeding line scurried by with .50-calibers blazing. Unharmed, the entire file vanished. Aga Khan Road was growing near. A final turn to the left at the next intersection and they'd head for the beleaguered hotel.

On the bloody ground behind them, the first of Mayfield's Marines went silent. A haphazard bullet in the center of his face had ended the unfortunate lance corporal's life. With the intensity of the hundreds of rifles firing in their direction, he most certainly wouldn't be the last of the Americans to fall on this night. The remaining fifteen fought on with incredible bravery, hoping to hold the relentless attackers until help arrived.

Six hundred meters south, Ambrose's final forty, running as fast as they could, spied the thunderous conflict unfolding ahead. Ricocheting shells, wild and unpredictable, began striking the area a few hundred yards in front of the oncoming Marines. Each hit the unyielding pavement and continued upon its way. More than one whistling bullet brushed far too close to a scurrying American's ear.

Ambrose reacted immediately. "Everyone keep running, but head over to the grassy areas to the left," he ordered. "That should take us out of the line of fire."

Even weighed down by the soft, clinging grasses, three minutes, no more, and they'd reach the evolving battle.

9

The hand grenade flew high, landing within a few feet of its target. In a blinding flash, the British machine gun guarding the main entryway into the Marriott was torn apart. Its gunner was felled. The faltering members of the desperate detachment fired their assault rifles again and again at the endless lines of onrushing figures. Masked in heavy gray, a handful of deviants went down. But the overriding remainder continued their assault upon the hapless defenders.

Dragging as many of their dead and wounded with them as they could, for a third time the British sergeant ordered his men to fall back. Less than ten of the original thirty were still in the fight. And their numbers were dwindling. Forty feet from the hotel's glass doors and floor-to-ceiling windows, the stubbornly retreating force stopped. There was nowhere left to go. The surviving few turned and formed a semicircle around the entryway. They had no choice but to make their final stand where they were. And to hope the American Marines were drawing near. If not, they'd every intention of going down fighting. They were determined to drag into the netherworld as many of the raging opposition as they could.

The dejected sergeant took up a defensive position directly in front of the lobby's wide entrance. He glanced at the blood pouring from his left side, the horrific result of a recently fired enemy round. That portion of his uniform was turning a sickly red. The bullet had broken his ribs as it made its disjointed journey through his exposed torso. Every labored effort, each shallow breath, was filled with agony. Still, his injuries, no matter how severe, didn't dissuade him. He'd keep on fighting until the bitter end. The remnants of an earlier head wound continued to stream into his eyes. A pervading sadness was written on his blood-streaked face.

The opposition's advance had been far too rapid and much too powerful. It was well beyond anything he'd expected. Still, when the debased ones broke through, they'd have to do so by taking him down. He had every intention of making sure that was no easy task.

Still limited in their severe actions by the stifling fog, his grinning foe began gathering for a final push. In moments they'd begin an enormous onslaught.

The concluding assault roared forth. A discordant chorus of small-arms fire beset the Marriott and its frantic occupants. There could be no denying that the horrific end was nearly here. The ruthless jihadists would be soon upon them. Running figures, their automatic rifles blazing, rushed toward the building without the slightest hesitation. With their night vision to guide their concluding actions, the languishing British cut them down. The dedicated assailants, however, kept coming.

In the middle of the chaotic lobby's highly polished floor, Lauren Wells gripped the microphone with all her might. For once, she didn't care that her hair was disheveled and her appearance haggard. She had little doubt the sparkling marble beneath her feet would soon be stained with the blood of thousands of slain people whose only crime had been finding themselves in the wrong place at the wrong time.

Behind her, terrified individuals were everywhere. She tried to appear calm and professional as she stared into the camera, but the harsh reality of the situation was imprinted upon her every movement. She'd been in tough spots before. There were almost too many to count. Over the years, she'd witnessed far too many people die in the most hideous of manners. With more than one bullet flying in her direction, she'd become acutely aware of the inherent frailties of life. Yet, until now, she'd somehow survived each dangerous encounter unscathed. Nonetheless, this time the ruinous feeling sinking deep within her was different. A morose pall had enveloped the struggling reporter's core.

She knew the truth. The perverse beings attempting to breach the hotel's defenses cared nothing about the untold humanity within its sheltering walls. Like those around her, it wouldn't matter who she was or what she was here to do: they'd gleefully take her life in the most horrifying of ways. Death's shroud, dark and strangling, hung over the despairing scene. It weighed heavily upon the doomed hotel like a hellish, soul-devouring tapestry.

Chuck Mendes fought to hold the camera steady. He signaled he was ready.

She could scarcely be heard over the urgent screams and frantic directives of those around her. "This is Lauren Wells. I'm speaking to you from the Islamabad Marriott," she said in a stiff monotone. "I hope what I'm relaying is somehow found and that my words will eventually find their way to our television audience. It is shortly before two a.m. on November first. The hotel and its thousands of occupants have been under an overwhelming siege by an undetermined force for nearly ten minutes. The British soldiers guarding the enclosure are attempting to hold them back. They're fighting with incredible bravery. At the moment, however, there appears to be little hope of them emerging victorious. There are too many rifle-carrying marauders outside. We're about to be overrun. What the hopeless defenders face is simply too much for them to overcome. In a matter of minutes, possibly less, they'll likely be defeated and the sadists will prevail. A crazed legion of Basra's fanatics, sadistic smiles on their bearded faces, will enter the hotel. Once they breach the entrance, there's little doubt what the result will be."

She made a nervous glance about the room. "The lobby and first floor are full of desperate people unsure of what to do. We've barricaded all the doors into the hotel except the ones in the front. With its nearly endless windows and wide glass entranceway, there hasn't been time to do so. Many of those present are opposed to blocking the main entrance even if we could find a way. They're convinced the insurgents, seeing their lethal path blocked, would set the hotel on fire and kill us that way. Thousands of people have run upstairs, hoping against hope to find some sort of hiding place. Others have remained here, believing their best chance, their only chance, is to somehow slip out during the first confusing moments of the butchers' incursions inside these walls."

Wells sighed, convinced of the certainty of what she was saying. "But it won't matter which decision we make . . . stay on the lowest floors, or hide in the farthest reaches. They'll find us. With smoking rifles and sharp-edged swords, they'll go from room to room relentlessly destroying. Without exception, everyone will be massacred. Even if we're somehow missed in their murderous rampage, we'll soon find ourselves trapped in the roaring fires these twisted souls will set. It's quite likely that all of our lives are already over. There appears to be little any of us can do to change that. Like so many others, I'm trapped here with no means of escape. Early in the attack, a few dozen people tried to hide in the fog and break through to safety. But each failed. Men, women, children . . . the Fedayeen Islam cut them down without mercy. Their bodies lay scattered about the areas in front of the hotel. The stain of blood is everywhere."

Behind her, a number of men and women of many different nationalities could be seen rushing about and shouting to each other. All were preparing to make a desperate stand once the rabble reached the hotel's foyer. Wells nervously glanced toward the main doors and the long rows of plate glass windows on each side of them. The defenders inside the Marriott, the last line of the despondent defenses, were taking up positions near the entranceway.

Ten feet behind Wells, the camera captured a couple with a young child standing near the registration desk. The man and his wife were engaged in a highly agitated conversation. She caught their interaction out of the corner of her eye. It distracted her momentarily. The attractive American pair in their early thirties and their captivating four-year-old daughter had been among those she'd spoken with during the follow-up interviews she'd conducted to supplement her earlier reporting. Their names were Collin and Kari McCaffrey and they were from Minneapolis. The child was named MaKenna. Both parents had impressed her with their compelling story and the fundamental decency with which they lived. The family had been in Pakistan for nearly twenty-four months. Collin, a highly skilled surgeon, and Kari, a registered nurse, had been a part of a medical team that had come to work in the most backward areas of the country to provide urgently needed care. Their time here was nearing its end. Their two years serving in this far-off place were almost up. Until the world around them erupted, they'd been scheduled to depart in a few weeks.

Collin was holding a stout table leg and gesturing toward those heading toward the foyer. It was clear from his actions that he planned on joining in defending the huddling thousands trapped inside. It was equally obvious that Kari was vehemently opposed to her husband's decision. But he couldn't be dissuaded. With a final shake of the head, he directed his wife and child to take cover behind the lobby's lengthy check-in desk. He turned and headed toward the front of the building.

Wells continued her reporting, intent on including as much of what was happening as she possibly could before it was too late. "Fifty men and women have banded together in a last-ditch attempt to stop the attackers once they enter the hotel. They've seized anything they can find to use against the Fedayeen. Some have armed themselves with knives and cleavers from the hotel's kitchen. Others are tearing apart the lobby's tables and chairs to create makeshift weapons. They're grabbing everything really— lamps and heavy fixtures—whatever they can find. They're planning on hiding near the hotel's entrance and surprising whoever enters. The defenders are fiercely determined. Even so, the majority are realists. Few have the slightest delusion of prevailing. That, nevertheless, no longer matters. They recognize they won't be able to stop the overwhelming cadre of thieves and murderers headed this way, but each hopes their efforts will slow them just a bit more. They're not willing to go down without one hell of a fight. We were told a few hours ago that the Marines would be arriving at the Marriott right about now to rescue us and take us to the United States embassy. But there's been no sign of them. We've no idea if they've even reached Islamabad. It's possible they were forced to turn back. We've no information whatsoever on where they are or if they're actually coming."

Outside, the assault continued. Scores of long bursts spewed forth from the assailants' rifles. Half the remaining British soldiers were felled within moments of each other. In an instant, the massive glass windows and immense doors burst into thousands of shattering pieces beneath scores of viciously striking bullets. Inside the Marriott, every head instinctively ducked. Yet, for more than a dozen, the deadly game had reached its end. As Wells had anticipated, the pristine white marble began to turn a bright red.

The mindless attackers came on. They were moments away from breaking through.

10

1:55 A.M., NOVEMBER 1
ALPHA COMPANY, 3RD BATTALION,
6TH MARINE REGIMENT, 2ND MARINE DIVISION
LEAVING CONSTITUTION AVENUE
ISLAMABAD, PAKISTAN

The first of the Humvees slammed around the corner and raced onto Aga Khan Road. One thousand feet to the hotel's entrance. The imposing structure was coming into view.

Behind Erickson, seven more turned onto the apprehensive avenue. With their swiftly rotating tires, spewing water and devouring the passing mist, they continued their maniacal quest to reach the Marriott before it was too late.

In the distance, Erickson's night vision, cutting through the suffocating fog, identified ample muzzle flashes and distant apparitions scurrying through the corrupting night. They were everywhere the Marine captain's eyes surveyed. There were far too many to calculate. All were heading toward the hotel. The echoing sounds of the frightful struggle reached out to seize the approaching Marines. Turmoil and anarchy crushed the blighted scene.

During his long years of military service, the talented company commander had faced similar moments. And as in all of them, he'd no idea what the latest frightful encounter might bring.

Whether the sneering slaughter inside the hotel was underway, he'd no way of knowing. With the pitched battle ongoing, he knew there was some chance he'd be able to save many of those within the battered architecture. But for that to happen, he had to get there soon.

The onrushing rescuers' vehicles were closing. Half a minute . . . no more . . . and he would cross his foe's lines and reach the hotel's doorstep. His six Humvee-mounted machine guns were already within range. The only problem was that, while he assumed the majority of the frenetic figures he saw were enemy combatants, in the spiraling confusion he couldn't be certain. Until he cut the distance significantly, and he became more confident about who and what they faced, he wouldn't engage.

His anxiety continued to rise. The furious images were much too close to the immense complex. But he couldn't order his gunners to unleash their weapons and risk killing one of the British soldiers or a desperate civilian attempting to flee.

"Faster, Mullins, faster," he directed the lead Humvee's driver. He did nothing to hide his mounting concern. His words were rushed, his determination obvious. "Machine gunners, select targets and prepare to open fire. But don't do so until I give the command. Let's make sure of what our night vision is telling us before we let loose with everything we have. When we get there, the first pair of Humvees will focus on fighting their way through to the front of the hotel and attempting to secure it. The rest of you are to play it by ear. Have your teams exit the vehicles and join the battle the moment we run into significant resistance. Take out the bastards wherever you find them. Once we've seized some level of control, I want you to set up an outer defensive perimeter and get ready for potential counterattacks. After we subdue the attackers, place two vehicles to the southwest, the remaining four to the west and northwest. We've no idea what's lurking in the night, so be prepared for absolutely anything. Humvee commanders, is that clear?"

"Yes, sir," each said.

"Sergeant Howard, you'll have command of our forces on the perimeter until help arrives. I'll handle the defense of the hotel and any threat arising from the north or east."

"Got it, sir," came Howard's response from the third vehicle in the rushing line. Fifteen seconds and they'd be in a position to attack. And like those the Marines on Constitution Avenue had surprised, the marauding bands they would soon confront had no idea the Americans were on the way. Even if they could've heard the Humvees approaching, in the conflict's din they had no ability to determine what direction the approaching force was coming from and who they were.

The British sergeant stood scarcely an arm's length from the hotel's main doorway as he made a final, desperate attempt to hold off the significant force coming toward him. He took a quick look around, a consuming sorrow seizing him. That he could see, none of his bested men were still fighting. The last had succumbed moments earlier.

A dozen insurgents were headed his way. Behind them, more were appearing out of the cloaking night. He opened fire, hoping to take them out before the extremists could respond. Screaming in anguish, the foremost four fell upon the contested ground. The fifth in the disordered gathering brought his weapon up and fired a long burst from his assault rifle. Two bullets ripped into the final British soldier. The first splintered his collarbone. The second missed his heart by inches, tearing open his left lung. The sergeant fell facedown a few feet to the right of the Marriott's broad doors. His tortured breath was fleeting and unsteady. Each moment's searing pain was all-consuming. He lay unmoving, unable to do anything further to stop the advancing aggressors.

Seeing him fall, the initial grouping rushed forward. In their haste to storm the building, they ignored the downed sergeant. There'd be ample time later to deal with him.

Doing their best to not give away their presence, the defenders inside the hotel waited in every corner of the sweeping foyer and initial portions of the spacious lobby. The one nearest the doorway saw the sergeant go down. He signaled the others. From their tenuous hiding places, they waited in ambush.

With murder in their hearts and hatred in their souls, the zealots scrambled up the steps. The first four kept their rifles at the ready. Those behind them drew their macabre curved swords. Each was certain the sacrificial blood flowing from their terrifying blades would soon be thick and heavy. There was a cruel, cocksure smile on every face.

From his hiding place, the desperate individual at the forefront of the defenders whispered, "Get ready. Here they come!"

Standing thirty feet away, still giving her report, Wells had frozen moments earlier as the windows and doors shattered. She and her cameraman had instinctively turned toward the sound of the crashing cascade of lethal glass. The still-running camera, poised on Chuck's shoulder, would record the subsequent series of events exactly as each transpired.

A few feet from what remained of the foyer's obliterated center door, the leader of the vindictive group turned to the youngest of those holding a rifle. He said something to him. The disappointed teenager stopped. His unhappiness with what he'd been told was obvious. Even so, he complied. He took up a position outside the doorway. He'd remain there to ensure none of those cowering within the hotel escaped the approaching tumult. When the hundreds of others in the attacking force reached him, he hoped to be allowed to join his conquering comrades as they methodically dispatched the reviled heretics. He was certain that in fleeting minutes all those hiding inside the huge structure would be dead. And he ardently wished to be a part of the glorious triumph over the sordid enemies of Islam.

Three abreast, the victorious killers holding rifles stepped through the scattered glass of the mangled doors. The figures clutching swords were right behind. Each took two steps toward the lobby. They could see many of those they'd come to dispatch— men, women, and children—running from the extended room toward the expansive hallway at its end. All were making their way toward the distant stairs. Their unmerciful conquest at hand, the oncoming warriors' malicious smiles grew. They knew fleeing would do little good. Their countrymen had the hotel surrounded. Every possible exit was blocked. Those they'd come to annihilate were accomplishing little more than postponing the inevitable. Their rapturous conquest was at hand. The attackers boldly moved deeper inside.

It happened in slow motion, but it happened at the speed of light. From out of nowhere, a dozen or more of those lying in wait pounced. An equal number soon followed, rushing from their hiding places. They swarmed over the seven assassins. The unprepared deviants were able to fire a few belated rounds from their AK-47s before they went down in a surging current of resolute defenders.

Three of those scrambling forward in defense of the hotel were struck by the spraying bullets. In an instant, the wounded trio fell upon the merciless marble. Collin McCaffrey was among them. The strong-minded American would be the first of those defending the Marriott to die. Hit in the middle of his chest, just forty feet from his concealed wife and child, the young doctor's final moments passed. Next to him, a pair of severely injured, a German and a Swede, began to bleed out. Their life's grievous end taunted them as it grew near.

The abhorrent rabble had stopped three of the hotel's defenders. That, however, wasn't going to be nearly enough. Filled with a torrential fury, the throng was coming at them from every direction. The unsuspecting invaders' belated efforts would be far too little and much too late. In a swirling, wrath-filled instant, all seven were overwhelmed.

The vehement fighting, up close and personal, was unimaginably ruthless and immodestly brutal. A butcher knife was plunged deep into an imprudent heart. With devastating effect, an imposing lamp was smashed over an exposed head. A solid table leg was swung with maximum enterprise. Wrenched from his grasp, a struggling peasant's throat was slit with his own sword. Strong hands found an astonished terrorist's neck. A lethal pair of boots, strategically placed, stomped one of the fallen cultists. Their blinding anger toward those who'd come to destroy their families spewed forth. Their endless ire surged unabated.

In a handful of confusing seconds, it was over. The defenders, through sheer numbers and determination, had won. All seven zealots lay dying. Their distorted carcasses were spread across the cold floor. Their lifeblood was spattered far and wide upon the stained walls and gleaming marble. But the precipitous victory wasn't without cost. Beside them, an additional pair of those attempting to protect the hotel were gone, victims of their startled foes' belated efforts to reach the nonbelievers with their fearful swords. Numerous others were injured. Even so, it mattered not to any. Like so many on this caustic night, they'd fight until the bitter end.

Outside, the teenager guarding the entryway saw what was

occurring. He scrambled from his sentry post, waving for help from those close enough to the immense structure to see his compelling movements. On the run, a significant force of more than two score responded. Assault rifles at the ready, they rushed toward the scene.

Inside, the surviving defenders picked themselves up and began preparing for the next murderous incursion. Each understood further suffering would soon be upon them. This time they had seven deadly rifles and an equal number of swords to aid their efforts. All the same, each realized their sudden bounty wasn't going to be enough. During the next assault, they wouldn't be able to catch the extremists unaware. With what they faced, none of those protecting the battered building fooled themselves in the slightest. The odds were too great. Even with the additional weapons, their unwavering efforts would eventually fail.

They had scarcely more than scant ticks of the clock before the next determined assault would be upon them. The defenders who'd seized the enemy's rifles rushed out the crippled doors. They took up positions on the steps in front of the hotel. With their newly acquired weapons' single magazines holding no more than thirty rounds, those who'd taken protective positions outside the hotel were planning on waiting until the last possible moment to open fire. Their surviving cohorts returned to their hiding places. Each understood that an irrepressible tsunami of death and destruction would soon wash over them.

At this point, however, it mattered not to any. They'd give no quarter. They'd never back down. The doomed defenders were planning on taking many of the black-clad figures with them to their looming destiny.

Thirty meters from the hotel, the jihadists suddenly stopped and dropped to a kneeling position. Each took aim and opened fire. An additional fifty emerged from the fog and joined them.

They released a second enormous volley of murder and discord upon those waiting inside.

More than a thousand scalding bullets smashed into the mutilated building. Surging arrays of lethal little killers, spewing from the ends of the homicidal rifles, soared through the broken windows and doors in search of defenseless prey. Outside, three of the seven defenders holding the recently acquired AK-47s went down. The weapons dropped from their hands as they died in a clamor of unspeakable ferocity. Many others waiting within the illusory protection of the hotel's stout walls were felled by the massive strike. The defenders' struggling numbers dropped by a third as dead and wounded appeared throughout the gleaming enclosure. Behind them in the first floor's open spaces, more of the unfortunate were gone. The crimson-stained marble grew to immense proportions.

Wells stood in the open lobby as round after round whizzed past. She could hear eternity's whisper tugging at her existence, calling to her to join those who lived no more. But to her great surprise, and still without a scratch, she somehow survived the brush with mortality.

Others weren't so lucky. A raucous round grazed Chuck's shoulder, clipping the still-running camera with a glancing blow. He instinctively dropped it on the floor. From this strange angle, it continued recording the distorted scene. A trail of red ran down his arm, trickling to his elbow and falling upon the marble.

"You all right, Chuck?" the clearly shaken Wells asked.

He grimaced in pain as he glanced at his wound. "I'm okay. It could have been a lot worse, I guess."

Outside, the four survivors cradling rifles opened fire on the swelling masses. One by one, they began taking down the incensed insurgents caught in the open. Three additional defenders rushed from inside to grab their fallen comrades' rifles. They took up positions near the others and raised them to engage the approaching enemy.

The relentless jihadists inserted new thirty-round magazines into their weapons. The moment they did, they sprinted toward the hotel entrance. Each was screaming at the top of his lungs and firing frenzied bursts as he went.

The figures holding rifles were former soldiers from armies around the globe. Not one panicked. All were experienced at handling AK-47s or similar weapons. They continued to take careful aim and let loose at the wicked forms scrambling through the unyielding nightmare. Each enacted a severe toll on the surging marauders. But the swarming enemy did so in kind, taking out the seven, until none remained on the hotel steps.

With the protective rifles silenced, the lead group of onrushing aggressors, thirty in number, rushed up the steps. Without the slightest hesitation they burst into the foyer.

They were met by an equal number of steadfast defenders fighting with the menacing swords they'd liberated from the ravaged dead, along with their makeshift weapons. Even though their numbers were roughly equal, the forlorn groupings of ones and twos waiting inside the grisly lobby were vastly outgunned. Each recognized they had little chance against such an imposing adversary. The moment had arrived for a final, hopeless stand.

Face-to-face, in the limited space before the broad lobby, the opposing warriors tore at each other. The concluding attack was brutally swift and exceptionally brutal. It lasted hardly more than a handful of fleeting seconds. The surging subversives, rifles firing, swarmed over those attempting to block their path. But the wavering defenders gave it their all, fighting with a steeled intention that defied all odds.

The opposing forces battled without the slightest compassion. Anguish and wrath overwhelmed them. Carnage and blood were everywhere.

Throughout the gruesome foyer, the grappling defenders blunted the onslaught ever so slightly. Nonetheless, the inevitable was about to occur. The survivors began to falter and then fall, death seizing them. Openings in their disjointed defenses appeared. The frail lines began to crack. There was little doubt the ruthless jihadists were about to break through.

Instinctively, Wells staggered backward, edging away from the horrid contest. The hideous struggle followed her, moving deeper into the spacious room as the final stumbling defenders attempted to hold on.

It was nearly over. A portentous massacre was at hand.

11

Up the roadway the Humvees roared. Barely one hundred meters remained until they'd reach the front entrance. The gunfire outside the hotel had stopped. Erickson knew it wasn't a good sign. In every direction the company commander looked, heavily armed figures were running toward the Marriott. A number were entering the building.

There could be no doubt about what was transpiring. He keyed his headset. "Okay, I've seen enough. There's nothing out here but sorry sonsabitches that need to be eliminated. Open fire. Hold nothing back."

The Marines' six heavy machine guns ripped into the running hordes. In clusters and clumps, in overwhelmed gatherings, shadowy forms began to fall. The startling result was sudden and certain. With each passing moment, a dozen or more were being cut down. Once again, an oblivious opponent was about to feel the immense power of the adept Americans. Even as they succumbed in staggering numbers, with the masking landscape smothering the onrushing formation, the zealots paid little attention to the intense gunfire. Most believed it was coming from nearby Fedayeen Islam units. Without hesitation, the surging Humvees leaped into the center of the menacing bands. Sinister images were everywhere the Marines looked. Erickson's men slashed at them with their irresistible weapons. Still, in immense numbers the vindictive provincial army kept moving toward the hotel.

Over the stirring bass sounds of the Americans' guns, Erickson screamed into his headset. "At fifty meters, stop, discharge your teams, and lay down a blanket of suppressing fire. For the moment, drivers are to remain with their vehicles and fight from there. The rest of you aren't to wander far from the Humvees. Until we get things under control, we're going to need all the mobility we can muster. Which means we've got to be on the move whenever the opportunity arises. More than anything, I need you to get me to the hotel's entrance as fast as you can. Concentrate on cutting a swath straight to the Marriott's front doors. We've got to take out those who've gotten inside before it's too late. Team leaders, after we've created a path to the building, the first two Humvees will continue on. Turn the final six and begin heading outward, destroying everything that strays into view. Take down the enemy and secure the perimeter as rapidly as you can. Is that understood?"

"Got it, sir," was the response from Sergeant Howard.

"Once we reach the entrance, I want both of the leading Humvees to turn around and create a barrier for those inside. Position your .30-calibers on both flanks to support the heavy machine guns guarding the center. You're to keep the insurgents from getting anywhere near the place. Is that understood?"

Sergeant Zepeda and Corporal Moore, team leader for the second vehicle, both answered, "Absolutely, sir."

"Moore, you're to handle any threat approaching the front of the hotel while I enter to deal with any jihadists who've gotten inside. Sergeant Zepeda, you're on me."

Fifty meters. Six of the fire teams slammed to a stop. Their .50-calibers continued to lay down a blanket of suppressing fire while eighteen Marines jumped from the vehicles and took up defensive positions. In scant moments their grenade launchers, M4s, and light machine guns were bringing a lethal curtain down upon the confused attackers. The toll among the swarming aggressors rose into the hundreds.

While the Americans took down the thrashing cultists, the leading pair of Humvees continued on, destroying everything entering their crosshairs. The instant they reached the hotel's entry, Erickson leaped from the lead vehicle. He raced toward the steps with Zepeda right behind. Both were ready for any eventuality. Behind them, the remaining Americans began creating a defensive wall that nothing but the most immense attack could penetrate.

Erickson spotted the British sergeant and ten others in civilian dress scattered about the area in front of the shattered doors. Despite the sounds of the struggle emanating from within the building, Erickson resisted the all-encompassing urge to rush through the opening. To blindly do so could prove fatal. He hurried to the wounded soldier, hoping against hope he was still alive. If possible, he needed to find out what they could anticipate once they entered the hotel. While the wary Zepeda kept watch, the company commander knelt and turned the distressed Brit over. The wretchedly injured sergeant grimaced, the agony of his mortal wounds all-devouring. His concluding breaths were halting and sporadic. To Erickson's relief, he was still conscious. His eyes, the extreme pain fully present, were open.

"Sergeant, how many have gotten inside?"

The briefest of smiles appeared at the edges of the sergeant's mouth. His words little more than a whisper, he haltingly answered. "You made it, Yank."

"How many inside and how long have they been there?"

"Too many to count . . . Went in seconds ago, I think. They should be nearby. Kill 'em . . . Yank. Kill 'em all." And with that, the final British soldier died.

Inside the tumultuous lobby, lingering fighting and absolute confusion reigned. At the head of the surging assailants, the young peasant who'd originally been ordered to stay behind broke free from the melee. It was time to seek revenge against those who'd murdered the seven devout followers from his village as they tried to enter the hotel. He glanced around the vast room, taking in the scene. The unending opulence disgusted him. His entire village was worth less than even a single garish fixture within the lavish hotel. In the coming hours, he was going to enjoy watching the ravishing fires as the debased structure burned to the ground.

With rifle poised, he spotted Wells and Mendes on his left. For the moment, he ignored them. An evil smile came to his face. The beautiful foreign woman and the man standing near her could wait. He knew they already were dead. Their graves were waiting. Standing in an open area with nothing to shield them, they had no chance of getting away. With nowhere to go, there was little need to hurry their demise. If either attempted to run, they wouldn't get more than a few hurried steps before he or one of his companions cut them down.

Instead, with tunnel vision and his rifle at the ready, the grinning fifteen-year-old headed for the lengthy check-in counter. He guessed correctly that there'd likely be inviting targets sheltering behind it and he didn't want to risk them being overlooked in the coming disorder. He'd clean out that area before moving on to his next victims.

Wells saw him heading toward the polished counter. From where she stood, she had a clear view of the woman and the small child she sheltered. The woman was still unaware that her husband had perished. Wells knew the approaching sycophant wouldn't hesitate to kill whomever he found there. There was no way Kari McCaffrey, crouching to protect her daughter, could see the wild-eyed individual coming toward her.

Wells realized any action she took would focus further attention in her direction. But she couldn't stand there doing nothing. Despite the risk, she needed to warn the endangered nurse before it was too late.

"Run!" Wells yelled.

The young mother looked up at her, her eyes full of fear.

"Run!" Wells yelled again. She frantically motioned toward the rear of the extended floor.

In a flash, Kari reacted. She scooped up MaKenna, sprang to her feet, and began sprinting toward the long hallway.

Despite her desperate efforts, however, she and her little girl wouldn't get far. The wayward figure took aim from ten feet away and, without the slightest hesitation, placed three rounds into the fleeing woman's back. She died instantly. Kari's four-year-old child was knocked from her arms as she slammed onto the cold marble. MaKenna tumbled onto the unyielding tiles. The fall stunned the little girl. Lip bleeding, body scraped and bruised, she lay facedown, crying, uncomprehending of what had occurred. She was only a few feet from her fallen mother. The tiny form, her back to Kari, was unaware of the harsh reality that had befallen her parents. And she was far too young to understand.

The pitiless one raised his rifle once again, intent on killing the weeping child. His second victim squarely within his sights, he began to squeeze the trigger.

From out of nowhere, the determined reporter hit him with a body blow that would've made an NFL linebacker proud. She rammed headlong into his exposed side, knocking them both from their feet. His rifle fell from his hands, skidding across the polished floor. In a tangled mass, the pair crashed to the ground.

Each did their best to scramble to their feet. But the boy beat her to it. Before she could catch her stolen breath and find a way to stand, he drew his sword and raised it to slay her. Dressed in little more than rags, the twisted assassin loomed over the fallen woman, menacingly straddling her helpless form. He was a fraction away from finishing his pious task.

There'd be no chance of escape. She knew that despite his best efforts, Chuck was too far away to reach her in time. Wells looked up, the final moment of her life full upon her. Yet, strangely, she didn't have the slightest fear. Despite an exceptionally abusive upbringing by her immensely wealthy father, she'd never yielded to anyone. Even with death poised to seize her, such an unwavering approach wasn't about to change. The defiance in her wondrous eyes was unmistakable. That was when, to her amazement, she saw him. Fifty feet away, the man she loved was standing there. His rifle was raised.

"Sam!" she screamed.

12

As he stood on the edge of the lobby's dreadful melee, Erickson was beyond stunned to see her. Until this moment he'd had no idea Lauren was within seven thousand miles of what was taking place here. When they'd spoken earlier in the week, she'd made no mention of any plans to leave New York. In a flash, the talented Marine recovered. He blew the menacing jihadist's head off.

The malevolent sword, raised and ready to take Wells' life, harmlessly fell from the teenager's hands. He collapsed onto the polished marble. He was dead before he hit the floor.

The assailed reporter struggled to her feet, the shock of the passing seconds overwhelming her. On trembling legs she rushed over and scooped up the struggling child. Cradling the little girl, she ran as fast as her dazed senses would allow toward the rear of the hotel. Chuck joined her, trying his best to protect them as they scurried away.

Erickson turned, searching out his next victim from the brutal conflict's disjointed scene. Even though they were outnumbered by more than ten to one, he recognized that the exceptionally skilled duo standing in the foray had a huge advantage. With few exceptions, the marauders inside the hotel had their backs turned to the suddenly appearing Marines. Each assailant had assumed the only people entering the hotel behind them would be their arriving comrades. They were completely unaware of the Americans' presence. Even so, Erickson and Zepeda didn't have a moment to waste. They had to act before the miscreants figured out what was happening and turned to respond.

The pair began taking down the enemy. Zepeda fired a three-shot burst into two figures attempting to finish off one of the few surviving defenders. Both went down. The Marine sergeant turned toward the next inviting target and squeezed the trigger. With the jihadists scarcely more than arm's length away, there was no need to take careful aim. Moving from target to target, the proficient Marine destroyed one after the next. His echoing shots plowed through his ill-fated quarry. He continued without pause, relentlessly completing the grim endeavor.

Beside him, Erickson took out another of the desperate individuals. Then another. And yet one more. Before their rivals could respond, the menacing twosome ravaged the overwhelmed majority.

It took little more than a few passing heartbeats for the Marines to tear them apart. Without ever realizing what had happened, two-thirds of the hotel's self-assured attackers were gone. Their bloody figures were scattered across the wide lobby as if tossed there by a vengeful god.

Only six of the zealots remained. Finally recognizing that something had gone horribly wrong, the final half dozen turned to face the rifle-wielding figures. For most, however, they were going to be far too slow, and much too late. Before a brief life's tortured end claimed them, only two of the startled interlopers got off even a single round.

Still, the Marines' efforts weren't without cost. Zepeda was felled, a final bullet from a jihadist's lengthy burst striking him, smashing into his upper thigh. As he tumbled onto the harsh floor, blood spurted from the fresh wound.

Without hesitation, the company commander destroyed the surviving antagonists, each with a single, certain shot. After a hurried look around to ensure none of the murderous opposition remained, he rushed to Zepeda's side. A cursory examination of the wound left no doubt it was serious. The loss of blood was mounting from both the smaller hole made by the round's entry and the extensive damage done as the enemy's tumbling bullet exited through the back of his leg.

Erickson keyed his headset, directing his comments to those who'd arrived in the two Humvees outside the doorway. "We've gotten the situation within the hotel under control. All of the Fedayeen have been eliminated, but Sergeant Zepeda's been hit. I need one of you inside to address his wounds while I try to create a semblance of order in here. There are thousands of terrified people in this building and I need to get a handle on the situation before we can even think about moving them to safety."

He'd scarcely finished the words when the junior member of Zepeda's squad, Private First Class Dowling, appeared. He hurried over to where his company commander was kneeling next to the fallen sergeant.

"He's bleeding pretty badly," Erickson said. "You've got to handle this on your own while I ensure the hotel's actually secure. Get a tourniquet on his leg and then do what you can to apply first aid to the entry and exit wounds."

The young Marine didn't hesitate. He stripped off his belt, placed it around his team leader's thigh above the flowing wound, and tightened it. The loss of blood dropped to a manageable trickle. He took out his own first aid packet, removed Zepeda's, and began applying bandages to both the front and back of his wounded squad leader's leg.

Pleased with Dowling's efforts, Erickson refocused on the harried scene in the lobby. Ready to fire at a moment's notice, he moved through the first floor's initial areas, kicking the fallen Fedayeen weapons away while searching for any signs of a potential threat. None appeared, however.

While Erickson surveyed the distant corners of the chaotic room, his grief grew. The immense failure he felt momentarily overwhelmed him. There was little doubt that many of those who'd made the heroic stand within the hotel lived no more.

Still, from the low moans and anguished cries, he also was certain that more than one, while badly wounded, was still alive.

Outside, the sounds of the swift, uneven battle continued, growing more distant as the Marines eliminated those closest to the lengthy structure and moved on. Erickson could tell from the excited radio chatter that his men had caught the perplexed enemy unprepared for the raging death that came for them.

13

Wells cautiously approached the lobby holding the sobbing, injured child. Chuck was with her. As she passed the bodies of MaKenna's mother and father, she shielded the little girl, making certain she couldn't see what had happened. When she drew near, Sam could see the profound trauma set deep within Lauren's eyes. She walked up to him as he viewed the horrific scene. Over one hundred bodies, defenders, attackers, and noncombatants alike, were scattered about the bloody space.

She gave him a gentle kiss on the cheek. "Oh, my God, Sam, I no idea it was you who was coming. It's a miracle you got here when you did. Another ten minutes and we would've all been dead."

She could see his disappointment as he surveyed the hellscape spreading out before him. His sorrow spewed forth. "This is my fault," he said in a low tone. "If we could've gotten here a couple of minutes sooner, none of this would've happened and these people would be alive."

"I know, but you saved so many."

Yet for him it wasn't enough. The loss of a single life among those he'd vowed to protect weighed heavy upon him. And there were a great deal more than that both inside and outside the hotel. As much as he would've liked to have taken a moment to be with her after a year's separation, now wasn't the moment. There were a million things to do and no time for any of it.

"I'm aware of that, Lauren." He took another look around the lobby. The dead and soon to die were everywhere. "But what occurred here is my responsibility. As it is, there are people in here who're still alive. And we can't spare a moment if we're going to save them. We need care for the wounded and we need it now. With this many people in the hotel, there's got to be at least a few with some sort of medical training."

Wells looked at the beautiful child with shoulder-length blond hair cradled in her arms. "There are. This one's parents were part of a team of doctors, nurses, and support personnel who had been providing assistance in the farthest corners of the country. I've no idea who they are or where they might be within the building. But there are definitely people who can help."

"We don't have much time. Can you gather some volunteers? Priority one will be identifying the medical personnel and getting them down here. Once you've finished that, send people to the upper floors to let those hiding up there know they're safe. Tell them we need everyone to gather on the conference level. With who knows what stalking the night, we have to leave this place as quickly as possible. Make sure those you send to the upper floors understand there can be no mistakes. They have to keep going until they find everyone."

"I'm on it, Sam." She turned to her still-bleeding cameraman. "Chuck, do you think you can make it up the stairs and send down anyone you find with medical training? While you're doing that, I'll check this floor for them."

"On it," he answered.

With the child cradled in her arms, she turned and followed, purposely walking toward the rear of the hotel. She knew a number of people were hiding in the kitchen, restaurants, and areas at the far ends of the floor. Hopefully, members of the medical team were among them.

Erickson called to the pair as they hurried away: "I don't want any more people than absolutely necessary to see what's happened here. So, except for those coming to treat the wounded, have everyone on the ground floor gather near the stairs and head to the conference areas. Chuck, the same for the people on the upper floors. Don't let them near the lobby."

Both signaled their understanding as they continued on their way.

While he waited for the duo to send the much-needed help, he turned toward Dowling, wanting to check on his injured sergeant. "How's he doing?"

"His breathing's steady, sir. But I'm pretty sure he's in shock. I've elevated his legs, got the bleeding stopped, and the bandages I applied appear to be holding."

"About as much as we could hope for at this point."

"Don't worry about me, sir," Zepeda said through clenched teeth. "I'll be okay." He turned his head, viewing the monumental carnage. "Take care of the others."

"Keep a good eye on him, Dowling, while I try to determine how many of those who battled the sorry bastards are still alive."

Erickson began moving about the oppressive space, examining the battered defenders. He started identifying which were holding on and attempted to determine what level of care each would require. For the majority, there was no decision to make. Most were dead, their bodies vanquished, their sightless eyes set in a fixed stare. A baker's dozen were clinging to life, though few would last much longer without significant help. As he neared the conclusion of the forbidding undertaking, he could see relieved people moving toward the wide stairs leading to the conference level. At first, it was just ones and twos heading up the steps. Their numbers, however, soon swelled.

As requested, those with medical training began gathering. Lauren, her task completed, joined them. While they stood at the bottom of the stairway, it didn't take long for one of the folks who'd been a part of the McCaffreys' medical team to notice who Wells was holding.

"MaKenna?" the perplexed woman asked. The sobbing, traumatized child never looked up or responded in the slightest. "Where are her parents?"

Lauren shook her head. "We need all of you in the lobby to deal with the wounded."

The growing group started toward the front of the hotel. The arriving doctors' and nurses' relief to be alive was rapidly replaced by the pervasive horror they spied. Even the most hardened was taken aback by the tossed room's dreadful landscape. Few, including those with significant emergency room experience, had ever encountered anything half as appalling as this. All stopped before reaching the registration desk, unwilling to be drawn further into the lurid spectacle spreading before them. The abject slaughter was beyond comprehension. More continued arriving. In moments, their numbers were sufficient for each of the wounded to begin receiving care.

Erickson motioned to the vacillating group. "You won't do these people any good over there," he said. "I know this isn't pretty, but it's time for you to do your job. I've identified those who're still alive. As I point them out, I need each of you to take one and do what you can. We've got a dozen or more wounded, plus my sergeant over there."

They began to walk toward him, their reluctance to enter the horrific melee still evident.

"How many of you are doctors?"

Five hands, three men and two women, were raised.

"I'm a trauma surgeon and I've handled far worse than this," an older man at their head said, doing his best through his false bravado to encourage the others. "Give me the most difficult case you can find."

Without saying a word, Erickson pointed to a beaten defender lying a few feet from him. The fallen figure gave every appearance of being on the edge of death.

The doctor walked over, took one look at what he faced, and called to two of the team's medical technicians. "Aaron . . . Gary . . . get up to the fifth floor as fast as you can and grab every piece of equipment and all the medical supplies you're able to carry. We need the first of it down here in the next two minutes if any of these people are going to survive." He knelt and began examining his severely wounded patient.

The technicians responded immediately, turning and running toward the stairs.

"There are medical supplies in the hotel?" Erickson asked the doctor.

Never taking his eyes off his despairing patient, the man answered. "Yeah. Forty of us, doctors, nurses, medics, and technicians, belong to a group that's been over here for the past two years providing urgent care in some of the most primitive portions of the country. We've been traveling from village to village with a mobile hospital full of equipment. It's crammed in a couple of rooms on the fifth floor. We can bring it down here in the next ten minutes if you can find some people to help my guys."

As Erickson pointed out the other wounded, the remainder of the doctors began selecting their patients. The nurses soon followed. Without a word, Erickson moved over to the hallway. He could see Lauren standing near the other end, working to get the last of the people she'd found up to the next level.

"Lauren," he shouted. "See if you can get a half dozen or so people to go to the fifth floor and help the medical technicians bring down their equipment."

"On it, Sam," she responded.

Lauren's volunteers were soon on the way, taking the steps three at a time.

Erickson returned to the lobby. The doctors and nurses were doing their best despite the long odds. Even this early in their efforts, the majority recognized that when the medical supplies arrived they weren't going to be able to save those under their care. While they continued to treat the wounded, all could hear the fierce contest continuing in distant milieus outside the hotel. The Marines' efforts to quell the sadists weren't finished quite yet.

The world around the hotel went quiet. Erickson's headset crackled to life. "Sir," Sergeant Howard told him, "we've eliminated everything for three hundred meters in each direction. There's not a Fedayeen rifle still firing. We're moving out to set up a defensive perimeter. So far, there's been no signs of additional combatants heading our way."

"What's the status of your men?" Erickson asked.

"We caught the assholes by complete surprise. Killed hundreds of 'em. I've got two wounded, one of them fairly severely, and no dead. That's it. But it won't stay that way for long if a thousand more aggressors show up. Next time, once they spot their dead comrades, they'll likely be far better prepared than this force was."

"Understood. Get your wounded to the lobby. There's a medical team here."

"Yes, sir."

"Then get that perimeter established."

"We'll do our best, sir."

With scarcely two dozen of his men protecting the hotel, the company commander recognized the situation was far from secure. "Let's hope Lieutenant Ambrose gets here real soon."

"From the sounds of gunfire south of us, sir, I'd say they've got their hands full," Howard responded.

14

On Constitution Avenue, Mayfield and his men continued to battle those who'd relentlessly appeared in the well-manicured area beyond the last of the government buildings. With each passing instant, the forty Marines on foot were closing with the furious struggle. In scarcely two hundred meters, they'd reach the evolving conflict.

The perplexed enemy, blinded by the suffocating fog and unaware of the Americans' presence, remained unsure who or what had attacked them. But whoever it was, their unrelenting foe knew what they were doing. The floundering extremists' losses had been severe. Well more than one hundred were dead or wounded. And that number was increasing. Nevertheless, the curtain of gunfire the jihadists laid down was taking its toll upon Mayfield's force. With two dead and three wounded, the remaining eleven fought on with incredible resolve. Yet, with hundreds of aggressors attacking their positions, the desperateness of their situation was becoming evident.

As they approached, Ambrose surveyed the murderous quagmire the running Marines would soon enter. Even with his reinforcements, the Americans were going to be outnumbered ten to one. He recognized that if they were going to destroy the gathering throngs, he needed to come up with an aggressive plan to overcome the lopsided odds.

While the platoons scurried through the grasses on the left side of the roadway, he soon identified the four Humvees engaged in the furious engagement and those fighting in and around them. His night vision told him the vehicles were spread out across the pavement ahead and slightly to the right of his formation. To his left, he could see the outlines of a row of government office buildings, each two to five stories tall. The structures were eerily silent. There was no activity within their hazy forms. The images he found on the ground, however, were far different. Ahead, there was movement everywhere. Significant enemy forces had taken up positions beyond the final building. The running platoon leader surveyed the area, trying to determine if further Fedayeen were arriving. But as the Marines drew closer, there was no indication of additional forces joining in.

Masked in a blanket of clinging gray, Ambrose recognized the zealots would have no idea of the existence of the oncoming Americans. Like those arriving before him, he'd use that to his advantage. In a passing moment, he recognized what he needed to do. If his plan worked, in a minute, possibly two, his men would be in a position to destroy the entirety of the opposing force with only minimal losses of their own.

He keyed his headset. "Zack, we're greatly outnumbered, but I've got an idea that should more than even the odds. I need you to take your platoon and circle around the other side of the buildings."

"Roger," Marshall responded. "Second Platoon, on me."

The trailing nineteen turned to the west, heading toward the opening between the nearest structures. Ambrose's voice returned. "From what I can see, our guys are presently engaging all of the rabble in the area. There appears to be about four hundred of the cultists involved, maybe a bit more. They're firing from the open grassy areas beyond the final building. They obviously don't understand even the most basic concepts about conducting a successful assault. They've ignored every advantage the buildings and their surroundings give them. And they've made a fatal mistake. They're far too tightly bunched and completely exposed. On top of that, they're making no effort to flank the Humvees and take them out. Instead, they seem to be counting on winning through sheer numbers and brute force. In essence, they're making what is fundamentally a head-on suicide attack that, even if victorious, will cost them dearly. Stupid. They're begging us to pick their bones clean. And I can't think of a single reason why we shouldn't do that."

"No reason at all, Jeff," was Marshall's reply.

"In the last minute or so, I've seen no indications of additional jihadists arriving. Hopefully, this is all there is. They can't possibly know we're here. That, and the fact they've made all of these tactical errors, is our big advantage. I want you and your platoon to flank them and come in behind the bastards."

"We're on it," was Marshall's response.

"Bring your men up to the farthest edge of the last building. Carefully spread them out behind the insurgents without exposing your guys to getting hit by friendly fire from my platoon or Mayfield's Humvees. Once you're in place, we'll have them in a cross fire. We'll tear them to pieces without subjecting ourselves to more than a meager response from the enemies' rifles. With what I have planned, hopefully we can end this quickly and emerge nearly unscathed. In no time, we'll be heading to the Marriott."

"I'm all for that."

"Even so, be real careful as you near the targeted area. Make sure I'm right that no other aggressors are nearby. Check the areas to the west closely for any sign of unfriendlies before committing to the attack. Otherwise, it'll be your men entering the trap rather than the other way around. We need to surprise them, not have them surprise us."

"Roger, we're on it."

"Wait for us to launch our attack. Once we engage and the cultists turn their focus toward my platoon, open fire. Hit them with everything you've got."

With the noise from Mayfield's ongoing battle, and the consuming mist hiding their movements, 1st and 2nd Platoons slipped into place.

"Zack, you all set over there?" Ambrose whispered into his headset.

"Ready as we'll ever be."

The words had scarcely left the young lieutenant's mouth when Ambrose screamed, "First Platoon, open fire!"

His men unleashed four searching grenades at precisely the same instant. They soared through the dour gloom, reaching out for their oblivious opponent. Each arrived with rapturous effect. Death-laden explosions rocked the center of the fanatics' lines. The world around the ensnared humanity shuddered and yawed with ferocious intensity. The striking ordnance, its fragmented lading spreading in every direction, tore them apart. Razor-sharp shrapnel reached out to consume the unlucky.

Before the surprised interlopers could react, an equal number of malice-spitting light machine guns opened fire. Three times their number in M4s joined in. A blinding whirlwind of seeking rifles and chattering machine guns took them out in ever-expanding numbers. In the blink of an eye, scores of hapless attackers were gone. The confounded survivors attempted to answer back. Their distorted efforts were, however, of little use.

The moment the flailing enemy took the bait and attempted to respond, Marshall ordered his platoon to open fire upon their staggered opponent. The terrifying assault increased twofold. The frightful trap was sprung. The almighty force that hit them tore the primitive revolutionaries to shreds. With each passing second, the ghastly horror continued unabated as grenades, machine guns, and automatic rifles cut them down. Perdition's fires consumed them. For far too many, their solemn journey across the River Styx had begun.

In two minutes, no more, the slaughter reached its end. Not one of those the Marines had come to destroy was still firing.

"Cease fire! Cease fire!" Ambrose screamed into his headset.

Both platoons responded. With the sounds of the clash ringing in their ears, they got to their feet. They could hear the anguished screams and tortured cries of the critically wounded among the defeated force. They recognized the dying gasps of those whose final, hideous moments were upon them. They could see motionless forms spread far and wide upon the sinister landscape.

Ambrose spoke into his headset: "Zack, what're your losses?"

Marshall searched his stretching line. "One wounded, but it's fairly serious."

"Mayfield, what about your men?" the senior lieutenant asked.

After a quick examination of the scene, the sergeant answered. "Two dead and three wounded, sir."

Ambrose looked around. "I have one dead and two more wounded."

Considering the size of the force they'd destroyed, it was a remarkable result.

"Let's see what the company commander wants us to do," Ambrose said into his headset, then called out to Erickson: "Sir, we've eliminated the enemy along the roadway. Estimate their losses at around four hundred."

"Roger," Erickson responded. "What're ours?"

"Three dead and six wounded. Two of the wounded are serious."

The lieutenant's response was met with silence. Erickson knew a death among his men, even a single one, was nothing to be celebrated. And he understood in all likelihood the company's losses in the coming days were far from over.

"What're your orders, sir?" Ambrose asked.

"I need you to join us at the Marriott. Leave three fire teams from Lieutenant Marshall's platoon behind. We've no time or ability to care for any enemy wounded. Have them take those who're still breathing into the nearest building and put guards on the door. As they're doing that, the rest are to collect the enemies' rifles, ammunition, swords, and any other weapons they find. No reason to leave them behind. Stack them next to the roadway so we can pick them up on our way back. Carry our dead over and place them near the weapons so they can be loaded into one of the returning Humvees. Then have them spread out along the escape route to act as a tripwire."

"Got it, sir."

"The rest of you are to get up here as fast as you can. We've eliminated the immediate threat to the hotel but have no idea what size force, if any, is nearing. Before they stumble upon us and can bring additional suffering to those we're here to protect, we need to get the evacuation underway. Send Sergeant Mayfield's Humvees up here immediately to reinforce Sergeant Howard's men." Erickson looked around the chaotic lobby. "Load your wounded into the four Humvees and have him bring them with him."

"Roger, sir, we're on the way."

15

With the dead from both sides splayed across the cold marble, Sam Erickson stood watching the doctors and nurses, the majority of their medical equipment present, frantically working. So far, three of those they'd attempted to save had succumbed, their wounds too serious to overcome. There was little doubt more would follow. Yet, until all hope was lost, they wouldn't cease their desperate measures.

Momentarily leaving MaKenna in another woman's comforting arms, Lauren returned to Sam's side. For now, Chuck, his gunshot wound tended to by one of the medical technicians, would handle things on the level above the lobby.

The people sent to the upper floors to gather the concealed evacuees were steadily going about their task. Tromping up and down the halls, banging on doors, and yelling at the top of their lungs, they began coaxing the terrified to come out into the hallways and head for the conference center. An endless stream of relieved people were gathering. As they did, Chuck assigned each a conference room.

A few harried minutes after death's sneering figure had turned its back on her and melted away, Wells's fragile composure was beginning to return. And her involvement in getting four thousand people ready to leave was an excellent diversion. She knew the horrifying events inside the Marriott would soon find an unexpected moment to reach out and shake her to her core. Yet for now, however, she was reasonably okay.

"Where do you need me next, Sam?"

"Find me a couple dozen people to get all the food in the kitchen packed. We're going to need every bit of it in the coming days."

"Waste of time," she answered.

"What? Why?"

"There's no food. The delivery trucks stopped showing up days ago. Right now, everyone's beyond hungry. Some haven't had anything to eat in the last thirty-six hours."

There'd been no further attacks or signs of the jihadists in the short time since the end of the struggle for the hotel. Having checked on the two teams guarding the entrance to the building, Erickson was waiting on the hotel steps when Mayfield's Humvees arrived. Four of the medical technicians stood ready to carry the two most critically wounded Marines inside. The moment the vehicles eased to a stop, they sprang into action, triaging and readying the worst cases for transport. In less than a minute, the wounded were being carried into the hotel or hobbling through the entrance on their own. A trio of nurses were waiting.

Erickson walked over to where Mayfield stood next to his

idling Humvee. One look at its battered front, and the company commander recognized how intense the defeated assailants' attack had been. The signs of the fearsome struggle were everywhere. The three Humvees behind it were no different.

"Where do you want us, sir?" Mayfield asked.

"First drive around the perimeter and collect the enemy weapons and ammunition. Drag any wounded Fedayeen a safe distance from the hotel. Place some guards around them. Don't risk your men while doing so. If any of the sonsabitches makes the slightest move that appears halfway threatening, don't hesitate to take them out. It's unlikely any are still alive, but keep an eye out for any of the British soldiers who were defending the hotel."

"Yes, sir."

"If we're not ready to leave by the time you're finished, I want one Humvee to the south. There's a huge area on that side of the hotel with no one defending it. Place two in positions to support Sergeant Howard's teams in the west. The final one's to go to Aga Khan Road. Set up an outpost there. Make sure everyone's focused and ready. We've no idea how many of those brainwashed idiots are nearby."

"Will do, sir."

"We're leaving this place in thirty minutes, no more," Erickson said.

Mayfield got back into his Humvee. The battered vehicles disappeared into the shifting fog. As they did, the Marines on foot arrived.

Entering the lobby with Marshall's and Ambrose's men, Erickson's first action was to direct them to remove the ravished bodies of the enemy dead. Each vanquished jihadist was taken outside and tossed into a jumbled pile. They then carried the remains of the overcome innocents from both the grounds around the hotel and the disheveled first floor into the kitchen. They carefully laid those who'd forfeited their lives in long rows. Lieutenant Marshall and a handful of his men went through the dead's identification, writing down the information so it could be passed on to their countries of origin. They'd have preferred to have taken each of the defeated British soldiers and dead evacuees back to the embassy, but with the vehicles filled with captured enemy weapons and the wounded needing transport, there wasn't any way to do so. While Erickson made final preparations to abandon the hotel, Marshall gathered the aggrieved families of those who'd fallen and took them into the kitchen, giving them a few minutes to say their goodbyes.

The company commander waited until all of the valiant defenders and ravaged Fedayeen were removed before signaling for the first of the departing masses to leave the conference center. The last thing he needed as they moved through the lobby was the anxious thousands seeing the unspeakable spectacle's horrific results. There was no time to do anything further to mask the struggle.

In an endless procession, Alpha Company's Marines sent the survivors down the stairs. With the expansive lobby forever stained a bitter red and the bloodied furniture and shattered fixtures, there could be no mistaking what had happened. While they passed, not one of the evacuees missed the signs of the accursed event.

With only the driver and machine gunner remaining in the vehicles, the medical staff loaded the surviving handfuls of harshly injured into the leading Humvees. A doctor or nurse would ride in each.

In a never-ending trail, with the sounds of not-so-distant battles tearing at their senses and a fiery world filling the horizon, the anguished evacuees started out of the shattered doorways. None looked forward to the lengthy walk through who knew what. With so many in their number, the going would be painfully slow. Every moment would be filled with immense fear. Yet, after what had happened at the hotel, none was eager to remain where they were. Each understood that if they wanted to see the coming day, there was no choice but to confront whatever might be waiting.

At last, all were ready. They stood in well-spaced rows, ten across, from the edge of Aga Khan Road's entrance into the hotel all the way to the sorrowful lobby and up the distant stairs. The immense gathering, with fussing children, weighty medical equipment, and suitcases and other belongings, awaited the word to move out. None could deny that the heaviest thing they carried was their apprehension for what the coming hours would bring.

At their head, Erickson looked back at the massive line of frightened individuals. It seemed to go on forever. Like Moses, his own extended exodus was about to begin. And as in the Bible's vivid tale, he had a brutal pharaoh's army in pursuit.

The Humvees would create an outer shield for their precious cargo. Inside the widespread vehicles' defensive ring, the Marines on foot and the three hundred men and women who'd indicated some level of expertise with assault rifles would fill the gaps. Each of the volunteers was holding a conquered Fedayeen's weapon. Even without night vision equipment, they were more than eager to assist Erickson's men in engaging any jihadists who might appear.

Within the Marriott, Zack Marshall took his place at the end of the line. He spoke into his headset. "My men have double-checked the hotel, sir. The upper floors are empty and we're ready to leave."

"Roger. No time like the present," Erickson replied.

Ambrose's lead fire team stepped onto Aga Khan Road. Rifle at the ready, thirty yards behind them, Erickson headed away from the hotel. Row by row, person by person, those in his charge followed. Nearly two and a half endless miles before they'd reach the summoning embassy's grounds. While they took their initial steps, none could shake the unyielding nightmare they were walking through. Erickson's Marines weren't supposed to be here. Yet here they were.

Thousands of miles away, others also were hearing about the potential for such a reality.

16

While Erickson was starting toward the embassy, three thousand miles away, Army Sergeant First Class Darren Walton was fast asleep. At least until his cell phone began ringing. His wife elbowed him in the ribs. After doing so a second time, he sat up.

In a fog, Walton grabbed the phone. "Hello?"

"Sergeant Walton, this is Lieutenant Cramer."

"Yes, sir?"

"Sorry to bother you. But with you and your family leaving early in the morning for a weekend of skiing in Garmisch, it couldn't wait. As of a short time ago, all leaves have been canceled. The entire division's been put on alert."

"Alert, sir? Did they tell you why?"

"Pakistan. Should the president decide to intervene, the 3rd Infantry's one of the divisions that have been selected to go. Can't imagine it's going to happen. But even so, first thing tomorrow we're to begin getting our Bradleys and the platoon's equipment ready. I need you to meet me in the motor pool at seven."

"Seven. Yes, sir."

"Good. I'll see you there." Cramer hung up the phone.

Walton's wife, having heard pieces of what was going on, asked, "What was that?"

"Don't bother getting the girls up. We're not going anywhere."

17

Sitting under a swaying pine tree, Staff Sergeant Charlie Sanders stared out at nothing in particular. As he did, he spotted his Green Beret A Team's senior sergeant, Michael Noll, approaching.

"Aw, there you are, Sanders," Noll said. "Sergeant Porter around?" He knew Porter and Sanders were never far apart.

"Just went into the barracks to change clothes. I'm about to do the same. We're planning on grabbing some chow and heading downtown in search of wine, women, and song. Emphasis on the wine and women."

"Belay that. There's been a change of plans. Captain wants us to form up in the company area in ten minutes."

"What? We've already been dismissed for the night."

"Like I said, change of plans. So tell Sergeant Porter to put his uniform back on and line up in the usual spot in ten minutes."

Eleven soldiers stood in a straight line in front of their team leader, Captain Neil Short. Not one of them had the slightest idea why they were there.

"Men, sorry for the confusion. But we just got word that as of five o'clock the entire group's been placed on a one-hour alert," the A Team leader said. "You all know the drill. Married men, go home, grab your gear, and return immediately. From this moment on, you're confined to the company area until further notice. There's a chance we might be heading to Pakistan."

18

Thirty-two-year-old Captain Beatrice "Bea" Washington was getting into her car to head home when her company's charge of quarters came running toward her.

"Captain Washington! Captain Washington!"

"What is it, Sergeant McNeill?"

"Battalion commander called. Said he needs to speak to all the company commanders right away."

"Oh, God, what now?" she said.

"He didn't say, ma'am."

"I hope it's nothing important. I promised my daughters I'd be home in time to go trick-or-treating." She knew that the summons could be anything. "All right, Sergeant McNeill. If he calls again, tell him I'm on my way."

Captain Washington finally arrived home at a few minutes past seven. Her eight- and ten-year-old girls, having been in their costumes for the past three hours, were beyond frantic. The moment she opened the door, they rushed over to her. "Mommy, where have you been?" her oldest, Joanne, said. "All the best candy's probably gone by now."

"Yeah, Mom," her youngest, Aniyah, asked. "We've been waiting for hours. Why did you do this to us?"

"Sorry, girls, but something came up. With my job, you know your mom can't just leave whenever she wants. But I'm here, and there's still time for you to pile up tons of candy before people run out. So, rather than standing here fretting about it, let's go."

The words were scarcely out of her month when the girls blew by her and out the door.

When they returned home, it took some time for them to go through their stash and go to bed. Once they had done so, Washington picked up the phone and made a call.

It was answered after the fourth ring. "Mom?"

"Oh, hi, Bea," her mother responded. "Hadn't expected to hear from you tonight. Is everything all right?"

"Yeah, no problems. The girls and I are okay. But I need a favor."

"Oh, what's that?"

"The entire division's being placed on alert status."

"Oh? And what does that mean?"

"Maybe nothing. But it might mean a great deal. The president's not ready to intervene in Pakistan quite yet. Still, he apparently doesn't want to get caught unprepared. If he needs to send units, he wants to be ready. Should it come to that, he's selected the 10th Mountain to be a part of that force."

"You're going to Pakistan?"

"No, Mom. At least not yet. And there's a good chance we never will. But you never know how these things are going to turn out. That's why I called. If they tell us we have to go, we'll only have twenty-four hours to get all of our equipment and every soldier onto trains to head for Bayonne, New Jersey. Once there, we'll be loaded on ships and on our way."

"But Pakistan. I've been watching what's going on there. It's horrible. I don't want you anywhere near that place."

"Neither do I, Mom. But I'm a soldier. I fly helicopters. I command people who fly helicopters. It's what I do. You know that. . . . Look, it's probably not going to happen, but if it does, can you jump on a plane and get here as fast as you can? The girls will need you."

"Of course, dear. Just as long as when you get back you don't get upset if your daughters seem more than a bit spoiled. 'Cause you know my rule: what happens with Grandma stays with Grandma."

"All right, Mom. I promise to bite my lip and say nothing about what's happened while I was away."

"Then it's a deal, Bea. Just let me know if you need me and I'll be on the way."

"Thanks, Mom. I can't tell you how much I appreciate it."

19

The ominous world surrounding them as they walked down Constitution Avenue was beyond frightful. With the roaring flames devouring the city, it was as if the unyielding fog were on fire.

Behind the fleeing thousands, the Marriott's ferocious inferno soared. Arriving scant minutes after those within the Marines' care disappeared, the initial insurgents to reach the location had seen to that. The first thing the wary force found were their countrymen's bodies scattered far and wide across the eerie grounds. And a modest gathering of wounded two hundred meters west of the hotel. The precise composition of the malignant force their comrades had encountered, and exactly what had transpired, the struggling injured were unable to say. Americans, some of the survivors thought. But none was certain. They were positive of one thing, however. Whoever the attackers had been, they were extremely proficient. And quite lethal.

The rampaging peasant army, their victories without end, had seldom demonstrated caution as the weeks passed. Yet, after surveying the Marriott's gruesome scene, the stunned gathering hesitated. Even though the arriving revolutionaries were vast in number, none was eager to wander into the night in search of a similar fate. So they justified staying where they were in order to explore the distant corners of the hotel. Once their languishing efforts were complete, they set the multimillion-dollar structure ablaze. No one made the slightest attempt to do any more than remain where he was and gleefully watch the hypnotic flames.

The Marines had anticipated an unrelenting enemy onslaught as they shepherded the struggling masses' toward the embassy. Each was convinced they'd be embroiled in one vicious fight after another. But, to their surprise, it didn't happen.

They were nearly there. Scant minutes remained before the harrowing journey would reach its end. Still, the company commander knew he couldn't let down his guard. Until the undetermined moment, untold hours distant, when he and his men stepped onto the final departing King Stallion, it was a luxury he couldn't afford.

Even so, he had to admit they'd been lucky. Only a few half-hearted marauders had appeared through the mist to challenge the Marines' efforts. Each had been spotted well before they could reach the critical caravan. The highly mobile Humvees had rushed out to brush their attacker aside without suffering a single casualty among Erickson's charges.

As they neared the end of their march, the plodding line reached the first of the abandoned embassies. The company commander motioned for Lieutenant Ambrose, twenty yards behind, to join him. Ambrose hurried to the front of the formation.

"The turnoff to the diplomatic enclave's just ahead," Erickson said. "That's going to be your platoon's destination. Grab three of the machine-gun–mounted Humvees without wounded in them and one of the two equipped with TOW missiles. You'll also take a number of the evacuees. No matter their nationality, the fifteen hundred at the end of the line will be sheltering within the enclave's apartment buildings. Include at least a hundred of the civilians carrying AK-47s. Make sure each is given enough ammunition to last for at least a couple of days. Leave any women with children under five, along with their siblings, with me. After we unload the food the King Stallions are bringing, I'm going to put those women and children on the CH-53s and get them out of here."

"Yes, sir."

"Don't put up with any objections from those you're handling. Threaten to shoot anyone who refuses to follow your orders. I'll take the remainder of the evacuees, retrace our earlier steps, and lead them into the embassy grounds."

"I'll get right on it, sir."

"The XO will be waiting for you. While we were gone, Scott's been creating the stoutest fortifications possible to tie the embassy and the enclave together. He'll show you where he wants your men and the civilians in your group carrying rifles. He'll have your share of the antitank stuff. We're allocating each platoon two Javelins and one TOW tripod with six missiles."

"Got it, sir."

"We don't have a handle on what forces the enemy has in the area. But intelligence reports indicate the Fedayeen overran a number of Pakistani armored units while sweeping across the country. While they destroyed hundreds of tanks, they captured a number of them intact. There could be dozens, armed and ready, in the northeast portion of the country. They probably have at least as many functioning armored personnel carriers. So we need to be alert for not only the possibility of significant infantry attacks but also for the sudden appearance of armored forces."

"We'll do our best to be prepared for anything, sir."

"All right, Jeff. Good luck."

"Good luck to you, sir."

When they reached the enclave road, Ambrose ordered his men to stop and wait to receive the last fifteen hundred evacuees. He rushed to the rear to identify those who were being placed in his care.

Erickson continued on. Ten minutes, no more, and the first of the anxious thousands would enter the embassy's shielding walls.

The enemy, no doubt, wouldn't be far behind.

20

When the company commander had arrived with his charges, he found Scott Tomlin and Eric Joyce had done a magnificent job in creating strategically layered defenses on all four sides of the embassy and enclave. While awaiting his return, the eighty-seven Marines who had remained had dug their own foxholes between the rows of trees that surrounded the embassy and begun those for their comrades.

The majority of the spreading strongholds were in the north and west. Those guarding the enclave's eastern side, along with those in the southern woods, were, by necessity, more widely spaced. The sandbagged American Humvees and Marine foxholes reached as far as three hundred meters from both compounds. Two to a foxhole, Ambrose's platoon would have the foremost defilades to the northeast, protecting the enclave. To their left, in front of the northern portion of the embassy, were the remaining British security forces along with the Canadians and Australians. The small contingents of Japanese, Swedish, Swiss, and Spanish were on the eastern side along with 1st and 2nd Squads from Lieutenant Matt Peters's 4th Platoon.

The Dutch, French, and Germans held the far south of the combined defenses. The majority were on the edges of the tree-filled field below the American embassy. Beyond them lay the ghostly Kashmir Highway.

Lieutenant Bates's 3rd Platoon and Marshall's 2nd Platoon were to the west of the American compound. With them, the Italians were in the southwest corner in front of their own embassy. A single three-man Marine mortar team was assigned to each of the four sides.

Closer in, around both the embassy and enclave, Tomlin placed the civilians who'd arrived from the Marriott holding the conquered Fedayeen's AK-47s.

Fifty yards west of the embassy's main gate the command bunker, consisting of Erickson, First Sergeant Vickers, and Radioman Genovese, was soundly reinforced.

Nearest the embassy, Steven Gray's fifty men waited as the last line of defense. With the exception of the Marines, British, and French, who were equipped with night vision equipment, none of the others had any more ability than the flailing attackers to see twenty yards in the harsh conditions. For that reason, until the layering clouds lifted, the defense of the thousands awaiting rescue would rest primarily upon Erickson's men.

In all, there were 750 waiting with assault rifles, machine guns, mortars, and antitank weapons to challenge the approaching hordes.

They wouldn't have long to wait. The first attack would soon be upon them.

There'd been no signs of the formidable peasant army for a significant portion of the past hour. That, however, hadn't been true in the frantic period preceding it. Within minutes of the last evacuees entering the compounds, both had been set upon by a series of probing measures. Each incursion had been larger than the last. The intensifying skirmishes had been followed by a pair of major assaults marked by waves of suicide attacks by explosive-laden zealots.

The explosive response by those defending the grounds had been swift and certain. They tore the subversives apart with astonishing proficiency. Every attack, no matter how passionate, had been brushed aside by the skillful Marines. With the jihadists firing blindly at their fog-hidden foe and the Americans able to see the attackers as if it were the brightest of days, the futile battles had been uneven matches. The entrenched fire teams had spotted the ghoulish figures long before they could get anywhere near the stout barricades. There'd been little more than a handful of minor wounds among the embassy's protectors. And more than two hundred Fedayeen dead.

Quite unexpectedly, at the height of the second notable foray, the frustrated radicals set fire to everything outside the Marines' defenses. Once they had, they vanished. To where, none of those behind the battlements had any way of knowing. As suddenly as the extremists had appeared, the sounds of battle went quiet. And at least for the moment, there were no signs the surprising situation would soon change. The only movement the Marines were picking up was coming from the untold numbers of wounded jihadists attempting to drag themselves from the battlefield.

For the first time in weeks, the insurgents' crude approach was catching up with them. Throughout their conquests the strategy employed by Basra's followers had been simple. No matter their losses, they'd conduct unyielding assaults to overwhelm and destroy. So far, these subjugating maneuvers had worked with incredible success. Brute force had won the day. At least until they'd attempted to replicate those tactics to conquer the well-armed heretics. For this was no dispirited Pakistani army they faced.

Few who led the menacing throngs were quick learners. It'd taken far longer than it should to figure out the fatal flaw in their approach. Like their followers, most were ill-informed illiterates who carried with them no more than the rudimentary perspectives of their backward villages. They understood nothing about conducting modern warfare against a first-rate foe.

All who'd entered the initial fray against the nonbelievers had been convinced by morning their swords would run red. Their conquest would come with ease. Unaware of the Marines' presence, it had taken far too long for them to realize their style wasn't working. After so many effortless victories, it was a hard lesson for most to grasp. But in the confounding fog, as they were hideously slaughtered, they began to realize the adversary they faced could somehow conduct their actions with absolute precision despite the conditions. After a heated debate, even the most strident had to admit their misguided attempts were useless. Continuing the hapless incursions was beyond foolish. Each rationalized the decision by professing those behind the high walls could die as easily in daylight as they could in the dark.

They'd withdraw and sleep until the morning sun burned away the fog. Once the blanketing world was gone, they'd attack with relish and fury and bring an end to this.

The Marines couldn't know it, but they'd have five hours of absolute calm before the renewed offensives would begin in earnest.

While the fearful night dragged on, all of the Pakistani government buildings and the abandoned embassies continued to be ravaged by fierce explosions and rising flames. With a satisfied smile,

Erickson watched the fires burning in the distance. For by their actions the enemy had done him a significant favor. Each of those locations would have been ideal for emplacing snipers to pin the Americans down. They also would have provided immense cover when launching the vindictive attacks. But the fanatics' scorn had overwhelmed all other actions. And it had caused them to make another fateful blunder. They put the reviled structures to the torch without giving it a passing thought. Once the fires finished razing the buildings and the trees and grounds around them, there'd be nothing left but hundreds of yards of open ground in front of the Marines' defenses. In the coming days, the American marksmen would make sure the enemy paid in blood for their mistake.

To the east, little more than a half mile distant, the Chinese and Russian embassies also burned. The bodies of their dead lay scattered across the devastated grounds. Neither embassy had been strong enough to withstand the tides of hatred and vitriol that washed over them. The sadistic cruelty inflicted upon the defeated ones had been extreme. Not one had survived the encounter.

Even dampened by the earth-hugging clouds, the blazes roared, consuming each ill-fated structure. The funeral pyres were there for all to see. The dancing images taunted the dug-in Marines and those they protected. They knew a similar fate awaited them should they fail.

Lieutenant Peters approached his company commander's bunker. With him were the thirteen men from his platoon's 3rd Squad. With the command bunker's sandbagged walls to protect them, they crowded around Erickson.

"Matt, the King Stallions should be on the ground in the next few minutes," Erickson said. "Let's go over how we're going to do this one more time to make sure everyone's on the same page. With each arriving flight, we're going to attempt to handle things the same. You're to take 3rd Squad through the landing zone, reinforce the French, Dutch, and German detachments, and determine if things appear secure enough for the helicopters to land."

"Yes, sir," Peters replied.

"As soon as you're comfortable with the situation, radio the pilots and give them the authorization to come in. Same as it was when we landed: first two King Stallions near the southwest corner of the embassy, with the remaining four in the parking area close to the main gate. Once they touch down, our first priority will be emptying them as rapidly as possible. Is that understood?"

"Absolutely, sir. We'll do everything we can to ensure there are no delays."

"When that's completed, we'll begin filling them with evacuees and getting the CH-53s back into the air."

"You can depend on us, sir."

"Good. Before the King Stallions arrive, make contact with Gunny Joyce. His detachment will be escorting the civilians who've volunteered to empty the first two and carry the food and water through the embassy grounds and across to the enclave. Don't be surprised how quickly they grab those cartons of MREs along with the water cans. Within minutes of arriving here, the evacuees from the hotel cleaned out every food store the embassies had. But it wasn't enough to do anything more than temporarily relieve their hunger. So they're highly motivated to get those boxes and cans into both compounds. There'll be tons of anxious folks awaiting the contents. The thousands of pounds of food, even if not the fanciest, should make them happy."

"Sure not going to complain about those with Gunny Joyce working too quickly, sir."

"Once they make their way through the parking area with their loads, that should create enough space for a second group, with some of Steven Gray's men in support, to begin unloading the last four. Their contents are to be taken into the embassy. At the same time, more of Gray's men will carry the stretchers with the wounded out and place them in the first helicopter. Two of the nurses will be going with them to Spinager. After that's done, Gray's men will return to the embassy to escort mothers and children out to the next available CH-53. All the really little ones are in these groupings. So I need you to take special care to protect them and send them on their way. Can't imagine how any of us are going to feel if we're hit with a surprise attack while they and their mothers are loading."

"We'll do everything we can to keep that from happening, sir. My own son's that age. I don't even want to think about such a possibility."

"Do you or any of your men have any questions?"

Erickson looked into each solemn face. Not one of Peters's men said a word.

"No, sir," Peters replied. "We're ready. Not too sure what'll happen in the coming days, but with the fog as thick as it is right now, this one should be okay."

"I hope you're right, Matt, but I'm not going to count on anything. You'll need to stay alert out there. With all there is to do, it could take a half hour, possibly more, before the final helicopter's airborne. That's a lot of time for the bastards to figure out what we're up to. With any luck, if it's like their earlier attempts to breach our lines, our sentries should spot them and pick them off before they get anywhere near this place. Even so, ultimately it's going to be on your guys' shoulders to handle anything that rises up to challenge our actions."

"We've every intention of doing so, sir."

"All right, then, the King Stallions should be here shortly. Let's hope we're sending another four hundred to safety soon. Good luck to you and your men."

"Thank you, sir."

Peters motioned for the squad to move out. Ever wary, they hurried to reinforce the perimeter. They knew the enemy could be anywhere. Each understood Basra's followers could launch an attack at any moment. But as they edged into position, nothing rose up to greet them.

The King Stallions' landing gear would soon reach out for the damp asphalt. Despite Matt Peters's confidence that the arriving craft would be all right, even this early in the unfolding events the landings and takeoffs would be supremely hazardous. Every minute on the ground would be exceedingly dangerous. Yet, they had no other choice. It was this or nothing.

All was ready. At Peters's direction, the first of the King Stallions descended. The other five gathered, waiting their turn to land. As they did, the volunteers Joyce was leading headed out the main gate. Inside the embassy grounds, those carrying the stretchers gathered. As soon as the initial hold was emptied, they'd head out to the narrow roadway with their charges. Behind them, the women with the youngest children began to queue. Some had a single child, others as many as five or six.

If all went well, nearly four hundred of the most precious would soon be on their way.

21

Ambassador Alan Ingram was on the phone when Steven Gray entered his office. Outside, the silent hours in and around the cloud-shrouded complex continued into the solemn morning. All knew the lull meant nothing. At any moment, the horrors of an unyielding attack could resume. With the sun burning through the faltering fog, and the threat to their survival growing, the ambassador had thought the situation couldn't get any worse.

It had pleased him greatly to notify the State Department that their makeshift plan had sent eight hundred on their way overnight. But with more than five thousand people within the compounds' fortifications, and a murderous force more than fifty times their number surrounding them, he couldn't imagine being in more dire straits. However, he was about to be proven wrong. While he spoke on the phone, another searing nightmare was unfolding.

Ingram, his angst evident, motioned for his security officer to take a seat. Even with no fighting for the past four hours, he knew

Gray was extremely busy. Still, as soon as he heard who was on the other end of the line, he'd requested his subordinate join him.

He put the phone on speaker. "So you're certain of that, General Bhatti?" Ingram said. "How many nuclear weapons does the Fedayeen control?"

"Within the past hours, the majority of the two hundred in our inventory have been seized by the insurgents," the Pakistani general replied.

"What's the status of those weapons, General? Are Basra's men in a position to fire them?"

"Our nuclear weapons, both strategic and tactical, were made ready the moment the war with India began. So each is capable of being fired. All the terrorists need are the launch codes and there'll be nothing to keep them from releasing them against our enemies."

"Are the launch codes secure?"

"Mr. Ambassador, we've done our best to keep them out of unfriendly hands. But as you know, nothing in my country is secure forever. They're bound to get their hands on them. And the moment they do, I expect Salim Basra to undertake an all-out attack against India."

The disbelief on both Ingram's and Gray's faces said it all. The news being relayed by the head of the Strategic Arms Division was beyond belief. The consequences of what they were being told were unmistakable.

"What about Israel? Do you believe Basra will attempt to use them against them?"

"Israel, no. Our Shaheen-III missiles don't have the range to reach Israel. But I've little doubt that Basra would attack the Jews along with destroying India if he could. He'd release them against America if the missiles could reach your country. Fortunately, our weapons don't have the power to do so."

"How long do we have before he gets the codes?" the ambassador asked.

"Who knows? Minutes . . . hours . . . a few days. A week at most."

"General, if they launch those missiles, hundreds of millions in India will die. And there's no doubt they'll fire theirs in return and destroy Pakistan. The dead on both sides will be incalculable. Things for the remainder of the world also would become extremely dire. The effect of the nuclear winter that would follow could easily kill a billion or more. Yet you're saying before week's end that'll happen."

"Your assessment's correct, Mr. Ambassador. Both countries would suffer immense loss of life. And who knows how badly it would damage the remainder of the planet? It could take mankind a thousand years to overcome the destruction. That's why even though I'm in a highly tenuous position I had to stop and risk calling you. I'm sure you recognize with Basra's forces closing in I'm putting my life on the line. But my existence means nothing when compared with the horror these lunatics are about to inflict. I don't want to see my country devastated. I don't want a significant portion of this world destroyed."

"General, I assure you none of us wish for that to happen."

"These misguided peasants are too stupid to understand the consequences of their actions. Their twisted master, Basra, is a false prophet. Still, the foolish ones continue to lap up his words and blindly follow even if it leads to their own destruction."

"Do you know where each of the nuclear weapons is located?"

"At least for the moment, yes. I have placed Strategic Arms Division spies in the midst of those who willfully slaughter their countrymen in the misguided belief they're serving Allah. Most of the ignorant individuals who seized the nuclear arms are so backward, they've no idea how to move them. So, at least for now, the majority remain where they were placed. Until discovered by the Fedayeen, my spies are in a position to track their movements and report back to me. But they won't be able to keep them from being fired once the codes are received."

"Understood. Is the Strategic Arms Division capable of counterattacking and regaining control of some or all of the weapons?"

"I'm afraid not, Mr. Ambassador. The finest of my men died trying to protect them. The few who remain are too weak to attempt to do so."

"How many men do the terrorists have guarding them?"

"It varies from location to location, but you can be assured there are many of the insolent swine awaiting anyone challenging their control of the launch sites."

"General, are you willing to tell me where each nuclear armament is emplaced and to try to keep your military from interfering if we intervene to stop these horrific weapons from being fired?"

There was an extended pause. The answer was a reluctant one. "Yes, Mr. Ambassador. I'm prepared to tell you where they are."

Ingram grabbed a pen and tablet. "All right, General Bhatti. Let's begin. . . ."

And so the head of the Strategic Arms Division relayed the information on the locations and quantities of weapons one by one. The conversation went on for an hour as the ambassador wrote down the details. Finally, the deadly listing was complete.

"That's the last of them, Mr. Ambassador."

"Thank you, General. I'll do what I can to save the world from the horror it'll soon be facing. As your spies report in, can you update me on any movements of the missiles?"

"I remain on the run, Mr. Ambassador, but I'll try," was the reply. "With nearly all cell phone service out, it's taking a great deal of time to find a working landline."

"Understood, General Bhatti. Rest assured, you made the right decision by providing the information. But you still haven't answered the second part of what I'd asked. You're one of the most influential people in what remains of your country's leadership. Will you do what you can to convince your army and air force to allow us the freedom to do what we need to do to stop Basra from releasing the nuclear missiles?"

There was another lengthy pause. "Yes, I'll do what I can to convince the others. For now, I must take my leave. My present location's quite vulnerable, and if Basra gets his hands on me, I don't wish to think what will happen."

"General, try to stay safe."

"Again, I'll do what I can. Our military may look defeated, but there's still hope. We're headed toward the southern portion of the country, and when we arrive we will attempt to rally our forces and make our stand. It may take months, maybe years, but we'll take our country back from the rabble whose false beliefs betray everything we stand for."

"Thank you, General. I'm not sure if my president's willing to allow the American military to become involved, but I'll certainly speak with him if you wish. If you'd consider allowing us to assist you in this fight, you might get your country back much sooner than anyone believes. Will you talk with the others to see if they'd consider a military intervention by the Western powers?"

A final pause. "Yes, Mr. Ambassador. Given the situation, we may have no other choice. We cannot allow that madman to continue ravaging our country without doing everything possible to save our people." With that, Bhatti hung up.

The moment the phone went dead, Ingram looked up at Gray. The expression on his security officer's face was as grim as his. "With what we were just told, our problems with the fanatics outside these walls suddenly seem quite small," Ingram said. "The planet's going to explode in a massive nuclear war if we don't intercede. "

"What're you going to do?"

"What choice do I have? I'm going to do what I can to stop this from happening. Get on the phone immediately. I need to speak with the president. I doubt you were read in because it's always been on a strict need to know, but we've been preparing for this eventuality for years. There's a plan in place to deal with Pakistan's nuclear weapons falling into the wrong hands. I'd prayed we'd never use it, but at this moment there are no options left."

22

The protective fog was a fading whisper as a persistent sun consumed the final wisps of gray. Moments after the ambassador finished his conversation with General Bhatti, the dogmatists prepared to make their move. It would be a frontal attack directed toward the western and northern approaches to both enclosures. This time, however, the attackers knew the heretics wouldn't have the tactical advantages the night had provided.

Even though they had no idea who they were facing, it didn't matter to Allah's chosen. Once again, there'd be nothing sophisticated in the massive populist army's assault. Their plan was simple, their approach unrefined. It was a tried-and-tested method they'd used in battle after battle against the Pakistani military. Brute force would rule the day. No matter how severe their losses, they'd overwhelm the defenders through sheer numbers and the savagery of their assault.

In their bastions of fortified sand and shielding trees, the highly alert pairs of Marines knew it was only a matter of time.

Each was more than prepared. None would panic no matter how savage the barbarous attack. As the morose morning grew brighter, the defenders' machine guns, grenade launchers, and rifles were at the ready. Their mortar teams were fully prepared. Behind the Americans were stretching lines of civilians armed with the weapons they'd taken from the Marriott's dead jihadists. In the center of it all, Erickson waited. He would command the defenses on the southern and western sides of the compounds. Scott Tomlin would be responsible for attacks in the east and north.

The time for the first great struggle of the day had arrived. In the distance, 3rd Platoon's forward outposts spotted movement ... lots and lots of movement. Working their way through the fallen buildings and smoldering stones, the first running waves of screaming attackers, their bile rising, were approaching. The hatred in their eyes and animus in their voices was unmistakable.

Near the Italian embassy, a pair of Lieutenant Bates's Marines opened fire on the oncoming enemy. Three hundred yards away, a trio of assailants, the first of many to come, went down. A first whistling salvo from the Marines' northern mortar team reached into the heavens.

With an unyielding fury, the desperate battle exploded upon them all.

23

While Erickson and his defenders fought to hold off the first—and shortly thereafter the second—massive onslaught of the day, the president waited in the Oval Office. One by one, the secretary of defense, secretary of state, and chairman of the Joint Chiefs, Marine general Franklin Davies, arrived.

Without a word, all settled in their seats. "So what's got us out of bed in the middle of the night this time, Mr. President?" the secretary of defense asked. This wasn't the first time he'd found himself in the Oval Office at the midpoint of a foreboding evening. In each prior case, it had been under the worst of circumstances. He knew the present summons was going to be another full-blown crisis.

"Ambassador Ingram called an hour ago. He's received word that the Fedayeen Islam have seized the majority of Pakistan's nuclear weapons."

Neither the chairman nor either secretary did anything to

mask the shock they felt. "How reliable's his source, Mr. President?" the secretary of state asked.

"The information came from General Bhatti, head of the Strategic Arms Division."

"Mr. President, did the ambassador know what kind of shape those weapons are in?" General Davies asked. "Are they in a position to be fired?"

"All two hundred are armed and ready. For the moment, the only thing keeping Basra from releasing hell upon an unsuspecting world is the lack of launch codes."

"Are the launch codes safe?" the secretary of defense asked.

"The ambassador says they are but probably won't be much longer. With the chaos in Pakistan, he anticipates they'll fall into the insurgent's hands in a matter of days if not sooner."

"Does he think Basra's crazy enough to launch them?"

"Ingram knows Pakistan better than anyone. He says there's no doubt the crazy bastard will unleash them all."

"Is India aware of what's happening?" the secretary of state asked.

"So far, there've been no indications of that," the president said. "If they did, they'd likely have made a first strike of their own to take out the Pakistani missiles."

"Hundreds of millions are going to die at Basra's hands if something's not done to stop it," the secretary of state said.

"And who knows what the long-term effect will be," the secretary of defense added. "We've never experienced anything close to this, and even our best scientists aren't certain what the worldwide outcome would be from such a catastrophe."

"What're the Pakistani military's plans to address the situation?" General Davies asked.

"Apparently, with their army in disarray, there's little they can do," the president replied. "Which is why Bhatti came to us."

The secretaries and chairman looked at each other. It was the secretary of defense who spoke. "For years, we've had our Special Forces preparing for what we're presently facing. Operational Plan Distant Thunder's ready if we decide to intervene."

"What choice do we have?" the president said. "If there's any chance we can keep this from happening, we've got to step in."

"Mr. President, did the ambassador say whether the Pakistani military would contest our actions if we entered their airspace?" General Davies asked. "Sure don't want to risk our Green Berets by sending them on a suicide mission."

"Ingram asked General Bhatti to intercede to keep that from happening. But with the total anarchy over there, he didn't know what our troops might face."

"Even so, I can't see where we've any other option," the secretary of state said. "Once we've identified where the launchers are positioned, we've got to go in and disable them before it's too late."

A half smile came to the president's face. "That was the one bit of good news Ingram had. Bhatti was able to not only alert him to the situation but also to provide each weapon's location. The ambassador's organizing the information as we speak. He'll be sending it our way within the hour. By the time you return to your offices, the details should be waiting."

"Good. I'll get my people on it the minute we return to the Pentagon," General Davies said. "With that data in hand, it won't take long to finalize our plan of attack."

"When do you anticipate we can undertake a response?" the president asked.

"Our Green Berets are ready to move on a moment's notice," General Davies replied. "If you order us to initiate Distant Thunder, it'll take no time to begin implementing it."

"Even in the middle of the night?"

"Yes, sir. We can notify them, put them on planes, and have

them on their way before sunrise. To carry out the mission, we'll need to also send along sufficient Apache attack helicopters and Black Hawks to support their actions. Still, if India will allow us to use Spinager as a jumping-off point, that shouldn't be a problem."

The president turned to the secretary of state. "Robert, get ahold of your counterpart in the Indian government to see if they'll allow us to land an additional force at Spinager to support an incursion into Pakistan."

"Anything in particular you want me to tell them, Mr. President?"

"Well, whatever you do, don't let them know Basra has control of Pakistan's nukes." He paused. "Tell them we're very appreciative of their cooperation so far, and for the restraint they've shown with regards to what's occurring in Pakistan. Let them know that if they'll allow us to temporarily expand our operations at Spinager, we've got what we believe is a viable plan to send our forces into Pakistan to render useless every nuclear weapon the Pakistanis have."

"Can't imagine they'll be displeased to hear that," the secretary responded.

"Certainly wouldn't think so. But given India's colonial history, you'll need to handle this with a great deal of sensitivity. Having foreign troops on their soil, even if it's in their best interest, isn't something they'll take lightly. You saw how much effort it took just to allow us to fly in a single company of Marines. This mission will involve much, much more."

"Reluctant or not, I don't believe they won't eventually see the potential good from such an effort. Especially since it'll be our soldiers' lives being risked, not theirs. From what I know of them, they'll agree to our proposal. It's just a matter of how much debate they'll need to work through to reach that conclusion."

"That's the thing, Robert. They need to understand there's no time for delay. Make it clear if our action's going to succeed, we need to set it in motion before our window of opportunity closes."

"Understood, Mr. President."

"Give them my word we'll withdraw our assets from India the moment this is over."

"Yes, Mr. President. I've always found Prime Minister Singh to be a reasonable man. Quite pragmatic in his approach to leading his country. There's no way he won't see the value in our proposed actions. If we succeed, his biggest concern will've been eliminated. Think I know the right buttons to push to get him and his ministers to acquiesce. And to do so quickly."

"Good. Make it so." The president turned to the chairman of the Joint Chiefs. "So, General Davies, if we promise Prime Minster Singh that what we have planned will work, how do you anticipate approaching this?"

"By moving fast. We'll start putting things into motion the moment I return to the Pentagon. I'll personally notify Special Operations Command to get a Green Beret group and the support elements we're going to need ready to move by morning. We've got enough C-17s and C-5s waiting that we can load the helicopters and all our Special Forces onto the same transports. We'll follow that up a day or so later by ferrying over a number of Chinook cargo helicopters. Once our Special Forces seize and disarm the nuclear armaments, the Chinooks will come in and remove the weapons from Pakistani soil. If things go as planned, it shouldn't take long before there's nothing left over there but empty launchpads. All we need is your okay. So, Mr. President, do we have your permission to undertake this operation?"

The president didn't hesitate. "I'm afraid our hands are tied. Start your preparations for Distant Thunder. As soon as India gives us the go-ahead, you can get our aircraft into the air."

"Yes, sir. If all goes as planned, our men and equipment will be on their way to Spinager by sunrise. Forty-eight hours from now, there won't be a single nuclear weapon in Pakistan capable of being fired. Our Special Forces engineers will've removed and destroyed the trigger mechanisms on each one, rendering all two hundred inoperable. Even if the Fedayeen obtain the launch codes and somehow regain control of the sites before we remove the missiles from Pakistan, there'll be no way to detonate them without the trigger mechanisms."

"Good. But that still leaves one major problem we'll eventually need to address."

"What's that, sir?" the secretary of defense asked.

"Coming up with a way to eliminate Salim Basra and end his so-called holy war."

24

While the rancorous assaults on the embassy continued, in the snowcapped mountains to the northeast, the Fedayeen Islam's leadership gathered at the rear of an ancient Toyota pickup. Since the war's first days, the insurgents had been using the dilapidated truck as their mobile command center. A nondescript figure approached the waiting group. Other than a scraggly beard whose farthest reaches grazed his chest, and a perverse presence in his eyes, he looked little different than millions of his countrymen.

The uneasy queue parted to allow the emaciated, stern-faced Salim Basra through. Even out in the open, those present were more concerned about their tempestuous leader and his fits of rage than the sudden appearance of life-stealing American drones or Pakistani fighter jets.

Basra was an evil, evil man; there was no other way to describe him. He carried with him not a single redeeming quality. Even in the best of moments, he was rash, heartless, vain, and depraved. Not a person who knew him liked him in the slightest. Prior to the war, he'd been scarcely more than a little dictator in the villages he controlled in the wildest of the tribal territories. His enemies had been many. His absolute cruelty had seen to that. Several had attempted to take his life. Yet he'd survived each failed attempt. And those who'd raised their hand against him soon regretted their actions. In each case, he'd made them watch as he and his men raped and tortured their wives and daughters prior to putting them and the failed assassins to the sword.

The self-involved Basra, with his insatiable ego and the unqualified violence that consumed him, was someone none wished to cross. He had no concern for those he commanded. He couldn't care less how many died in servitude to him. In his eyes, those he sent into battle were chattel to use and discard. Using his god as his shield, he'd conned them by the millions into joining his treacherous march. Seduced by his lies and false piety, the servile had fallen into line, waving his banners high.

As the impromptu meeting began, the Fedayeen leader's lack of patience showed. He turned to his subordinate commanders. "Have we obtained the firing sequences?" None was anxious to answer and feel his wrath. "Well?" he said, his frustration mounting.

"We're working on it," said his second-in-command, Bila Chachar. "We thought we'd located them early this morning, but the lead went nowhere."

Basra looked into each of their faces, his glare unyielding. "You have forty-eight hours to place those codes in my hands."

None had the slightest doubt of the meaning of Basra's not-so-veiled threat. Two days from now, in the most hideous manner, they'd all be dead if they didn't obtain the launch codes.

25

Huge C-17 and C-5 cargo aircraft were spread across the tarmac. The waiting planes and the areas around them were bustling with activity.

In the predawn darkness, along with the other eleven members of his A Team, Staff Sergeant Charlie Sanders trudged up the rear ramp of one of the C-17s. All around them other Special Forces units were doing the same. The planes' deafening jet engines were running. Sanders dropped his equipment in the pile near the rear of the aircraft. He eased his way past the two partially disassembled Apache attack helicopters nestled in the aircraft's hold. Next to their plane, a huge C-5 was being loaded with their mission's Black Hawk helicopters.

Even in the dim light he couldn't help but notice that all the identifying markers had been removed from the Apaches. Each had been painted over. The pungent smell of fresh paint was everywhere.

Sanders selected a spot in the side-wall seats on the left of the fuselage. Next to him, Sergeant First Class Aaron Porter stared straight ahead, his mind in the first stages of preparing for what was to come. The plane continued to fill with 6th Special Forces Group Green Berets and helicopter crews. Within its hold two twelve-man Special Forces detachments, a pair of Apache pilots along with their weapons officers, and sixteen Black Hawk crew members found seats. When the last had settled in, forty-four of the aircraft's fifty-four seats would be filled.

The task of seizing the launch facilities and disabling the nuclear weapons would fall upon the eleven hundred men of the 6th Special Forces Group. With so vast an arsenal of death-dealing weapons to disable, the entire group had been committed to the mission. It was an assignment for which they were acutely ready. It was one they'd practiced for often.

"God, it smells awful in here. Why the hell did they paint over the Apaches like that?" Sanders asked.

"Guess you didn't notice, but they did the same to all the C-17s and C-5s," Porter responded. "None of them has a single identifier on it. Captain said the Indian government demanded we do so before they'd allow us to fly into one of their air bases. They didn't want to make it easy for anyone to figure out the planes and helicopters were American."

While Porter relayed what he'd learned, the time to depart had arrived. The C-17's ramp was raised. As the planes began to taxi, Sanders turned to look at Porter. It was time to go through a ritual the pair superstitiously undertook at the start of every exceedingly dangerous operation.

"You ready for this?" Sanders asked.

He knew what the answer would be. The same as it always was. Rather than immediately responding, Porter reached for the sheath dangling at his side. He pulled out the menacing knife he'd used to cut many an unwary throat. He absent-mindedly began sharpening the razor-edged blade. "When have I not been ready?"

"Yeah, but this looks like a tough one."

"When have they not been tough? Just like our last mission was and the one that'll come after this one will be."

Ritual over, Sanders leaned back in his seat and closed his eyes. In minutes, their C-17 took to the air. Sanders, dressed for the cold, noisy flight, settled in for the fourteen-hour journey to northeastern India. Despite the ominous task they faced, he was soon asleep. The Special Forces engineering specialist would remain that way for a great deal of the flight. The twenty-six-year-old battle-scarred soldier had experienced far too much life-on-the-edge combat to let one more forbidding assignment overly concern him.

He'd once been the most gregarious and outgoing member of Alpha 6333. But the tragic events of the Pan-Arab War three years earlier had changed that for the deadly African American soldier. Now he was sullen, selecting his friends carefully and being the most standoffish member of the A Team. Yet, despite any shortcomings, he was without a doubt one of the best in the world at what he did. When it came to blowing things up, Charlie Sanders was at the top of his field.

During his earlier years he'd felt invincible, steadfastly convinced no bullet would ever find him. Nonetheless, as he'd watched his comrades fall during countless bloody battles, those feelings had dissipated. At this point he viewed his existence as fleeting. He understood that in his line of work you measured your life in terrifying seconds and never looked past the here and now. So he slept.

Others in the aircraft weren't so lucky. For many, this was their first taste of a Special Forces operation. And their anxiousness caused their eyes to remain wide-open.

As the aircraft started over the Atlantic, in the side seats toward the aircraft's front, the Detachment 6333 and 6334 leadership teams gathered to go over the assignment. As the senior officer, Captain Neil Short, the 6333 commander, would be in charge of the raid. For over an hour he briefed the 6334 commander, Eric Henry, along with each team's warrant officer and the senior and junior operations sergeants. All eight were soon involved in an animated discussion of the difficult task they'd face. Their assignment was one of the most fiercely challenging any in the Special Forces Group would ever undertake. And unlike most of their previous efforts, with the lack of intelligence, they'd be entering the coming battle partially blind.

Each knew that in the coming days some, possibly many, of those in the aircraft would take their final breaths. Despite having the Apaches and Black Hawks to support their assault, their losses could be severe. Yet it mattered not how hazardous the task was: this was an assignment none could ignore. The world, even if unaware, was depending upon them. They had to stop Basra from blowing an immense hole in the planet and dragging mankind into an abyss from which there'd be no return.

As the C-17 continued its journey, a relentless clock ticked, each tedious minute the same as the last for those within its windowless world. Inside each of the aircraft armada's metal shells, with every passing hour they drew five hundred miles nearer to whatever the fates held.

26

So far, the evening's evacuations had gone smoothly. With the adjustments Erickson had made, the first round trip for the King Stallions had been accomplished without a hitch. Rather than all six coming in at once, with the skulking enemy on all sides, the company commander had modified his approach. Now the King Stallions arrived in pairs at fifteen-minute intervals. It was enough time for the two on the ground to be emptied and refilled with escapees prior to the next pair landing. As two churned into the skies, the next duo would appear.

Three hours earlier, using this adjusted system, immense offerings of food and water had arrived. They'd been exchanged for four hundred eager souls. With a single exception, all the children under the age of eight were gone.

Only four-year-old MaKenna was still here. Sam had done all he could to convince Lauren to take her and join those leaving. Wells, however, wouldn't hear of it. Like the stately Marine she adored, the determined reporter had a job to do. And with such an incredible story unfolding, she had no intention of leaving until the tale's concluding moments. Her plan was to walk up the final helicopter's ramp next to the man she loved.

She'd done her best to convince MaKenna to leave with one of the departing mothers. The traumatized child, however, had clung to Wells as if her life depended upon it.

In the apprehensive gloom, once again skimming the diverse landscape's towering mountain and windswept valleys, the helicopter pairs approached. In brief minutes the first were scheduled to arrive.

For the moment, things were relatively calm. With the disappearance of the horrid afternoon's sun, ten hours of brutish assaults had dissipated. As the last of the daylight faded, it took the ferocious scene's monstrous intensity with it. Once the sun set, only sporadic, half-hearted clashes by small groups of prodding attackers had occurred. After the previous night's slaughter, the Fedayeen had figured out that full-scale attacks prior to the next sunrise would be foolhardy. The reviled defenders owned the night. Their fighting abilities were too great to overcome. So the majority of the fanatics had retreated to their distant holes to wait out the uneasy darkness.

Both sides recognized it was little more than a momentary pause in the pitiless siege. Thousands upon thousands of raiders languished in the shadowy night, preparing for the coming morning. At first light, a swirling maelstrom of all-out assaults filled with unimaginable anguish would begin anew.

Even with the fragile lull, the conflict's notable casualties ensured the overwrought medical staff had their hands full. Inside the compound, in the modest, single-story building that served as a makeshift hospital, the taint of fresh blood was everywhere. The same was true at the smaller first aid station within the enclave. They were surrounded by a maniacal foe intent on taking their lives. And all understood that the situation, filled with suffering and death, wouldn't get any better.

Forty-three defenders, including nine of Erickson's Marines, had perished in the previous day's frenetic clashes. More than three times that were wounded. Half of those, their injuries treated, had returned to the front lines. With the threat so great, there was no other choice. If they were capable of firing a rifle, the doctors let them go.

By Erickson's calculations, enemy wounded and dead were more than twenty times those of the defenders. Wave after wave of futile charges had seen to that. Stilled forms, some as close as twenty-five meters from the outer Marine fortifications, lay scattered about as if flung there by a pitiless deity's hand. In some locations, those who'd lost their lives were piled three high.

Yet, despite their losses, the zealots' resolve hadn't wavered. If anything, as the long hours passed, their self-destructive incursions had bolstered their bloodlust. The Marine commander had little doubt that in the days to come things would grow worse. Life in this fraught corner of the planet had little importance. No matter how high the rotting corpses were stacked, no matter how many were chewed up by their grinding tactics, there was little chance of them being dissuaded. Even if those protecting the embassy slayed a hundred thousand, the dirt-poor, imprudent peasants wouldn't be deterred from completing their divine mission. Their lifetimes of pent-up anger and insatiable rage would never be sated until the last of the foreigners was dead. The nonbelievers had to be vanquished, their lives forfeited in the name of a righteous god.

The American compound and the enclave, their thick, pockmarked walls showing the effects of yesterday's numerous rocket-propelled grenade strikes, were holding on. The Americans' seven-story main embassy building, nestled near the western edge of the sprawling complex, had been struck by RPGs and small-arms fire so often that it was impossible to calculate the holes. With the exception of the ambassador, who'd refused to budge, his entire staff and those who'd been sheltering in the structure had moved to less inviting targets.

Inside the main gate, the men and women who'd volunteered to unload the approaching King Stallions waited. The moment the first one landed, they'd scurry into its hold to begin the perilous task. Behind them, the four hundred scheduled for this evening's second round of evacuations queued. The remaining women with children under the age of twelve would be in this grouping.

There'd be no fog to mask the King Stallions. And the weather reports were predicting none for a few additional sunsets. There was, however, a lingering front, marked with a steady drizzle and intermittent showers, scheduled to arrive in the coming hours. With the country entering the final month of its monsoon season, it was no surprise.

For now, a moonless, star-filled sky hung over their hushed world. A brisk breeze tugged at the huge American flag fluttering in the center of the scene. Fog or no fog, with the dead and wounded mounting, Erickson had no choice but to continue the rescue attempts. The resupplying of both compounds and evacuation of well over one thousand on this night were of paramount importance. He'd depend upon the pervasive darkness, and a stout defensive force, to protect the arriving craft. And he'd hope for the best in the less-than-ideal conditions. Before today's dawn, three successful trips into and out of Islamabad had to be accomplished if the last of the survivors were going to leave this place within the week.

———

With the harried medical staff still treating two of his wounded, Lieutenant Matt Peters, along with the remaining eleven members of his platoon's 3rd Squad, moved into the open parking area west of the embassy walls. The first of the King Stallions was nearly here.

On this rushed incursion, the forward pair of CH-53Ks would be carrying additional fuel for the embassy's generators and the Humvees. It would be more than enough to last for seven days. The final four would be loaded with additional food, water, and medical supplies for those remaining behind.

Third Squad's Marines were soon in place, taking up positions in the woods on the southern edges of the parking lot's asphalt. They'd be doing all they could to defend the craft as the civilian volunteers emptied the helicopters' lading. Once that was completed, the CH-53Ks would take on the latest loads of fleeing people and disappear into the night. As they did, the next King Stallions would land.

"Sergeant Patterson, you all set?" Matt Peters asked.

"Everyone's in place," 3rd Squad's sergeant answered.

In the center of the parking area, through his night vision, the lieutenant took a lengthy look around, searching in every direction. Like Erickson, his concern was quite real. But his careful examination revealed nothing. With no sign of the enemy, and the world around them stilled, the time had come to contact the helicopters. "Rescue One, Rescue One, bring it on in," Peters said into the radio he carried.

"Roger, we're on the way," the lead pilot responded.

Timing their appearance precisely, Gunny Joyce's widely spaced Marines ran out the front gate. One hundred volunteers were with them. Seventy-five yards away, the initial King Stallion eased toward the ground. Upon settling onto the parking area's pavement, its pilots shut down the engines. The anxious volunteers rushed toward it. There was no time to waste. At Peters's direction, the second cargo helicopter started to settle.

Well into a second night of fevered enterprise, each defender and volunteer knew their role. Without wasted effort they'd empty the arriving helicopters. Weighed down by the heavy loads, they'd carry the welcome contents into the compound. Once that was completed, they'd rush back to meet the next arriving pair. And eventually the ones that followed. Finally finished, they'd return to the American compound to rest. They'd steel themselves to do it again in another four hours.

They scrambled toward the King Stallions' dark forms. Inside the embassy's harboring walls, Steven Gray readied the first group of evacuees, thirty-five severely wounded and close to one hundred women and children. Others, scheduled to leave on the third, fourth, fifth, and sixth helicopters were lined up behind them. Uneasiness was sketched upon every face.

Even so, the beginning stages of another rescue attempt were going smoothly. In the coming hour, more critical supplies would be secured. And four hundred additional individuals would be on their way to freedom. Appearances, however, are often deceiving. For none had recognized the harsh reality they'd soon be facing. Satan's sadistic image was hiding within their midst.

Despite the futility of their earlier efforts, the Fedayeen had hit upon an idea to keep more from escaping. Concealed three hundred yards away, in the filthy, trash-laden culvert on the far side of the Kashmir Highway, a malignant force was waiting. For the past few hours, they'd used their countrymen's distracting probes, along with the masking terrain near the highway, to aid their efforts. They'd started well beyond where the defenders night vision could see. In both the east and west, the stealthy gathering had slipped a number of small trucks into the deep depression. The rear of each was crammed with heavily armed assassins. Ever so methodically, the concealed vehicles had crept through the wide ditch until they reached the point from which they planned to unleash a startling ambush.

It'd felt like forever, but the moment for which the hiding force had prayed was here. At the same instant, from both directions they'd roar up the embankment and leap onto the highway. Using the road's elevation to fire through the highest of the trees, the grinning dogmatists would have a decent shot at the stationary targets. No matter the losses they suffered, their plan couldn't fail. They'd attack with all the animus they could muster. They'd kill and destroy.

As the second of the landing helicopters turned off its engines, an ill-fated destiny arrived. The leader of the hidden force signaled. The drivers started their vehicles. In unison, each pushed the pedal to the floor. Tires spinning, they soared up the steep embankment.

In the east, from out of nowhere a line of trucks crammed with Fedayeen fighters appeared upon the multilane asphalt. A score or more were in their number. With their lights off, the deadly column was racing at full speed. Like rising cobras, with a lightning strike they were ready to inflict their lethal poisons. An identical force rushed onto the roadway from the west. Both formations raced down the highway.

The startling attackers were well-armed and ready. The jihadists were cradling rocket-propelled grenade launchers, Stinger air defense missiles, light machine guns, and assault rifles. To a man, they were confident of victory. Even if the RPGs somehow failed and the helicopters took to the air, at this distance there'd be no time for the pilots to institute defense measures. The heat-seeking Stingers would take them down.

In little more than an instant, the stunned defenders spotted the evolving threat. In the east, a pair of French defenders opened fire on the speeding convoy. More than one round struck the onrushing vehicles. A mortally wounded figure, screaming as he fell, tumbled from the rear of the lead truck and slammed to the unforgiving pavement. But the undeterred killers kept on coming. Behind the French, two German-manned bunkers joined in, firing at the rapidly approaching formation. To the west, the Dutch spotted the second line of nimble marauders. In a flashing heartbeat, a firefight erupted, with scores of combatants from both sides joining the mounting tumult. Spitting muzzle flashes, carrying certain death, lit up the night. The tracer rounds' vivid hues danced in the darkness in search of prey.

Aiming at the inviting windshields, the defenders gave it all they had. Third Squad's eleven men rushed through the trees to join them. Whenever the branches parted, the running Marines unleashed long bursts toward the insurgents.

In the east, a first driver, and shortly thereafter a second, took a round to the face. Both pickups, closely positioned, swerved. Out of control, they smashed into each other, tumbling over and again on the harsh thoroughfare. One and then the next burst into flames. Riding in the rear, multiple necks were snapped and bones broken by the vicious fall. Their passengers lay sprawled on the wide, sticky tar as the defeated vehicles' fires moved to consume them.

The others, their losses mounting, continued on. Each passing instant they grew closer to their prize. With little time to respond, there were far too many for the defenders to fully suppress.

Both groups of dogmatists were soon within range of the inviting targets. They slammed to a stop. Hasty figures, sixty or more, leaped from the trucks and took up firing positions on the expansive roadway. While their countrymen spread out to cover them, a dozen RPGs were raised.

The defenders' response was immediate and unmistakable. They let loose with everything they had. One by one and in small clusters, they cut down their surging foe. But the situation was unfolding much too fast for them to ever hope to get them all.

As the startling gunfire lit up the night, Matt Peters, scarcely twenty yards from the second of the helicopters, didn't hesitate. He instantly spoke into the small field radio. "Significant enemy force on the highway. Abort your landings! Abort! Abort!"

Despite his best efforts, the astonished lieutenant was too late to change the lurid outcome. There wasn't enough time for the pilots and their crews to respond to his urgent cries. Their fates had been forever sealed the moment the menacing force appeared.

Even with those around them falling beneath the persistent gunfire, on the highway a pair of triggers were pulled. RPGs rocketed from insurgent shoulders. They soared from the ends of their narrow tubes. The menacing rounds were a blur as they ripped across the low sky, trimming the treetops' farthest reaches as they did. In a flash, both struck.

The assailed helicopters and their highly volatile contents erupted. A deafening thunder crushed the night. An unimaginable devastation reached out to devour everything within reach. Inside both craft, their crew members disappeared, their essence vaporized.

Standing much too close to the second King Stallion, 3rd Platoon's leader was swept into the swirling witch's cauldron. His badly burned form was tossed thirty feet into the air by the violent outburst. He slammed onto the ground. Matt Peters's ragged form lay motionless in the center of the parking lot. The severely injured lieutenant was still alive, but just barely.

Still, the obscene result was far from over. The ferocious blast reached out to seize many of the volunteers headed toward the crippled craft. In the same instant, the voracious explosions blew a huge hole in the embassy's western wall.

Billowing flames climbed high, crushing the night's shadows. They seared the heavens, silhouetting as they did the numerous human forms caught in the gruesome landscape's death grip. Razor-edged pieces of wreckage, and a scowling conflagration, surged in all directions to maim and destroy. Those in the whirl-wind's path had no time to react. And scant chance of redemption.

The deepest of hells had nothing on the rapidly unfolding scene. Like a sharpened blade cutting a pliant bounty, the inferno leveled everything for fifty yards in each direction. It cut down Joyce's detachment and many of the civilians they were escorting. Near the middle of the formation, the embassy detachment's gun-nery sergeant, bleeding and battered by the lethal debris, was knocked backward by the unrelenting holocaust. Yet somehow he survived. Three of his Marines, one woman and two men, weren't so fortunate. Nor were scores of others. Those at the front of the gathering had no chance. Near the helicopters' disintegrating skeletons, fiery forms appeared, staggering a brief distance from the fiendish vista and dropping to the ground. Most moved no more. In the south, the four at the rear of 3rd Squad's scurrying Marines and the German forces fighting from the inner line of foxholes were struck by the crushing blow. A third of the area's civilian defenders were felled. Half of the southern trees, ripped and shredded, were ablaze. The same was true for the thick mul-berries sheltering the last line of civilian foxholes to the west.

Having taken a few steps out of the main gate, Steven Gray was knocked off his feet by the power of the terrifying blow. While he struggled to stand, he could feel the blood running down his face. He could sense the firestorm assailing him. Those at the head of the emerging line of evacuees would taste the stinging scene's wounds. But at this distance none of their injuries would be life-threatening. The same, however, couldn't be said for a great many. In the singed grasses and raging fires, the hideous results were unmistakable. The death toll was immediate. And immense.

27

Erickson didn't hesitate. He motioned for the first sergeant to remain in the command center. Before the flames reached their apexes the company commander was out of the bunker and running at full speed across the fire-emblazoned track. Scarcely one hundred yards from the corrupting nightmare, he could feel the roaring furnace's scorching heat.

While he rushed toward it, a horrifying scene was unfolding in front of him. There were mangled bodies everywhere his eyes surveyed. Some were silent. Others were writhing about in soul-seizing torment. Even at this distance, the company commander could hear the frightful screams of the severely burned and injured.

While he ran, Erickson keyed his headset. "Lieutenant Marshall, I need every other man from your platoon to leave their foxholes and head for the parking lot. They're to bring some of the civilian defenders with them. We've got to reach the wounded as soon as we can."

"We're on it, sir," Marshall responded. "Second Platoon, you heard the company commander. One of you remain in your foxhole, the other head for the wounded without delay." Eighteen Marines scrambled from their sandbagged worlds and rushed to join Erickson. They grabbed a number of civilian defenders as they sprinted past.

"Lieutenant Bates," Erickson said, "you're to command our western defenses while I attempt to get the situation under control. I want every man on alert. I wouldn't be surprised if the Fedayeen followed up with a full-blown attack while we're at our most vulnerable."

"Understood. We'll be ready for anything they throw at us, sir."

"First thing we've got to do is get the fighting in the south under control. We're not going to be able to help the wounded if we're trying to dodge a mountain of bullets at the same time. I need you to send one of your squads south to support those fighting the Fedayeen on the highway. They're to eliminate the threat and secure the southern perimeter. Is that clear?"

"We'll handle it, sir. Jones, this one's on you. Take your men and reinforce the French, Dutch, Germans, and any of Lieutenant Peters's guys who're still in the fight."

"Yes, sir!" Sergeant Jones replied. "First Squad, on your feet." In an instant, his squad was out of their defenses and scurrying through the burning fields and trees toward the Kashmir Highway. As they went, Jones barked out further orders to his fire teams. "Wilson, you're to reinforce the Dutch. Belcher, you've got the Germans. Nolan, you're with the French. Suppress the enemy fire. Take 'em out. Then wait for further orders."

In the enduring bunkers in the southern portion of the woods, the startling explosions had staggered the defenders. The profane spectacle, its appalling images forever imprinted on their brains, gripped the aghast fighters. While the flames rose high, for a lengthy moment the rifle fire from both sides ceased. Yet the pause soon ended as individual by individual they realized the bitter contest with those on the roadway was far from over. A surging curtain of tracer fire returned.

In under a minute, Jones's arriving Marines joined the fray. With one hundred spitting rifles piercing the darkness, the killing on both sides soon reached its crescendo. The howling fires and constant secondary explosions shredded the night, adding their merciless voices to the demonic scene.

It didn't take long for the fearsome clash to become one-sided. Out in the open, the insurgents had little chance. Still, even with death swirling around them, the gleeful despots stood their ground. Seeking an immeasurable revenge, the Marines, French, Dutch, and Germans cut them down with ease. To a man, each Fedayeen went to his grave with a satisfied smile on his face. What they'd come to do had succeeded beyond the wildest of imaginations.

At the edge of the parking lot, despite everything he tried, Erickson was forced back by the searing heat. He couldn't get to those he'd come to save. Moment by moment, his desperation grew. The crippling sight was even worse than he'd imagined. There were so many in need of help. And the scant time remaining in many a life was fading.

Erickson fitfully waited, hopelessly praying for the inferno to subside. As the gunfire south of him ended, his headset crackled to life. "Sir, we've eliminated the insurgents on the Kashmir Highway," Sergeant Jones announced. "What're your orders?"

"What're your squad's losses?

"Not certain, sir. Things are a bit crazy over here at the moment. I believe most of my guys made it through okay. But the French and Germans have both suffered casualties. Not sure about the Dutch."

"Patterson, what about your men?" Erickson asked.

"Four were cut down by the explosion, sir. A couple of others were hit during the firefight. But neither's wounds appear life-threatening."

Erickson knew what the answer to his next question would be, but he asked anyway. "What about Lieutenant Peters?"

"No idea about the lieutenant, sir. Last time I glanced in his direction, he was pretty close to the King Stallions."

"Okay." The Marine commander looked behind him. With the ambassador at their head, the hospital's medics were scrambling out of the compound and heading his way. A dozen civilians were right behind. From the west, Lieutenant Marshall's force was growing near. "Help's on the way."

The moment the flames ebbed, the frantic rescuers, with Erickson in the lead and Ingram not far behind, rushed to aid the fallen. But, for many, their efforts would be much too little and far too late.

It felt so surreal, so freakishly disassociating, to those rushing to assist the injured. As they edged deeper into the growing perdition, a sledgehammer of reality reached out for them. The enormity of what they faced staggered even the most callous of individuals.

Thirty yards into the parking lot, Erickson located one of Joyce's volunteers who had fallen. He knelt next to the sobbing, frightened woman in her late twenties. There was flowing blood on her forehead and a nasty gash in her torso under her ribs.

Knocked violently from her feet, her twisted right leg, the pain sharp and insistent, was pinned beneath her. From its strange angle, Erickson had little doubt it was broken. To his relief, her burns were less severe than he had expected. He quickly examined her wounds. She needed medical help before the loss of blood became significant. He looked around, hoping to spot one of the approaching medics. However, none were close by.

While Erickson examined the woman, others passed, heading deeper into the death and destruction. He looked into her eyes. Her pain was undeniable. He tried his best to reassure her, gently taking her hand as he spoke. "I know how bad this must feel. But you're going to be all right. Let's get you back to the embassy so the doctors can patch you up." Erickson spied one of his men, clearly overwhelmed by the enormity of it all, standing nearby. "Adams, give me a hand."

"Yes, sir." The inexperienced private, one of the newest members of his unit, approached. The disbelief on the nineteen-year-old's face said it all.

"I need you to carry this woman to the hospital building. Once you've done that, hurry back. There'll no doubt be lots of others who'll need your help to get inside the compound."

The idea that he'd be helping people to safety, rather than facing the pernicious carnage, pleased Adams greatly. "Absolutely, sir. I'll be back for the next one as soon as I can." The company commander directed his next comment toward the injured woman. "You ready?" he asked.

She looked at the young Marine waiting for her to be positioned on his back. She gritted her teeth and nodded. Erickson did his best to gently lift her. Even so, the slightest movements forced her to let out a piercing scream. The company commander had little choice but to continue. It took no time for Adams to lift her and start toward the compound, securely holding her agonized form.

Erickson got to his feet. After taking a look around to ensure he was satisfied with the ongoing actions, he began searching for the next in what would be a lengthy list of people in need of help. In no pattern, untold numbers lay upon the scorched landscape. The horror of it all overwhelmed him as he waded into the morass of humanity.

Twenty feet away another distressed soul waited. Erickson knelt down, examining what he faced. Despite the efforts of all involved, far too many remained unattended. To his surprise, the man was one of the lucky few. His injuries weren't too extensive: burns, a couple of deep cuts, and numerous bruises, but nothing more. He knew he'd be unlikely to find many more this fortunate. In no more than a minute, he managed to slow the bleeding. Adams, having returned, assisted the injured individual as he struggled toward the gate.

The Marine commander focused on where he was needed next. The minutes passed. The deeper he got into the horrifying multitudes, the worse the situation grew. A ghoulish hour passed without him pausing in the slightest.

28

Outside the hospital, there were bodies everywhere. Some were still breathing. Many were not. Three of the nurses, doing their best to control the uncontrollable, were triaging those being brought in. While they moved through the gruesome milieu, they shouted frantic orders to the lab technicians working alongside them.

Lauren, shielding MaKenna to keep her from seeing what was occurring, was standing near the hospital entrance as a continual stream of wounded arrived. For once, the story was too grim for her to record. Instead, Chuck had put down his camera and been one of the first to head out to help.

She saw Sam approaching. He was carrying a dreadfully disfigured individual who could only vaguely be described as human. He stopped in front of her and gently placed the mangled form on the ground. The company commander's uniform was covered in blood. Thinking her love had been wounded, panic seized her. It didn't take long, however, for Wells to realize that none of the vile stains had come from him.

His shoulders slumped as he surveyed the macabre scene. Hopelessness and confusion gripped his features. From the remaining bits of charred clothing, Lauren could tell the person Sam had been carrying was a Marine. The anguished look on his face confirmed any remaining questions she had about the horrors outside the embassy's walls.

Erickson spotted one of the nurses nearby. She'd just finished her initial examination of one of the wounded lying on the ground next to the building. It was another of the women who'd been among the volunteers cut down by the blast. Like so many, she had suffered significant injuries. The nurse looked up, trying to prioritize the woman's needs.

Erickson seized that brief window. "Nurse! Nurse! He's hurt real bad. We need to get him inside right away!" he said while motioning to the pitiful figure.

The nurse let out a deep sigh and walked over to where Erickson and Wells were standing. She looked down at the ragged flesh. Without a word she reached out to feel for a pulse. She'd known before she acted that her efforts would be for naught. Even so, she took the time to ensure she wasn't mistaken. Erickson looked into her eyes, his apprehensiveness evident. Her eyes turned emotionless. The nurse shook her head.

"What? I don't understand. He was in real bad shape when I found him, but I'm certain he was breathing when I picked him up to bring him here."

The exhausted nurse didn't respond. The past hour weighed heavy upon her, overwhelming her tortured existence. Piled upon the difficult day that had just passed, it tore at her crumbling essence. After an extended pause she said in a voice devoid of emotion, "Take him over there." Struggling to lift her arm, she pointed to an open area deeper in the compound where a number of bodies lay. "We're gathering the dead and placing them there for now."

She turned and headed back to the woman she'd been examining. With a continuous stream of wounded and dead arriving, she had too much to do and no time for any of it.

Unable to move, the dejected captain stood in silence, an incomprehensible expression on his features. Lauren, unsure of what to do, waited. Finally, he did what the nurse had directed. He picked up the disfigured body and started toward the extended line of those who lived no more. Kicking up the clinging dirt, he shuffled over to the spot she had indicated. He laid the vanquished flesh on the ground at the edge of those who'd fallen. The battle-hardened Marine stood over the body, his lips moving in a whispered prayer. The entreaty complete, he turned and headed back to where Lauren stood.

Unsure of what to do, Wells attempted to distract him with a sliver of good news. "I saw them bring in Gunny Joyce a little while ago."

"How's he doing?" he asked, his consuming weariness far too apparent.

"Got some deep cuts and some second-degree burns. But nothing life-threatening. The nurse said he should be all right. He's inside now. They're working on him."

Erickson didn't respond. It was clear Wells's attempt to divert him had failed. He rubbed his bloodshot eyes and turned to view the unspeakable scene once more. In a steady stream, more assailed people, some alive, some not, were arriving. "This is my fault," he said. "I knew how dangerous this would be but went ahead with it anyway. I rolled the dice and all these people died."

"You didn't have any choice, Sam. This is the hand you were dealt and you had to play it. Despite the risk, you couldn't just sit here doing nothing as the Fedayeen picked us off. Risk or not, you had to attempt to do exactly what you did."

"But these people would be alive if I hadn't taken the chances I did. I gambled with their lives, and they ended up paying for it."

"You can't look at it that way. Look at how many lives you've already saved. Look at how many you saved at the Marriott. How many you've gotten onto the helicopters and out of this horrible place." The anticipated drizzle was beginning, with the heavier showers soon to arrive.

"I need to get away from here," he said, speaking in a stilted tone she'd never before heard from him. He looked around once again, taking in the frantic gathering. "I know it doesn't look like it, but the ambassador has things under control outside. And my guys have put out most of the fires. They should be able to finish up without me."

It was the first time in two horrendous wars Wells had heard him admit anything was too much for him. She looked into his eyes. All she could find was an unfocused stare. He gave the appearance of having aged ten years since she'd last seen him a few hours earlier. The veteran reporter looked around until she spotted a small, secluded building on the eastern side of the compound. It was far enough away from the inexorable turmoil to allow him to clear his mind and rest for the first time since the mission began.

"When's the last time you slept, Sam?"

He struggled to respond. "Uh . . . not really sure. Got a couple hours a few nights ago, I think."

She shook her head, her concern obvious. "I know you think you're superman, Samuel Erickson. But as much as you try to deny it, you really do have your limits. From the look of things, you've reached yours. With what's happened, it doesn't appear we'll be getting out of this mess anytime soon. And we're going to need you more than ever. You're not going to be of use to any of us if you run yourself into the ground. Why don't we find a quiet place to sleep for a couple of hours? It'll do you good."

Erickson looked at her, unresponsive. He couldn't deny the truth in what she was saying. There were going to be a multitude of critical decisions needing to be made in the coming days. More life-and-death judgments he'd need to undertake. Right now, he couldn't trust himself with even the most basic. With the angst outside the walls nearing its end, and no attempts by the Fedayeen to capitalize on the chaos, now was a perfect time to do what Lauren was urging. He keyed his headset. "XO?"

"Yes, sir," Tomlin responded.

"I'm going to try to grab a little sleep. I need you to take charge of our defenses for a couple of hours," he said, knowing his executive officer was more than capable of handling even the most unanticipated situation until he arrived.

"Absolutely, sir."

"Wake me if you need me."

"Will do, sir."

Wells took him by the hand. "This way, Sam," she said, her voice as gentle as any he'd ever heard. Still cradling MaKenna, she led him across the embassy's grounds, heading for the distant spot. Neither said a word as they turned their backs and walked away from the madness.

Lauren took him to the far side of a two-story building, out of sight of the reviling images. The spot she'd picked was perfect. It was one of the few locales inside the ten-foot-high walls with no one nearby. And the roof's overhang was adequate to shield them from the approaching weather. "Let's rest here for a while." Without waiting for him to respond, she sat down and scooted closer to the building. She propped her back against the wall.

He did the same. His weariness, bordering on complete collapse, was evident in his stiff movements as he dropped to the ground. Eyes fixed, he stared straight ahead. Finally, he turned to look at her. As much as he tried, he was unable to form any words.

"You going to be all right, Sam?" she asked, her need for reassurance obvious.

He didn't respond for the longest time. Finally he began to talk, his voice as exhausted as his body. "At this point, I've no idea what all right is."

She wrapped her arm around him and held him as tightly as she could without suffocating MaKenna. "Who was that you were carrying?" she asked. She was confident it was a Marine. Little did she know his answer would stagger her.

"Matt Peters," was his somber response.

"Lieutenant Peters? Oh, my God, Sam," she said in complete surprise. "I was talking with him right before he left the compound. He was smiling and showing me pictures of his wife and little boy."

"Never had a chance. He was twenty yards from what was left of the second helicopter when I found him. Matt had been with me since I took charge of the company a year ago. Was a great guy and an even better Marine. Had his whole life in front of him."

"I know, Sam. But you did all you could to save him. Try to get some sleep."

Erickson awoke with a start, his tortured dreams dissipating. He lifted his head from Wells's shoulder, the reality of where he was and what was occurring hitting him head-on. The first hint of the coming dawn was still an hour away. Lauren hadn't closed her eyes throughout the languishing night as she watched over both her charges.

"How long have I been asleep?" he asked, his concern evident.

"About four hours."

"Four hours? Why'd you let me sleep so long?"

"Because things have been nothing but quiet. And you needed every minute of it. How're you feeling?"

He rubbed his eyes. "Okay, I guess." He pulled up a blood-stained sleeve and peered at his watch in the darkness. It was nearly six. He hurriedly stood. "I need to get out there."

"Nonsense. There's still a little time. What you really need is to wait right here while I find us something to eat."

Sam seemed quite distracted while he ate in silence. Lauren didn't have the slightest idea that the unsettling news he'd received while she'd been away was the reason why. Both were finishing a last morsel when a figure came around the corner of the building.

"Oh, there you are," Ambassador Ingram said. "Someone told me they'd seen the two of you over here."

"Was about to leave, sir. Need to head back to the command bunker," Erickson said.

"Glad I caught you before you did. I was speaking with Steven Gray and wanted to go over the modifications we've made to keep the evacuations going. It's going to take a bit longer than we planned to get everyone out of here, but Steven's people have been able to clear an area inside the compound for the helicopters to land. There'll only be enough room to bring in one at a time, but we should be able to rotate the surviving ones throughout the night to get the job done."

"That sounds wonderful, Mr. Ambassador," Wells said. She'd spent a great deal of the previous hours wondering what they were going to do now that they'd lost two of the King Stallions. She was obviously pleased with Ingram's news.

Erickson looked around to ensure no one was nearby. "Won't work," he said.

"What?" Ingram replied.

"Why not, Sam?" she asked.

"Because while you were getting us breakfast, I received a status report from Scott."

"And?"

"He told me that among the weapons we seized from the dead Fedayeen on the highway, Sergeant Patterson found three Stinger air defense missiles. Which means those surrounding us likely have quite a few more. If that's the case, it won't matter how dark or foggy it becomes. Even if they employ all of their defensive measures, the King Stallions won't have a chance if they try to land."

In an instant Wells and Ingram recognized the implications of what he was saying. In the predawn darkness, the shock on their faces was unmistakable.

"Won't the embassy's walls protect them while they're landing?" the ambassador asked.

"I'm afraid not. They're older Stingers, but they have a three-mile effective range. The guys we're facing probably have little idea how to use them, but they're pretty simple to operate. It won't take but a few tries to figure things out. They'll knock down the helicopters long before they get anywhere near this place."

"So how are we going to get out of here, Sam?" Wells asked.

"I wish I knew."

Alone, he walked out the front gate, heading for his bunker. The dreaded sunrise would soon be upon them. As he steadied himself for the coming day, Erickson understood that inside the two side-by-side compounds, five thousand desperate individuals were trapped. And the arrival of another day's killing light was nearly here.

29

1:09 A.M., NOVEMBER 3
OPERATIONAL DETACHMENT ALPHA 6333,
CHARLIE COMPANY, 3RD BATTALION,
6TH SPECIAL FORCES GROUP (AIRBORNE)
CAMP NOWHERE
THE SPĪN GHAR MOUNTAINS OF NORTH-CENTRAL PAKISTAN

In the dark night's howling gale, the buffeted Black Hawk settled into the deep drifts. It was certainly not the first of the critical transports to land at the location. Nor would it be the last. Scores of Black Hawks and Apaches, their stark images masked by the savage snows, covered the high plateau. The pilots cut the engine and the craft's blades slowed. The moment the crew chiefs opened the doors, the subzero temperatures and swirling winds rocked the six Green Berets sheltering within its modest hold.

"Jesus Christ!" Aaron Porter exclaimed.

"Our next stop, gentlemen," Captain Short announced.

Those inside the helicopter peered at the barren landscape. In the near-whiteout conditions, they couldn't see far. This high in the jagged mountains there was nothing but a blinding, treeless world to greet them. But the desolate scene was far from lifeless. All around them, there was furious activity. And the constant sounds of Black Hawks and Apaches landing. Throughout the crag-laden plateau, unseen by those on the ground, more were approaching. The entire Special Forces Group was here or would be shortly. If their attacks were going to succeed, everything had to occur on a precise schedule, one that, given the mission, would be a daunting challenge.

While Green Berets who had arrived earlier headed for shelter, a number of half-frozen soldiers scurried about, refueling the immense helicopter fleet. Some distance away, scores of scattered tents tugged against their moorings.

Behind their Black Hawk, three others, carrying the remaining eighteen Green Berets assigned to their mission, found landing places nearby. A pair of deadly Apaches, armed with Hydra-70 rockets, Hellfire missiles, and 30mm chain gun rounds, were right behind.

"Where the hell are we, sir?" Sanders asked.

"Nowhere," was the reply.

"I can see that, sir, but really, where are we?"

"I told you, Sanders. We're at Camp Nowhere. That's the name the guys who set it up yesterday afternoon named it. It's our final stop before we reach the target. The Apaches don't have the range to make it to the nuclear sites, fight for an extended period, and return to Spinager without refueling. And India made it clear they didn't want us launching attacks from inside their borders. So we had no choice but to establish a fuel depot and group headquarters closer to the battle zone. As isolated as it is, this is the one place in Pakistan where we can probably operate for weeks without being spotted."

Sanders took another look around. "Nowhere . . . That makes sense."

"Now, if you don't mind, Sergeant Sanders, while the refueling takes place, why don't we find ourselves a heated tent? We've got an hour and a half before we're scheduled to depart, and I'd rather not spend any more of it out here than we have to."

None of those inside the pummeled craft needed further encouragement. In seconds, cradling their M4s and packs, they were crawling out of the Black Hawk and making a head-down fight through the deep drifts and blizzard-swept landscape. Fifty yards away a large tent awaited. The remaining members of their assault force joined them.

The moment they entered the tent, the soldiers headed straight for the heater. Despite the horrid conditions, the device, a modernized, simplified version of a potbellied stove, was more than adequate to warm the enclosed space.

Both teams were soon inside. Captain Short was the last to enter its thick canvas walls. He quickly pulled the tent's flaps shut and secured them. "Get yourselves warmed up. Once you've done that, we need to go over the plan of attack a final time. Then we'll break into specialties to further coordinate the two teams' efforts."

Like the detachments huddling inside the tent, the basic setup of a Special Forces A Team was the same. Each was composed of two officers—a captain in command and a warrant officer—two operations sergeants, two weapons specialists, two communication specialists, two medics, and two engineers. The engineers were exceptionally well trained in both building and destroying. Every Green Beret was cross-trained in a secondary specialty to provide redundancy for each assignment.

"Okay," Short said, beginning the final run-through of how they'd gain control of the hilltop they'd been assigned. "Once we arrive, the Apaches will . . ."

The Green Berets broke into smaller groups to go over how they planned to divide their responsibilities. In the far corner of the tent, Charlie Sanders, as the senior engineer, gathered the three others: Staff Sergeant David Meeks and Sergeants Pierce and Davidson. He began laying out how he wanted to approach the multiple tasks they'd face once the Americans had seized the nuclear weapons. He looked first at Pierce and Davidson. As a fellow member of Detachment 6333, he'd supervised Pierce's actions numerous times while they practiced the removal of the trigger devices during the simulated scenarios. On every occasion, Pierce had been flawless in his actions. Sanders was confident he'd perform well under the pressures of facing actual nuclear devices. However, he'd never had the opportunity to observe Davidson, a member of their sister team.

The senior sergeant knew a single misstep by the engineers could trigger an immense nuclear explosion. Such a mistake would be their last, instantly leveling the hilltop and incinerating the members of both teams. As Sanders began talking, they could hear the helicopters with the greatest distances to travel taking off. The American plan was getting underway.

"Davidson, how long have you served with 6334?"

"Two years, Sarge."

"How much practice have you had in removing triggers from both strategic and tactical nuclear weapons?"

"More than enough. I can handle this," was Davidson's response.

Sanders glanced at Staff Sergeant Meeks. As Davidson's superior, Meeks would be intimately familiar with his junior sergeant's abilities. Without being too obvious, Meeks shook his head yes, confirming Davidson's assertion.

"Okay. After we've seized control of the compound, I want you and Pierce to locate the tactical nukes. Once you have them in your hands, work as a team, disconnecting the triggers one at a time. You both know the drill. One of you removes the device, the other acts as guide, announcing the next step prior to any action and observing as the other performs it. Is that clear?"

"Yeah, Sarge," both said.

"Take your time. Don't rush this. While you're working on the tactical stuff, Sergeant Meeks and I will disable the three Shaheens. Once we're finished, we'll head over to help you disarm any of the smaller ones that remain."

"After we remove it, do you want us to destroy each trigger prior to moving on to the next?" Pierce asked.

"Negative. That can wait. Removal will be our first priority. Once they're out, the weapons will be useless. Even if additional enemy forces appear and somehow succeed in regaining control of the encampment, there's no way a bunch of backward farmers will know how to reinstall the triggers. You heard Captain Short. There's a light rain falling that's only going to get heavier. It's not expected to stop until midmorning. So it's going to be dark and miserable while we're working. Given the situation, we can't risk any more light than that of our flashlights, so this isn't going to be easy. Even so, don't panic and make a mistake. But get those triggers out. Once they're removed, we'll carry the entire load a safe distance away and destroy them."

Pierce glanced at Davidson. The pair had gone through Green Beret training together and knew the other's abilities well. "Got it, Sarge," was Pierce's reply.

"Good. So all we need now is to get our hands on those babies and disable them," Sanders said.

The first of Alpha 6333's refueled helicopters fought its way into the low skies. Inside, Sanders went through his rucksack filled with explosives and tools, going over which he'd use to remove and detonate the trigger devices. Three additional Black Hawks and a pair of Apaches joined the initial one as they headed to the southwest through one of a trio of serviceable passes in the cloud-swathed mountains.

In front of them, fanning out to the west, south, and east, the darkened silhouettes of the lethal caravan reached beyond the night-hewn horizon. Behind 6333, like avenging angels, still more took to the skies. In a steady stream, they headed for their targets. All of the members of the Special Forces Group's 1st, 2nd, and 3rd Battalions would be committed to the multiple assaults.

The final battalion, the 4th, would wait at Camp Nowhere, ready to leap into action at a moment's notice. When word came that one or more of the objectives remained in enemy hands or the losses incurred by the initial teams were significant enough to call for reinforcements, they'd rush to join them. Given the uncertainty of the situation and the odds their departing comrades faced, those in the battalion had little doubt they'd be called upon to join the fray. To a man, they were eager to do so.

They had only vague ideas about how many Fedayeen were waiting at each nuclear site. The Americans assumed that at even the smallest locations the arriving Green Berets would be greatly outnumbered. They suspected enemy communications were unsophisticated at best. So whatever force they faced wouldn't be able to call for help in time to thwart the determined assailants. Still, they couldn't know that with any certainty. To minimize the possibility of hundreds, even thousands, of additional fighters showing up, each attack was scheduled to begin at the same moment. Otherwise, they ran the risk of one of the targets alerting the other nuclear facilities and any additional units sheltering nearby. If that happened, it could prove disastrous for the elite soldiers.

They needed to catch their foe unaware. They needed to strike while the majority were sleeping. At 3:00 a.m., using the drizzle and darkness to cover their actions, untold assaults would begin.

With their target reasonably close, Detachments 6333 and 6334 waited while the entirety of 1st and 2nd Battalions departed. Finally, it was their turn. At 2:37 the soldiers stepped back into the cold and headed for their Black Hawks. As they did, in preparation for the grim task, a significant number of medevac helicopters, red crosses emblazoned on their tops and sides, arrived on the icy mountainside. Like the soldiers of the 4th Battalion, they expected to be called upon soon.

30

At his desk, Alan Ingram fell fast asleep. There'd been too many things to address in the past seventy-two hours for anything more than the briefest of catnaps. With another night-induced lull in the fighting, he was hoping to rest for as much as an hour, possibly two.

Unfortunately, his plan was about to be thwarted. He had been unconscious for only a few minutes when the phone rang. He awoke with a start, momentarily confused by both his surroundings and the sudden intrusion. He did his best to shake the cobwebs, picking up the phone after the third ring. Little could he know what awaited.

"Alan Ingram," he mumbled.

"So sorry to intrude at this late hour, Mr. Ambassador, but the urgency of the situation leaves me no choice." There was obvious concern, bordering on panic, in the uneasy voice. Even in his addled state, Ingram instantly recognized who was on the other end of the line.

"Not a problem, General Bhatti. What can I do for you?"

"Mr. Ambassador, I've dreadful news. Basra's people have gotten their hands on the launch codes."

Hearing those fateful words, the failed attempt to sleep vanished from Ingram's brain. "Oh, my God!" He hesitated, struggling to compose himself as he fought to address the implications of what he'd heard. "Are you sure, General?"

"Yes, quite sure, unfortunately," Bhatti said. "The information came from one of my most trusted sources—someone I'd planted within Basra's leadership team who's been providing us with significant information on the Fedayeen's battle plans. I've no doubt of what he told me. Within the past hours, Basra received the codes. My man was standing next to him when they arrived."

"So the missiles are ready to be launched?"

"Not yet, but it won't be much longer. Because his forces have destroyed the infrastructure in the areas they've seized, they've no way of communicating directly with the nuclear sites. And he'd likely not use radios or cell phones even if he had them for fear your country would pinpoint his location and send drones to destroy him. Instead, he's depending on a courier system he spent years developing using motorcycles and trucks. Not the most efficient way to conduct a war as widespread as this one, but it's how he's always done things and we don't see that changing. Each of those carrying the codes has received rudimentary training on how to enter the information, then activate and launch the weapons."

"Have the couriers left? Maybe if they haven't and your spy can provide us with the location of Basra's camp, it might not be too late to send drones to stop them."

"Unfortunately, that's not possible. My man is quite unfamiliar with the area where they've been traveling, so he's been unable to provide anything on their location we could use. They're in the mountains; that's all he knows. Even if he were capable of providing the exact location, Basra's extremely paranoid. His camp never stays in the same spot for more than a few hours. And I'm afraid it's too late anyway."

"So the couriers are on the way?"

"Yes, all are on the way."

Little did either know that identifying the Fedayeen camp would do little good. For Basra was no longer there. The moment he'd received the launch information, he put his plan into motion to ensure he'd be safe from India's response to his nuclear attack.

Before responding to the incredible news about the receipt of the launch codes, he turned to his oldest son, Muhsin, who'd been a part of his leadership cabal since the beginning of the war. Basra handed him what he claimed was an urgent message to be delivered without haste to the leader of his forces near the border with Kashmir.

"You must take these orders to Ayamin Patel without delay."

His son, of course, was in on Basra's scheme. "Yes, Father. I'll leave immediately."

Within minutes, Muhsin was gone, driving east as he left the encampment. Once he was certain he was far enough away to not be detected, he turned and headed northwest.

None of Basra's followers suspected what was happening. His insistence on the constant, unpredictable movements had been not just to avoid arriving American drones or Pakistani F-16 strikes but also to ensure when the nuclear codes arrived he'd be no more than an hour from where his family was hiding.

Two hours later, unaware of the ongoing American efforts to thwart the missile launches, the second part of Basra's plan began to play out. From out of the darkness a vehicle appeared. Behind the wheel was Basra's second son, Kashif. The instant he reached the edge of the camp, he brought the pickup to a stop and leaped from the cab.

"Where's my father?" Kashif said to the first person he saw. "I must speak to him immediately!"

"He's over there," was the response. The man pointed.

Without replying, Kashif ran in the direction indicated. He spotted his father sitting next to his second-in-command, Bila Chachar. Basra did his best to appear surprised by his son's arrival.

"Kashif, what're you doing here?"

"Father, you must come quickly."

"What are talking about, my son?" Basra responded, doing his best to sound perplexed. Neither father nor son was a great actor. Yet their little play would serve its purpose with so unsuspecting an audience.

"Mother's ill. She appears to be dying and may not last the night. She's asked to see you a final time. Her remaining wish is to have you at her bedside when the end comes."

"What's wrong with her?"

"No one seems to know. For days her fever has raged and she's no longer able to stand. She's coughing up blood and every breath is difficult and painful. To make matters worse, my younger brothers and sisters are becoming quite ill and are showing the same signs that mother did in the beginning. You must come immediately or it'll be too late."

With many of his followers aware of his wife's near death a few months earlier, Basra knew the story would sound quite convincing. There was little doubt if the traveling American medical team hadn't chosen that moment to appear in the tribal territories' primitive outpost, she would have had no chance for survival. As it was, even with the delicate surgery the doctors performed, it'd been touch and go for at least a week. One of the nurses, the lead surgeon's wife and an exceptionally kind woman, had stayed by her side night and day until the crisis passed. Basra had been particularly taken with the couple's precocious, golden-haired four-year-old daughter as she scampered about, playing with the village children and chattering away in the foreign tongue he couldn't understand.

"Kashif, you know that's impossible. I am needed here, to direct our armies against those foolish enough to stand in our way."

There was a momentary lull, but an unsuspecting Bila Chachar chimed in right on cue. "Nonsense. Your place is with your wife and children. The battles continue to go well and those present can handle things in your absence."

"Are you certain? If things are as serious as my son describes, I may need to be away for a few days."

"Don't concern yourself. Go. The one true God will watch over us until you return."

Basra hesitated, trying to give every appearance of mulling over the decision. "All right, Bila, I'll do as you suggest."

Chachar smiled. He had demonstrated to those present that at least on this occasion Salim Basra would listen to his counsel.

"Thank you, Father," his son said. "We must hurry before it's too late."

"Bila, there's no time to waste. Hand out the launch information to our couriers and get them on their way. May Allah watch over their righteous endeavors. I'll return as soon as possible."

Without another word, father and son turned and headed toward the truck. The pickup was soon driving away from the camp. Basra's ruse had worked. By 8:00 a.m., when the massed rockets would launch, he'd be twenty miles away, deep within a protective cave with his family. His plan was to remain there for the next three days to ensure the fallout levels from India's retaliation were reasonably safe before coming out.

The crucial phone call between Ingram and Bhatti continued. "How long do you estimate it'll take for the couriers to arrive with the launch codes?" the ambassador asked.

"Given the widespread locations of our nuclear weapons, it'll vary. But we've little time. Four of the sites are probably within fifty kilometers of Basra's camp, and we anticipate the codes reaching those locations within the hour. Minutes after that, the weapons will be readied. It'll take a few hours more for most to reach their destinations and encode the firing data. Even so, every facility, no matter how distant, will be capable of launching their missiles by the time the sun rises."

"Do you anticipate Basra unleashing each the moment it's ready? Or will he wait until they're all online?"

"Basra's always been unpredictable. Still, even he understands the moment he launches the first of the missiles, India's going to respond. My spy said the orders the couriers are carrying direct each facility to go ahead and fire on their own if they come under attack. Otherwise, they're to wait until all are ready. If possible, the launch of Pakistan's two hundred strategic nuclear weapons will occur as a single event at eight o'clock tomorrow morning. And my country's fate will be forever sealed."

"That gives us five hours before a full-scale nuclear war begins," Ingram said.

"That's correct, Mr. Ambassador. Unless the United States can somehow stop this, by shortly after sunrise the land I love will be little more than a smoking crater. The nuclear winter that will follow will likely kill millions and possibly billions more. Even your great nation's citizenry will be unable able to avoid the widespread famine that will seize the planet."

"General, are you certain Basra will launch? Even he has to know what the consequences will be if he does so. Few of his countrymen will survive."

"Basra will launch. He's a madman. He doesn't care what happens to Pakistan or its people. To him, they're little more than pawns he'll use to reach his sadistic goals. He won't shed a tear for those who are lost. His primal hatred of India and the world outside his impoverished village is beyond anything anyone can comprehend. He believes that destroying India is worth whatever price is paid. And he's certain the slaughter of so many devout followers of Islam in India's retaliation will be the event that triggers nearly two billion followers of Allah's chosen religion to rise up in a worldwide holy war. Along with the effects of the nuclear event he's planning, such a war may soon consume this planet and lead to mankind's end."

Ingram understood the fervor such a perverse goal would create in Basra. And he could hear the truth in General Bhatti's words. "He's got to care about something, General. Something we can eventually use to defeat him."

"The only thing he'll be concerned with is saving his own skin. He's a bully, and like most bullies, he's also an abject coward. So nothing else will matter to him."

"If only his followers were able to see it."

"Until he's dead, there's no chance of them recognizing the serpent in their midst. They've fallen under his spell and in their simplemindedness can see nothing. Their adoration for him knows no bounds. But he truly is the worst of villains. And his own survival will be his only concern. Knowing what's coming, I've no doubt he's running as far away as he can. He's bound to have a safe place filled with provisions in one of our mountain ranges to guarantee he'll live through what's going to occur. He must be stopped. We have minutes before the first of the couriers arrives. Is there anything America can do before it's too late?"

"General Bhatti, I hope you understand I'm not in a position to provide you with the details of our actions, but you can be assured that if things go as planned, we're going to be able to keep this from happening. If things go like they're supposed to, in less than five hours, at the moment Basra intends to unleash them, all of the nuclear facilities should be in American hands."

Bhatti let out an audible sigh. "Mr. Ambassador, I cannot tell you how relieved I am to hear such news. Yet, even if such is true, we've far less time to keep my country from being destroyed. Once the codes reach the initial handful of sites, they'll launch at the first sign of trouble and the die will be forever cast. At the closest locations, we're talking about the unleashing of a dozen Shaheen missiles. That's more than enough to trigger an all-out response by India. So, in reality, if those four locations aren't rendered harmless, we've less than an hour before the world will face the roaring fires of an unimaginable event."

"Which are those, General?

"Mehrgarh, Maurya, Seleucid, and Mishira."

"I'll do what I can to alert our forces," Ingram's said. With that, he ended the call. And made a new one.

31

Held together by fraying duct tape and bailing wire, the bouncing truck churned toward the nuclear site. The pickup's dents and scratches were too numerous to tally. Its patch-marked paint was so faded, it was impossible to determine what color the vehicle had been. Or how old it was. A spidery crack, widening as the years passed, ran across the windshield. The aging windows and door handles rattled and shook with every modest movement. Its windshield wipers barely worked. The tired truck's sputtering engine threatened to make every effort its last.

Yet the determined courier was nearly there. Three kilometers, no more, and he'd be able to release his death grip on the steering wheel. In ten minutes, those in the isolated camp would be roused to begin the process of entering the system data into the trio of Shaheen launchers. In half an hour the nuclear armaments would be primed to strike.

The narrow path, scarcely more than an overgrown goat trail, made reaching the plateau in the darkness and drizzle a difficult task. Like the hundreds of unpredictable obstacles the derelict road had presented, the next deep rut the messenger encountered could stop him in his tracks. Even so, the jostled driver was skillfully handling the endeavor. His years in the harsh conditions of the tribal regions, where pavement was nonexistent and navigating never easy, were serving him well. With the launch codes resting in the passenger seat, he continued steadfastly on his journey.

For the entirety of the drive a crooked smile had been affixed to his timeworn face. To be entrusted with such a critical assignment caused the driver to burst with pride. When morning arrived, he, as Allah's reverent servant, would send forth an unspeakable result to smite their abhorrent adversary. Mishira's life-devouring payloads would explode in a trio of spectacular airbursts over Mumbai, killing a significant portion of the sprawling metropolis's inhabitants.

The time was here to seek their revenge for the wrongs his people had endured at the hands of the despicable Hindus. At 8:00 a.m., the triumphant moment would come. And his hallowed task would be complete.

As the helicopters neared Mishira, Alan Ingram's warning was reaching the Special Forces Group. Alpha 6333 was yet unaware the nuclear codes were nearly there, and their mission more desperate than any realized. That word wouldn't arrive until moments before they touched down on Pakistani soil.

Throughout the driver's challenging journey, the raucous engine's clatter and the night's whistling winds had drowned out the world around him. Until the low-flying Apache passed directly overhead, he had no idea of the thundering slayers' presence. The menacing form was inches above the pickup as it screamed toward the sleeping encampment. Before the astonished emissary could react, an identical black shape roared past. As suddenly as they had appeared, they vanished into the mist-swept night. For the briefest of moments, the startled messenger did his best to disavow what had happened. Still, there could be no mistaking what he had witnessed. Neither sinister shape had an identifying marking on it. From where the roaring avengers had come, and who they were, he had no idea. But he recognized with absolute certainty what was unfolding in front of him. The broad plateau was seconds away from being attacked.

The courier slammed on his brakes and the creaking pickup skidded to a muddy stop. Four more unmarked helicopters raced past, each taking a similar tack to the Apaches. Inside the courier's truck's cab, he'd have a front-row seat for the horror about to seize the hazy hilltop.

On the wide mesa, only a half dozen of the four hundred insurgents were awake. And even they were far from alert as hour after hour they trudged along the edges of the shielding barbed barriers.

With little rhyme or reason, across the jumbled mesa the remains of burned-out military vehicles and empty wooden crates sprawled. Two dozen or more indiscriminately placed pickups and at least that number of aging motorcycles further cluttered the landscape. Garbage and waste were everywhere. Sanitary conditions were nonexistent. The place looked more like a squalid collection of vagrants than a military outpost. Only in the middle of the compound where the trio of transporter-erector-launchers were nestled was there anything approaching orderliness.

The Fedayeen camp commander's intentions had been to set up stout defenses capable of withstanding all but the most determined attacks. Yet once his men had seized the hilltop, his participation in their revelry had gone on for more than a day. At the celebration's end, few were willing to commit to the backbreaking labor necessary to create the much-needed fortifications.

Because the facility was now miles behind the front lines, and there'd been no threat from any source, their commander had let down his guard. He'd been too busy accepting congratulations for his victory to concern himself with anything else. He had not even assigned his growing force defensive positions. Furthermore, no effort had been made to bring a single air defense weapon to the plateau. Both were unalterable mistakes.

None of those sleeping on the rainy plateau were concerned with their surroundings. The closest bedraggled Pakistani army units were two hundred kilometers away. Other than the constant need to pillage the nearest villages for whatever food they could find, there was nothing worrying them in the slightest. Their location, all four hundred were certain, was safe and secure.

The last thing they expected was an assault. Especially one as startling as what was moments away from reaching them. A majority of those on the hilltop were out in the open and quite exposed. Only the boldest of the insurgents had claimed a spot in the handful of tents. The remainder slept on the expansive mesa's clinging grasses beneath tattered, filthy blankets. In groups of ten or more they were scattered around the sputtering fires across the compound.

They'd left the least experienced to patrol the fence throughout the night. By 3:00 a.m., the six teenagers were struggling against the boredom and their minds' persistent urging that they find a secluded corner to curl up and sleep. Yet each, head down, continued slowly walking, aware that if they left their posts a lash's sting in front of the entire camp would be their reward. The well-defined American plan, about to be precisely executed, was timed to catch them at the lowest ebb of the interminable night.

At the last possible instant the half-awake, casually wandering sentries heard the oncoming Americans' resounding engines. Even so, it was much too late to have any hope of changing the ill-prepared hilltop's fate. Confusion followed by sudden panic tore through them. As the first teenager turned to yell a tardy warning, the Apaches raced over the treetops.

The weapons officer in each AH-64, sitting in front of and below the pilot, began lining up the unending targets. With their sophisticated system's all-weather capabilities, the night's haze and insolent rains wouldn't hinder their efforts in the slightest. While they prepared to release an irrepressible hell, each was extremely exacting in his targeting. The last thing they wanted was to strike one of the nuclear weapons.

With stunning effect, the ferocious executioners pounced. From the stubby pods on both sides of the lethal pair, Hydra-70 rockets and Hellfire missiles went forth to seek and destroy. Their initial target would be the northern perimeter's imposing wire. Faster than the eye could follow, a line of ravaging killers slammed into the water-soaked ground at the outer edge of the enclosure. They continued their murderous dance toward those nestled on the exposed grasses. Death reached out for the corrupting mesa. Explosion after explosion tore into the razor wire. With a rearing dragon's roar, rocket after rocket poured into the crumbling barricades, shredding the concertina in a dozen places and blowing huge holes in the wire. From within each exploding Hydra thousands of high-velocity steel fragments went in search of prey.

A rapid blink later, a jumble of small trucks in the northeast corner of the compound were ripped apart by Hellfires. Sharp-edged, defeated metal reached out for everything within its path.

The rupturing vehicles began to burn. The flaming wreckage spread far and wide. Its white-hot, serrating explosions consumed the world around them. Beneath the tattered cloth, three dozen jihadists were dead without ever knowing what had occurred. Under their modest, bloody coverings, they moved no more.

In many ways, they were the lucky ones. For unyielding anguish was coming for the ill-destined. The scorching Hydras' shrapnel scored seething hits around the erupting campfires on the northern end. Devastation reached out for the reposing forms. The assailed screamed in torment, the unyielding anguish devouring their worlds.

The American crews had neither the time to admire their handiwork nor any interest in doing so. The avowed assassins, their weapons at the ready, soared over the Shaheens. Seconds later, the ambushing Apaches struck the southern wire. Once again, Hydras and Hellfires exploded with crippling effect. An additional handful of pickups and a trio of motorcycles exploded, cutting down all nearby. The crippling rockets tore their adversaries apart. Yet the Apaches' lightning strike was far from finished. They split up, banking left and right, focused on aligning for the next run. Behind them, the striking ordnance's blazes lit up the night. Carnage and devastation was everywhere. Torrents of fresh blood poured. The pair quickly devastated the razor-sharp wire on all four sides. Anarchy reigned.

Throughout the enclosure, four hundred vivid dreams were shattered. A scalding incubus's devilish display arose in their midst. Panic seized them. Black-clad figures, more asleep than awake, staggered to their feet. Grabbing for their rifles, the majority of the frantic images stumbled toward the fence line. It was the worst thing they could have done. Their sole chance of surviving could only be found by falling back toward the one location the Apaches wouldn't attack: the core of the compound.

Yet large numbers of individuals were headed in the opposite direction.

Half dressed, the insurgents' commander stumbled from his tent and screamed orders to his disheveled force. In the uncontrollable chaos, none of the frantic jihadists paid him the slightest attention.

With the attack helicopters' detonating weapons masking their presence, two Black Hawks settled to earth a quarter mile north of the nuclear missiles' perverse forms. Before their landing gear touched down, with their night vision positioned and their rifles at the ready, six Greet Berets leaped from each. Undetected, Alpha 6333 had reached Pakistani soil. At the identical moment, a few football fields east of the compound, 6334 also arrived.

The Green Berets deposited, all four Black Hawks raced skyward, intent on carrying out the next phase in the savage onslaught. The helicopter crews knew that for the modest force of Green Berets to have any chance they needed to keep the pressure on. They had to destroy as many of the fanatics as they could.

Hidden by the night, both Special Forces units began organizing their assaults. Alone or in pairs, 6333 spread out until the entire length of the northern fence was in one or more of the soldiers' field of fire. With Porter seven yards to his left, Sanders waited for Captain Short to direct the team to move forward. Ideally, the senior engineer, his value to the mission absolute, would have remained behind until the enemy was vanquished. Yet, with so few in their number and every rifle critical, there was little choice but to include him in the striking force.

Given Sanders's disposition, even if he had been ordered to stay behind, it was unlikely he would have done so. After so many years, always in the center of every undertaking, he no longer knew any other way to react to the sounds of gunfire. He'd participate in the resolute advance. But Porter would be close at hand.

When the last of the team's men was in place, they began weaving through the tangled trees' low-hanging branches. For the mission to succeed, they needed to get close without being detected. In the east, the arriving Green Berets' second detachment also started taking up positions. But after reaching their assigned locations, instead of moving forward, they dropped into the smothering bushes and knee-high grasses to wait for the peasants to take the bait.

The Apaches struck in the north a second time. With scurrying figures everywhere, the American duo opened up with their essence-devouring 30mm chain guns. At six hundred rounds per minute, the weapons acquisitions officers fired lightning bursts into the disheveled assemblage. In ones and twos and falling handfuls, those caught by the body-crushing shells were torn apart. Few would survive even a glancing blow. When struck, small numbers of still-breathing wounded screamed in agony as they dropped to the ground. Most of the fallen, however, moved not at all.

A third, fourth, and fifth unpredictable run by the marauding avengers followed. Across the wide plateau the frenetic duo soared, their determined firing precise and unrelenting. Each time, as they neared the center, their guns would go silent. The moment they were clear of the Shaheens, more targets would come into view. The pounding chain guns opened up again and again.

With the enemy crushed by the Apaches' immense blows, all four Black Hawks thundered in from the west. Flying low over the withering scene, the door gunners opened up with their machine guns. The soul-crushing malice reaching out for those on the ground was unrelenting. The Angel of Death's foreboding shadow came to gather them in immense hordes.

The Apaches, their fuel and ammunition running low, turned for a final run from the south. Those caught in the open had no chance. Only those who clawed their way back toward the crest's protective center were able to ward off a certain death.

The devouring birds of prey vanished into the night. The Black Hawks followed. Scarcely half the destitute defenders, their ring growing tighter in the middle of the protective void, were still in the fight. Each dove behind whatever fleeting cover they could find. This time they listened to their commander's orders. The hasty lines he created were sound. In every direction those protecting the camp's inner circle were soon in place, ready to confront anything appearing before them.

With the Apaches forced to leave and no way for the Black Hawks to get to those who remained, it would be up to the vaunted Special Forces to ferret out and destroy the survivors. Outnumbered eight to one, even the exceptionally proficient soldiers would find it a difficult task.

While the trailing Apache rushed north toward Camp Nowhere, it spotted a small truck near the base of the hilltop. Its idling engine was emitting a come-and-get-me heat signature. The weapons acquisition officer had no idea who was in the vehicle. Nonetheless, given its location and the direction it had been traveling, he correctly assumed it belonged to the bad guys. He fired a burst into the stationary pickup, tearing it and its sole occupant apart.

Struck in the chest by a mighty round, Basra's courier took a final halting breath before he lived no more. A second squeeze of the chain gun's trigger and the target exploded. Thick smoke wafted into the pestilent skies. Inside its cab, the mounting inferno consumed Mishira's firing codes.

Even if none knew it, with the critical paperwork gone, the Americans had bought some time to disable the mankind-killing missiles. All they had to do was overcome the daunting numbers waiting within the compound.

32

While the gruesome scene unfolded, Alpha 6333 edged through the forest's mounting rain. Movement by cautious movement, they closed with the target. It didn't take long to cut the distance between where they'd landed and what remained of the tattered northern concertina.

Under normal circumstances, the light emanating from the hilltop's fires would have helped identify the spectral figures edging through the woods. But none of the jihadists were looking in the Green Berets' direction. Eyes wide, two hundred wary heads were fearfully raised as they searched the heavens for another airborne assault.

When he reached the point where the shielding timber all but disappeared, Porter found the spot he wanted. Little shelter remained before they'd hit open ground and the true challenge would begin. A couple of hundred yards from the rising missiles, he and Sanders dropped to one knee behind the final trees' sodden branches. The initial rows of shattered barbed wire were fifty yards away. Both raised their M4s and took aim. The deft weapons specialist spoke a single syllable into his headset, using the code word that would let the remainder of the detachment know he and Sanders were in place. One by one, others began to do likewise until all of Alpha 6333 had reported they were ready. In the distance, their night vision identified the outlines of the monstrous weapons pointing skyward.

All in the spanning line took aim, waiting for Captain Short to direct them to open fire. The A Team commander started to give the order. At the last moment, however, he hesitated. The peasants were unaware of the Green Berets' presence. Short wanted to see if his team's inexperienced adversary would make another mistake.

"Wait one," Short said. "I'll bet if we give 'em a few seconds, they'll think they're safe and begin to show. If the opportunity presents itself, might as well take out as many as we can before they realize we're here."

Sure enough, as the sounds of the helicopters faded and then vanished altogether, a dozen tentative heads peeked out from their hiding places. They were wholly unaware of the mortal presence lurking in the shadows. Shortly thereafter, their torsos found their way into the Special Forces' sights. In front of Porter and Sanders, circumspect individuals on the eastern edge of the lurid defenses stood and took a few halting steps. Others began crawling from the shallow holes and makeshift barricades.

The Americans waited. Their captain's decision was starting to pay dividends. In less than a minute, across a few hundred yards of tussled landscape, forty were exposed and vulnerable. That number soon doubled. The Fedayeen commander motioned for twenty unsure individuals to start moving toward the wire in each direction. Eighty hesitant figures started edging forward. It didn't take long for the creeping majority to be within reach of Alpha 6333's rifles. Only the twenty headed south were shielded from the

American guns. Leaving the protective center and heading toward the outer perimeter, sixty hapless quail were in the detachment's sights. And the anxious Americans were eager to feast upon them. Yet no order came from their patient leader.

Short wanted to see if they could trap even more in the deadly snare. Nonetheless, as the seconds passed, those in hiding made no effort to join the ones who'd ventured forth. Stunned by the garish death that had seized so many, the final 120 were frozen in place in the center of the compound. Each was waiting to see what might befall their exposed comrades.

"I'll take the trio out front," Porter whispered as he examined the first five on the left. All were moving toward the concertina. "You've got the two behind. We'll play it by ear from there."

Even in these conditions, there was little chance a single round from the highly skilled fighters would miss. The remainder of Alpha 6333 selected inviting targets and waited for their captain to issue the command.

It was becoming apparent that no additional targets would show themselves. Still, their captain's willingness to allow the enemy to expose a significant portion of their force had given his soldiers the critical edge they needed. Forty . . . fifty . . . possibly sixty dead might not fully tip the scale in the Americans' favor but it would give Short's men a far better chance. As he watched the anxious figures edging toward the shredded concertina, he knew the time to unleash his rifles had come. It was now or never. Short keyed his headset a second time. "Open fire!" he screamed.

The instant he did, murderous rounds ripped across the landscape. Faster than the mind could record, Porter cut down the first of his targets . . . and the next, and yet a third, before any of the ill-fated jihadists could react. A trio of kill shots hit dead center. Sanders's did the same, with two swift squeezes of the trigger ending a misguided pair of lives.

Both identified additional targets. In the woods, ten additional rifles added to the turmoil. The dead and wounded fell all along the line. Agonizing screams and anguished movement added to the hideous night's scene.

In seconds, more than fifty were added to the rolls of mortally wounded. Moments prior, as they watched their countrymen move across the bloody ground, many of those sheltering in the center had let out a sigh. Each was beginning to believe the evil that had befallen them was over. But it wasn't nearly so.

Nonetheless, from the center, the reaction from the thirty sheltered survivors guarding the northern approach was swift. With only a moment's hesitation, those hidden by the launchers, skeletal vehicles, and billowing tents began returning the aggressors' fire. On each of the remaining three sides others joined the discordant serenade, firing in all directions at every imaginary invader they could find. The hilltop erupted once again with the fierce struggle, crushing the distorted plateau around them. The unconstrained firing went on for a frenetic half-minute before their overwhelmed commander realized the only true threat was coming from the north. It took him far too many screeched directives to get the ones shooting at nothing to stop.

He ordered a third of those in the western, southern, and eastern sides to leave their positions and join those facing the true peril. While they attempted to do so, the Green Berets cut down many of the scurrying figures. One by one, the precise Americans began capitalizing on every mistake—a miscreant's torso too exposed, the signal given off by a firing rifle, an attempt to move toward deeper cover—all leading to even more suffering.

Without night vision equipment, all the jihadists had to identify the sources of the gunfire were the lines of tracers spewing from the ends of the Green Berets' rifles. That, along with the plateau's uncontrollable fires, was guiding their desperate efforts.

However, in many ways the fires were hurting rather than helping. The smoke-filled scene's distorted images were creating false images everywhere Basra's followers looked. Even so, as they narrowed the general direction of the offending rifles, the peasants began to zero in.

Beneath the persistent Fedayeen response somewhere on the far right, a Green Beret fell. Two of the camp's defenders joined him. A sadistic battle of attrition was underway. The attackers had vastly superior abilities, the defenders an immense advantage in numbers.

The plan called for Alpha 6333 to move forward until they reached the shredded barbed wire. The moment they did, they'd toss a series of smoke grenades and open up with everything they had. That would be the cue for 6334 to head toward the openings the Apaches had created in the eastern perimeter.

Once inside the compound, with the enemy caught in a cross fire, both teams would fight their way to the nuclear arsenal. Having received word moments before they leaped from the Black Hawks that the Fedayeen had gained access to the firing codes, the urgency of their actions was at the forefront of every mind. Unaware of the destruction of the launch paperwork, each believed they needed to strike without hesitation. For all they knew, the possibility existed that the Shaheens' programming was complete and they were ready to fire.

Alpha 6333's leader spoke a third time, cognizant that the order he was about to give could cost many of his men. "Forward," Short directed. "We need to get inside that camp without delay." His team would be the bait to draw out the enemy, forcing them to focus on the attack from the north. Once they did, the Green Berets would enter the next phase of the operation, trapping their unsuspecting quarry and slamming the door shut.

Alpha 6333's survivors leaped to their feet and, firing as they went, headed toward the eighty entrenched dogmatists shooting in their direction. Seldom moving in a straight line for more than the briefest of moments, the determined soldiers came on. The remaining bits of cover where they could find them helped. Still, they weren't going to be nearly enough. Ten surreal yards were crossed by the first of them. Then twenty was reached by a few. Far too often the attackers found themselves diving into the muddy grass. With the enemy fire so intense, they had little choice but to crawl forward for extended periods with their noses pressed against the rain-soaked ground.

They were drawing near the wire. A second in their number went down from a blindly fired round. His wounds, though not yet fatal, were too serious for him to continue. While they moved toward the encampment, Porter was doing everything he could to shield Sanders from the line of fire. The weapons specialist understood if worse came to worst, the other engineers could handle the assignment without his longtime friend. Yet in the direst of battles he'd seen firsthand that Charlie was the best there was when it came to a job like this. Porter had every intention of ensuring the team's senior engineer would be making the critical decisions when the time came to disable the holocaustic weapons. He recognized all too well that whoever was removing the trigger devices would be holding their lives in his hands. And he wanted it to be Sanders.

The Green Beret losses were mounting. The toll on the Americans, however, was nothing compared to that inflicted on the enemy they faced. For every Special Forces soldier who succumbed, those they assaulted suffered tenfold. The superior abilities of their antagonists were too much for the struggling primitives. Every time an American stopped and opened fire, another floundering form forfeited his life. Even in the harried situation, few ringing shots from their M4s would miss.

Twenty additional yards were crossed by Short's determined fighters. As they did, two more Americans fell. Still, the proficient Green Berets had taken a severe toll. By the time Alpha 6333 reached the wire, the enemy's numbers had dropped by an additional third.

The eight surviving Green Berets had achieved their initial objective. They could reach out and touch the concertina. They breached the crumbling barriers and continued on.

Few of the Fedayeen protecting the north were still in the fight. In total, barely seventy of the four hundred blissfully sleeping jihadists remained. Since it appeared that the attack was coming solely from the north, the majority of the hilltop's remaining protectors started edging away from their fortifications and moving into position to engage what appeared to be the only threat.

The now-wounded jihadist commander had no choice but to shift even more of his force to the northern bastions. Only small numbers remained to protect the exposed sides and rear. Little did he know that a second coiling serpent was hiding in their midst.

"Pop smoke! Pop smoke!" Short screamed.

Sanders and Porter grabbed the smoke grenades dangling from their body armor. Each pulled the pin and tossed them. Three others did the same. Clouds of colored smoke billowed forth. It was the moment for which the second Green Beret detachment had been waiting.

"Forward," Captain Henry ordered. In the east, the undetected second force, their rifles silent, entered the compound unopposed.

The Americans were inside the wire. But the ruinous mission was far from over. None of 6333's members had been thrilled when briefed about the next phase of the engagement. They had, however, no choice if they were going to distract their foe long enough for those in the second A Team to close in. In front of Short's detachment, separating them from the Shaheens, was 150 yards of ground with only a few scattered boxes to protect them.

Once they breached the billowing smoke's thick cover, they'd be too close to the compound's center to depend on anything sheltering them for more than the briefest of periods. They understood that the nearer they got to the prize, the more the ravishing fires would betray them. And the less the chance of surviving.

They were, however, out of options. They'd have to continue the head-on assault for their plan to succeed. They'd have to endure until Captain Henry's men reached the middle of the compound and, catching their victims unaware, annihilated the last of the Fedayeen. Those at the northern fence knew it would cost them dearly.

"Once 6334 has taken out the enemy," Short said into his headset, "Porter, I want you to remain with Sanders and head for the launchers."

"Yes, sir."

"The rest of you are to spread out, identify any remaining resistance, and dispatch it."

"We'll handle it, sir," Master Sergeant Noll replied.

The briefest reluctance hung in the air. They knew the demanding task they faced. And the life-forfeiting action they were undertaking.

"On your feet!" Captain Short screamed.

The Green Berets leaped up and rushed toward the enemy's streaming rifles. They hadn't taken a second step before another in their number was cut down. Still, not one was dissuaded. They had to seize those launchers before it was too late. For what an unsuspecting world faced if they failed was beyond comprehension.

33

It had taken a monumental effort, but Alpha 6334's survivors had fought their way to the center of the compound. They spread out, taking up defensive positions around the critical armaments.

Sanders and Porter reached the middle of the hilltop and joined Captain Henry's team. Neither had suffered more than superficial wounds. When the duo arrived, the 6334 commander and six of his men were wading through the compound's center with rifles ready, finishing off the remaining Fedayeen. They'd take no prisoners. For as they quickly discovered, no matter how badly wounded, their foe wouldn't stop fighting until each had taken his final breath. The Fedayeen's consuming hatred wouldn't allow for anything else.

The distasteful task was nearing its end. Henry sent his medics, some of the world's best at battlefield surgery, to deal with the Green Berets' wounded. One was trying to stabilize an injured team member's severe injuries. The other had headed out in search of their sister team's survivors.

The harried captain saw Sanders and Porter approaching. For the first time since they'd left North Carolina, the waiting team leader felt certain their desperate mission at Mishira stood a real chance of succeeding. If all went as planned, long before the miserable rain stopped, Sanders would have disabled the nuclear weapons and destroyed the triggers.

Yet, with the area far from secure, the first thing the thirty-year-old junior commander needed was to establish a perimeter to protect the engineers while they removed the trigger device from each nuclear weapon. "Davidson, stay here to assist Sergeant Sanders," Henry said. "Porter, watch over them. The rest of you, fan out and take up defensive positions around the tents and nukes. No slipups. I know we nailed these bastards good, but there are bound to be a few still clinging to the darkness who'd like nothing more before they die than to lop off some heads. Let's make sure that doesn't happen and our engineers' work isn't interrupted by anyone or anything. We've got to get these things deactivated as quickly as we can."

With sporadic gunfire still emanating, the Green Berets did as they'd been directed, swiftly identifying potential enemy ambush points and defeating them. Satisfied, Captain Henry moved out to join them. Porter stayed where he was, his deadly rifle in hand. Not once in the most challenging of combat had he failed to spot even a hint of danger and deal with it. And he wasn't about to fail now.

Once the others were gone, Sanders looked at Davidson. "Where's Staff Sergeant Meeks?" he asked.

Davidson hesitated. "He's over there." He gestured to an area not all that far away. "As we rushed forward, an enemy grenade came out of nowhere. It landed right in front of him. Before he could respond, it exploded. Sergeant Meeks never had a chance.

What's left of him is facedown in the mud about thirty yards from here. What about Sergeant Pierce?"

Sanders shook his head. "No idea. But with the hell we went through in reaching this place, I'd be more than surprised if he shows. And even if he somehow did, he'll probably not be in any shape to help. So it looks like it's going to be you and me handling this one."

He took off his night vision equipment and let out a huge sigh while looking up at the first of the rockets. Perched upon the large transporter-erector-launcher, the two-stage ballistic missile's nuclear tip was almost impossible to see in the darkness and rain.

"No time like the present, I guess," Sanders said. "Let's get started."

He and Davidson sidled up to the Shaheen's controls. Sanders, knowing he'd have his back turned while he worked, was more than uneasy as he surveyed the tumultuous world around them. He took a final look at Porter. "You got our asses covered, Aaron?" The question was more than a bit rhetorical. Nonetheless, Sanders wanted his partner's assurance.

"What do you think?" was the curt response.

With Porter ever vigilant, Sanders started lowering the missile. As he did, Captain Short, thick blood splattered across the front and back of his uniform, appeared. An enemy bullet had crushed his left shoulder. The dark liquid trailed down to Short's filthy fingertips and fell upon the sordid ground. The detachment commander's arm hung lifeless at his side. There was no one with him. His grim countenance was impossible to miss.

Short stared at Porter and Sanders and, like Captain Henry, his relief was evident. The A Team leader staggered over and leaned against the transporter's heavy metal frame. "Thank God you two made it."

Sanders stopped in mid-effort and looked at him. The thick red was unmistakable. "You all right, sir?"

"Hanging on at the moment." Short looked down at his uniform. "When one of the medics has time, I'll have him take a look at it."

"Do you know where Sergeant Pierce is? I sure wouldn't mind having another pair of hands, sir."

"About halfway between here and the concertina, I'm afraid. Just when the enemy gunfire had slacked off, a trio of insurgents, firing like crazy, came running out of nowhere. Pierce took a bullet to the head before either of us could react. I was able to drop the sorry bastards but not before a stray round tore through my shoulder. I did what I could for Pierce, but it doesn't look good. He was barely breathing when one of the medics took over from me."

Sanders's suspicions had been correct. The enduring pair of engineers were going to be facing this on their own.

"Good news is help's on the way," Short said. "Medevacs have been dispatched from Camp Nowhere. Should be here in less than thirty to pick him up along with the other wounded and dead."

"Do we know what our losses are so far, sir?" Porter asked.

"Ran into Captain Henry on the way here. Neither of us is certain, but it's likely we've lost close to half of the two A Teams. No surprise that our detachment took the brunt of it. Not sure how many are left, but it doesn't look good. Probably one or two I'm not aware of might've survived. But I'd be amazed if it's any more than that. The gunfire you hear," Short added, "is Master Sergeant Noll dealing with the final enemy pockets. Noll's been hit, but his wounds aren't extensive enough to put him out of action."

Porter glanced at Sanders. "Charlie, how long's it going to take for you and Davidson to deactivate the nukes?"

"With just the two of us, probably two to three hours."

"No sooner?"

"Not a chance. Not if anybody on this hilltop wants to be alive in the morning."

Porter turned back to his commander. "Two to three hours is going to be a helluva long time, sir. With so few of us remaining, I'm not certain we'll be able to hold that long if the bad guys reappear. With half our force out of the fight and the possibility of a significant counterattack occurring if any Fedayeen units are nearby, we're extremely vulnerable."

"I've already taken steps to rectify the situation," Short said. "Reinforcements are on the way."

"That's a relief. How many A Teams are they sending?"

"Even after I relayed our losses and our tenuous grip on Mishira, they were able to free up only one of the remaining teams to support us. Alpha 6421 is loading on their helicopters as we speak. But that's all the help we can expect. Most of 4th Battalion has already left Camp Nowhere to join in on the fighting at other locations. From what I can make out from the chatter on the radio, there are at least eight sites we haven't been able to conquer. So most of the reserve battalion's on the way to rectify that. Group seemed confident the reinforcements will turn the tide and all of the nukes will be in our hands within the next hour or two."

"Sounds encouraging, sir," Porter said, his relief obvious. "And while I would've liked to have seen more rifles headed our way, one additional A Team on this hilltop should be enough to handle all but the most determined attacks." There was a noticeable pause as all present measured Porter's words. Fortunately, his assessment rang true. "So, do you know, sir, whether Captain Henry or the arriving Alpha 6421 commander is senior?" Porter asked.

"No idea. Why?"

"Just wanted to know who's going to be in command once you're gone."

"I'm not going anywhere, Sergeant," Short replied.

Knowing what they knew about their team leader, even with the seriousness of his wounds, Porter and Sanders weren't surprised. "I certainly can't tell you what to do, sir," said Sanders, who was nearly as proficient in his secondary specialty as a combat medic as he was as an engineer. "With as bad as you're bleeding you need to get on one of those medevacs as soon as you can. You might kill yourself if you don't. At the very least, why don't you let me take a few minutes to address your wounds before I start on this?"

"Not a chance, Sergeant Sanders. You've got far more important things to attend to. Your first priority—your only priority—is disarming these weapons. Until that's done, nothing else matters. So let's focus on the task at hand and stop worrying about me. One of Captain Henry's medics is going to stitch me up as soon as they get the dead and seriously wounded onto the medevacs. That should hold me until we're out of here for good."

Sanders looked at his commander, trying to judge the situation. It was obvious the captain was in severe pain and the blood loss was significant. Yet he knew there was no way he could change Short's mind. Still, there was something he could do that his commander would probably accept. And it might be enough to save his life. The sergeant reached into his rucksack, pushing aside the plastic explosives and fishing around for the plasma he and every Green Beret carried when heading into combat.

"Okay, sir. Have it your way. But with as many wounded as there are, it might be quite a while before the medics have the time to get to you. I don't care what you say: Before I continue with the Shaheens, let me get some plasma into you. It'll only take a second to get the line in."

With Meeks dead and Pierce clinging to life, the original plan to have the two senior engineers work on the strategic nuclear weapons while the junior pair started on the tactical ones had to be scrapped. Instead, Sanders and Davidson would have to disable them all. With the trio of launchers lowered, the time had come to cripple the Shaheens.

The triggers for the nuclear weapons consisted of a system of conventional explosives that, when activated, would set off a chain reaction within the missile, detonating the nuclear component. With the conventional explosives removed, there'd be no way to ignite the deadly ordnance, rendering each of them harmless. Once that was completed, they'd move on to the smaller tactical weapons and disarm them one by one.

Sanders took the detailed diagram of the nuclear missiles and the instructions on how to remove the trigger mechanisms out of his back pocket. He unfolded them and handed the ones for the strategic nuclear devices to Davidson. He shoved the other set, for use with the tactical missiles, back into his pocket. As the intemperate rains picked up, Davidson took out his flashlight and shined it on the deactivation paperwork for the Shaheens. There was no option but to work out in the open. Given the deteriorating conditions, this wasn't an ideal situation under which to perform such a pernicious task. But they had no choice.

Sanders opened his rucksack a second time and located the tools he'd need to complete the job. Shortly thereafter, instruments in hand, he turned toward Davidson. "Okay, nice and slow, read each step and observe my actions as I perform them," the senior engineer said. "Sing out at the first sign of a possible misstep. I know we've got a great deal to handle, but let's not rush this. One mistake and there'll be nothing left of this place except a rising mushroom cloud. Even with the possibility of a counter-attack, better to be thorough and precise than fast and wrong. With what these two teams went through tonight, the last thing I want is the rest of them dying because of a mistake by either of us."

"Absolutely, Sarge," Davidson said, while trying to hide the apprehension within him as the terrifying undertaking came into view. This was no longer a harmless practice session. This was the real thing. An error by either, and they'd never know what hit them. Every life form on the plateau, and for great distances beyond, would be forfeited in a flashing instant. "I know what's expected."

In actuality, there was little chance of Sanders making a mistake, fatal or otherwise. He'd practiced the procedures so often that they were imprinted on his brain. He could do them in his sleep. Even in the less-than-ideal weather and vulnerable situation there was no possibility of him failing. Still, he had every intention of playing this by the book.

"Ready?" Sanders said.

"Ready," was the reply. "Step one, locate the . . ."

"Okay," Sanders said as he carefully placed the final Shaheen trigger onto the ground next to the earlier pair. "Three down, twelve to go. Let's go find the tactical ones."

"Any idea where they're at?"

"Information we received said they'd probably be in one of the tents."

Davidson looked up at the taller Sanders. "They give ya any idea which one?"

"Nope. Guess we'll have to start checking until we find them."

The engineers headed for the first of the modest tents to search for the malignant devices. The tent contained a cot and sleeping bag along with a dozen or so coarse blankets scattered about on the floor. Beyond that, it was empty. On they went to the second. . . .

It wasn't until the fourth tent that they stumbled upon their prize. As they stood inside the entrance with the flap open, Davidson shined his flashlight on the long crates stacked in three piles. There could be no doubting this was what they were after. He began to count as he shined the flashlight on each one.

"One, two, three, four, five, six, seven, eight, nine, ten . . ."

Sanders could see the puzzlement on the younger sergeant's face as he shined the flashlight into every corner of the modest enclosure.

"I thought they said there were twelve."

"They did," Sanders confirmed.

"But there are only ten in here?"

"Maybe the other two are in one of the tents we haven't yet checked."

"Yeah, maybe."

"Let's see if we can find the others before we disable these. That way we can take care of them all at once."

Their rummaging inside the remaining tents and in every corner of the hilltop's core areas yielded nothing. They searched the center of the camp from one end to the other for the missing armaments. There were no others to be found.

Their fruitless efforts over, they returned to the original crates. While they stood over them, Davidson asked, "What do you think happened to the other two?"

Sanders, the aftereffects of the intense battle washing over him, shrugged. "Not a clue. Most likely the numbers we were given were wrong to start with and this is all there ever were." He let out a long, pain-tinged groan as he eyed the wooden boxes. His weary arms felt like they weighed a ton. His aching legs were scarcely better. "Either way, we've still got a lot of work to do before this night's over."

"At least we'll be out of the rain while we work on these."

While Davidson watched, Sanders pried open the crates containing the tactical nuclear weapons. When he'd removed the last lid, the pair started lifting them one by one from the containers and placing them on the ground inside the tent.

When all ten were removed, Sanders took out the instructions for disarming the tactical nuclear missiles. Without a word, he handed them to Davidson. Once again, they understood they couldn't make a mistake. These were lesser nuclear devices, but each was capable of leveling everything for a mile or more in all directions. More than enough if detonated to ensure not a trace of any of the Green Berets would remain.

Davidson, every bit as drained as Sanders, shined his flashlight on the new set of instructions. Tiredness clung to his voice as he spoke. . . . "Step one, locate the . . ."

Two hours later, with Porter and the weapons specialists from Detachment 6334, Sergeant First Class Shaun McCoy and Sergeant Aiden Hernandez, watching over them, Sanders and Davidson carried the first of the trigger mechanisms away from the hilltop. Down an overgrown, winding path leading to a broad field west of the encampment the stumbling party moved.

They walked through the caustic rains for what they perceived to be a significant distance. The five-minute journey through the lightless, unfamiliar landscape felt a hundred times longer. In reality, they were a quarter mile from the western concertina. Still, it was more than sufficient to safely destroy the conventional ordnance. Sanders stopped and looked around.

Satisfied, he laid the trigger mechanism from the first Shaheen on the damp ground. When he was finished, he took the one Davidson was cradling and did the same. He positioned and then repositioned both to ensure that they and the ones to follow would be destroyed once he attached the plastic explosives and hit the switch. "Okay, let's go back and get the next load."

"How many trips do you think it'll take to lug all the triggers out here?" Porter asked.

"Two more should do it. I'll bring out the last Shaheen trigger next. At the same time, Davidson should have no problem carrying three or four of the tactical ones. We'll bring out the rest on the trip after that. Once that's done, I'll need ten minutes to set the charges and blow the load. Half hour from now, there'll be nothing but an unrecognizable hole here and no chance of any of the nukes on this hill being fired without new triggers arriving and being installed. Then we wait."

"Did they say how long it'll be before we're out of here and headed home?" Davidson asked.

"They're going to go after the weapons at the most distant locations first," Porter said. "Being one of the closest to Camp Nowhere, we're near the bottom of the list. Even so, the Chinooks should reach us in a few days. Once they carry the missiles and tactical nukes away, and they're safely out of country, the Black Hawks will come get us and we'll be on our way out of here. In less than a week we should be sleeping in our own beds again."

34

As the fourth afternoon's assaults continued, the engagements were beyond anything Sam Erickson could have imagined. In fifteen years as a combat Marine, he'd seen some of the vilest things mankind could inflict upon his ilk. Yet the abject carnage that surrounded them on this gruesome field was some of the worst his recoiling mind had ever experienced.

The beleaguered Americans were exhausted. Not one had enjoyed more than a few hours of fitful sleep since they'd arrived at the isolated outpost. Yet none were ready to give up. They were determined to fight with all the fury they could muster until their final gasp was upon them.

The stretcher-bearers, with the ambassador at their head, had had little time to breathe. And none at all to rest. Their trips to and fro to collect the wounded and gather the dead went on without the slightest pause. While they performed their merciful mission, more than one had fallen beneath the enemy attack. The survivors' legs ached. Their straining backs begged for a moment of relief. But without complaint they continued their endless trips between the front lines and the hospital.

This ghastly day had been the most intense of all. For eight hours the insurgents had been hammering the Marines. As the unending anguish refused to yield, the steady clatter of torment-tinged rifle and machine-gun fire continued its relentless drone. An unending devil's concert of detonating grenades and screaming mortar rounds added to the frightful chorus. Explosion after explosion rocked the appalling scene, shaking to its core the tumultuous world around them. The frightful sounds of suffering were everywhere. One after the next, the undeterred fanatics came on.

The previous three days had contained ebbs and flows in the action and directional attacks focused on particular portions of the embassy's defenses. This day, however, had been different. From the morning's first light there'd been no reprieve. There'd been no probes or parries, no cautious or calculated actions. The barbarous onslaught, coming from every direction, had been uncompromising. And on both sides the grievous toll grew.

Ten, twenty, thirty, or more of the enemy had fallen for each defender struck. And it mattered not. Every insurgent felled was replaced by another, and another, and another. . . . Their determined efforts were without end.

Life held little importance in this sordid corner of humanity. It was something in his contempt and scorn Salim Basra understood quite well. On every battlefront, he treated his followers as scarcely more than cannon fodder in his grand scheme. He was more than willing to sacrifice them on the altar of his insatiable ego without giving it a passing thought. Even so, like lemmings plunging into the sea, his adherents continued to follow his commands without question.

For as far as the eye could see, Islamabad was in ruins. Where once a magnificent city had stood, the accursed landscape was scarred and battered. Not one of the stout trees the defenders had used to strengthen their defenses had survived unharmed. Most were splintered and unrecognizable. Four days of combat had seen to that.

From great distances or mere arm's lengths, the vicious fighting went on. Within the bloodstained rubble, lifeless, mangled bodies were everywhere.

Inside the command bunker the radio crackled with frantic chatter as Erickson's men did their best to coordinate their actions. Their commander listened intently, interjecting as needed, but unable to do much to control the uncontrollable. This was the moment for which Erickson had trained his Marines well. He had little choice but to depend on his skilled lieutenants, platoon sergeants, and squad and fire team leaders to handle the frenetic actions. Not one was letting him down.

While the debased battle continued, the urgent calls were unending. "Man down! Man down! My partner's been hit. Corpsman needed in the forward bunker in the southwest corner near the Italian lines! Corpsman! Corpsman!" a voice from Lieutenant Bates's forces pleaded. It wasn't the first time someone had called out, "Man down!" Nor would it be the last.

"On it," was the response from 3rd Platoon's corpsman near the center of the western defenses as he finished applying the dressings to a shrapnel-laced head wound. Bathed in the blood of others, beneath the withering enemy fire, the overtaxed medic scurried across the terrifying landscape. In a low crouch, weaving in and out of the mangled trees, he soon reached his latest challenge.

"Corporal Taylor, what's the status of those in your fire team's other bunker?" Lieutenant Ambrose asked moments later.

"Not sure, sir. Neither seems to be firing his weapon. Abrams? Nelson? You okay?" Taylor asked. His query was met with silence.

"I'm getting no response, sir. Let me crawl over and check on them."

"Private Simpson, use your grenade launcher to eliminate the enemy squad that's firing from the outcroppings to the northeast," Scott Tomlin directed as he attempted to control 4th Platoon's efforts in the east.

"It's my last one, sir."

"Use it anyway, but don't miss," the company's executive officer ordered. "Those bastards already have taken out a couple of the Japanese defenders on my left."

On it went. Throughout the day the radio was seldom silent. The frightful milieu refused to release its hideous grip, and the sorrowful weather showed no signs of relenting. In the killing fields, essence-seizing black smoke, tinged with traces of burnished blood and ravaged sinew, rose to meet the depressing heavens. Yet throughout the hellscape surrounding the embassy the lurid endeavor's combatants scarcely noticed the miserable conditions. They were far too busy trying to survive the perverse fray. On the mud-choked battleground, death's unmerciful specter refused to release its immense grasp. Eternity fell without reason upon the unlucky.

On both sides, the numbers of those who lived no more soared. One-quarter of the Marines, either dead or severely wounded, no longer manned the critical defenses. Felled by RPG rounds, three of the company's Humvees were gone. A significant number of soldiers provided by the other defending countries also fought no longer. A hundred of the civilian fighters were out of the fray. Along with that, Fedayeen mortars had killed fifty people within the embassy grounds and more than two dozen sheltering in the enclave.

The floor of the embittered hospital was awash in ankle-deep pools of glistening red. Its walls were forever stained. To make matters worse, the Marine company's beset men had been forced to expend vast quantities of munitions to hold off the uncompromising attacks. It was more than twice what they'd used on the previous three days. For the moment, there were adequate amounts of 7.62 rounds for the AK-47s the civilians were firing. But the 5.56mm M4 ammunition intended to last the Marines for a week was perilously low. Few of the fire teams' grenade launchers still had rounds. The surviving Humvees' .50-caliber shells were nearly spent. And two of the four American mortar teams had fired their final rounds earlier in the afternoon.

Behind the company commander's bunker, the embassy's western wall showed the effects of the endlessly striking ordnance. There were holes, large and small, everywhere Erickson looked. He had little doubt the other sides of the compounds had similarly suffered. And yet the embattled enclosures still stood. And the survivors held on. The last of their food was gone, consumed early that morning. Collected rainwater was momentarily easing their thirst, but the water cans the King Stallions had provided were empty. Should things stay as they were, starvation and thirst would become a real possibility for the trapped individuals within the strongholds.

With the cloud-smothered night still four hours away, the survivors clung to their positions, praying for another sheltering evening and the reprieve it would bring. The Pentagon had their brightest minds working on it, but they'd yet to find a way to effect their rescue. Despite the desperateness of the situation, there was a small glimmer of hope. By the end of November's fourth day, the Americans had tripled their support forces in India, and others were arriving. The first attempts at critical C-130 airdrops to resupply the battered garrison were scheduled for 2:00 a.m. Hopefully, they'd occur at regular intervals in the nights to follow.

Still, there was a harsh reality Erickson understood far too well. Should the cargo planes fail to complete tonight's mission, there'd be no denying the consequences. Early tomorrow morning, the last of the defenders' munitions would be expended and their grievous fates sealed. But before they could concern themselves with tomorrow, they had to survive the present day. And that was in no way certain. For all, it felt as if the crushing nightmare would never end. Every moment was an eternity in combat so intense. Every pounding heartbeat possibly their last. Four endless hours before night would find them. . . .

35

More casualties were being added to the distraught rolls with each passing minute. The agony of it all devoured them. They knew nothing else. For those in the foxholes, their existence had been turned upside down. The things they'd been taught throughout their lives had no meaning. Nothing had meaning. Their surroundings held only death. Their struggling minds drew back and shuttered. The despairing defenders were convinced the swirling vortex wouldn't end until it consumed them all. Their visceral reaction to the ghastly environment had long ago become instinctual. The primitive parts of their consciousness ruled every action. Kill or be killed was all their repulsed lives understood. There was nothing but the here and now. Their memories were gone, wiped clean by their ignoble existence. They had been in this horrid place forever, and forever they'd remain.

They continued firing their rifles, taking down their onrushing foes. Fingers on their triggers, they waited for the next cultist to appear in their sights. Once he did, they'd dispatch another wayward being into the next realm. This would never end. Of that they were certain. Yet suddenly, in the middle of the anguish, a dozen distant whistles pierced the ear-shattering din. The moment the shrill sounds reached them, the approaching transgressors stopped firing. In unison, the jihadists ceased their attack. To the last murky figure they retreated, slipping away. Working their way through the twisted steel and jagged rocks, they edged back toward their encampments.

For half a minute, the astonished Marines continued to cut down those unfortunate enough to wander into their crosshairs. Still, as the seconds passed, the targets disappeared until none remained. The enemy had vanished without explanation, fading into the dismal afternoon.

"Cease fire! Cease fire!" Erickson screamed into the radio. He was as confounded as any by the precipitous result. Still, there could be no doubt that the jihadists were gone.

The horrid scene went silent. Not a sound reached the defenders' ears. As their confused minds struggled to accept the sequence of events, the unanticipated stillness was as terrifying as the battle's horrifying echoes had been.

The radio traffic was calm for the first time in hours. The perplexed Erickson held his breath and waited to see if the startling ceasefire would hold. Tense moments passed, but the situation remained unchanged. The fanatics were gone. Despite everything he tried, the American commander's bewildered intellect couldn't come up with a rational explanation for any of this. Why their lethal adversary had withdrawn, none had a clue.

"XO and platoon leaders, report in," Erickson directed as the stillness took hold.

"No idea why, sir, but once those whistles blew, the Fedayeen slipped away," Tomlin announced.

"Same over here, sir," Ambrose said. "They're gone. Staff

Sergeant Reilly's heading over to check with the British, Canadians, and Australians to see if they can add anything to what we saw."

"No one in sight, sir," Lieutenant Marshall added.

"I sent Sergeant Michaels over a couple of minutes ago to talk to the Dutch, French and Germans and get their observations, sir," Lieutenant Bates said.

The moment Bates finished speaking, Michaels keyed his headset. "Just met with the three of them, sir. They've no more idea of what happened than we do."

"Okay, don't let down your guard. Keep your men in place and be ready for anything," Erickson directed. "If things stay like they are, in another few minutes, have your squad leaders report in on the status of their men and their remaining ammunition. If time permits, do a similar check of the civilians helping defend your sectors."

As it turned out, there was more than enough time to do the things the company commander had requested. An anxious hour passed. It felt much longer. There was no activity in the haunting world surrounding the battered Marines. Given what the day had held, none of this was making the slightest sense to the hundreds who awaited the next attack.

One hour turned into two. The final status reports arrived. As Erickson had expected, his men were short on everything. He did his best to redistribute the remaining munitions to ensure each platoon had roughly equal amounts. The C-130s couldn't get there soon enough.

Two hours turned into three. In their sandbagged worlds, many relaxed for the first time in forever. Less than sixty minutes remained until an uneasy darkness would grip their world. When it did, its relative safety would surround them. All began to believe they'd seen the final attack of the day. They could allow their minds to accept that they were likely to see tomorrow.

At this moment, they had no way of knowing how wrong they were. For the hideous afternoon had one more immense trick to play.

36

With the fading day's rains turning into a monsoonal downpour, the leaden skies refused to release their grip upon the morose vista. A grasping malaise hung over their somber world. It hid the sparkling hills and snow-covered mountains from view. Yet everyone had to admit the moment they'd been awaiting was drawing near. The first subtle hints of the coming night were tugging at the eastern horizon's darkening skies. The persistent passage of time was welcoming to one and all. An hour, no more, and they'd slip into darkness.

It was the pair of Marines in Ambrose's forwardmost bunker who were the first to determine that the situation wasn't quite as it seemed. Peering through the broken trees, they watched the disdaining nightmare returning to life.

"Sir, there's something odd going on out there," Lance Corporal Speers, in charge of the bunker, said into his headset. "We've got movement . . . lots of movement."

"Where?" Ambrose's replied.

"Everywhere we look. Whatever it is, it's still a thousand yards out and difficult to make out. But if we're seeing what we think we're seeing, there's a massive force building. Its size and composition are far beyond anything we've faced so far."

"On foot or in vehicles?"

"Right now on foot, just like it's been since we arrived."

Ambrose brought his field glasses up and scanned the distant landscape. His sentries were correct. Something enormous, human in nature, was gathering.

"Sir," Ambrose said into his headset, "we've got a huge amount of activity in both the north and northeast. Looks like the lead elements are preparing to move toward us."

"Roger," was Erickson's response. "Any indication of what they're up to?"

"No, sir. Way too early to know what the bastards have in mind. Could be nothing more than a show of force intended to remind us what tomorrow will bring. Or it could be the initial stages of the biggest attack we've seen."

"Just spotted the same thing over here, sir," Sergeant Michaels said. "Forces gathering in the south and moving toward us. They're a long way off, but it looks like they mean business."

"XO, what's happening in the east?" Erickson asked.

"Not certain yet, sir," Tomlin replied, "but something's not right. There's definitely activity. Nothing's started this way, but that could change at any moment."

"Sir, Italians tell us they're seeing lots of movement in the southwest," Lieutenant Bates added.

Inside the command bunker, the first sergeant grabbed Erickson's arm. "In front of us, sir," Vickers said while pointing west.

Erickson looked in the direction his senior sergeant had indicated. He peered through the torn trees and tumbled stones. It didn't take long to spot the images Vickers had identified. A significant force, bigger than anything they'd previously encountered, was amassing in the west. Despite believing they were in the clear, there was little doubt their life-taking trials were far from over. From the reports Erickson was receiving and what he'd witnessed, Basra's disciples were planning a decisive attack against all four walls at once.

Erickson spoke into the radio, trying to sound calm and confident. "Okay, nobody panic. Doesn't matter how many they throw at us: we'll handle this. And time's on our side. Get ready to repel a final assault before darkness arrives and things turn in our favor." As the words left his mouth, from every direction the frenzied mob started toward them.

From within their fragile defenses, the Marines could see line after line of enraged figures running across the riotous landscape. With incalculable numbers in their ranks, across the unholy ground the sandal-shoed, frayed-clothed legions came for them. Even a thousand yards from the compounds' pummeled ramparts, the gaunt multitude's cries of "Death to America!" filled the fading afternoon. There was anger in the incensed throngs' urgings and hatred in their hearts. Cradled in the onrushing jihadists' arms were satchel charges, rocket-propelled grenades, light machine guns, and automatic rifles. A curved sword, its blade sharpened to a razor's edge, hung from every waist.

As the terrifying moments passed, the maniacal rush never wavered. With every instant they grew closer to the modest force waiting behind their sandbagged positions. Across the scorched and ragged lands, yard by yard, crater after crater, they came nearer. In slightly under sixty seconds an eighth of a mile was crossed. Eight hundred yards remained until they'd reach the steeling defenses' forward elements. Eleven hundred yards before they'd arrive at the embassy's walls. The Marines and their supporters waited. The advancing force was unrelenting. With each waning minute they surged two hundred yards closer to their prize. Six hundred yards from the defenders as the terrifying moments passed . . .

On they came. In little time, a quarter mile to the forward outposts was all that remained.

A momentous storm of suffering and death was growing clearer. The Marines readied their weapons. Each selected targets from the murderous cavalcade. Those carrying RPGs would be their top priority.

Step by lurching step, this seething ocean was growing nigh. Their soaring voices continued rejoicing in their coming conquest. Without pausing, the forward rank of running executioners leveled their rifles and opened fire. Wild shots sprayed in every direction. An initial RPG round smashed into the deteriorating northern wall of the enclave. A second roaring rocket, somewhere in the south, ripped into the embassy's battered fortifications. To the wayward ones' surprise, not a shot was fired in response. The Marines and their supporting forces ducked their heads and waited for the command to open fire. Yet no such directive came.

Erickson had little choice. With no ammunition to spare, the combat-experienced captain delayed giving such an order. He needed to ensure every shot counted.

Another hundred yards was crossed. The fervent attackers were three hundred yards from the first of his defenses. The embassy's walls, battered by four days of fearsome attacks, were only six hundred yards away. The determined raiders came on, their efforts growing more self-assured as the pockmarked outposts came into view.

By all appearances, the onslaught would be considerable but straightforward. The only remarkable feature of this one was its size. At least, that was the belief of those readying for the attack. Little did they realize that the enemy was poised to spring multiple surprises. For this time they had something special planned. Something unpredictable. Something, given what had occurred over the past four days, none could anticipate.

Erickson and his men couldn't know it, but the attacks in the south, east, and west, while giving every impression of being severe, were intended to be little more than powerful feints designed to pin down the forces in those areas. The fiendish inferno's real goal was to concentrate an annihilating assembly against the diplomatic enclave's brittle defenses and the embassy's northern wall. As soon as the defenders took the bait and were fully engaged in the other portions of the battlefield, the jihadists would shift their focus to throwing everything they had against those protecting the vulnerable north. It would be Ambrose's platoon along with the thin lines of British, Canadians, and Australians who would face the brunt of the anguish-filled assault.

Twenty-five thousand foot soldiers, supported by fourteen Al-Khalid tanks, would attack. Ten lethal armored personnel carriers armed with missiles and machine guns would be with them. As a final blow, a dozen large, brightly colored "jingle" trucks loaded with explosives would rush into the melee, heading straight toward the enclave's main gate and any still-standing apartment buildings. Each was being driven by a suicide bomber.

The tanks and armored personnel carriers were presently hanging back, out of sight of those defending the two compounds. They were waiting to see if the massive infantry elements would be able to complete the conquest without them. The valuable armored vehicles would be dedicated to the conflict only if absolutely necessary. While the Pakistani army remained on the run, there were still many battles to come. And the seized armored force was too precious to waste. So if it could be helped, it would remain in reserve. The jingle trucks, however, were of far less importance and would be committed no matter what.

For decades, the flamboyant trucks had formed the transportation backbone upon which the country's two hundred million people depended. Piled high, they'd carried, day after day, year after year, vast quantities of supplies into and out of the largest cities and the meekest hamlets. Without them, the Pakistani economy would have collapsed. They were also one of Pakistan's primary art forms. Their owners painted them from head to foot with bright images of every sort, size, and description. Religious symbols, images of the country's heroes and politicians, along with popular movie stars, flowers, animals, anything and everything, adorned them. They were vividly decorated in every color of the rainbow. The more they stood out on the busy highways, the prouder their drivers became.

On this day, the twelve waiting out of sight of the enclave were intended to stand out in a far different way. For once the attackers smashed the infidels' defenses, the jingle trucks would rush in to finish the job. With the northeastern compound conquered and the embassy's northern wall breached, any surviving jingle trucks would roar across the short distance between the enjoining locations to punch further holes in the embassy's walls. The nonbelievers' defenses defeated, thousands of warriors would enter into the heart of the final obstacle. There, they'd slay all they encountered. None would be spared.

Unaware of the drama unfolding, Erickson began playing his few remaining cards. "Mortar teams, open fire. Don't stop until you've released your final round. Once the enemy's crossed another hundred yards, Humvee machine guns, join in. After that, fire team leaders, unleash your .30-calibers as you see fit. Those with individual weapons are to follow."

Unaware of the insurgents' grand plan, the mortar teams started releasing shells at a furious rate toward the approaching hordes. Slicing through the low-hanging heavens, the soaring succession of ordnance sailed across the unforgiving skies. One after another, the whistling shells reached out for the unfortunate with round after round of gut-ripping steel. The fierce detonations cut huge swaths through the exposed jihadists' numbers. By the scores, it cut them down in midstride. With every striking round, with every new explosion, the wounded and dying continued to mount. Nonetheless, it did nothing to slow the ardent attackers.

Critically short of mortar rounds, the lethal bombardment didn't last long. In less than a minute the last of the scant reserves were released. The Americans had lost a critical defensive element.

It couldn't be helped. The surging tsunami's leading edge was two hundred yards from the forward defenses and closing much too fast.

In the north, a trio of Humvee machine guns opened fire, adding to the blossoming contest's carnage. The Humvees protecting the other three sides soon contributed their own malevolence to the horrifying scene. They cut the murderous multitudes down at an appalling rate. Row after row of blood-splattered invaders were felled by the solid wall of .50-caliber rounds. By the score, the mortally injured fell. They joined the lifeless images spread far and wide across the roadways and fields throughout the profane panorama.

Yet the pitiless zealots were in no way dissuaded. Their leaders had brought them to a fevered pitch and their insatiable lust remained unabated. This was going to be the virtuous battle to slay the interlopers. An hour from now, as night took hold, those cowering inside the fortified walls would experience their final moment. And the victory the attackers were determined to achieve would arrive.

The first of Ambrose's Marines went down. Directly behind his position, a pair of civilian fighters, both hit by multiple rounds, joined him. They would be the first of many.

A ravaged Humvee was soon burning. The pernicious conflict's thunder consumed the devolving day. The reviling humanity came on. Inside their bunkers the Marines and their allies unleashed everything they had. Behind them, the rows of civilians waiting with automatic rifles joined in. A steady torrent of life-taking ordnance stung the blighted afternoon. Still, it did little to dissuade the fearsome onslaught.

The time to smash the barriers and massacre the heretics was here. All around the destitute defenders a mountain of mortal rounds struck the contested ground. Despite what was approaching, not one of the embassies' protectors panicked. Time, they were certain, was on their side. All they needed to do was hold out until darkness fell. With it would come the enormous advantages the night would provide.

In the west, a second Humvee exploded as an arriving RPG tore it apart. The agitated peasants, their numbers rising, continued their murderous rush. With each passing moment they closed for the ultimate conquest over Satan's spawn. The moment had come for the insurgents to spring the trap. Once more the strident whistles blew.

This time, however, it wasn't to signal the end of the battle. The sharp sounds were a sign of its actual beginning. The majority of those in the east, south, and west started to slink away. Skirting the American rifles, they swung north to join their valiant brothers.

With minimal losses, the French, Germans, and Dutch, along with their Marine and civilian supporters, abruptly found themselves more than holding their own. The same was true in the west, where the fighting had been extremely heavy. Suddenly, to the surprise of all, it wasn't nearly as intense as it had been. In fact, much of the massive force headed in their direction had evaporated. The experience of those protecting the east was similar.

Smaller groupings continued to attack in each of those directions, picking their way through the rubble while taking a far more cautious approach.

The north, however, was a different matter. There, things were growing worse. The vaunted enemy was swarming, their numbers expanding with each passing moment.

Forty minutes until night's veil would fall. Inside the command bunker, Erickson listened to Ambrose's men's excited chatter and their lieutenant's rapid commands. He could hear the platoon's thirty surviving Marines and the seventy-five civilian fighters protecting the enclave screaming animated directives to each other.

"Brown! There's three of them right on top of you. Keep your head down but toss a grenade a few yards in front of your bunker," one of the team leaders yelled.

"Dammit, I'm hit," a member of Ambrose's 3rd Squad screamed.

"How bad?" his team leader asked.

"Bad enough," was the reply as the wounded Marine fired his rifle at a quartet of approaching attackers. All four went down and moved no more. "But it's not so bad that I can't take out a few more of those sonsabitches."

"I'm down to my last two magazines," another announced. "Anybody got any ammunition they can spare?" His inquiry was met by silence. No one in the platoon had much more than he did.

"Sergeant Reilly, how do things look with the British?" Ambrose asked.

On the far left of the platoon's lines, the platoon sergeant, his concern obvious, responded. "Struggling like everybody else, sir. The buildup in front of them is every bit as intense as what we're facing. There appears to be thousands upon thousands headed their way."

While Erickson took in the unfolding events, he was growing more than a bit alarmed. Every frenzied clash he'd ever been in had had a level of unpredictability. But for some reason this one felt acutely so. The company commander scanned the areas he could see in the west. Marshall's and Bates's men were still engaged with the persistent attackers. However, with a modicum of effort, each was holding his own.

Erickson couldn't put his finger on it, but he didn't like how this was unfolding. Something was wrong here. Of that, he had no doubt. For the most part, each of their opponent's previous actions had followed the same unimaginative script. This time, however, the pieces didn't fit. For now, he wasn't certain why.

"XO," Erickson said when the animated talk momentarily died down, "is the enemy still attacking in the east?"

"Yes, sir," was the response from Scott Tomlin. "We're getting hit, but it's nothing like it was a couple of minutes ago."

"Same over here. It's still ongoing, but what started as one of the fiercest battles we've faced is presently half-hearted at best."

Tomlin glanced to his left, looking toward the enclave and the relentless action occurring in the areas to the northeast. He didn't like what he saw. Instead of evaporating as it had in the other locations, the intensity of the attack was building. And the situation was deteriorating much too fast. He could see Marines, the pressure immense, falling back from the forward bunkers.

"From my position I've got a clear view of a great deal of the enclave's defenses. They're being hit big time, sir. And there's no indication it'll end anytime soon. Our guys appear to be in real trouble."

"Lieutenant Ambrose," Erickson called out. "What's your status?"

"Uh . . . we're trying to hold on, sir. Same goes for the British, Canadians, and Australians. The Fedayeen are crawling all over us. We're cutting them down as fast as we can, but they keep coming. At this rate, even if we're careful, we'll have expended our .50-caliber rounds in the next ten minutes and our small-arms stuff in twenty. I'm not sure we're going to be able to keep the enemy from breaching our lines and entering the enclave. There could be as many as twenty thousand in front of us." It was at that moment Ambrose saw the jingle trucks and cautiously advancing armor. "Oh, Christ! They're a long ways off, but there's no doubt about what I'm seeing, sir. There are a number of tanks headed this way."

"Have you got a count on how many?" Erickson asked.

"Negative, sir, not a precise one. Six . . . seven . . . eight . . . is what I've spotted. But they're too far away to get an accurate number. They're a mile from us and moving slowly. With them are armored personnel carriers. And we've picked up something else. It appears to be a widely spaced convoy of large trucks."

There was little doubt things were suddenly dire. Nevertheless, Erickson understood he needed to convey steadfastness and control. While Ambrose had never faced anything this severe, his subordinate did have significant combat experience.

"All right, whatever you do, don't panic," the company commander said. "Let me get further support headed your way. While I do, align all of your antitank weapons to face the immediate threat. We're not helpless here. If we can get it positioned in time, we've got enough firepower to handle what you've spotted."

Erickson had conveyed far more bravado than he was feeling. The situation demanded it. With such a force looming, his Marines were outgunned. Even so, his measured words provided the calming effect for which he was hoping.

"I'm on it, sir," Ambrose assured him. He began arranging his antitank weapons to meet the newfound threat. "Sergeant McGuire, get your Humvee aligned to take on the tanks in the middle of the formation the moment they move toward us. Wait for my order to take them out. After that, select your targets and fire on your own initiative."

"On it, sir," his TOW-mounted Humvee's commander reported.

"Corporal Alexander, same orders apply to your tripod mounted TOW. Focus on the middle."

"I'm zeroing in as we speak, sir," Alexander said.

"First and 2nd Squads, get your Javelins in place and ready to fire."

With a pair of Javelins available and the two TOW teams, both with multiple missiles, Ambrose had the firepower to take out many in the ominous force. The biggest problem would be finding the time to reload the TOW firing tubes once they had been fired. Even if his teams were exceptionally adroit, it would take a minimum of forty-five seconds to do so. And with so many enemy rifles searching for them, it would be impossible to rearm the missile tubes with any degree of proficiency. With the tanks scarcely more than a mile away, the platoon was already within range of the monsters' main guns.

Thirty minutes to go before night would surround them.

The president, recognizing the potential political consequences, had hoped to avoid becoming fully engaged in this so-called holy war without the Pakistani military's acquiescence. To that end, he'd directed the Marines protecting the innocents within the embassy's walls to do what they could to handle this on their own. Day after tedious day, hour after hour, Erickson had done his best to comply with those formidable orders. And until this moment, his men had addressed every situation no matter how severe.

Yet, as the fourth day neared its end, the Marine commander

was facing a harsh reality. This time his men wouldn't prevail. The odds were too great. There was little chance they'd be able to withstand so momentous a force. He turned to the Marine standing next to him in the command bunker. "Corporal Genovese, get to the embassy communication room as fast as you can and send out distress calls to anyone and everyone. Not likely we'll find any forces in a position to help, but don't let that deter you. Keep trying. Make it clear we need immediate assistance. With what we've got coming toward us, it's unlikely we can hold. We need any help they can provide."

"On it, sir!" Genovese was out of the bunker and sprinting toward the main gate before the words left his mouth. In barely a minute he would reach the main building's seventh floor. Out of breath, he would soon be making multiple distress calls in hopes of locating assistance for the destitute garrison.

"Scott," Erickson said into the radio as Genovese disappeared, "I know their contingents are small, but do you think the Swiss, Japanese, Spanish, and Swedes can handle things if I need to pull your guys and some of your civilian defenders to reinforce Ambrose's position?"

"Unless something changes, they should be able to, sir. There's only scattered fighting going on over here at the moment."

"All right. Leave your tripod-mounted TOW team where they are in case tanks appear in that direction, but send your other antiarmor weapons over to Ambrose at once. Get the remainder of 4th Platoon along with fifty or so of your civilian fighters ready to head toward the northern walls as soon as you can."

"Roger, sir, I'm on it. I'll send my heavier stuff now. Give us a few minutes to adjust the eastern defenses and get the civilians we're taking organized. We'll start moving toward Ambrose's position as soon as possible."

But Erickson wasn't finished. He turned to Claude Vickers.

"First Sergeant, even with the XO's men I'm not sure we can hold the enclave. Head into the embassy grounds. Grab Steven Gray and a handful of his men. I want you to take them and empty the enclave's apartment buildings. Move everyone through the back gate and into the embassy grounds. I need them out of there in the next twenty minutes if you can pull it off."

"On it, sir. But with that many people and so many floors in so many buildings, we'll be lucky to get half of them moved in that time."

"I know, but do what you can."

Without another word, the giant of a man ran from the bunker toward the main gate. As Vickers disappeared, Erickson returned to the task at hand.

37

Twenty minutes remained until nightfall would seize the harried scene. When it did, the Americans hoped the odds would turn toward them. At least that was true with regard to the Fedayeen foot soldiers. The tanks and armored personnel carriers were a far different matter. The coming night would have no effect on them. All had sophisticated thermal systems and were capable of fighting in any conditions. The jihadists, however, had no intention of handicapping their infantry by letting the battle drag into the nearing black world. In half that time, if the swarming infantry hadn't overwhelmed both compounds, the tanks would attack.

Fourth Platoon's remaining trio of Humvees had reached Ambrose. Each had taken up a solid defensive position. Their powerful machine guns were soon blazing. Two Marines lugging fifty-pound tank-killing Javelins joined the northeastern defenses. The added firepower helped, but they knew it wasn't going to be enough.

There was no time to waste. The remainder of 4th Platoon had to reach the wayward outpost before it was too late. "Sergeant Anderson, have you got the civilians who're accompanying us ready?" Tomlin asked.

"Yes, sir. As soon as our guys leave their foxholes and head toward the enclave, the civilians will follow."

"Let's go, then. Fourth Platoon on your feet. Without delay, locate a defensive position in front of the enclave and engage the enemy."

As the words left his mouth, Tomlin's reinforcements, Marines and civilians alike, left their sandbagged locations and started running along the enclave's eastern wall toward the raging conflict. They worked their way through the tumbled trees toward Ambrose's forward elements. With only two in their number felled as they approached, it didn't take long for each to find a home. They settled in and opened fire.

Fourth Platoon's appearance stemmed the assault's forward elements. The approaching humanity faltered beneath the scores of new rifles. But it wasn't long before the swarming masses regrouped and came on.

More and more zealots were appearing, with wave after wave slamming into the faltering Allied lines. Their numbers appeared to be without end. Even with Tomlin's support, in little time Ambrose's platoon, along with the British, Australians, and Canadians, were again struggling under the mounting pressure. Their spewing rifles were cutting down the dogged force in immense numbers, slaughtering anything wandering into their path. Huge numbers of wounded and dead choked the gruesome field's perverse grounds. Yet it didn't matter. The rigid fundamentalists kept on coming, with additional forms, having left their attacking positions in the east, south, and west joining them. The wanton strife wore on. Second by second a merciless clock ticked.

Ambrose had done an admirable job of controlling the

irrepressible events until the company's executive officer arrived. Now it would be up to Tomlin to somehow do the impossible.

In the distance, the line of explosive-laden trucks edged toward them. While he took in the evolving situation, Tomlin recognized his reinforcements weren't going to turn the tide. Without further help, before long the approaching masses would wash over them. And when they did, the lurking Fedayeen armored force would swoop in to finish the task. To his left, the thin British lines were especially vulnerable. They had five minutes, no more, before they would be overrun.

"Sir, my reinforcements are in place," Tomlin said into his headset. "But the situation's beyond desperate. The first two rows of Ambrose's Marines have fallen back. And the British, Canadians, and Australians are in even worse shape. They won't be able to hold much longer."

"Understood. Let me see what I can do," Erickson responded. "Lieutenant Marshall, get your platoon ready. We've got to reinforce the British protecting the northern wall. Leave your tripod-mounted TOW but bring everything else."

"Yes, sir," the platoon leader said. There was no mistaking the anxiousness in his response. "Second Platoon, out of your foxholes. Head straight for the northern defenses as quickly as you can."

"Sergeant McLain," Erickson said.

"Yes, sir," Marshall's platoon sergeant answered.

"Grab as many of the civilian fighters from your area as you can."

"Will do, sir."

"Once you're ready, let me know. I'll join you in leading them to reinforce those fighting in the north. Lieutenant Bates, have half your platoon slide over into 2nd Platoon's defenses. You're to take command of our efforts in the west."

The nine survivors of Marshall's 3rd Squad and a pair of Humvees reached the British just in time to keep them from breaking. His final two squads were close on their heels.

Three minutes later, Erickson, running at full speed, with one hundred rifle-carrying civilians, headed toward the distressing scene. With little more than the area's tattered trees to protect them, they advanced. But as they neared the northern wall they found themselves out in the open and quite vulnerable. A group of Fedayeen riflemen spotted the oncoming force. In unison, they raised their AK-47s and squeezed the triggers. The first of those heading toward the wall went down. A second and third followed. However, they wouldn't be the last.

Without realizing what had happened, a staggering Erickson took two steps forward and slumped to the ground. Confused and disoriented, he felt nothing. And then the pain arrived. An enemy round had ripped through his left shoulder. A second had ravaged his upper thigh. As he went down, a third grazed his neck and continued on. Blood spurted from the fresh wounds. Behind him, uncertain what to do, the entire line ground to a halt. The wounded captain, his agony evident, looked up.

"Keep going . . . keep going," he said while frantically motioning with his right arm.

He spotted Sergeant McLain running toward him. Before the firing insurgents could do further damage, McLain cut down those attacking the reinforcements. The platoon sergeant was soon kneeling over Erickson. "Company commander's down! Company commander's down!" he yelled into his headset. "How bad you hit, sir?"

"Never mind me: Get everyone to the north wall before it's too late."

"Yes, sir." McLain pointed at two of the gathered civilians, a man and a woman. "Do what you can for Captain Erickson. The rest of you, come with me." There was no time to waste. With a final glance at his fallen commander, McLain turned and headed toward the British lines. The remainder of the makeshift formation followed.

When they reached the wall, McLain ordered the first handful to move along its face until they linked up with Ambrose's left flank. Once there, they were to move forward, locating firing positions. The platoon sergeant continued directing each arriving civilian. In a hail of bullets those who survived the arduous journey settled into fighting holes and joined the unrelenting battle.

Once more, the arrival of additional reinforcements helped stabilize the battlements. Nevertheless, all understood it wasn't going to be enough. They were nearly out of ammunition. And while their defenses against an armored attack were significant, it was unlikely they'd be able to eliminate so powerful an advance. No matter how much damage the compounds' defenders inflicted, no matter how much death and suffering they caused, they wouldn't be able to withstand the inevitable. Within the hour they'd all be dead.

The two civilians left to care for the company commander knelt to examine his wounds. Even in the twilight they could see Erickson's upper sleeve was turning a vivid shade of red. A steady flow was running down his arm. The first drops were falling from his fingertips. His pant leg was becoming discolored. Blood also spurted from his neck wound. There was no question the injuries were serious. Without medical help, the blood loss would prove fatal.

"We need to get him back to the hospital as soon as we can," the woman said. She took a look around. She didn't like what she saw. "There doesn't seem to be a corpsman or stretcher-bearers anywhere. Looks like we'll have to figure out how to get him there on our own."

Neither was strong enough to carry the 190-pound Marine such a vast distance. "If we support you, do you think you can walk?" the man asked.

"I can walk. Get me up," Erickson responded. There was little doubt from his words that he was in agony.

Both reached down and brought him to his feet. As they did, despite their best efforts, an involuntary moan left Erickson's parsed lips. The surging pain nearly caused him to pass out. They turned to head back toward the embassy.

He resisted their efforts. "Not that way. This way," Erickson said while motioning toward the north.

Both looked at him in disbelief. "But your wounds are serious. You're losing a lot of blood," the woman said.

"Doesn't matter. Get me to the wall."

The man and woman hesitated.

"Hand me my rifle. Then get me to the north wall." It wasn't a request; it was an order.

There were no other option. They steadied his hobbling figure as he staggered toward the killing grounds. The moment the company commander arrived and got his first look at his struggling lines, he recognized the situation's harsh reality. The force they faced was even more devastating than he'd realized. One after another, his defenders were falling. In the distance, he recognized the idling tanks were starting to move.

With their lives, his men were doing little more than postponing the inevitable. Even if they somehow withstood the immense ground forces, once the Al-Khalids entered the contest, the defenders would be overwhelmed. The oncoming night wasn't going to save his depleted force this time. Instinctually, his mind flashed to an all-consuming picture of a horribly distorted Lauren and the child she cradled lying dead in the center of the accursed embassy grounds. Around her, for as far as the eye could see, were hundreds upon hundreds of those he'd sworn to protect. Desperation seized him.

He forced the profane image from his mind, returning to the roaring demons that consumed the one-sided battleground. His defenses were much too scattered and disjointed. He needed to consolidate the efforts of the original defenders and those who'd arrived.

"Fall back! Fall back!" he screamed into his headset.

Firing as they went, with rounds striking everywhere, each pulled away from the wavering front lines. One hundred yards from the battered compounds, his desperate forces dug in.

The enemy closed in for the kill. Knowing what their failure would mean, Erickson's impoverished force clawed at their looming destiny. To the last rifle, they were unwilling to go down without one hell of a fight.

The next few minutes passed exactly as the fanatics had anticipated, with enough sporadic action continuing in the east, south, and west to keep the defenders from providing further reinforcements. Even so, the unending marauders had yet to reach the northern walls. While they watched the skies darkening, the tanks and their menacing assembly had seen enough. The attack commander was under orders to not risk the Al-Khalids if it could be avoided. Nevertheless, he'd also been directed to take the compounds at any cost. Salim Basra wanted this done, and he wanted it done today.

It was time to make a mortal thrust into the besieged foreigners' hearts. The moment had arrived to unleash the menacing tanks and personnel carriers. The armored force picked up speed. Along with them, the jingle trucks drew ever closer.

The state-of-the-art Al-Khalids headed straight for the

vulnerable walls. All fourteen were well within range of the American defenses. So far, the first-rate tanks hadn't shown any indications of firing their cannons. That, however, was about to change. As the lead tank roared forward, it lowered its main gun and began sighting in its target. Others did the same.

The initial tank fired. The massive shell ripped across the anguished landscape. It headed straight for the enclave's centermost apartment building. The annihilating round tore the top three floors apart. The thunderous sound of the exploding ordnance could be heard for miles around. The building shuddered and yawed. It teetered for the briefest of moments before collapsing in upon itself. Immense pieces of falling rubble and fire-tinged debris spread far and wide.

Inside the partially evacuated structure, fifty people died. Claude Vickers was among them, caught while doing all he could to rescue those within the high building. An equal number of fleeing forms were wounded. Many found themselves trapped beneath thirty feet of wreckage. For only an instant the fighting stopped as all involved turned to take stock of the startling orchestration. Nonetheless, the fractious instant quickly passed. Once more, from every corner, the relentless killing continued. It was time for the Americans to get their revenge.

"Alexander, you got him?" Ambrose screamed into the headset.

"Dead center in my sights, sir."

"Take him out!"

Without responding, the tripod-mounted TOW commander fired. The three-and-a-half-foot killer ripped from the firing tube. As it flew, its fins popped out and a light came on in its tail. Standing next to the tube, Alexander tracked the armor slayer's flight through the fiber-optic cable that trailed from the missile's rear. Destroying a moving target was always a challenge, but it was one the corporal was more than capable of handling. Alexander adjusted the TOW's flight path to bring it dead center on the target. The resolute Marine didn't waver. A second riotous blast rocked the world as the forty-six-ton giant erupted beneath the missile's powerful warhead. Huge pieces of scorched metal soared high into the settling sky. Inside the tank's flaming corpse, its crew of three were dead.

Alexander never gave his actions a second thought. The instant the task was completed, he hurried to reload the firing tube. A second and third tank acquired targets and prepared to fire.

To have any chance, the staggered defenders needed to cripple the armored column, but Erickson didn't want to fire everything at once and leave themselves helpless while the TOW firing tubes were being rearmed. "Hold our remaining TOWs until absolutely necessary. Javelin operators, select your targets as you see fit and open fire."

As one, the six Marines spaced along the northern wall with Javelins perched on their shoulders fired. Each missile was set for a ruinous top-down kill that would allow it to destroy the target by piercing the tank's thinner top armor and exploding inside.

A half dozen swift Javelins were in the air. Even though their crews didn't know it, five additional tanks and an armored personnel carrier were about to suffer the same fate as the first. In rapid succession, the horizon lit up as the deadly missiles found their prey. In a blinding flash, with blast after vivid blast, the enemy armor went down.

Yet even so forceful an action didn't deter the ogres. Minus seven flaming brothers, the armored column roared forward. The jingle trucks' drivers picked up speed. It was time to put an end to the one-sided clash. The surviving Al-Khalids, along with the nine armored personnel carriers and a dozen murderous trucks, were headed toward the compounds. All the Americans had waiting for them were three Humvee-mounted TOWs and one tripod-mounted tube in the process of being reloaded.

A second tank fired. In an instant, its massive round blew a gaping hole in the enclave's deteriorating wall. Spurred on by the tank's actions, on the ground the attack commanders threw everything they had at the defenders. The mob redoubled its efforts, intent on pinning down the impoverished force. Thousands upon thousands came on. Gunfire from the north intensified. A mass of churning humanity and sixteen armored vehicles were headed their way. A dozen annihilating trucks were close at hand. Death was everywhere, felling those on both sides. The brutal scene's malevolent portrait, its colors goring red, was beyond heinous, with every sign indicating it would only become worse.

"Bailey, take out the bastard who just fired his main cannon," Tomlin ordered.

"On it, sir."

The lance corporal fired his Humvee's TOW. In seconds, the tank's crew would join those meeting a fateful end on this corrupting afternoon. The moment the tank was felled, Bailey began reloading his firing tube.

The unyielding pressure continued. Position by position, over and again, the Allies fell back until there was nowhere left to run. They were out of options. And little ammunition remained. Not one believed they'd be able to hold much longer.

38

It had been twenty-five minutes since Genovese had disappeared behind the embassy's walls. The fading wisps of the rain-soaked day's twilight were being overcome by the oppressive scene's approaching nightfall. In a steady stream, the enclave's evacuees were covering the short distance between the two compounds and entering the embassy ground. But a thousand remained within the housing area's battered enclosure. Many were still attempting to make their way down the crammed apartment stairwells.

The armored column was three-quarters of a mile away. The rushing jingle truck column, its bomb-loaded vehicles running full out, were seven hundred yards from the enclave.

A pair of RPGs ripped through the haze. The first well-placed projectile, coming in scant inches above a heavily fortified sandbagged barrier, slammed into the turret of the Humvee protecting the enclave's gate. With a wail of protest the vehicle exploded, its soaring inferno rising to singe the approaching night. The rocket ripped apart the protective layer of steel shielding the lance corporal firing its machine gun. When the smoke cleared, the machine gun's turret was nothing more than an unrecognizable mass of twisted metal.

The second RPG hit the embassy's northern wall, puncturing the thick concrete and producing another opening. This one was three feet wide.

Under the relentless onslaught's immense gunfire, the stream of wounded and dying was becoming a raging river as the Marines and their civilian supporters succumbed. "Man down! Man down!" the calls continued without pause.

The first of the large trucks rushed down the roadway leading to the enclave's wrought iron gates. One hundred yards behind it, a second of similar size and composition followed. And beyond it a third, fourth, and fifth, almost without end. The lumbering beasts were crammed with hundreds of pounds of explosives. Behind the wheels the self-destructive drivers, obscene smiles on their faces, slammed the gas pedals to the floor. The deadly caravan's speed continued to mount. Their journey to the wondrous place awaiting all the sainted martyrs was at hand. Each driver was determined to dispatch as many of the nonbelievers in the process as he possibly could.

The lead vehicle was drawing near. In the middle of the whirling struggle, Ambrose spotted the mounting threat. He recognized the situation's fateful consequences. If the lead truck was carrying even half the life-seizing explosives he suspected, it would take out much of the enclave with a single blow. Afterward, little more than smoldering rubble would remain. Hundreds of fleeing forms, caught in the open, would die. To a man, the Marines protecting them would join the mounting rolls. His platoon and the majority of the reinforcements would fall in a single blow.

In an instant, he was on his headset. "Simms, trucks headed this way in one hell of a hurry. Each appears to be loaded with explosive charges. You've got to eliminate the first one. And you've got to do it now."

Standing next to the TOW missile tube on the top of his Humvee, the Marine sergeant took aim. The lead truck was in his crosshairs. "Spotted him a few hundred yards back, sir. Been targeting him ever since."

"Take him out, Simms. There's no time to waste."

"He's as good as dead, sir."

"While Simms goes after the leader, 1st Squad, fire everything you've got at the second one," the lieutenant said. "You're the only ones with an angle on him. You've got to kill him as far from here was you can. If either of them gets anywhere near the enclave's entrance and detonates its load, the explosion will create a crater so large, it'll leave nothing but death and destruction."

"You heard the lieutenant: I need every rifle focused on the second truck," Sergeant Harvey, 1st Squad leader, directed his men. "Windshield and gas tank will be the most vulnerable. Do what you gotta do, but take him out."

In an instant, all six of the squad's survivors unleashed their rifles and a pair of light machine guns against the second of the onrushing assassins. Round after round smashed into the speeding truck.

While 1st Squad went after the trailing one, Simms tracked the leader as it rumbled across the landscape. The vehicle was four hundred yards from the compound and coming on fast. The fleeting seconds were passing. The Marine gunner had to hurry, but more importantly, he couldn't miss. Simms took a deep breath and fired. Spitting hellfire and damnation, the missile tore from the launch tube. With so short a distance between predator and prey, it would only take moments for it to reach its objective. But the onrushing truck and its murderous cargo were coming too close for comfort. The fully focused sergeant tracked the missile's relentless progress, making the corrections, both large and small, to zero in on its target. Never once did the truck stray from his sights.

The distance was soon covered. The noxious TOW's ordnance-laden nose rammed home, striking the onrushing leader head-on. The mountainous explosion, startling and cruel, was immense. Its crushing image, filled with animus and fury, was beyond imagination. It carried with it unutterable violence and glaring refrain. The detonating truck disappeared. A flaming cloud rose high into the sky, its peak reaching far into the receptive heavens. The feral blast rocked every corner of the scene, reaching out for great distances. Vindictive pieces of red-hot metal hastened far and wide, cutting down the unfortunate among the running peasants. It was accompanied by an eardrum-shattering resonance of immoral proportions. Thor's hammer, filled with thunder and lightning, fell upon the frail earth. Even in the middle of their frenetic actions, both sides turned toward the ghastly event unfolding little more than three hundred yards from the defenders' lines.

Like a great earthquake, the world around the depraved setting shuddered. The ground beneath the Marines growled and shook, knocking more than one off his feet. When the lurid smoke cleared, the debauched fissure that remained was thirty feet deep and more than three times as wide. The massive explosion reached out to annihilate and destroy. For fifty yards in every direction, not a hapless insurgent survived, not a blade of grass remained.

And the mocking insanity was far from over. As the vanishing truck's fires headed skyward, 1st Squad's youngest member sent an M4 round through the second avenger's windshield. The searching bullet struck the driver in the left cheekbone, shattering his jaw in multiple places. Its trajectory altered, the ricocheting bullet headed upward, slicing through his brain as it continued on its way. He slumped in the seat, blood and brain cells scattering far and wide across the truck's interior. With the driver's dead hands no longer gripping the steering wheel, the lurching monstrosity careened out of control. It swerved into the deep ditch on the edge of the roadway, tumbling over and again. A second awe-inspiring blast assaulted the combatants with a resounding roar that matched the first in every way. The horrific sounds and summoning fireball went forth to join its compatriot's singeing refrain. Another massive hole, equal in size and composition to the earlier one, appeared at the anguished spot where the runaway truck had slipped into the channel.

Like its brother, beneath a blinding flash the vividly colored truck vanished. Yet, despite the unspeakable outcome that had seized their comrades, the trailing convoy never faltered. One hundred yards behind, the next in line swerved into the blighted field, regained its footing, and continued on. No matter their losses, the deadly pack wasn't going to be denied.

That, however, wasn't the Americans' only concern. On the far left, two tanks' main guns were lowering. Each would soon zero in on its target and be ready to fire. From little more than four hundred yards away there was little chance either would miss.

"How many TOWs are ready to fire?" Erickson asked as he watched the devilish display of trucks and armored vehicles through pain-filled eyes.

"Mine, sir," Corporal Kitchens, 2nd Platoon's TOW Humvee gunner, answered.

"Just finished reloading, sir," Alexander responded.

"Won't be ready for another half a minute," came a final reply.

It wasn't going to be enough. Despite their massive losses, more and more of the jihadists were appearing. And with the majority of the defenders down to their final thirty-round magazine, the desperate battle's ghastly conclusion was upon them.

"Select a target and fire on your own initiative," Erickson

directed the TOW operators. "The remainder of you, concentrate on the enemy infantry. Make every shot count."

"Firing now, sir," Kitchens replied. In a flash, his TOW was on its way. Another tank crew was about to perish.

Alexander released a second missile. Another massive explosion rocked the grievous scene as a third jingle truck was ripped apart.

Half-crazed souls were running everywhere. Cradling his rifle under his good arm, Erickson squeezed the trigger. Thirty yards away, a pair of wild-eyed miscreants went down.

Moments later, the loss of blood seized him. The last thing he heard was another "Man down! Man down!" ringing in his ears. And then there was nothing. Erickson's world faded to black. He dropped to the ground unconscious.

One after another, his men fired their final rounds. The remainder of the death-laden trucks neared. Like a swarm of ravishing locusts, the jihadist foot soldiers lay down a blanket of gunfire so thick that nothing could withstand it. The surviving defenders had little choice but to dive deep within their makeshift bunkers. The game was nearly over.

39

"Fix bayonets!" Tomlin screamed into his headset.

An eighth of a mile remained before the armored column would reach the battered compounds. The now-leading jingle truck was three hundred yards from the enclave. The omnipresent running figures were seconds away from reaching the defenders' lines. As the third tank from the right roared forward, it lowered its massive main cannon. The target was soon within its gunner's sights.

"Fire!" the tank's commander yelled.

An overpowering shell ripped from the barrel of the recoiling tank. The lethal killer screamed over the Marines' bunkers, smashing head-on into what remained of the enclave's northern wall. Shattered cement, crushed stone, and steel rebar flew in every direction. Twenty feet in front of the gaping opening, a demolished bunker was ripped apart by the flying debris. Inside its false protection, two of Steven Gray's men lay dead.

The tank's automatic loader inserted another round. Along

with its brothers, the conquering beast continued its frenetic rush toward the prize. As it did, Ambrose watched the tank's main gun elevate. It didn't take long for the next victim to find itself dead center in its sophisticated targeting system. In seconds, the Al-Khalid's crew would send out another of death's messengers. When it did, its noxious ordnance would obliterate another of the enclave's apartment buildings. This one would strike at the base of the structure. Inside, a hundred fleeing people would soon be feeling the effect of the mortal assault. Few within its walls would survive what was about to befall them.

"Somebody, take him out!" Ambrose screamed into his headset.

The beleaguered lieutenant was hoping against hope that another of his men's TOWs was in a position to fire. But he knew the awful truth. No one was able to do so. Helplessly, Ambrose stared out upon the dreadful field. The offending tank's cannon was ready. Once more the monstrous image's commander screamed, "Fire!"

The Al-Khalid's gunner was only an instant away from unleashing the terrifying round. Little did he know that he would never release the death-dealing killer. For he didn't have a moment to live.

In a brilliant flash the tank exploded. A thunderous fireball rose from yet another blast. Flaming pieces of defeated metal soared into the darkening skies. Two hundred yards from the embassy's battered wall, the tank disappeared in a feral blaze. The confused Ambrose looked to the left and back again, trying to figure out the crippling shot's origin.

A startling breath later, a second Hellfire air-to-ground missile devoured the Al-Khalid next to it. An additional outcome struck the hellish scene. A pair of armored personnel carriers fifty yards behind the fiery monsters joined in as Hydra rockets tore their upper armor apart. Once again, monumental explosions surged through the evolving day. The astonishing events stunned attacker and defender alike. As for what had caused the cataclysmic outbursts, no one had a clue.

From out of nowhere, three Apaches sliced through the rancid rains, roaring across the low skies. There was quarry in every direction the target acquisition officers looked. They went after the endless figures closest to reaching the Marines' lines. Silhouetted by the fading twilight, their 30mm chain guns ripped apart those they found struggling across the calloused scene. A curtain of death poured forth in lightning bursts at a rate of ten rounds a second. The large 30mm shells tore the jihadists' world apart. Like a well-choreographed demon chorus, all in the slayers' paths fell in the unmerciful onslaught. Beneath the surging American craft, they perished in uncountable numbers. The abject savagery was beyond belief. None in the first wave survived the daunting attack. Behind the defeated ones their comrades' actions ground to a halt.

Corporal Genovese's frantic calls had taken precious minutes to wind their way through various levels. Finally, his pleas had reached the powerful force gathered at Camp Nowhere. Unaware of the camp's existence, those defending the compounds were as confused as their foes by the Apaches' presence.

Each attack helicopter's half-frozen pilot and target acquisition officer had been waiting in their craft. Should word come, they were ready to leave on a moment's notice to support the Green Berets holding the invaluable nuclear facilities. The distress call they'd received was one they hadn't anticipated. But it was as urgent as any they could have envisioned from the Special Forces units. Thousands of lives were on the line. Without hesitation, they responded to the embassy's desperate pleas. Swiftly rising, they took to the dimming heavens. They were soon roaring, engines running full out, through the treacherous mountains toward Islamabad. Their fangs were bared and ready. They covered the forty miles between Camp Nowhere and the capital in fourteen minutes. None of the astonished crews could believe their eyes when they arrived on the scene. Inviting targets, like an irresistible siren's song, were everywhere.

A second trio of flight crews had raced to their helicopters and launched five minutes behind the first. They were closing with the aberrant spectacle.

It'd be up to the buzzing Apaches to turn back the incensed throngs. And they were more than equal to the task. The initial trio split, the first two banking sharply left and right, while the trailing one remained on the same path. It didn't take long to find further prey.

The astonished peasants did their best to fight back. In the heat of battle, a dozen Stingers were lifted onto insurgent shoulders. Most of those cradling the little heat-seekers had neither the patience nor the ability to wait for the firing tone to sound, telling them their air defense missile had acquired the target. One after another, they pointed the Stingers in the low-flying helicopters' direction and squeezed the trigger. Released before they were ready, the majority of the searching air defense missiles careened away. Only a couple of the nasty killers were being held by jihadists with both perseverance and some degree of skill. Within moments of rocketing off their shoulders, both came near to striking their targets. Still, the Apache pilots were more than prepared for such an eventuality. Each instantly released red-hot flares and chaff to fool the mindless threat. In every case, the purveyor of certain death chased one of the false images and sped away.

With the Fedayeen ground forces halted and most of the bedraggled foot soldiers poised to retreat, it was time to go after the armored force once again. Another Hellfire went out. And one more. Two savage explosions rocked the perverse scene as a pair of deadly trucks exploded. A rupturing Al-Khalid was added to the rolls by the trailing Apache. And shortly thereafter another . . .

The tank crews opened up with their antiaircraft machine guns. Still, it was no use. The Apaches couldn't be dissuaded.

Roaring in at treetop level, the second helicopter grouping arrived and joined in. At Camp Nowhere, more were being readied. The blood-streaked skies were swarming. The monumental slaughter of those bent on certain conquest reached its peak.

It would be well after a frightful nightfall before the executioners' final murderous round would be fired. Not an armored vehicle or jingle truck had survived. More than twenty thousand bodies lay upon the sorrowful landscape. The relentless gunfire and immense explosions would ring in many a survivor's ears for days to come. The absolute carnage the peasants had witnessed staggered them all. Their agonized minds rebelled against the hideous reality.

Late into the night, the burning Al-Khalids' fiery carcasses shattered the darkness. What the garish images betrayed were beyond comprehension. Everywhere their eyes could see was agony and disorder. On the killing fields the fanatics who had somehow survived staggered to their feet. Confused and dispirited, they wandered away hoping against hope to find somewhere to lick their deep wounds. The dazed insurgents made no effort to recover their wounded or gather their dead, leaving them where they lay.

Throughout the night, the thousands of injured released primal screams and guttural anguish while pleading for a merciful end. Those angst-ridden sounds were carried great distances upon the merciless winds. In their reconstructed worlds, the Marines silently took in the unending misery.

Along with their earlier defeats, over a third of the one hundred thousand Basra had sent to destroy the nonbelievers were no longer in the fight. For the first time, the indomitable spirit propelling his unquestioning cult wavered. After six weeks of battle, the confounded peasants were beyond fatigued. With no system in place to feed or shelter them, they were hungry and miserable. All understood that was unlikely to change.

To toss their lives away with little gained and far too much lost was becoming difficult for many to accept. Still, their soulless leader understood that few had the ability to critically examine even the simplest of precepts. They'd been scarcely more than windblown apparitions their entire lives, going where they were led without question. And despite their misgivings, Basra was confident that would be enough to keep the majority in the fight. At least for the foreseeable future.

With their loathing for all things different from themselves, and their belief they were doing God's work, most would stay where they were. Even so, there were signs the smallest of fractures were forming in this populist army. For the moment, however, they weren't enough to change the course of battle.

Nonetheless, for the first time a few had had their fill. They slipped into the smoldering night and faded away.

40

It had been touch and go. Erickson's wounds had nearly proven fatal, but the doctors had been able to pull him back from the abyss. The same hadn't been true for far too many others. Zack Marshall, the second of the platoon leaders to fall in defense of the embassy, lived no more. Fourth Platoon had lost its platoon sergeant. Over half the Marine Company was dead or severely wounded

Once more, MaKenna fell asleep in Wells's arms. For the first time in hours, with the medical team's assurances that Sam would survive, Lauren allowed herself to take a deep breath. There was no longer any reason to hang around the hideous hospital. She was exhausted, and they'd just be in the way as the frenzied efforts to treat the critically wounded continued.

Tomorrow she'd return to give blood. Until then, she'd try to rest for a few hours. As she walked out into the rain, she spotted her cameraman approaching. He was covered from head to toe in dirt and grime. "All done, Chuck?" she asked.

"For now."

"Why don't we find some shelter in one of the buildings that's still standing?" she said.

Having returned from locating survivors in the enclave's toppled building, the exhausted cameraman glanced at his watch. "Sounds good to me. I've got a couple of hours before I need to show up at the main gate to help bring in the stuff from the airdrop." He paused and looked around. "With the enclave evacuated, most of the embassy buildings are crammed with people, but maybe we can squeeze in somewhere. What about trying that one?" He motioned toward an unimposing two-story structure not far from the hospital.

"That'll work."

The building was packed, every room at its limit. When Wells peered into the doorway to the final room on the second floor, she let out a deep sigh and quietly asked, "What do you want to do, Chuck?" Her voice was as weary as her body.

"We're probably going to find the same thing no matter where we try. Why don't we go back downstairs and settle in there? There was still a small amount of space on the floor near the entrance."

Without a word, she turned and headed toward the stairs. The entry floor's hallway was better than nothing. And at least they'd be dry.

They were soon back on the first floor, a few feet from the doorway. With an audible groan, both sat down and propped their backs against the wall. Wells laid MaKenna on the floor next to her. Within minutes, all three wayward beings were fast asleep.

They'd been unconscious for a short time when the narrow door creaked as someone entered. Just feet away, Wells opened her eyes in response to the annoying sound. The person in the doorway was one of the medical team's female doctors. Even in the twilight, the significant blood on her soiled scrubs was unmistakable. The haggard figure looked miserable. Wells had little doubt that while she and her fellow evacuees were living a nightmare that appeared to have no end, the doctors and nurses were walking through the deepest pits of hell.

The doctor recognized Wells from the bedlam at the hotel and her concerned presence at the hospital earlier in the evening. She spotted MaKenna lying on the floor next to her. "Mind if I join you?" the woman said in what was little more than a whisper. The complete exhaustion in her voice and stilted movements were unmistakable.

"Please," Wells replied while scooting closer to MaKenna to make room for the building's latest arrival.

There was just enough space for the doctor to squeeze between her and Chuck. "Angela Morgan," the doctor said to introduce herself.

"Lauren Wells."

"Yes, I know. I've seen you on television. Would say it's an honor to meet you, but given the situation we find ourselves in, honor has no place here."

"How're things going in the hospital?" Lauren asked. "Everything under control after today's turmoil?"

"Not a chance. Still got tons of people waiting for care. I felt quite guilty leaving, but apparently I fell asleep not once but twice while standing over a table, treating the wounded. Fortunately, neither case was overly serious, so no one suffered from my lapses. Haven't had a minute's sleep in days and have to admit I was starting to do more harm than good. So, despite my protests, they told me to go find a place to grab a few hours' sleep before even thinking about showing my face. How's she doing?" the doctor asked, gesturing toward MaKenna.

"Okay, I guess," was Wells's response. "She gets extremely anxious and starts to tremble every time she hears gunfire."

"Don't we all? With what she went through, who can blame her?"

"Seems to be sleeping a bit better, though. Even so, she hasn't said a word since I first picked her up in the hotel hobby. Does she know how to talk?"

Morgan let out a tired laugh. "MaKenna? She's a little chatterbox. Has an immense vocabulary for her age. And an adorable voice. In the two years I've known her and her parents, she's never stopped talking except to eat or sleep. Otherwise, she barely pauses long enough to take a breath before moving on to the next thing appearing in her vivid imagination. It was a running joke on the team. If you needed Collin or Kari, all you had to do was listen for MaKenna. She'd lead you right to them."

Wells looked at the sleeping form. She let out a lengthy sigh, her concern for the child growing stronger. "Hopefully, I'll hear that sweet voice someday."

"Give her time. She'll get there." Morgan looked around. "And it's not like any of us are going to be leaving here anytime soon."

"Yeah. I'm feeling more than a bit guilty about that. MaKenna shouldn't be here right now. I should've put her on that helicopter and gotten her out of here while I could. By now she'd be safe and sound and back with family."

"Family? I don't believe she has much of one."

"What do you mean?"

"From what they told me, Collin's and Kari's parents had died by the time they finished college. I'm not certain of any family beyond that. I think Kari mentioned a sister once. The lack of family was one of the reasons they signed on to spend a couple of years over here before settling in and starting Collin's medical practice outside Minneapolis. There was nothing tying them down back in the States."

Wells took a long look at the sleeping child before turning back to the doctor. "So if we get out of this, what's going to happen to her?"

"I don't know. If I'm wrong about the sister, I guess child services will put her in foster care or a group home once we get back."

Wells had thought the morass surrounding her every waking moment and the all-consuming angst she felt couldn't get any worse. Yet Morgan's words had proven her wrong. Should she survive this, she'd return to her cushy job, lavish apartment, and exciting life. Yet for MaKenna, there was a decent chance her tortured existence would never end.

41

The C-130 cargo aircraft were designed for such a mission. With the way their holds were configured, their crews could release sixteen fully loaded pallets weighing up to thirty-seven thousand pounds in total from the rear ramp in a matter of seconds.

Having received word the C-130s were close at hand, Steven Gray and a couple of his men walked along the inside of the embassy's southern wall. As they did so, each lit flares and dropped them. When they were finished, a dozen shined brightly. Even on a night as miserable as this, they couldn't be missed.

The four fully loaded C-130s would use them to guide their cargo drops. Their instructions were to eject the crammed pallets so the majority would land one hundred yards south of the flares. If accurate, that would put them in the center of the field between the embassy and the Kashmir Highway.

Each aircraft was within range of the jihadists' Stinger missiles, so the American crews knew they were vulnerable to an air defense attack. Fortunately, the darkness and drizzle masked the blacked-out planes' presence as they soared across the heavens. And all four were loaded with flares and chaff should defensive measures become necessary. An unsophisticated Stinger's chances of breaking through the false targets were almost nil.

Even if the noise from each aircraft's quartet of propeller-driven engines gave away this first attempt to resupply the thousands of desperate individuals, it was unlikely those holding Stingers would be able to locate the planes and launch an attack. At least on this night the risk for the C-130s was small.

Scott Tomlin stood waiting in the middle of the broad field's singed grasses. The airdrops were too critical for anyone else to handle. Inside the compound's gate, a line of wary volunteers, rain dripping down their faces, waited for the ambassador to lead them to the bounty. Once the parachute-laden pallets touched Pakistani soil, they'd head out to retrieve the invaluable lading. They were aware of the fate that had befallen the last people who'd attempted to gather arriving supplies. But with necessity trumping everything, they had little choice. They either succeeded tonight or, out of ammunition, died a horrible death in the morning.

For this first drop, and more to come on future nights, those items needed to wage war would be the top priority. Water would be second most critical, medical supplies third, and food the final component.

Overhead, Tomlin heard the first of the turboprop transports. Soon the noise in the miserable skies became even greater as one after another the trailing aircraft drew near. He looked up, attempting to spot the approaching planes. Given the conditions and omnipresent night, it was a useless gesture. He wouldn't know for certain that the supplies were on the way until the pallets, dangling from huge parachutes, were seconds from reaching the ground. Piled six feet high, the sixteen pallets carried by each aircraft would hit the ground one right after another.

He could hear the droning C-130s growing louder. Although he couldn't be certain, they seemed to be directly overhead. With any luck the heavily loaded pallets were moments away. The decisive moment had arrived.

Tomlin recognized the chances were slim of this going perfectly. The odds were high that some of the critical supplies would be lost in the attempt. Even with the wide field as their target, the C-130 crew chiefs could release their cargo too soon, causing them to land inside the crowded compound. If they did, they could severely damage one or more buildings and kill some of those sheltering within the embassy's walls. Equally as undesirable were the supplies being released too late, causing their parachutes to drift beyond the targeted area. If that happened, it would deposit them out of the reach of those awaiting them and into enemy hands.

Tomlin would soon know, for the floating loads were on the way. Without warning, there was a large thud near the eastern end of the open grasses. A first had reached the ground. So far they were batting a thousand. The pallet had landed at a safe location inside the defenders' lines. Tomlin turned in response to the sudden sound in time to see the stretching parachute crumple to the ground seventy-five yards away. One down, sixty-three to go. A second followed, fifty feet closer to where he stood. He looked up to see more on the way.

He keyed his headset. "Corporal Genovese, the supplies are arriving. All should be on the ground shortly. As soon as the last of the flares goes out and they're covered in darkness, have the ambassador bring the first twelve volunteers out to get the materials ready to carry inside. I'll let you know when to bring out the others."

Genovese turned to those at the head of the lengthy line. "Okay, stuff's coming down. Flares should sputter and die shortly.

Initial group, get ready to head out. Lieutenant Tomlin will be waiting to give you your assignments."

All around Tomlin, as the planes released their loads, the cascading parachutes continued to appear. In half a minute, the entire resupply was dropping from the skies. Task completed, the plodding planes circled and headed back to India. Shortly after sunrise, they'd begin loading tomorrow night's gifts for the waiting multitudes and working out a second flight plan. Their intentions were to never come in from the same direction or at the same time.

As the last of the loads touched down and a final flare died, Tomlin said, "Okay, Corporal, send the first dozen."

Genovese gestured for Alan Ingram and his team to move out. The ambassador headed out the gate, wisely clinging to what remained of the outside of the embassy wall to disguise his team's presence. Chuck Mendes was right behind. Ten more civilians, from a hodgepodge of nationalities, were with them. The time had come to face their fears and do what needed to be done. None could deny it was an exceptionally dangerous task. They all recognized they'd be exposed and vulnerable during the extended time it would take to complete the job.

All twelve carried a long, sharp knife. Their initial job would be to move in pairs from pallet to pallet, cutting each parachute's cords. They would follow that by using the heavy blades to saw through the thick straps binding the heavy loads to the pallets. Once the bindings were gone, Genovese would send the much larger group into the field to gather the supplies.

The waterlogged grass was the scene of a flurry of activity as the fifty volunteers grabbed as much as they could carry and headed for the embassy. Some labored alone, others in pairs, with a few in small groups working to handle the heaviest containers. Many of the scurrying workers were on their second trip. Cartons and containers filled with grenades and bullets; long wooden crates concealing Javelin and TOW missiles; five-gallon cans loaded with precious water; much-needed medical supplies; and boxes crammed with MREs were being taken inside where others waited to organize the distribution process. While their efforts continued, on the outskirts of the field the French, Dutch, and Germans, along with 3rd Squad's survivors, were ready for anything as they searched the night for signs of trouble. Most suspected that, this being the first drop, the jihadists would be more than a bit confused by what was transpiring. Still, with what had occurred already here, not one defender was going to let down his guard for the briefest moment.

They'd been lucky. Fifty-four of the sixty-four crates had landed inside their lines. Six more had dropped onto the Kashmir Highway. The farthest had fallen some distance from the embassy's defenses. Even so, it was worth the risk to attempt to retrieve them. It had been a tenuous situation, but what the pallets carried was too precious. Leaving their bunkers, eight of the French and German soldiers, along with two of 3rd Squad's Marines, had headed onto the highway to collect each one. They'd gathered the goods each contained and returned unharmed. Only four pallets had fallen too far away to retrieve. Still, over ninety percent of the load had been recovered and was making its way to where it was needed.

As each crate's contents were opened and sorted, additional volunteers moved into the battle zone, distributing ammunition, food, and water. By morning, the food and water for the noncombatants sheltering inside the grounds also would be handed out.

Nothing pleased the ambassador more than knowing that while all were hungry, each had waited for their turn to come. Their portions of both food and water would be small but adequate to sustain them for another day.

Ingram had recognized that these were people worth saving. Yet, on this night, their actions left no doubt.

The initial effort had been a success, pleasing them all. By 5:00 a.m., the last of the much-needed supplies had disappeared into the embassy grounds. Not a shot had been fired nor an individual harmed. Still, they understood things were unlikely to stay this way. With a few of the pallets dropping into their hands, the Fedayeen now realized what the sounds of aircraft engines meant. The airborne resupplies were a threat to the cultists' ability to overwhelm their abhorrent foe. Next time they hoped to be ready to respond.

The sheltering darkness wore on, dragging toward morning. Another sunrise was not far away.

42

Alan Ingram had spent the morning, along with a hundred others, being trained in how to use the captured AK-47s and the Marines' M4s. Too many of the compounds' original defenders were dead or wounded. They had little choice but to reinforce the survivors with new volunteers. Men, women, and teenagers as young as sixteen would soon be heading out to take up positions around the embassy. For many, it was the first time they'd held an assault rifle. With ammunition precious, even after a second night's successful drops, none of the trainees had experienced what it felt like to pull the trigger and release a round from an automatic weapon. The first time that would occur would be while facing a furious human form intent on taking their life.

As Ingram headed down the seventh-floor hallway toward his office, he heard the phone ringing. He broke into a run, reaching his desk and scooping up the telephone shortly after the fifth ring. "Alan Ingram."

"Ah . . . Mr. Ambassador," the voice on the other end of the line said. "After trying all morning, I've finally reached you."

"General Bhatti, it's good to hear your voice."

"And yours. When you didn't answer my earlier calls, I was growing quite concerned for you and your people."

"We're still here, still being battered by Basra's hordes. But we're holding on and hoping to hear America's leadership has come up with a plan to effect our rescue. How are your efforts going?"

"About as well as can be expected. Honestly, given the desperate situation when we last talked, I'd little hope either of us would be alive at this moment. Or that my country would still exist. But your Special Forces did a magnificent job, both in their initial attack and in defeating the Fedayeen counterattacks. Your country's to be congratulated on both the boldness of your plan and the bravery of your soldiers."

"Thank you, General Bhatti. I'll pass your kind words on to the president."

"Yes, do that, please. You can also tell him I recently heard from my spy in Basra's inner circle. This morning the sorry bastard finally came out of hiding from a horrendous assault that never came. Once he heard your Special Forces had not only seized our nuclear arsenal but had rendered the weapons useless, he flew into a rage and lashed out in every direction. Early this morning, half his leadership team were beheaded before he calmed down."

"Can't say I'm sorry to hear that."

"Neither was I. Eventually, his cruelty will be the fatal flaw that leads to his demise."

"Let's hope you're right, General. Honestly, I can't understand why so many continue to follow that horrid man."

"Nor can I. But apparently once people commit to something,

even when they know it's wrong, they continue to submit with absolute loyalty and are incapable of turning away. They'd rather die for their false prophet than admit their mistake."

"You're probably right, General. Hopefully that'll change someday and mankind will rid itself of the dark forces like Salim Basra whose evil infests this world." The ambassador had no idea how long the shaky phone connection might last. And there were questions about the situation in the remainder of the country he needed to ask. So he changed the subject ever so slightly. "We get so little news here, locked behind these battered walls. How's your army doing? Are you still in the fight against Basra?"

"The situation isn't great, but it's also not disastrous. Your Special Forces thwarting the horrifying destruction of my country bought us some time. While we're still falling back, we've rallied what remains of our military in the south and are setting up stout defenses around Karachi. It's where, with our back to the sea, we'll make our stand—and, when we're strong enough, strike out to defeat him."

"When do you think you'll be capable of doing so?"

"At this moment, on our own against the Fedayeen, we've no idea. It could take months, even years. So far our lines around the city seem to be holding. And we think they're going to. When our people started hearing about Basra's unspeakable atrocities, many turned their support toward us. That's especially true in the larger cities. Within Karachi, ninety percent of the population is aiding our efforts to save our country from Basra's deluded butchers. Right now we're playing for time as the tide begins to turn against him."

"Sounds rather encouraging."

"Basra's forces continue to grow, but at a much slower rate. And we believe he's made a potentially fatal mistake. As backward as he is, he has no concept of how to lead and sustain a massive army in the field. His men have been living off the land. But unless they can continue their conquests and find additional food and supplies, once they've cleaned out the resources from the places they now control, they'll have no way of replenishing them. Many of the fools should soon grow even hungrier, and we suspect the louder their stomachs' growl, the less enthusiasm they'll have for his corrupt holy war. We're finding a few are actually recognizing Basra's promises are nothing but lies. Their numbers are growing. At the moment, it's only a trickle of discontent. But eventually, who knows?"

"That's wonderful news, General," the ambassador said.

"Unfortunately, our forces aren't strong enough to exploit the cracks in the Fedayeen's army of fanatics. Still, after your country was able to drag Pakistan back from the precipice, I've been working on our leadership day and night to allow America to join with us to defeat the interlopers. Given the situation, do you think your president might be willing to commit his forces to helping destroy Basra?"

Ingram instantly recognized what was being offered. Nonetheless, he needed to answer honestly, even if it could jeopardize the opportunity in front of him. The president had informed Ingram of his willingness to send two divisions of combat troops if the Pakistanis were receptive. But the ambassador didn't feel he was in a position to speak for him. "I can't promise it, General. But I think America might have reached that point. The public support for such an action is growing. Still, your leaders will need to understand something before we step forward to help. It's possible after they hear what I'm about to tell you they may change their minds. Once we'd disabled all of the nuclear devices, the president felt we should take things beyond where they stood and remove the weapons from Pakistani soil. We were afraid if we left them where they were that, given time, Basra might grab some of your scientists, retake the nuclear sites, and force them to create and install new triggers. We'd be back where we started. Once Basra's defeated and your country stabilized, you have my word we'll return those weapons to you. Under those conditions, do you think your fellow leaders would still be interested in our help?"

"Does India know of your actions? Even with the threat China poses to them, if they discover our nuclear weapons are gone, I've no doubt they'll feel the need to invade my country to destroy Basra and the threat he poses. Once they've defeated him, they'll turn Pakistan into a puppet state with them pulling the strings. They may go so far as to ban the practice of our religious beliefs and turn our children away from Islam."

For the first time, Ingram decided the truth wouldn't help. He liked General Bhatti and felt badly about lying to him. But he also understood it was in both sides' interests for him to do so. "No, General, we're not going to tell India. All we've told them is that while it's hard, they need to have patience. We've promised that America will ensure the situation is resolved in a manner both your countries can agree to."

"Have they accepted your assurances?"

"Naturally, they're quite anxious, but so far they have. Once they see American ground forces have arrived, they'll have all the proof they need of our intent to carry out our promises."

"Good. That's more than acceptable. With your guarantee the nuclear missiles will be given back to us once this is over, I'm confident I can convince even the most reluctant of our leadership to agree. The past few weeks have opened a great many eyes to the reality of the situation. And to who our true friends are. Upon the condition all foreign forces are to be withdrawn without delay after Basra's army is defeated, we're willing to accept not only your assistance but the help of the French and British if they're able to come to our aid."

Having lived under the thumb of British colonialism for a significant portion of the previous two centuries, Ingram understood such an offer to be quite a concession by the remaining Pakistani military. Despite the good face General Bhatti was presenting, to allow a notable British force to return to their soil, the Pakistanis had to be in greater trouble than he was letting on.

"Let me contact Washington and I'll call you back."

"Of course, Mr. Ambassador."

"Give me a number where I can reach you." After Bhatti gave him the number, the ambassador hung up the phone.

By midafternoon, Ingram had the answer. It was time to call General Bhatti. "General, you can tell your leadership America has committed to sending two combat divisions, along with one each from the French and English. Our plans are in place and we're ready to move as soon as you give the word."

"You have it, Mr. Ambassador. When do you anticipate being in a position to attack?"

"Our military doesn't believe we'll be able to get a strong enough force onto Pakistani soil until at least the seventeenth. Possibly even a few days more."

"The seventeenth's more than acceptable. You've my promise we'll do all we can to hold on to the land we control as we await your arrival."

"How do you think your populace will react to the presence of our soldiers?"

"Some will understand, especially in the southern portion of the country, where Basra's despised for what he's doing. Many of those in the rural areas will no doubt be angry. Still, you leave them to me. Along with the attacks on the Fedayeen, we're planning a major propaganda campaign to address those issues."

"Okay, let me contact the Pentagon and our allies to work out the details."

"Thank you, Mr. Ambassador. We'll be forever grateful for your efforts on our behalf."

"General, with the situation as tenuous as it is here in Islamabad, once I get things set up, it might be best for you and those in Washington to communicate directly rather than going through me. Do I have your permission to instruct them to begin working with you?"

"Absolutely."

"All right, then. I'll get on this without delay. Best of luck to you, General Bhatti."

"And to you, sir. May our victorious paths soon cross."

43

In the middle of the night word came. Roused from a troubled sleep, the division's soldiers were directed to return to their units. The first trains, loaded to their limits, were to leave by noon. The next third would be on their way shortly after sunset. The remainder would depart by the following dawn.

Bea Washington's helicopter company would be among the initial to depart for Bayonne. Surrounded by piles of gear, the apprehensive men and women under her command worked in the early morning darkness to prepare their UH-60 Black Hawk helicopters to load onto the huge trucks that would take them to the railhead. Her helicopter crews weren't the only ones. Everywhere she looked, the hurried actions were ongoing as the lead elements of the highly mobile light infantry division were being readied for the journey to Pakistan.

Washington's copilot, Chief Warrant Officer Shaun White,

came up to join her. "Trucks are on the way, ma'am. Unit's ready to load as soon as they arrive."

Washington glanced at her watch. "Forty-five minutes before we're scheduled to leave. The moment the last of the Black Hawks is secured, you can give the word for everyone to load the remaining equipment and prepare to depart."

"Yes, ma'am."

The air was thick, every soldier's anxiousness apparent. It was always like this moments before heading toward the next war zone.

It was White who ended the uneasy pause. "Were you able to find someone to watch over the girls while you're away?"

"Luckily, my mother came in yesterday afternoon. Neither of them was that happy when I woke them to say goodbye. Still, it's not the first time they've been through this. And it probably won't be the last. With Nana to watch over them, they'll be okay. How did Jenn react when the phone rang?"

"With the baby due any day, she wasn't happy. But it is what it is."

A cordon of large trucks turned the corner and headed down the narrow streets. Washington spied them. "Looks like the trucks are here."

If they arrived first, they'd wait in Karachi for the 3rd Infantry to show. Once they arrived, the 3rd Infantry would strike out from there. At the same time, the 10th Mountain's massive helicopter force would ferry its troops across the hostile landscape to the mountains of northern Pakistan. From there, they'd attack south, intent on eventually meeting up with the approaching 3rd Infantry's lead elements and crushing Basra.

It was a bold plan, filled with peril. If it worked, Pakistan would be back in friendly hands in as little as a couple of furious weeks. Yet all understood if things didn't go the way the Pentagon hoped, the Americans could become bogged down in another costly war of attrition lasting for a decade or more. It was, however, a risk worth taking even if the outcome was uncertain.

While they loaded the first Black Hawk, even the most nervous among them couldn't envision the hornet's nest they'd soon be facing.

44

7:48 A.M., NOVEMBER 7
4TH PLATOON, BRAVO COMPANY, 2ND BATTALION,
69TH ARMOR REGIMENT,
2ND ARMORED BRIGADE COMBAT TEAM (SPARTANS),
3RD INFANTRY DIVISION
WÜRZBURG, GERMANY

As the 10th Mountain loaded their equipment, another of the Americans' divisions was doing the same. Being six hours ahead of New York, they were doing so at a more reasonable hour.

Four thousand miles away, Darren Walton was watching as his unit's equipment was being prepped. The entire 3rd Infantry Division was taking its first steps toward reaching Pakistan. His thirty-three-ton Bradley fighting vehicle, along with hundreds of other armored elements and supporting equipment, was being readied for the trip across town to the Würzburg depot. Once the trains were loaded, they'd settle in for the trip north to Bremerhaven and the Baltic Sea. There the ships would be waiting.

This wasn't the veteran platoon sergeant's first taste of war. And he knew what they might face on the killing grounds. Over the years, he'd seen the worst mankind was capable of inflicting upon his brothers. He'd killed and in return watched his closest friends die. Like Bea Washington, he had no illusions about the glory of war or what he'd soon be facing.

His platoon leader, Second Lieutenant Ethan Cramer, approached where Walton was standing in the motor pool as the platoon's soldiers worked around him. "Things coming along okay?" Cramer asked.

"Yes, sir. We're right on schedule. All four Bradleys are nearly ready to roll. Equipment's loaded and the guys are putting the pads on the tracks so we can drive them across town. Should be ready in the next half hour. How'd the company meeting go?"

"Fine. Nothing new since yesterday's briefing. Things are subject to change, of course. But if the tactical situation remains the same, once we reach Karachi, our battalion won't wait for the rest of the division to unload. We'll head straight from the docks to reinforce the Pakistani army units protecting the city while the others prepare to attack. When the division's in place, we'll hit them with everything we've got and not stop until we've destroyed Basra's army."

"Are they still estimating a couple of weeks of intense fighting and we'll be on our way home?"

"That's what they're saying. Nice and simple. Clean up this mess, load back on the ships, and be home before Christmas. With what we're going to unleash on Basra's followers, they won't know what hit them."

"Let's hope they're right, sir. Sure would like to avoid another Christmas spent away from my wife and kids."

45

Charlie Sanders watched as the Chinook cargo helicopter lifted the final Shaheen missile a few feet into the air. The Chinook whirled about, the rocket dangling beneath it, and headed east toward the snow-covered mountains. Once in India, the disabled nuclear weapons would be placed on air force cargo planes and flown to Germany.

Within minutes, the Chinook and its payload, its image growing smaller, disappeared over the horizon. Sanders let out a deep sigh. With the three rockets and the ten crates holding the smaller tactical nuclear weapons gone, the immense threat was over. Without them, the transporter-erector-launchers were of little importance. The departing Green Berets would leave them in the center of the compound as they made their escape.

The past few days had had their moments, but all of the Americans were in agreement that this portion of the operation had been easier than any had expected. They'd fended off a series of Fedayeen attacks, most highly disorganized and half-hearted. One had been significant, the remainder modest in scope. The assault's ferocity had lessened with each subsequent attempt to regain control of Mishira. A handful of additional wounded, and no dead, was all the surviving Green Berets had experienced. And on this steamy afternoon things couldn't have gone better. For the first time since they'd seized the hilltop, not a shot had been fired by any of the Special Forces soldiers. By midmorning, with the world around them calm, Sanders had been able to focus on the task at hand: getting the deadly slayers he and Davidson had disabled out of there. With the final helicopter gone, another critical mission was nearly over.

Before sundown, the same Black Hawks that had deposited them on the contested plateau would arrive to extract them. Even Camp Nowhere, the first stop on the extended journey home, didn't seem like such an unappealing place when compared to where they were and what they'd been doing. He turned to retreat to the bunker on the northeast corner of the perimeter he'd shared with Aaron Porter for the past three days. Once there, he'd gather his gear in anticipation of the Black Hawks' appearance. In a couple of hours, the helicopters would arrive and whisk them away from this hellhole. It wouldn't be long before he'd be sitting in his favorite Fayetteville bar, cold beer in one hand and, with any luck, a smiling woman in the other.

An uneventful ninety minutes passed as the afternoon droned on. The time for their departure was growing near.

The square-jawed Neil Short, his bandaged left arm and shoulder in a heavy sling, approached. Inside the bunker, Porter sat sharpening his knife while Sanders stared at the snowcaps rising in the distance. The younger sergeant had been aimlessly attempting to figure out which of them contained the secret location where Camp Nowhere was hidden from all but friendly eyes. Both looked up to see the A Team commander hovering over them.

"Black Hawks on the way, sir?" the upbeat Sanders asked.

"That's what I came to tell you. Our orders have been changed."

"What?" Porter said, his surprise evident. Both sergeants understood it was unlikely they'd be pleased by what Short was about to tell them.

"For now, we're staying right here. Higher-ups believe the threat the Fedayeen poses is too great to let stand. For the good of all, we need to put the Pakistani government back in power and do what we can to stabilize the situation."

Porter and Sanders gave each other sideways glances. Neither liked the sound of where this was heading.

"We've been in discussion with the Pakistan military for a few days now," the captain said. "After the guys in our group saved their asses by disabling the nuclear weapons, the Pakistanis have agreed a joint effort to put an end to this mess needs to be launched. If everything goes as planned, in less than two weeks the 6th Special Forces Group is going to be part of a massive Allied assault that will sweep across Pakistan to destroy Salim Basra and his followers. The 3rd Infantry is heading out by ship. They're scheduled to reach Karachi and begin unloading on the seventeenth. A French armored division and a British one will arrive around the same time. As we speak, the 10th Mountain's loading onto trains and heading for Bayonne. They'll reach Pakistan and be ready to attack on the same day the 3rd Infantry arrives."

"That's fine, sir," Sanders said. "After what we've gone through, nothing would please me more than seeing these sorry bastards wiped out. But what does the 3rd Infantry's and 10th Mountain's attacks have to do with us? We've done what they sent us here to do. It's time to go home and settle in for some well-deserved rest and relaxation."

"The details of the plan are still being finalized, but one thing's clear: there'll be no R and R for this team anytime soon," was the captain's response. "We're going to be right in the thick of things. The entire group's going to do their best to fend off any Fedayeen attacks and hold right where they are for the next ten days. A day or two before the division-level attacks begin, each A Team will head out and start raising hell everywhere they can. Wherever we find them, we're going to take out the fanatics and sow a mountain of discord behind their lines. The 3rd Infantry, French, and British will be coming from one direction, the 10th Mountain from the other. With us in the middle striking every which way they turn, the rabble won't stand a chance."

"How long do they think this will take, sir?" Porter asked, knowing every additional hour of combat decreased the chances of finding their way out of here.

"Group's estimating it'll likely be the end of the month, possibly a few days more, before we put an end to this. Once we do, we'll head for home."

From the captain's tone and mannerisms, it was apparent he was pleased with the change of plans. Despite what they'd endured, he was eager to continue the fight. Nevertheless, there was little doubt from their expressions that neither of the grizzled soldiers shared his enthusiasm. They'd stared into death's eyes on many an occasion. With their captain's edict, each understood the chances were great that before the month was over they'd do so once again.

46

9:58 A.M., NOVEMBER 8
OPERATIONAL DETACHMENT ALPHA 6333, CHARLIE COMPANY,
3RD BATTALION, 6TH SPECIAL FORCES GROUP (AIRBORNE)
MISHIRA NUCLEAR ARMAMENTS MOBILE LAUNCH FACILITY
THIRTY MILES SOUTHWEST OF ISLAMABAD, PAKISTAN

As always, Porter sensed the danger before he saw it. He peered out on the expansive valley searching for its source. It didn't take long for him to locate it. "Someone headed this way," he said.

Sanders looked in the general direction his partner had indicated. They'd intentionally selected this location in the northeast corner of the plateau to establish their defensive position. Here the trees were thin and wouldn't limit their view of the sloping scene below. Despite his exceptional abilities, Sanders was no match for his partner when it came to identifying potential danger. The junior sergeant's search found nothing.

"How many of them?"

"Just one," Porter said.

"Where?"

"About ten o'clock. See the bent sapling well down the hill sticking out of the tall grasses?"

About a half mile away, Sanders spotted the pitiful little tree. "Yeah."

"Follow it down the slope for a few hundred yards. Hard to see because the person's clothing kind of blends into with the landscape, but there's someone down there."

Sanders located the movement. "I've got 'em." He watched the distant figure struggling up the steep grade toward them. Whoever it was seemed to be wandering somewhat aimlessly. The stumbling form appeared confused and lost. Once or twice each minute, the figure would stop and look around, focusing primarily on what, if anything, was behind them.

The erratic movement continued for a further ten minutes with the person more or less heading in the general direction of the Special Forces encampment. Whoever it was had cut in half the distance between where Porter had first spotted them and the American defenses.

The wayward image was close enough for the team's senior weapons specialist to hazard a guess as to whether they were male or female and what kind of threat they appeared to pose. "Given what they're wearing, it's got to be a woman or girl." Porter paused, examining the approaching person once more. "There's no indication she's carrying a weapon."

The person stopped and looked around once more, attempting to get her bearings. This time the unsteady effort succeeded. Straight as an arrow, she headed toward where Porter and Sanders were waiting.

"Halt!" Porter ordered when the striving Pakistani was thirty yards away. She responded instantly, complying with his directive.

It was a girl of eleven or twelve. Porter motioned with his rifle for her to approach the bunker. Both could see she was trembling, her dark eyes wide with fear as she walked toward them. When she got closer, they spotted blood on her tattered clothing along with heavy bruises and irregular cuts and scrapes on her face. With the remainder of her body covered by what she was wearing, they couldn't tell any more than that. She didn't appear to be a threat, but the situation called for prudence. With her wearing traditional Pakistani clothing consisting of loose-fitting salwar pants, a kameez shirt, and a dupatta scarf, she could easily be concealing a bomb beneath them.

When she was fifteen feet away Porter said, "That's close enough." The girl stopped. "Hands up," was his next command.

She did as she was told, uneasily raising her arms into the air. It was apparent she'd understood his commands. With 40 percent of the Pakistani population reasonably fluent in English, it wasn't overly surprising.

"Charlie, pat her down for weapons and explosives."

Rifle at the ready, Sanders got up and headed over to where the girl was standing. The terror hadn't left her eyes. He needed to ensure nothing was out of place, but given her appearance, he wanted to be as delicate as the situation would allow. He gently patted her down.

"She's clean."

"All right, bring her in."

Sanders took her by the arm and led her over to the bunker.

"May I have some water, please?" the anxious girl said. Her parched lips and clinging mouth showed she was badly dehydrated. Her meek voice was hoarse and raw. Sanders took out his canteen and handed it to her. She emptied the half-full container in a few hasty swallows. She handed it back.

"Thank you. I've been wandering around for hours and haven't had anything to drink since yesterday afternoon."

"What's your name, girl?" Porter asked.

"Fareeda."

"Okay, what the hell are you doing out here on your own, Fareeda?"

"I was looking for you," was the unanticipated answer.

"Us? Why us? How did you even know we were here?"

"I heard the Fedayeen Islam men who came to my school talking about the Americans that were nearby. They were planning an attack against you once they finished with us and could gather hundreds of their soldiers to assist them. They're going to kill you."

"Let 'em try," Sanders said.

He motioned to the north. Fifty yards away lay the huge pile of jihadists they'd eliminated while taking the site. With them scheduled to board the helicopters and depart yesterday, the original plan had been to leave the bloated carcasses where they were. Now that they weren't leaving for another ten days, those plans had changed. The vile smell and unwanted pests the corpses were attracting was becoming untenable. Enough fuel had been drained from the transporter-erector-launchers to douse them all. An hour from now, a huge funeral pyre would blaze in the late morning sun. Hopefully, the fearsome fires and rising smoke wouldn't attract a pest of a different kind—one holding a rifle.

It took the girl more than a moment to recover from the mass of jumbled images to which the African American soldier had pointed. Finally, her focus returned and she spoke again. "Please, you've got to help. I escaped when they weren't looking. Before they go find others to help slay you, they're planning on killing my teacher and all of my classmates. If you don't stop them, all will die."

"How do you know the Fedayeen will kill them?" Porter asked.

"Because they hate us."

"Why do they hate you?" Sanders asked.

"Many of the backward men who live in the tribal territories believe educating girls is a sin against the Koran. Most of our country isn't like that, but our attending school and learning to read and write goes against what those kinds of people have been taught. And for them, there's only one possible punishment for our sins: death. They're evil, ignorant men who care nothing about any life but their own."

Porter looked at the dried blood on her shirt and legs. Along with the multiple rips he spotted on her clothing, when he put it all together, there appeared to be a pattern. "Fareeda, did they rape you?" he said as quietly as he could.

She dropped her head, unable to look into the Americans' eyes. Her voice, filled with shame, was scarcely a whisper. "Yes, many times. The other students and our teacher too."

"Shit!" Sanders said. "Every last one of those sorry sonsabitches needs to die in the most awful way imaginable." His disgust was evident as he spit out the words. "And I know a couple of guys who'd be happy to oblige them."

Nonetheless, Porter kept his voice calm and steady. He knew the hard-core among the uneducated peasants looked with great disdain at girls attending school. He also understood the sexes weren't allowed to attend class together, so there'd be no boys among them. "How many girls are there, Fareeda?"

"Counting me, thirty. Please, there's little time. They're going to kill all my friends and my teacher. Please, before it's too late, help us." There was anguish in the pleading girl's voice. And an unrelenting pain in her eyes.

"How many Fedayeen are there?"

"I don't know . . . forty . . . fifty, maybe."

"Where's your school?"

"In the valley below, about five or six kilometers from here." She pointed to the east.

"Is it close to any villages?" Porter asked. He knew if further fanatics were nearby it would make any rescue attempt impossible.

"Until they destroyed it, my village wasn't too far away. It would take me thirty minutes, but I could walk home each evening. The people of my village built the school where they did to keep it hidden from those who might object to such a place. So it really isn't too near anything. Until the day before yesterday, my friends and I were lucky. The Fedayeen moving through the area didn't spot us. We'd hoped it would remain so. But as this group was foraging for food, they found our school."

"What about other Fedayeen? Are there any close by?"

"On the way to find you I saw no one. Still, over the past days there have been more than a few passing through the valley. So it's possible some are nearby."

Porter was running through his options, already beginning to develop a semblance of a rescue plan. "Are there trees or other things in that part of the valley to protect us if we try to help?"

"No. My school's by a little stream in the middle of a wide grass field with nothing at all to shelter it."

"How tall is the grass?" Porter asked.

Rather than answering, she held her arm out, indicating it was around three feet high.

He looked at Sanders with the hint of a sneer on his face. "High enough to get close without the bastards knowing we're there." He looked back at the girl. "Do you think you could find it again if we went with you to save your friends?"

"Yes, I can lead you there."

"Do you understand? It would mean risking your own life if you did."

"I've no choice. Many will die if I don't take you. The Fedayeen will kill them. Please, we need your help."

Both soldiers could sense from her sincerity and the urgency of her plea that she was telling the truth. "Aaron, do you think the captain would even consider letting us try?" Sanders asked.

"No idea, but I'm gonna ask. In all the years I've been doing this, I've never allowed innocents to die. And I'm sure as hell not about to start now."

The girl stood off to the side as the animated discussion continued. Her uneasiness showed.

The first soldier had taken her into the compound, where she did her best to answer the questions of the bandaged man who was obviously the leader of the Americans. Despite her pleadings, it was apparent the one in charge was reluctant to do anything to help.

Porter was doing his best, but so far hadn't been able to convince Captain Short to authorize the incursion. With Captain Henry and the Alpha 4124 commander, Captain Burns, observing, the animated discussion continued.

"Come on, sir. We need to do this," Porter said. "You and I both know they're going to kill those girls if they're not stopped."

"There's a reason we're positioned on this plateau, Sergeant Porter. And walking into a trap isn't it. Once word comes, we're to undertake a covert operation behind enemy lines to harass and destroy the jihadists wherever we find them. Got to tie down as many as we can while the 10th Mountain and 3rd Infantry get established and start ripping into their lines."

"Sir, that's not going to happen for a number of days. Until then, we're sitting here, doing nothing. And you heard what the girl said: the sorry bastards at the school know we're here. Once they finish with them, they're planning on gathering a huge force and attacking us. Why wait for another assault when we can go into the valley and take them out before they get organized. If we don't, and they hook up with additional units before heading this way, they could cause us some real problems. Who knows how many they'll be able to collect before they come for us? Hell, thousands could show up. Our mission could be in jeopardy if we don't act now."

Porter had hit upon an argument with which the captain could agree. The fanatics at the school had the potential to pose a serious threat to his Green Berets. You could see from the look on the A Team commander's face that he was giving his sergeant's words some thought.

Porter saw his opening. "Come on, sir. You know we need to do this. It's not only right; it's smart. Let me lead a team down there and take 'em out."

"What if they're waiting for us? They could've sent the girl here hoping she'll lead us into an ambush."

Porter glanced at Fareeda. "Look at her, sir. You know as well as I do she's telling the truth. And if it really is a trap, I'll spot it and take it out before the jihadists know what hit them."

Short knew Porter's comments were more than an idle boast. In all his time in the Army, he'd never seen anyone with the talent for identifying danger and eliminating it like those his senior weapons specialist demonstrated. In his two years as the Alpha 6333 commander, he'd never seen anything the lethal assassin couldn't handle. Still, while he shared Porter's concerns, he wasn't willing to jeopardize their future actions in undertaking the rescue.

"All right, Sergeant Porter. Go do what you can to save those girls and scout what we're up against."

"How many men should I take with me, sir?"

"There aren't that many to start with and I sure don't want to weaken this hilltop any further. Should a major attack come, we're going to need every rifle. If you insist on doing this, you and

Sanders will have to handle it on your own. I've got no one else I can spare. Find out what we're facing down there so we can figure out what to do next. If there's any way possible, save the girls while you're at it."

"But, sir, I—"

"It's you and Sanders or it's nobody. Those are your choices, Sergeant."

Hastening past the bunker, Aaron Porter, with Fareeda in tow, didn't slow down. "Grab your gear, Charlie. It's time to save some little girls and see what we can do to wipe out a pile of human excrement in the process."

Without a word, Sanders snatched his rifle and rucksack. He rushed to catch up.

47

11:44 A.M., NOVEMBER 8

OPERATIONAL DETACHMENT ALPHA 6333, CHARLIE COMPANY,

3RD BATTALION, 6TH SPECIAL FORCES GROUP (AIRBORNE)

IN THE VALLEY BELOW THE MISHIRA NUCLEAR ARMAMENTS

MOBILE LAUNCH FACILITY

TWENTY-EIGHT MILES SOUTHWEST OF ISLAMABAD, PAKISTAN

They were two miles into the valley, two-thirds of the way there. Cautious and wary, they continued their steady descent. Minutes after leaving camp, they'd found themselves on an open hillside with nothing but wild grass, some higher than their waists, for as far as they could see. The swaying plain went on unbroken until it reached a winding road a mile to their left. From their location, they could see the snaking asphalt making its way through the gorge's floor. Normally, the roadway would've been filled with jingle trucks, cars, and motorcycles headed toward or away from Islamabad. But the war's chaos had put an end to such activity.

While the Green Berets did their best to scan its length, the ghostly roadway sat eerily vacant. There were no signs of a human presence. Even so, both would have felt better if there had been some kind of cover to mask their efforts.

Beyond the road, a thick forest spread in every direction. Nestled in its midst was a sparkling lake of vivid blue. On the far side of the shimmering waters, the Americans could make out a non-descript gathering of a few hundred homes.

"Is that your village, Fareeda?" Porter asked.

His question had a dual purpose: to get his bearings in the unfamiliar territory and to distract the girl from what lay ahead. For the past few minutes a trail of black smoke had been rising from the undulating fields in front of them. It was growing thicker by the minute. There was little doubt the telltale haze was coming from the area where the school was located. Without being too obvious, the Green Berets had given each other telling sidelong glances. They were still too far away to see the source of the smoke, but each feared the worst. It was looking more and more likely they were going to be too late.

Porter's attempt to focus the girl's attention elsewhere failed. "Yes," Fareeda answered, her nervousness undeniable. "Until the evil ones came, it had been my home. Please, we need to hurry," she begged, panic clinging to every word. "The only place the smoke could be coming from is my school. There's nothing else it could be."

"Fareeda, we're going as fast as we dare," Porter said. "We want to get there as quickly as possible. But we have to be extremely careful in the open like this. Any faster and we could find ourselves unprepared for any Fedayeen who might be waiting."

When they came up over a small rise six hundred yards from the school's sole building, they dropped to one knee, using the grass to conceal their presence. From their vantage point they could see all but the eastern side of the distant building. The horrific display came into view. They'd suspected what they were going to find. Still, as it appeared before them, an undeniable reality set in.

The modest building's walls were engulfed in flames, but the roof wasn't yet burning. Nonetheless, it wouldn't be long before it would be entirely ablaze. The growing fire reached into a cloudless sky. In front of the crippled structure, near the door, a large grouping of individuals were dancing and screaming at the top of their lungs. Each was rejoicing in their corrupt undertaking. They were far too busy with their capricious celebration to notice the dealers in certain death watching their every action.

A dazed Fareeda fell to the ground, her hands covering her face. After what she'd been through, it was too much to endure. She began sobbing uncontrollably.

Porter looked over at her pitiful form, knowing there was little he could do to ease her suffering. He assumed the situation was beyond hopeless, but he wasn't willing to admit they'd failed.

"Fareeda . . . Fareeda . . . ," he said, trying to console her. "I know how awful this must be, but we can't stop now. If we hurry, it might be possible to save some of your friends. Does the school have any other doors besides the one those men are in front of? Any way we could come around from behind and rescue your classmates?"

"No, there's just that one," she was able to tell him through her tears.

Porter took a quick look around. He could see no windows in the staid building.

"What about windows? Are there any on the other side?"

Fareeda shook her head no.

He glanced at Sanders. His hatred and disgust for the despicable throng who'd done this incomprehensible thing was beyond measure. "Charlie, have you seen any indication there are more of them on the far side of the building?" Porter asked.

"Don't know for sure, but I haven't spotted a one coming or going in that direction."

"What about sentries?"

"Not a hundred percent certain, but there've been no signs of any. These guys are so certain no harm's going to befall them that I doubt putting out sentries would've crossed their minds."

"So most likely those we see are all there is. With no other way to access the building, looks like we've little choice but to take them out—and do it fast if we're going to reach those girls."

"It's a pretty big group, Aaron. Do you think we can handle so many on our own?"

"What choice do we have? We can and we will," Porter said, trying to sound more confident than he actually felt. He spotted a huge pile of automatic weapons thirty yards from where the revolting revelry was taking place. Some in their number were holding their rifles, occasionally stopping to fire frenzied bursts into the air to punctuate the ruinous festivities. He took a rapid count of those in front of the burning school holding AK-47s. It was less than a dozen. "Look over on the right. Most of them left their weapons at the edge of that little stream. With us catching them by surprise, they'll be too far away to reach them before we cut down the majority of the bastards."

"Sounds good to me," Sanders replied.

"Fareeda, stay here. Hide in the grass and wait. If we don't come back, don't move until dark. Then head back to our encampment. Find Captain Short, the man I was talking to when you were with me, and tell him what happened. Do you understand what I'm telling you? Stay here until it's dark then go back to the plateau. You got that?"

She nodded her head yes. The reality of the ghastly scene around the school was clinging to her like a ghoulish spirit. Its unrelenting grip was all-encompassing.

In a low crouch that shielded the circumspect duo from the careless eyes of those below, they moved forward. Three hundred yards from the assailed building, still undetected, Porter and Sanders stopped.

"I'll start with the ones nearest the doors," Porter said. "You've got the big grouping closest to the stream. Focus on taking out those holding rifles. Once they figure out we're here, the majority are bound to head toward the pile of AK-47s lying by the stream. Be ready for that. Cut down as many as you can before they get their hands on those weapons. We might not be able to get them all before that happens, but I'd sure like to eliminate as many as we can."

"I'll handle it," Sanders replied through clenched teeth as he stared at the unholy display. "Those sorry excuses are as good as dead."

Porter could feel Sanders's anger rising and the determination in his dark eyes. He'd only seen Charlie this incensed on a handful of occasions, and each time it had made his partner more lethal than he already was.

The talented Americans began zeroing in on the bountiful targets. Even from so great a distance, few of their apt shots would miss. On many an occasion, beneath the unrelenting pressure of the fiercest combat, Porter had put a hole in the center of the smallest of targets from farther away than this. With so many from which to choose, it didn't take long to select their initial victims. There were sixty rounds between them in their fully loaded magazines. Ten more than they'd need if none of the bullets missed. It was possible their actions would be so precise that neither would need to reload before they'd finished destroying the sadists below the rise.

"Ready?" Porter said.

"Yep."

"Now!" Porter fired an exceptionally accurate three-shot burst at a tightly bunched grouping clutching rifles ten feet from the burning school's door. Three sorrowful individuals, their rapturous celebration halted in midmovement, went down. Their AK-47s fell from their hands. The first had taken a bullet between the eyes. He was dead before his buckling knees touched the sandy soil. The second, the taller of the fated threesome, was hit in the center of his chest, the bullet striking his fourth rib a glancing blow and tearing through his heart. He was still breathing but wouldn't be for long. A few seconds, no more, and his heaving image would stop its fruitless efforts. The final bullet went into an exposed neck, crushing the twisted image's larynx, severing the spine, and paralyzing its victim. He sprawled in the dirt beside his mortal comrades, his suffering beyond description. His confused eyes, uncertain of what had occurred, stared skyward.

Two of the rounds, without slowing in the slightest, found further homes. One crushed an exposed thighbone in a second victim, while the other ripped through the gaunt belly of the wayward being next to him. Those with leg and gut wounds also fell into the clinging dirt, wailing in unspeakable distress. Blood spurted from both wounds. With a trio of rounds Porter had slain two, with another near death and a pair severely wounded. It was a result that didn't surprise the practiced Green Beret in the slightest. He'd expected no less and, in fact, was disappointed he hadn't been able to do more damage with his initial attempt.

A passing fraction after his teammate, Sanders added to the startling aggression. A quick squeeze and three rounds headed for the ill-minded creatures carrying rifles on the southern edges of the gathering. With stunning results, another tight grouping of bullets had found their mark. Because of the noise emanating from the depraved merriment drowning out the world around them, not one in the stained valley had heard the stinging sounds.

None of the additional prey settling into Porter's sights had reacted to the bizarre actions of their fallen comrades. It took the

American weapons specialist less than a fleeting moment to find his next quarry. The Special Forces marksman fired again. Three shots . . . three kills for the virulent sniper. Two additional forms holding rifles near the tormented schoolhouse, and a third without one, went down.

Sanders grabbed hold of those he would assault next. Satisfied with the targets he'd selected, he squeezed the trigger a second time. As he did, many of the evildoers suddenly registered that something had gone horribly wrong. Still, it was much too late for most to react. A fourth trio went down. All but two of those clutching rifles had been eliminated.

With devastating effect, Porter fired again. Sanders followed. The dead and dying continued to mount. A horrid reality grabbed those who had so far survived. They had no idea who was assaulting them, but they all understood that they were in serious trouble. Many, out of their minds with fear, scattered to the four winds before realizing their only hope was reaching the stream and the redeeming weapons nestled there. While Sanders and Porter cut them down, they ran toward the muddy bank. Thirty yards away lay their sole chance for salvation. Yet for every yard of ground, one or more of the frantic figures fell beneath the relentless siege. Round after round spewed from the Americans' rifles. In ten seconds, two-thirds of their overmatched opponents had been struck.

While the duo fired burst after burst at their terrified bounty, a curling smile came to Porter's lips. This was going better than he could have imagined. They'd caught the misguided creatures unprepared. So far, not one had gotten off an effective round. And with their weapons scattered along the bloodying waters, it was unlikely any would reach them in time to do so. Maybe the relentlessly firing duo would emerge victorious soon enough to have a chance of finding some alive within the ravaged building.

———

Sanders gave the flaming door a kick. The deteriorating door-frame gave way. The entrance flew open wide. The instant it did, roaring fires burst forth. Sanders leaped back as the flames reached out to lick at his staggering image. He could feel the intense temperatures assailing him. He realized in a passing instant that no one could have survived so fierce an inferno. He could sense all hope slipping way.

"Hello!" he yelled. "Anyone?" No response greeted him. Shielding his face, he got as close to the fiery doorway as he dared. He did his best to peer inside the modest room, but with the fearsome blaze blocking his view, he could see little more than a few feet into the structure. And could do so only for the briefest of intervals. The roaring fire was consuming everything.

He'd never be certain what he saw and would always deny what his mind was relaying in those dread-devoured moments. But there were multiple bodies, smaller than adult size, on the scorched floor. There was the pungent smell of burning flesh. And there was nothing more he and Porter could do.

The pair led the inconsolable girl away from the dismal setting. With her hands covering her face and Porter cradling her as she walked, the somber trio continued on. When they were certain she could no longer see the horrific scene, they stopped.

Sanders mouthed to Porter, "What're we going to do with her?"

The senior sergeant shrugged. He looked into her eyes. "Fareeda, your home's over by that lake, right?"

Through gasping breaths she answered. "Yes."

Porter weighed his options, trying to decide if he should risk taking her there. "Maybe we should bring you to your family, where you'll be safe. Do you think if we wait until dark it'll be possible to reach your village without being seen?"

"Yes. But it'll do no good."

"Why not?"

"Because I no longer have a family. I no longer have a village. When the first Fedayeen came through the valley, they demanded my father and all the men join their army. When those in my village refused, they killed them. They then killed everyone else. My father, mother, grandmother, brothers, and sister are dead. If I hadn't been at school, they would've killed me too."

"Are you certain of this?"

"I'm certain. Our teacher sent one of the older girls to check on them. When she returned, she told us what she found."

"Do you have somewhere you can go? Somewhere we can take you? A friend or someone?"

She shook her head. "No. They killed them all. There's no one left and nowhere for me."

They brought the anguished girl back to Mishira. They couldn't leave her where she'd be at the mercy of the next deviants to wander through the area. It was obvious the defenseless girl was in shock. None of the three said a word throughout the mournful trip back to the plateau.

48

Sitting on the edge of the makeshift bed, Erickson grimaced as he bent down to tie his boots. With his left arm essentially useless, it had taken multiple attempts and far too long for him to put on his uniform. Yet now he faced a task he couldn't accomplish alone. "Lauren, would you do me a favor and tie my boots?"

Standing over him, Wells's disapproval spread across her face. "Sam, you shouldn't be doing this," she said. "You're not ready. The doctors said you could reopen your wounds and do yourself a great deal of harm if you insist on leaving the hospital."

"Doesn't matter. I'm not waiting one minute more before I return to my men. For a week I've been trapped in this bed, listening to the sounds of battle without being able to do anything about it. I've laid here watching as they brought in one wounded Marine after another. Enough is enough. I need to be out there. I can't command my company from where I am. So please do what I ask and help me with my boots."

"All right," she said as she reluctantly bent down to do what he'd requested. "I love you so much, Sam. And because of that, there's no way I want you to do this. But I know you too well. Once you make up your mind, there's nothing anyone can do to stop you."

Lauren's efforts completed, Erickson staggered to his feet. He fought with all he had against the light-headedness that threatened to devour him. He paused, waiting for the overpowering feeling to pass. Finally, he reached over and picked up his rifle. Ready to return to the command bunker, he took a severely limping step toward the door. His stiff movements were beyond unsteady. His struggles couldn't be missed. On his own he was unlikely to make it to the doorway without falling. Without assistance, he had no chance of reaching the distant bunker.

Lauren looked over at MaKenna. Her tiny form was curled up on the floor beneath a thick blanket as she took a fitful afternoon nap. "Will you at least let me help you get out to the command bunker?"

"What about MaKenna?"

"I'll have Chuck watch her while I'm gone."

Although the distance from the hospital to the main gate was scarcely one hundred yards, it took the struggling pair ten minutes to arrive. Lauren leaned against the battered wall next to the gate, pausing to catch her breath. Fifty yards to the command bunker. Outside, there were the sounds of distant gunfire. Once they left the high walls, both recognized there was always the possibility of a stray bullet finding them. Yet for the moment, the world in front of them seemed relatively secure.

Inside the bunker, Corporal Genovese snapped to attention as he saw Erickson and Wells entering. Next to him a partially recovered Gunny Joyce did likewise.

His attention focused on a minor skirmish taking place on the edge of the Marines' western defenses, Scott Tomlin had his back turned to the arriving pair. It took a few seconds for him to sense someone had entered the enclosure. He turned to see who was there. To his surprise, it was the company commander, along with Lauren Wells.

"Oh, sir, I didn't see you there," he said. He could see the first signs of fresh blood on Erickson bandages and a growing hint of it on his pant leg. He looked at Wells. "Last time we spoke, you said the doctors had indicated it'd be a few more days before they'd even consider letting him out of bed. Said if he did so, it might kill him."

"That's exactly what they said. But you know Sam: the only counsel he's going to listen to is his own. And his advice was to head out here and take that chance."

"Hey, if it kills me, it kills me," Erickson replied with an air of indifference. "It's a risk I need to take. There are more important things to worry about than whether I should be here. I've no doubt you've done an incredible job in leading the company in my absence, Scott, but these are my men and I need to be with them."

"Understood, sir," Tomlin said. "In your position I'd probably feel the same way. But with Gunny Joyce's and Corporal Genovese's help we've been more than capable of handling things for the past few days." He took a look at his company commander. There was no mistaking how miserable Erickson felt. "We've got this. For your own good, you really should return to the hospital for a few more days. Just until the doctors give you the go-ahead."

Erickson, the crippling pain intense, would never have admitted it, but he could stand no more. He reached out and, with Lauren's help, sat down on the edge of one of the bunker's stiff cots. Once he was settled, he felt a thousand times better. He ignored Tomlin's pleas. "Why don't you get me up to speed on what's happened while I was gone," Erickson said.

"Absolutely, sir. . . . We're holding on okay. Each night's airdrops have, to varying degrees, been successful. So we've got plenty of ammunition, along with adequate food and water."

"Few problems with the resupplies, then?" Erickson asked.

"I wouldn't say that, sir. The drops have been good but certainly not perfect. Didn't take long for the Fedayeen to figure out what we were up to and to do what they could to interrupt them. We've lost more than a few of those who were brave enough to go into the fields to retrieve the supplies. We're doing all we can to protect them while they work, but it's nearly impossible with the parachutes landing all over the place. Even so, over eighty percent of the stuff the C-130s have brought has reached us. Last couple of nights have included a trio of Humvees in each load. So we've been able to add a half dozen .50-calibers to our defenses to make up for those we've lost. Another three are being included in tonight's lading. So while the number of defenders continue to fall, in some ways we're growing stronger."

"How many significant attacks have there been?"

"Not one, sir. Nothing even close. After what the Apaches did to them, we suspect the bastards recognized the hell that would befall them if they attempted to do so. With the Apaches supporting us, the Fedayeen have been forced to change their tactics. Now it's a constant stream of small skirmishes probing for weak points. So far it's been nothing we can't handle. Even though we're surrounded by a massive force, they're now attacking by the dozens rather than the thousands. They understand anything larger and the death from the skies will return. So rather than our losing large numbers in massive attacks, they've been picking us off in ones and twos. Even the slightest mistakes have cost us."

"How many Marines are still in the fight?"

"Around seventy or so, sir. Along with that, there are twice that number from the supporting countries and a couple hundred civilian defenders out on the line. Steven Gray has trained at least that many more on how to handle an automatic weapon. They're ready and waiting whenever we request their assistance. So far we haven't needed more than about a quarter of them. So we're holding most in reserve to handle attrition as it occurs."

"Of the six thousand, how many people have we lost?"

"Hard to keep up, sir, but it was about fifteen hundred at last count. With the twelve hundred we were able to evacuate on the first two nights, that leaves us with about thirty-three hundred waiting for us to find a way out of here."

"Fifteen hundred," Erickson said as he pondered the implications. "At this rate, few of us will be alive a month from now."

"Yes, sir," Tomlin replied. "But there's been some good news on that front. Help's on the way—or at least it should be in the next week or so. President committed to entering this war. Two Army divisions are headed to Pakistan. Supposed to reach Karachi within the week. British and French are joining them. Once they do, they're going to hit Basra with everything they've got. First priority will be getting to Islamabad."

"How long before they'll reach us?"

"They're hoping to arrive here by the end of the month."

"End of the month?"

"Yes, sir. Give or take a few days."

"What day is it?"

"The eleventh."

"So hold on for nineteen days."

"Yes, sir, nineteen more or less."

"Can we last that long, Scott?"

"We'll need some luck, sir. But it's possible. If our forces reach Karachi when they're supposed to, we've got some chance of saving many of the people who remain."

"Then let's cross our fingers and hope for that luck. Anything else I need to know?"

"Not that I can think of, sir."

"Okay. Why don't you go into the embassy and grab some sleep. I'll take over out here for now."

"You sure, sir?"

"Absolutely. And should I run into any problems, Joyce and Genovese will be here."

Tomlin began gathering his gear. He'd done his best to talk his commander out of this. There was nothing more he could do. He grabbed his rifle.

As he did, Erickson said, "And, Scott?"

"Yes, sir?"

"Great job in my absence."

"Thank you, sir."

Tomlin headed out of the command bunker. When he was gone, Wells looked into Joyce's eyes. "Promise me, if he starts to falter, you'll let me know right away."

"Yes, ma'am," he replied.

"That's a direct order, Gunny," she said. "I don't care how much he protests: Don't let him do himself further harm without help arriving. If you do, you'll be answering to me."

"Understood, ma'am."

She gave Erickson a gentle kiss on the forehead. "Stay alive, Sam." She let go of his arm, turned, and started toward the main gate. She hadn't gone ten yards when a wayward round whizzed past her right ear. It smashed into the embassy's wall.

49

Around the encampment, nervous sentries roamed. It wasn't the threat from an outside source that worried them. It was the possibility of Salim Basra showing his disdain for their real or imagined failures that lay heavy upon the guards' every action. The result would be death for any their leader perceived hadn't performed in the manner he desired.

In the southern portion of the camp, nearly one hundred shivering couriers slept in their cars and pickups, waiting for the next assignment. With Basra banning even the smallest fires, it was the warmest place to shelter from the elements. The Fedayeen leader, in his growing paranoia, had moved his command element higher into the magnificent snow-covered mountains. Convinced that every passing cloud was an American drone coming to devour him, the wandering bands' movements were growing more erratic and unpredictable. They seldom stayed in a location longer than it took for a quick uncooked meal and a brief nap.

Filled with beautiful, sparkling lakes and jagged, snow-crested mountains, the area was beyond breathtaking. None of Basra's leadership, however, paid the slightest attention to the incredible world around them.

As they had swept across the mountains, plains, and valleys, all but one of those present were convinced their conquest was a certainty. Their rapturous victory was close at hand. A new fundamentalist Islamic state, returning the country to the ways of earlier centuries, would take hold. Yet a harsh reality had set in. None had believed they could be defeated, and for most those fervent views remained. They'd wear down the foreigners cowering in Islamabad along with the Pakistani units in the south. But from their mounting setbacks all now understood this was going to be more difficult than they had imagined.

While they had roared across the country, only Bila Chachar recognized the makeup of their forces and their approach to conquest contained within them potentially fatal flaws. He was aware that many populist uprisings had overcome their internal weaknesses and prevailed. Still, he understood that most had crumbled from within. He'd spent the past weeks trying to make Basra understand what it would take not only to seize Pakistan but to hold on to what they'd conquered. The narcissistic leader, however, took advice from no one. Certain of his infallibility, he wouldn't listen to the one man among them who could provide him with the greatest chance for victory.

Well into his middle years, Chachar was one of the few with the ability to read and write. Having served as a battalion commander in the Pakistani army in his younger years, he was the only individual with an understanding of modern warfare. And twenty-first-century life. He was the sole person in Basra's inner circle who hadn't grown up in the primitive tribal territories. Chachar had been born in Karachi to a moneyed merchant family. He'd attended the finest schools. To his family's displeasure, his final military assignment had caused him to fall in love with a girl half his age from the sparsely populated mountains. Willing to do anything to be with her, he had resigned his commission and, despite being disowned, had wed the girl and moved to one of the most backwards places on the planet. For the past twenty years he had remained there, slowly earning the trust of those whose fear of outsiders was extreme.

Since the war's earliest hours, he'd been trying to warn Basra. Their crude tactics had worked well in surprising and over-whelming a discouraged Pakistani military. But Bila recognized even with the millions fighting beneath their banner they wouldn't prevail against any well-organized force rising up to face them. The startling news they'd received in the past hour confirmed what Chachar had been saying.

Basra's younger son, Kashif, had returned with an unsettling report that the destruction of the American embassy and the slaughter of all who sheltered within wasn't complete. After hearing that the heretics' bastion still stood, the Fedayeen leader had flown into a rage. It was a predictable behavior all had seen often.

That anger had grown when his older son, Muhsin, arrived with the news that the Pakistani army had rallied in the south. They'd formed a defensive ring around Karachi that none of the jihadists' attacks, no matter how extreme, had been able to defeat.

Wrapped in coarse blankets as a defense against the snow that had been falling all day, they gathered in the center of the camp. There was deep worry on every face. The would-be despot turned to his youngest son and spit out his accusatory words. "Explain yourself, Kashif. Why do you return with such information? You were ordered to verify the nonbelievers were dead. It was your job to make sure our commanders finished the task. Yet you've failed. The embassy still stands. The reviled ones still live."

"Father, you need to be reasonable. Last week I observed a

major attempt to breach the American walls. Our men fought bravely. Still, no matter what we tried, we were unable to penetrate the enemy's defenses. Your commanders are doing their best. From the first night, they'd anticipated the defeat of those whose presence stains this land. But the enemy's resistance has been more rigorous than any of our fighters were prepared for. Those who oppose us now have a significant force of attack helicopters supporting them. So we've had no choice but to modify or efforts in order to avoid the senseless slaughter of thousands more of Allah's chosen."

"Helicopters? From where did such things come? Were they Pakistani? Indian? Who? From where have they received such help?"

"Our commanders don't know. All markings on them had been painted over. But they believed they were likely American. From where they'd come, we've no idea. All we know is every time we attempt an attack of any size, they appear in the skies above us."

"I don't care. There can be no excuses. You're to return at once and take the heads of our commanders who've failed. Those who replace them are to understand they'll meet the same fate if they don't destroy the defiled ones who mock Allah. They've three days to do as I've ordered."

"Father, please. I beg you not to do this. It's not our commanders' fault. I've seen the heretics' defenses. They're quite stout. And those inside their walls have been able to respond to every attack. We've no idea where they came from, but there's little doubt their efforts are being led by American Marines supported by soldiers from many countries. In the past days, the attack helicopters have joined them to thwart our every attempt. We've killed and wounded many, but none of that has weakened their resolve. Everything we've tried has failed. The tanks you sent to finish them were destroyed. To make matters worse, many of our men are out of ammunition. Most haven't eaten in days. I fear to report our commanders believe as much as ten percent have become disillusioned and slipped away. They're doing what they can to keep the rest from deserting, but no matter what they try, things are growing worse."

"Kashif's correct, Father," Muhsin added. "It's the same on the southern battlefields. Our commanders are doing their best. But our fighters are hungry and low on ammunition. For many, their belief in our sainted cause is wavering."

After hearing Basra's sons, Chachar knew time was running out. He had to intercede. He had to turn what was little more than a vengeful mob into an actual army. Or all would be lost. The first step he needed to take was to create a rudimentary logistics system capable of supporting an army in the field. Hungry soldiers without ammunition, no matter how motivated, would have little choice but to eventually turn their backs and walk away.

Bila had to choose his words carefully if he was going to get Basra to commit to doing what was needed. No matter what, he had to avoid chastising the ravenous egotist in front of the others. They could still win. But that wasn't going to happen without becoming far more organized. Taking what you needed by pillaging and plundering had been fine in the initial stages. Even so, once the ragtag army was no longer on the move, the fatal defects in such an approach were exposed. If he could get Basra's sons on his side, maybe, just maybe, their half-crazed father would relent and let him do what needed to be done.

"Despite what you've told us," Chachar said while looking at Basra's sons, "stalemated or not, we'll win. And we'll do so soon. But for that to happen, we need to provide our fighters with food and ammunition without delay. Believe it or not, our efforts under our great leader, Salim Basra, were actually too successful. We conquered with ease. We moved too fast. No army, even one as powerful as ours, can take to the field without a system in place to support their efforts. Now that we've met significant resistance, we need to come up with a system to keep our men supplied. Such an approach will allow us to provide our fighters with the things they need to complete the final conquest. If we can create such a system, victory is ours."

Such a plan, even in its simplest form, was beyond anything those gathered around him could conceive. None had ever had to think beyond the limits of their modest villages and the here and now. Fortunately, Chachar had no such limitations. He'd thought through a basic but workable system he could get even the most backward to understand.

"How do you propose doing what you suggest?" Muhsin asked.

"I'd suspected there might be a need for such a plan. I've been working on it for a while now. It'll put both food and additional ammunition in the hands of every Fedayeen fighter—and do so within two days. It'll continue to provide such supplies for as long as is required." He turned and looked at those present. "But I cannot do this alone. I'll need the help of each of you." This time Bila looked directly at Basra. "If you'll allow me to use most of those present to implement what I have in mind, we can begin this moment to overcome our limitations and finish this war. We can make you the ruler of the new Islamic country you've envisioned."

There was a look of disapproval on Basra's face. He trusted no one. It was obvious he was suspicious of what was being presented. More than anything, the idea of turning any of his absolute control over to his second-in-command went against everything the harsh tribal dictator believed.

At just the right moment, Muhsin came to Chachar's aid. "Father, I don't know if Bila's plan will work, but he's correct in his assessment. I've seen the situation on the battlefields. We must do something or risk our eventual defeat."

"Father, please understand. We need to do this," Kashif added.

There was an uncomfortable silence as Basra fought against his instincts to ignore all counsel but his own. Even so, it was apparent those present were buying into Bila's assessment.

"Are you certain your plan will work?" he asked.

Chachar gave him an honest answer. "Certain? No. There are no certainties in war. But if we can pull off what I have in mind, it'll give us a real chance of conquering all who stand against us."

There was little enthusiasm in Basra's answer. "Then you have my blessing." Basra looked into the faces of the forty or so gathered. "You're to make yourselves available to Bila Chachar. That includes my sons. His orders are my orders. Follow them to the letter. There'll be no hesitation on your part. Is that clear?" When none responded, he said, "I'll leave you to your work." He turned and left.

He'd never been usurped and didn't like it happening now. But, for once, he'd been outmaneuvered. Nevertheless, he didn't let his displeasure show.

Chachar's influence was growing. And the danger he'd pose to Basra's absolute sway was undeniable. He'd left his sons under Bila's command for a reason. They'd act as his eyes and ears. Eventually, he'd have to deal with the threat posed by his talented second-in-command. It was time to begin planning how, when the time was right and he no longer needed him, he'd bring about Chachar's end.

50

There wasn't a moment to spare. Chachar motioned for those present to gather around him. "Okay, we have immediate, medium-, and long-term problems needing to be addressed if we're going to prevail. So we're going to break into three teams to handle them. Kashif will lead those who are assigned to the immediate problem."

Basra's younger son nodded, trying to act nonchalant. Nonetheless, a growing smile belayed his satisfaction at being given a leadership role. Although in his midtwenties, his father continued to treat him like an ignorant child. Chachar, however, had selected him to command a major portion of the highly important plan, and it pleased Kashif greatly. It was the perfect opportunity for him to prove to his father who he really was.

"I'll lead the medium-term group," Chachar said. "And Muhsin will command those who're to address our long-term issues."

He looked at those gathered. He needed to ensure at least one in each group could read so they could interpret the details of what he'd created for the others.

"In group one will be Kashif, Omar, Mohammad, Ali, Hakim..." When he finished calling out ten names, he named his group. "With me will be Uday, Ahmed, Rashid . . . With Muhsin will be . . . Let's start with our immediate needs, those things we must complete in the next two or three days. Soldiers with taut bellies and no ammunition have little taste for the fight. We must come up with a way to bring weapons, fuel, and ammunition along with food and water to those on the front lines. If we fail to do so, the desertions could get out of hand and our army disintegrate. That task will be the responsibility of Kashif and his team. I want those in Kashif's group to form a circle around me so we can go over what you're to do. My group should stand behind them with Muhsin's men forming the outer ring."

Chachar took a number of hand-drawn maps out of his knapsack and unfolded them. He spread them on the ground and sat down behind them. "Kashif's men, come closer so you can see what I've drawn."

Bila indicated that he wanted Kashif to sit on his right, in the place of honor. All could see the pages included a number of brightly colored stars and a great deal of information. He turned to Kashif and those assigned to him. "Your role's going to be to solve our immediate problem. It's critical that you do so. You cannot fail. Without you, we stand no chance. You have to begin delivering supplies to our men in the next forty-eight hours. You must provide our fighters with what they need to sustain them for the next five days. In doing so, you'll give me adequate time to set up a logistical system to keep them supplied as they move forward to defeat our enemies."

Kashif smiled. His importance, and Bila's faith in him, was there for all to see. Now was his chance to prove his worth.

"The top two maps I've created," Chachar continued, "one page for the northeast and one for the south, will guide your actions. There are five red stars on both pages. Can all of you see them?" He looked at those in Kashif's cadre. The inner circle, their interest piqued, all nodded.

"Each indicates where one of you will place your headquarters to coordinate the actions in your area. Kashif, once we've talked about what this part of the plan entails, you'll need to take both maps and hand out the assignments."

Kashif nodded once again. Every mention of his name filled him with pride. Even if his father couldn't see his potential, Bila Chachar did.

"Here's what I want you to do," Chachar said, looking straight at him. "Within the hour, send couriers to our field commanders. Those you send are to tell them they are acting under the direct authority of Salim Basra. Each is to take twenty percent of that commander's forces. Those they gather are to go with the couriers to the nearest designated point I've drawn on the map. Those locations are strategically placed a few miles behind our lines. There they'll meet up with one of your team. Once you have your men, you're to seize as many jingle trucks as you can get your hands on. Is that clear?"

"Yes," all mumbled. Most still had little idea what Bila had in mind.

"All we require is within reach. As our fighters conquered, they took what they needed from the Pakistani army units they destroyed and the villages they passed through. But they could only take what they could carry. They had no choice but to leave the remainder behind. In our haste to defeat the army, we bypassed many towns and villages. The food in those locations remains untouched. Huge sources for what we desire remain in hundreds and hundreds of places across the countryside." He could see a light coming on in their eyes.

"Such is true," Kashif said. "When I've traveled to the front lines, I've seen exactly what you describe. What we must obtain is within our grasp. All we have to do is claim it."

Bila smiled. "You'll need at least one truck for every two hundred men you must supply. So make sure you have plenty of trucks. Send men with each truck to load them. Go to the nearest villages and the abandoned battlefields closest to our front lines. Seize what you need. Go to the places nearby where major battles occurred. Strip bare the rotting bodies, taking every weapon, bullet, hand grenade, and canteen. Collect anything that can be of use. As each truck is filled with food and ammunition, send it to the front lines so our men can see the things they need are on the way. Make sure every soldier is supplied with enough to last them until the end of the week. By then, my actions to keep them supplied in the foreseeable future will be underway."

"We'll make it happen," Kashif replied.

"Then do so now, there's no time to waste." He handed the maps to Kashif.

When the first group got up and walked away, intent on selecting their assignments and gathering their messengers, Bila wasted no time. He spread the next two pieces of paper on the ground. Like the previous ones, there were drawings and stars.

"Come in closer," he said to those he'd directly command. He'd done his best to pick the ten he felt were most capable. "Our role's going to be to establish a logistics system to keep our forces supplied for however long is necessary to complete our triumph. While Kashif's people strip clean the areas nearest the front lines, we'll range farther out. We'll start with the portions of our country Kashif doesn't touch. We'll work our way back from there, scouring for hundreds of kilometers if we need to. There can be no limits to how far we'll reach to find what our soldiers need. Your first assignment will be to identify a location in the section of the map I'll assign you. There you're to create a supply depot. It'll need to be a much larger operation than that of the short-term fix Kashif will be providing. Find a secluded place away from prying eyes. Then send your couriers deep into the countryside to locate jingle trucks. Find any soldiers we've left in those areas. You'll need a significant supply of both trucks and men. Is that clear?"

"Yes," the ten he'd selected said.

"Once you have them, send some of the men and half the trucks to gather supplies. At the same time, you'll need a number of couriers whose task it will be to go to the battlefronts, meet with our commanders, and identify their continuing needs. Keep a final, third group with you to work the supply center you're establishing. At the depots their job will be to take the supplies from the arriving trucks, sort what's coming in, and load the trucks headed for our field commands. You're to work this process night and day. There can be no pause. There can be no end. It's your responsibility to keep our fighters supplied. You've five days, no more, to begin supplying our men. Can you handle such a task?" He looked at them one by one, waiting for them to respond.

"Yes," was the answer from each.

"Good. Go pack your belongings and identify which of our couriers you wish to take with you. I'll join you as soon as I brief Muhsin's men on their assignments."

Once again, a group of ten got up and left. Chachar motioned, and the final gathering took their places around him. He took an additional set of maps and laid them out.

"Muhsin, eventually my men will exhaust the supplies we can lay their hands on. We'll have cleaned out every battlefield and town we can reach. That's where you and your team come in. Your job will be to establish a long-term system to keep us supplied once we have conquered and have settled into ruling this land. You'll need to establish routes, gather thousands of trucks, and seize supplies to sustain our new Islamic government for the years to come. You'll have to create massive supply distribution centers with huge warehouses in every corner of this land. On this map, I've created ten zones for doing so. Assign one of your followers to each and have them begin developing the long-term logistical setup we'll need. Once you've completed that and we've gained total control, we can look at creating better ways of communicating and creating the infrastructure needed to effectively rule. So it's critical you get your system in place in the coming weeks. Your father's a great wartime leader, but it'll be up to us to make sure his leadership translates into a system of government that'll work once the final bullet's fired."

Muhsin knew Chachar was correct. His father's way of ruling an isolated village with a few hundred people wouldn't work when it came to controlling over two hundred million. He also understood his father was going to resist every suggestion Bila proposed. But he was more than willing to stand at Chachar's side when he was needed.

"Okay, we'll begin working on that," Muhsin said as he stared at the maps. "There are bound to be issues that come up. When they do, where can I find you?"

"I've got something I need to do before heading out to set up the northeast's primary supply depot. Going to locate some things along the way to deliver to Islamabad. Will take me a dozen or so hours to do so. Then I'll be heading out to set up the process we talked about. I don't know exactly where I'm going to establish my own supply center, but it should be somewhere in this area." He pointed to a spot on the map. "Send messengers out to find me when questions arise."

When Muhsin and his team walked away, Chachar headed over to those he hadn't selected to work on the logistics teams. It didn't take long to find the person he wanted. "Rana Lanaki, may I speak with you, please?" Chachar started moving away. What he was about to tell Rana wasn't for any ears but his.

Lanaki had considered himself to be one of Chachar's most trusted advisers. He'd been more than disappointed when his name hadn't been called. Until that moment, he'd believed Bila to be a friend.

"Yes, of course," Lanaki said.

He followed Chachar across the clearing. When they were far enough away, Chachar stopped. In a low voice he said, "This is for only you to hear."

Lanaki signaled his understanding.

"You're to gather fifteen men and get ready to move. Pick some who are willing to work hard and ask few questions. Gather on the far side of the camp as soon as all are ready."

Lanaki knew better than to ask why. "It will be done," he said.

"I have a special assignment for you."

Within minutes, the first of the couriers headed out. They were going to the front lines to gather the force Kashif needed. In a steady stream, others started their vehicles. In less than an hour, much of the camp emptied.

Bila waited, answering last-minute questions and ensuring the operation got underway. The moment the last departed, he headed over to where Rana Lanaki and those he'd gathered were waiting. After verifying that their sadistic leader wasn't watching, they loaded into three small pickups and headed out. Those with him had no way of knowing where they were heading. Or what they were being tasked to do.

The Fedayeen's second-in-command had a huge grin on his face as they departed. He'd done his best to overcome the obstacles Basra had created. Chachar's plan had given their disheveled army an opportunity to continue their successes. What he had no way of knowing was that his rabble were only days away from facing the bloodiest battles of the war. They'd soon encounter an overpowering foe in the mountains, fields, and forests of their war-torn country. One for which Chachar hadn't prepared.

The Americans, French, and British were on the way. Once they arrived, the true battle for the devolving nation would be upon them.

51

Bila Chachar hadn't asked Basra for permission to do what he was doing. Nor did he care. He needed to get the supply system established, but there was something he was compelled to accomplish first. He'd come up with what he believed was a foolproof plan to destroy the American embassy and those cowering inside. And he didn't want Basra foiling it. He had little doubt his vainglorious leader would shoot it down because of arrogance alone. He'd reluctantly allowed Chachar to take charge of the development of the logistics system. Yet Chachar knew Basra all too well. And he recognized that would be as far as he'd go. There was little chance he'd let him do more. So Chachar said nothing and went forward with the concept on his own.

With him were the fifteen men Rana had selected. While they walked onto what had been a major battlefield, there were signs of carnage everywhere. Lots of abandoned Pakistani equipment lay strewn about with few discernible patterns to the madness. Some of it was little more than burned-out metal husks of no use to anyone. Others, however, had endured scarcely more than minor damage before the Pakistani army ran away.

While Chachar walked through the decomposing bodies and discarded equipment, it didn't take long to spot what he needed. There were a dozen military trucks in disarray not far away. "Go over there and see if you can get those trucks started," he directed Rana's men. "We can use as many as are in working order."

His force scurried over to the scattered trucks. One had a massive hole through its engine block. Another appeared to be in better shape but wouldn't start. The engine on the third turned right over.

They went through them one by one. In the end, having endured the furious battle, three were in working order. Each was driven to where Chachar waited. When they arrived, the driver of the first looked down and said, "These are the only ones that would start."

Chachar took a look around the vast killing ground. He found no other trucks large enough to be of use. "Three trucks. I guess they'll have to do. I spotted some howitzers at the far end of the battlefield. Let's head over to where they are. Hopefully, we can find three in working order and ample shells to go with them." He jumped into the passenger seat. "After that, we'll gather all the camouflage netting we can find and take it with us."

Towing the massive guns, they'd swung around the outskirts of the city. Darkness was settling. Seven miles south of the embassy grounds Chachar located the perfect spot. To the right, a wide jumble of shattered rocks, twisted steel, and assailed concrete from a once-magnificent high-rise formed a cave-like area running for sixty yards in both directions. It was deep enough to cover the sixteen-foot barrels of the huge guns.

He'd hide the howitzers there. "Stop here," he directed.

The driver did as he was told. The other trucks eased in behind it. In addition to pulling the howitzers, each truck was loaded with 155mm artillery shells. Given the unmovable obstacles in front of them, there was no way they could get the trucks any closer.

"Have our men get out and disconnect the howitzers. Once they have, they're to drag them over there." He pointed to where he wanted Rana to place them.

It took a mammoth effort to make it even a few feet through the distorted scene with each impressive weapon. Working them over or around every waiting barrier, every piece of mangled steel or jagged boulder, was an immense undertaking. But with brute force and unwavering determination, inch by inch they fought their way across the grotesque maze.

It took an hour, but finally the first was sitting at the edge of the cavernous opening. One at a time, they worked with the remaining guns. Finally, after a great deal of time and a stringent amount of toil, the third reached the critical spot. They slid them into the hole, positioning each precisely. When they were finished, Chachar was more than satisfied with the results. Within the ponderous cavern, the artillery pieces were well hidden with only a small portion of their barrels showing. Even so, they could be fired with ease, with plenty of space for the recoil created by each soaring round.

With a low-slung, hazy moon shining down upon them, he looked at their handiwork. He turned to Rana Lanaki. "Very good. Couldn't have worked out better. From this point on I want you to take charge. Have your men unload the shells and bring them over here. Focus on emptying the initial truck first so I can leave as soon as possible. When they've unloaded all three, have them finish the job by placing the camouflage netting over the guns. The way we've positioned them, they're almost impossible to find. With the netting, it'll take a miracle to see them from the air."

"It will be done," Lanaki responded.

"Drive the remaining trucks away from here. That way they won't lead the American helicopters to this place."

"The moment they're unloaded, I'll do so."

"Just one more thing."

"What's that?"

"We'll need men with experience in operating howitzers. Shouldn't take long to locate some among the Pakistani soldiers who've joined us. I want them to open fire in the morning."

"I'll make that happen," Rana replied.

"Fire only during daylight to avoid the muzzle flashes giving their position away. Fire for a few minutes at a time. And never when the American helicopters are nearby. Make your attacks unpredictable. Vary the time and number of rounds to limit the enemy's ability to find you."

Rana nodded. "This, too, will be done. I'll see to finding those to operate the guns and make sure they understand your orders." He looked up, ready to take charge. "Get the shells out of the first truck and bring them here," he directed his exhausted men.

Each got up and plodded toward the rear of the truck. A pair climbed up and began passing the monstrous shells down. With each weighing ninety-five pounds, carrying them the thirty scrambling feet was going to involve another intense struggle. But the peasants were accustomed to backbreaking labor. So while the task wasn't easy, they didn't complain at all. Shell after shell was soon being piled inside the man-made bunker. With hundreds to unload, it would take untold torturous journeys before the last would reach the sheltering hole. It was after midnight before the first truck was emptied.

"Once all the trucks are gone and everything's in place, I want you to create significant defenses throughout the area. The Americans may have no choice but to come looking for the guns. And when they do, you must stop them. You can expect helicopters to swarm over every millimeter of ground between here and their embassy. I want Stinger missiles being manned by men who know how to use them, RPGs, and a ring of machine guns and automatic weapons to defend these guns."

"This, too, will be done," Rana said. "We'll protect them with our lives."

"I'm taking five of your men to assist me with the next portion of my mission." Chachar turned to the others. "Abid, Tanvir, Yusuf, Nawaz, and Danish, get into this truck and come with me. The rest of you move on to emptying trucks two and three."

He hurried over to the truck and got into the driver's seat. The moment those he'd selected had climbed on board, he headed out.

52

Cradling hot lunches for Sam, Gunny Joyce, and Corporal Geno-vese, Lauren had entered the command bunker moments before the first shell landed two hundred yards south of the Kashmir Highway. The roaring projectile's explosion startled them all. Sec-onds later, shell number two hit closer to the highway. A third soon followed.

"Shit!" Erickson said.

"What is it?" Wells asked.

"Artillery. First time they've used that." Erickson spoke into his headset. "Anyone see where the shells are coming from?" His question was met with silence.

Three more massive explosions smashed into the highway and the area around it. The frightening display brought terror to the thousands in and around the embassy. The mangled ground near the fierce blasts buckled. The fragmented southern wall trembled and shook.

So far, the number of firing howitzers had been small. But

Erickson couldn't be certain. For all he knew, dozens were preparing to fire. The terrifying ordnance had yet to find the range. It did, however, appear to be coming closer with every firing.

The company commander knew they were in deep trouble. It wasn't the first time he'd endured an artillery bombardment. And it probably wouldn't be the last. Such knowledge, however, didn't make the situation any easier. He recognized the threat the big guns posed. Given enough time, they'd pound the embassy until little remained except smoldering rubble. Their survival was on the line.

He turned to Genovese. "It won't be long until they find us. Once they do, they'll rip this place apart. Get on the radio. We need Apaches down here. They've got to eliminate those guns. For now, tell them to focus on the areas south of the embassy. Given where the shells are landing, that's the most likely place they'll be."

"On it, sir." The company radioman contacted Camp Nowhere. He relayed Erickson's message. "Apaches will be on the way shortly, sir."

Another barrage reached the assailed compound. This time they landed inside the defenders' lines.

They seized an initial life.

53

9:19 A.M., NOVEMBER 17
4TH PLATOON, ALPHA COMPANY, 2ND BATTALION,
69TH ARMOR REGIMENT, 2ND ARMORED
BRIGADE COMBAT TEAM (SPARTANS), 3RD INFANTRY DIVISION
ON THE DOCKS
KARACHI, PAKISTAN

Darren Walton sat in the open commander's hatch of his Bradley fighting vehicle as Private First Class Aiden Lester eased the armored vehicle down the teeming dock at Pakistan's busiest port. The lengthy pier was crammed with people moving in all directions. The unloading of the massive American armored division was beginning in earnest. There seemed to be a method to the madness on the waterfront, but so far the Americans couldn't decipher it. Standing in the hatch next to Walton, Specialist Four Evan Minter let out an unrepressed yawn. After nine days on the noisy transport ship, it was a relief to be on solid ground. Along with its commander, gunner, and driver, each of the platoon's quartet of Bradleys carried six infantrymen in its rear compartment.

From the driver's position in the separate area at the front of the vehicle, Lester was following their platoon leader, Second Lieutenant Ethan Cramer's Bradley. Cramer was following the last fighting vehicle from 3rd Platoon.

In the smoke-clogged distance, Walton could see the crazy scene within the stretching venue's teeming streets. Karachi, Pakistan's largest city and the sixth most populous in the world, waited beyond the hectic waterfront. With the influx of frantic refugees, the immense metropolis now contained more than twice its normal population. Forty million were sheltering behind the Pakistani army's defensive lines. Every home was crammed beyond capacity. Every inch of sidewalk was filled with displaced people unsure of what fate would bring.

The distant sounds of artillery and armored clashes assailed them. With each exploding round, with every sound of man-made thunder, the panic grew for Karachi's sheltering millions. The northern fringes of the city were on fire or were little more than crumbling refuse.

The combat-savvy Walton knew what those distant signs of conflict meant. For the moment, however, he was more concerned with getting his tracked vehicle off the pier without killing someone. "Aiden, stick with the lieutenant if you can. But as crazy as this place is, don't rush things," the platoon sergeant directed. "Better to fall behind than to run over those scurrying around the docks."

"No worries, Sarge. I can handle it, even in this mess."

Walton smiled. He'd been assigned one of the best drivers in the brigade, even if the twenty-year-old Lester could be somewhat cocky. The platoon sergeant turned to get a good look at the frenetic activity around them. The docks were filled with the division's ships. The offloading of their huge holds continued at a rapid pace. There were hundreds of M1 Abrams tanks, M2 Bradley fighting vehicles, Stryker eight-wheeled armored vehicles, Humvees, artillery pieces, attack and transport helicopters, air defense systems, and support elements of every kind. Fifteen thousand American soldiers, along with the French and British armored divisions unloading twenty miles away at Port Quasim, were preparing to lay waste to anything standing against them.

In forty-eight hours, organized and ready, the three divisions would head out. They'd move inland. The British would head north. The French would travel east. Between the two, the Americans would strike northeast into the heart of the ravaged country. At the same moment, the 10th Mountain Division's massive array of helicopters would take to the air. Their eventual destination would be the mountains of the north and northeast.

Walton's battalion, however, wouldn't be waiting the two days the division needed to get everything in place. While the remainder prepared, its three companies would head to the front lines to shore up the grappling Pakistani army. By sundown, they'd be embroiled in a desperate struggle. Twenty miles away, their objective waited. And their first taste of conflict in this war.

The moment Alpha Company left the docks, Pakistani military police escorts appeared. With a pair of MP guide vehicles at their head and two more at the rear, the armored company headed out. They were moving northeast. While they did, Bravo Company's forces were forming behind them and preparing to head east. The majority of Charlie Company, scheduled to shore up the defenses on the northern edge of the city, was nearing the end of the docks. In minutes, further MPs would be guiding each as they crept through the dismaying labyrinth that was the city.

While each edged forward, to their surprise they were met with rousing cheers by those crammed twenty deep onto the sidewalks. The soldiers had anticipated being greeted with suspicion and hostility. Yet within the city they found otherwise.

Karachi's citizens prided themselves on the modern and, at least by Pakistani standards, progressive metropolis where they lived. They considered themselves, with their fast-paced lives and bustling streets, the Pakistani version of New York City. Just as

New York was far different from the remainder of America, Karachi was quite dissimilar from the rest of Pakistan. And the city's citizens were proud of it. Unlike the strict Muslim religious adherence throughout the remainder of the country, in Karachi some diversity in beliefs was tolerated.

There was little support here for the Fedayeen Islam's henchmen. They hated Basra and the horror he was bringing to their nation. While they weren't elated by the idea of foreign soldiers on their soil, they found the alternative abhorrent. So they waved and cheered as the Americans passed. However, once the Allies made their way to the insular villages and open countryside, that would change. These closely structured societies would be filled with animus beyond anything the foreign troops could imagine.

54

It had taken three frustrating hours for the platoon to arrive at the major crossroads they'd been directed to control. There were significant sounds of gunfire and explosions—and not too far away. On their left a battle raged. It was headed in their direction.

When the Americans appeared, it took no coaxing for the forward pair of Pakistani armored personnel carriers to back out of their positions. For weeks they'd been involved in delaying actions against those who'd endlessly pursued them. When they'd arrived on this spot ten days earlier, there'd been four M113s in their number. Only two had survived. The relieved survivors were eager for the reprieve Walton's platoon would be providing. They hurriedly disappeared, moving some distance behind the lines.

"Platoon Sergeant, place your Bradley on the right flank," Lieutenant Cramer said.

"We're on it, sir. Aiden," Walton said into the intercom, "let's set up where the APC with the checkered flag on its antenna had been sitting."

"I'll take the left," Cramer said. "Sergeant Vigo, you'll set up to my right. Sergeant Devine, you're between Vigo's and Walton's crews." The four combat vehicles began to align. "Enemy's been attacking in this area, so be ready for anything. Infantry support, as soon as your Bradley comes to a stop, dismount and set up defensive positions while we emplace the Bradleys. Make it quick: the Pakistani combat engineers have a lot more platoons to serve than this one. Let's get those fighting holes dug and get ready for the next attack."

The moment Walton's Bradley stopped, the half dozen soldiers in its rear area rushed out to defend the platoon, rifles at the ready. Walton was right behind them, lifting himself from the commander's hatch and climbing down to ground level. He motioned for the closest bulldozer to move forward. From out of nowhere, a bullet ricocheted off the ground near where he stood. A second followed.

55

6:49 P.M., NOVEMBER 17
OPERATIONAL DETACHMENT ALPHA 6333,
CHARLIE COMPANY, 3RD BATTALION,
6TH SPECIAL FORCES GROUP (AIRBORNE)
MISHIRA NUCLEAR ARMAMENTS MOBILE LAUNCH FACILITY
THIRTY MILES SOUTHWEST OF ISLAMABAD, PAKISTAN

Another solemn sunset was setting in.

So far, they'd been lucky. They'd been inside enemy territory for two weeks. Yet, after the failure of the initial Fedayeen attacks to reclaim the plateau, the surviving Special Forces soldiers had faced only a handful of minor skirmishes. Most had been brushed off with a modicum of effort. There had, however, been one significant onslaught by a force a dozen times their size the day after Porter and Sanders returned from the schoolhouse. Despite the opposition's numbers, the Americans had been more than capable of holding their own while waiting for help to arrive. With the appearance of a trio of Apaches, they had annihilated the attackers with ruthless intensity. None had survived. Not one had gotten within fifty yards of the concertina. The rotting corpses were scattered about the slopes where they'd fallen. The Green Berets had left them as a warning to others who might contemplate similar actions.

In fourteen days at Mishira, the Americans' numbers had

dropped by three: a trio of seriously wounded were all the medevacs had gathered. Given the circumstances, it was a remarkable
result. How much longer their good fortune would hold, none was
willing to hazard.

For a few days there'd been constant noise on the far side of the
valley. The puzzled Americans had had no clue who it was or what
they were doing. Still, as the sounds continued, the possibilities
had become quite concerning. If the buildup was in preparation
for a massive assault, they could be in serious trouble even with
significant helicopter support.

Aaron Porter, Shaun McCoy, and Aiden Hernandez had been
sent out to scout the valley floor. They'd returned within the hour.
The accomplished weapons specialists had persisted throughout
the long afternoon, hiding in the tall grass and observing the insurgents' actions.

What they'd found wasn't what they'd anticipated. Rather
than a massing of forces in preparation for an attack, they'd un-
covered something else. Deep in the valley was a supply depot.
The Fedayeen had established the busy facility in the dense trees
on the northern edge of the roadway. The concealed Green Berets
had spent ample time observing the comings and goings of jingle
trucks. In doing so, they'd been able to map the location. To their
relief, the second part of their mission—determining the presence
of others in the area—had found no signs of anyone. With the exception of the frenzied activity at the depot, the isolated gorge was
silent and still.

Porter's report on what they'd discovered had defined their
next mission. With their gear scattered about them, the twenty-
one survivors of the Green Beret A Teams waited while the detachment commanders conferred some distance away. After Black
Hawks had arrived with a complete resupply, each of the soldiers'

packs was overflowing with everything they needed for what, by all appearances, would be an extended effort in the coming days.

What they'd been selected to do would be beyond challenging. And exceedingly dangerous. Exactly the kind of thing for which they'd spent untold hours preparing.

"Okay, listen up," Captain Short said to the gathered force. "It's time to leave this sorry place and get back to doing what we do best. We've gotten word on our next assignment. The 3rd Infantry and 10th Mountain are unloading in Karachi as we speak. British and French divisions are doing the same. The lead elements from the 10th Mountain will leave for Camp Nowhere in the morning in preparation of what's to come. As soon as everything's in place, our massed divisions are going to unleash simultaneous attacks on Basra's army from both the north and south. As you know, the plan calls for a third action to take place to create chaos in the center of his forces. That's where we and the remainder of the group come in. It's time to take the fight to the enemy. We're going to make their lives a living hell."

"After what Sergeant Sanders and I experienced at the schoolhouse, I'm all for that, sir," Porter interjected. "We should show no mercy. We need to kill every sorry bastard that strays into our sights."

"That's exactly what the higher-ups have in mind, Sergeant Porter. Attack and keep attacking until we're told to stop." Short looked toward Captain Henry.

"Satellite images confirm what our scouts found this afternoon," Henry said. "The Fedayeen have established a supply depot in the valley below us. By all appearances, it's a major distribution center for Basra's fighters in Islamabad and the northeast portion of the country. They've been bringing truck after truck down the little road Porter and Sanders first spotted. Intel photos confirm they're loaded with weapons, ammunition, and food. So our initial assignment's going to be a critical one. We're going to destroy that depot. We're going to eliminate their ability to provide those supplies to their front lines and make sure there's no possibility of rebuilding it. When we're finished, the floor of this valley will be nothing more than a smoldering pile. It'll be of no value to anyone."

"Sir, do we have an estimate of how many Fedayeen we'll be facing at the depot?" Master Sergeant Noll asked.

"No idea. Sergeant Porter, were you able to get a count while observing their actions?"

"Not a precise one, sir. There were too many comings and goings for us to do that. But from the size of it, there could easily be a couple hundred or more."

"That's a pretty big target," Noll responded. "May take a while to finish the job. If reinforcements arrive, we could find ourselves with our hands full."

"We don't anticipate that being a concern," Captain Henry said. "The satellite photos confirmed what Sergeant Porter and his team found. There's no sign of anyone for at least ten miles. So we believe we're going to have adequate time to complete the mission."

"Any idea what'll come after that?" Noll asked.

"Until we hear otherwise, we're to play it by ear," Captain Short responded. "We're to move in a northeast direction toward Islamabad, disrupting the enemy's operations and killing as many of the bastards as we can find. Beyond that, I haven't a clue."

The captains looked into the faces of those they commanded. It was clear that most were pleased with the idea of pursuing the perverse peasant army.

"We move out at midnight," Short added. "There can be no delays. Make sure you're ready to roll by then."

Porter turned toward the bunker in the northeast corner of the mesa. Fareeda stood a few feet from it. There was no mistaking her uneasiness.

"What about the girl, sir?" Porter said, motioning in her direction.

"What about her?" was Short's rather terse reply.

"We know what'll occur if we leave her here. She's already lived through a hell none of us can imagine. And I don't want to think about what might happen to her on her own."

"What choice do we have? With what we're about to face we can't take her with us."

Porter realized in the coming moments the girl's life would be in his hands. If they abandoned her, she was as good as dead. He wasn't willing to give up on changing the detachment leader's mind without a significant attempt.

"With us, she's at least got a chance, sir. And while I've been able to scout a bit of the valley, there's no way I know it like she does. She's lived here her entire life. She knows every tree and blade of grass. We shouldn't throw away that level of expertise."

Noll jumped in, hoping to use his influence as senior operations sergeant to help. Like most on the plateau, in the ten days Fareeda had been with them, he'd grown quite fond of her. "Sergeant Porter may be right, sir. The girl might be able to offer a great deal of help."

Short paused. He didn't want the handicap the child might create. Still, he recognized the validity of Noll's comments. The kid could be in a position to help them complete their assignment. His answer was a reluctant one. "All right, Sergeant Porter, for now we'll take her with us."

"Thank you, sir," Porter said, his relief evident.

"While we wait, your team leaders will go over the plan of attack and your roles. When they're finished, Sanders, I want you to prepare the engineers to blow the supply dump and roadway. You've got to make sure both are no longer usable by the enemy."

Sanders grinned. "You don't have to worry about that, sir. We'll take care of it."

Midnight. Faces emotionless, backs stooped beneath their heavy packs, they positioned their night vision equipment. As always, Porter took the point. There were few better at leading such a mission. If an ambush was waiting, the odds were high he'd identify it and strike to destroy whoever it was before the enemy realized the roles had been reversed. With Fareeda walking next to Sanders, they started into the immense darkness. The supply depot awaited.

56

3:43 A.M., NOVEMBER 18
OPERATIONAL DETACHMENT ALPHA 6333,
CHARLIE COMPANY, 3RD BATTALION,
6TH SPECIAL FORCES GROUP (AIRBORNE)
AT THE EDGE OF THE SMALL ROADWAY IN THE VALLEY'S CENTER
THIRTY MILES SOUTHWEST OF ISLAMABAD, PAKISTAN

Bila Chachar had done all he could to keep the distribution center from being spotted and destroyed by a swarm of buzzing drones. So far, his endeavor had been a success. The busy outpost had remained safe. In the past days, the evolving terminal had grown until it was two football fields long. Where the tangle of trees allowed, it ran sixty yards or more into the surrounding woods.

Without pause, his efforts to send the much-needed supplies forward continued. In the secluded space, whispery figures hurried about the late-night scene. While they did, others barked out orders and gave directions in Urdu, the country's primary language.

A dozen or more jingle trucks, most in the thinner trees along the western edge of the encampment, sat idling for the half hour it took to empty them. Some had come from distant battlefields where others worked to strip everything from the dead. Their orders were to overlook nothing. Weapons large and small, along with vast ammunition stores, were finding their way into the isolated valley. More trucks, filled with food, had come from far off towns. Each hamlet was being wiped clean.

The moment the massive stores were removed, the drivers would turn about and head back for the next load. As they did, those on the ground would sort the contents. Once they had, the supplies were carried to where further jingle trucks waited for their holds to be filled. When each was ready, it would roar away toward the battlefronts.

Every few minutes a new truck arrived and another departed. The furious activity was without end. Given the immense task, those on the ground were laboring eighteen hours a day. But despite the extreme exertion, few muttered the smallest complaint. The way they saw it, what they were doing was better than forfeiting their lives on the sordid battlefields. So they continued working with one truck after the next. When the time arrived for a brief rest, each slumping figure would grab some of the choicest food from the arriving trucks and attempt to catch a few hours' sleep.

The system was far from perfect and in many ways a bit crude, but it was getting the job done. The thousands upon thousands of fighters in the northeast areas were receiving the things needed to continue this war. Bellies full and ammunition magazines loaded, they were renewing the fight.

Even Basra was unable to deny Bila's plan was working. Because of his second-in-command's endeavors, his massive army would have the necessary resources for the indefinite future. And when the time came, there'd be a rudimentary system in place to allow them to govern what remained of the devastated country.

While they unloaded the arriving trucks and reloaded the departing ones, those within the busy center paid scant attention to the world around them. As the fifth night in the makeshift depot dragged on, they felt safe and secure. Their rifles lay scattered about their makeshift encampment deep within the woods. Of the two hundred present, only a handful of unconcerned sentries, more asleep than awake, patrolled the perimeter.

Chachar's goal had been to identify a location to use as the central repository for the distribution of materials to the northern battlements. Minutes after driving into the valley, he'd stumbled upon a large band of Fedayeen soldiers languishing in the woods. The motley group provided a simple story, claiming to be recent volunteers who'd been ordered to scour the area for food and weapons.

Not a single element of their tale was true. In reality, they were deserters intent on hiding in this desolate place until the war reached its end. Their account, however thin, had withstood Chachar's cursory examination. He was more interested in finding a spot that served his purposes than concerning himself with why the group was there. While listening to the gathering's claims, he realized the sheltering forest would be perfect for his needs. It was tucked away in a nondescript valley whose thick woods would mask their efforts. And the little roadway would be capable of holding the constant traffic that would soon be upon it. Along with that, he'd located a ready-made work crew. Little did he know, the statements they made claiming they'd searched the desolate location from one end to the other also were false.

While Chachar's men continued working, they'd seen and heard nothing. For five days, only the steady drone of arriving and departing trucks had reached their ears. Despite the marginal skills of those he commanded, he'd been able to create a reasonable level of efficiency in their labors. With the depot running smoothly, his intentions were to leave at first light. One of his lieutenants would remain behind to run things while he returned to the high mountains to rejoin Salim Basra. The plan was about to receive an abrupt awakening, however. For while he slept in the shielding forest, Chachar had no idea the Americans were headed his way.

Using a waning moon's faltering glow to protect them, one by one the Green Berets edged across the busy roadway and into the woods. Slipping in and out of the darkened world, the adept soldiers surrounded the distribution center. The deadly phantoms were about to spring their trap. To a man, they selected targets from the bountiful human forms within the compound. All that remained was for Sanders and his engineers to blow huge craters on both ends of the roadway. Once they had, the attack would be fiercely sudden and mercilessly quick.

With the attackers in place, the word went out to destroy the road. The engineers were ready. Sanders and Davidson waited in the thick grass a few feet from the roadway's embankment. The depot, hidden in the forest a half mile to the left, was a beehive of activity.

Not one of the Americans had the slightest idea that what they were observing was the central supply point in this portion of the country. There were, of course, other supply centers supporting the war in the northeast. And more in the south. But none was one-quarter the size of this one. Its destruction would be a major blow to the Fedayeen.

Sanders and Davidson had dug a hole in the embankment supporting the road. They'd continued expanding it until it ran a few feet beneath the asphalt. Sanders had packed every inch with explosives. There was enough crammed in the hole to blow a crater ten feet deep and twice as wide, rendering its tattered pavement impassable. They'd picked the location carefully. With the steep angle of the hill behind the hidden Green Berets, and the impassable woods on the other side, there'd be no way to circumvent the damage. The crippled roadway would be of no use to anyone.

Sanders keyed his headset. "Timmons, Sterns, you all set down there?"

"Explosives are in place," Timmons said. "Detonator's attached. We're ready."

"Roger. On my mark, set the timers to thirty seconds, then find yourselves a safe spot to crawl in."

Timmons reached for the detonator, adjusting the timer. Davidson did the same.

"Now!" Sanders yelled.

Both released the detonator's dial. On opposite ends of the depot, the engineers scrambled up the hill. With seconds to spare, Sanders and Davidson dove behind a protective ridge one hundred yards distant.

A pair of startling explosions ripped through the night. Massive fireballs rose into the sky. The intense light exposed the astounded figures laboring in the depot. Each instinctively froze. A huge chunk of roadway was gone.

Hearing the engineers' chatter, the remainder of the Green Berets were prepared to unleash everything they had. An initial burst of rifle fire ripped through the trees. On the western end, three jihadists went down.

Fifty yards to the right, a second torrent of M4 gunfire tore through the low-hanging branches. Still more ill-fated quarry were felled. The woods burst to life with roaring gunfire. Spitting from the ends of the Green Berets' rifles, lethal lightning and terrifying thunder pounded them. Death's refrain tore into those caught in the open. The initial survivors scattered, running in every direction.

In the east, a nearly filled truck's driver put the transmission into gear and attempted to scurry away. But he didn't get far before he realized his escape route had vanished. Reaching the gaping hole in the roadway he slammed on the brakes and screamed to a stop.

From the ridge above, Davidson opened fire on the ammunition-laden truck. As his rounds ripped into the immense target, in ear-shattering protest, its lethal contents detonated beneath a mighty blast. Flaming pieces rained down upon a pitiless world. The truck and its driver disappeared.

Spotting a trio of Fedayeen running in his direction, Porter lowered his M4 and released round after round. All three went down.

Somewhere on the left, a torrent of M4 fire ripped through the trees. A fleeing jihadist fell from a well-concealed Green Beret's actions. And another . . . and another, almost without end. Five on the left, two in the center, they were falling so rapidly it was impossible to keep track. Terrified figures, out of their minds with fear, attempted to flee. Still, it was no use.

In the west, an additional truck exploded. And yet one more. The frenetic blasts reached out for the idling beasts around them. On that end, every truck, its fire raging, was soon devoured. Fiery, ear-shattering blasts reached out once again.

In both the east and the west, the woods began to smolder and then to burn. Within minutes, the majority of the pine forest was ablaze. The uncontrollable flames, fierce and unyielding, were soon seething. Within them, trapped forms by the dozens succumbed in a hell-sent whirlwind.

The Americans kept the pressure on. Another truck erupted in the east. Then two more. A half minute after the assault began, not a jingle truck still stood. The human forms around them were dwindling. Fifty . . . a hundred or more . . . had perished by the end of the first minute. With each halting breath, additional figures joined them as the unrelenting Americans continued the lurid assault. The one-sided contest surged unabated.

Sleeping some distance from the confluence of the attack, Bila Chachar's initial instinct had been to leap to his feet and grab his rifle. He was, however, a veteran of more than one battle over the years. And that experience saved him from a fatal mistake. Unlike the others, he didn't panic. Ever so slowly, he pulled his blanket up over his head. In measured movements, he reached out, feeling for his rifle. He pulled it to him and released the safety. Hidden beneath the coarse blanket, he took stock of the startling travail. There were intense gunfire and savage detonations everywhere. Along with that, the woods near the roadway were being devoured in an all-consuming inferno.

With such a fearsome attack, and the majority of his men some distance from their AK-47s, Chachar understood there was little chance his fighters would prevail. He'd no idea who the attackers were or where they'd come from. It didn't matter. It took no more than a passing moment for him to realize that whoever it was knew what they were doing. He understood his only chance was to remain silent as the battle unfolded. But he couldn't wait much longer. The gunfire and flames were growing nearer. Either could take his life.

The Americans moved forward. All around were thousands of boxes of every sort, size, and description. There seemed to be little logic to where they were lying. As they neared, a number of individuals using them to mask their presence leaped up and attempted to get away. None got far before a bullet found them. While they edged into the woods as far as the flames would allow, the Special Forces soldiers realized few targets remained.

With the attackers consumed with taking down the last of those who'd been working in the depot, Bila Chachar got up and crept deeper into the woods. It felt like forever, but reaching a point where he sensed he was in the clear, he threw caution to the wind and ran. A couple of others joined him as he fled, but there wouldn't be many more. You could count on one hand those who had escaped the attackers' clutches. Over two hundred lived no more. Their bodies, silent and unmoving, covered the charring landscape.

57

Captain Neil Short understood the fire could be seen for vast distances. And Short was never a man to be ill-prepared. Their defenses anchored by light machine guns, the Green Berets were ready for whatever might rise up to confront them. To their surprise, however, no counterattack came.

There'd been hundreds of ammunition-laden boxes inside the depot at the moment of the attack. It had taken until the first rays of morning for the firestorm's explosions to subside. Once it was safe, the Green Berets destroyed the few things that survived.

Task completed, Aaron Porter returned to the swaying grass where Fareeda was hiding. With darkness gone and his night vision useless, everything looked quite different. When he reached an isolated crest, he stopped, searching the rolling landscape for the spot he'd hidden her.

She'd done as he'd directed, lying motionless throughout the horrifying night. Even the startling explosions and the one-sided firefight hadn't caused her to deviate from what she'd been ordered to do. She saw him approaching. A broad smile came to her face. Still, she stayed where she was until told otherwise.

Although he was only a short distance from her, he looked around, perplexed. It was an expression the highly skilled sergeant rarely showed. "Fareeda?" he called out.

"I'm right here," she said in a voice so quiet he barely heard it.

A smile to match hers came to his face. The girl was in the sheltering grass no more than ten feet away.

"Is it okay to get up?" she asked.

He took a look around. "Yeah. It should be. A few of the Fedayeen escaped, but the last we saw, they were running away as fast as they could. They're probably miles from here by now. Even so, I want you to be alert as we head toward the road."

"I will."

"Fareeda, there's something I need to tell you."

"What is it?"

"When we get down to the road, you're going to see some awful things. There are hundreds of bodies lying in the dirt near it. And none of them look very nice. Do you think you're going to be able to handle such things?"

"Are they men like the ones who killed my friends and teacher? Men like the ones who attacked my family?"

"Yes."

"Then I'll handle it just fine."

They turned and headed toward the roadway. Despite her assurances, he continued to worry about how she'd respond to the ghastly sight. She seemed so young and fragile. He knew there was little chance she wouldn't violently react to the gruesome scene on the far side of the pavement. Still, there was nothing he could do when it happened except hold her close and reassure her. It had taken him years to develop the callous outlook he held deep within him. He couldn't expect a traumatized eleven-year-old to view such a scene without a significant response.

To Porter's surprise, Fareeda didn't react to what she found waiting. Through passionless eyes, she stood there taking it in. Her expression never changed as the minutes passed. Her consuming hatred for people like these overwhelmed all other emotions.

The three teams' losses were minimal, considering the force they'd faced. One dead, a few seriously wounded, along with a half dozen more with minor to moderate injuries. Nearly all had been caused by the mountains of exploding Fedayeen ordnance. They took the wounded in need of significant care and placed them on the south side of the shattered pavement. It was an ideal place for the medevacs to land. While they waited for the Black Hawks, the A Teams' medics were doing their best to treat their countrymen.

In thirty minutes the helicopters arrived. Four of the wounded were placed on stretchers and carried to the waiting craft. The body of the dead Green Beret was the last to be loaded. While they did, Captain Short was on the radio. As the helicopters took to the skies, the teams gathered. Like always, their rifles were at the ready.

When the Black Hawks were gone, only sixteen remained, less than half the three teams' original numbers. Many of the survivors had injuries that ran the gamut from superficial to beyond.

"What now, sir?" Master Sergeant Noll asked the moment Short put down the headset.

They'd been here for hours. They couldn't stay where they were much longer. Even if they had yet to do so, a significant enemy force would eventually arrive. The Americans needed to vanish. And to do so soon.

"Group wants us to continue working our way toward the capital. They're gathering further intel. Once they do, they'll let us know where they need us."

They looked down the road. They understood the pavement stretching into the distance would take them in the direction they wanted to go. From what their maps told them, the little roadway would intersect with the Kashmir Highway in about ten miles. Yet the dew-covered asphalt, even if the most direct route to Islamabad, wasn't an option—not if they wanted to avoid facing overpowering enemy units. From this moment on, stealth would be key to carrying out their mission.

"Well, we can't go that way," Michael Noll said while gesturing up the road.

"Sergeant Porter, when you and Sergeant Sanders went with the girl the first time, didn't you say you identified a large lake on the far end of the woods and a village beyond?" Short asked.

"Yes, sir. Lake appeared to be a mile or so away, with the village scattered about near its northern shore," Porter said. "That sound about right, Charlie?"

"It was kind of difficult to tell from where we were, sir," Sanders said. "And it wasn't something we were focused on at the time. So I'm really not all that certain. But I'd say Aaron's estimate is fairly accurate."

Short took a look around, doing his best to judge the terrain. "We've stayed here as long as we dare. We're pressing our luck as it is. Sergeant Porter, you said you believed the village to be empty?"

"Of anyone still breathing? Not that we saw, sir. The village appeared to be of decent size, but we didn't see any activity in it. No signs of anyone coming or going. Fareeda was certain about what had happened there. When they passed through it a couple of weeks ago, the Fedayeen killed everyone in it."

"Okay, then let's head for the lake," Short said. "Porter, take McCoy and Hernandez and find us a workable path through the woods. You've got five minutes to locate a way to get us there."

In the days she'd been with them, Fareeda had attempted to be as unobtrusive as possible, doing chores and being helpful around their camp. She'd been raised in a male-dominated society and taught that her place was in the background, never out front. She'd only spoken to Porter and Sanders when it was absolutely necessary. She'd never said more than a few words to the other soldiers. But that was about to change.

She realized that no matter how great the American fighters were, they were in a tough spot, deep within a world they were unfamiliar with and surrounded by jihadists. They'd protected her, and she needed to reward their kindness no matter how uneasy she was in stepping forward. The time had come for her to speak up. "There's no need," Fareeda said while looking at the soldiers' leader.

"What?" Short replied.

She raised her arm and pointed to the east. "There's a dirt road wide enough for a jingle truck to get to my village, not too far away. It'll take you to the lake. The village is just beyond it."

"Are you certain?"

"Yes. I used it every day to go back and forth to school. Come, I'll show you."

Short hesitated. The girl had done nothing to cause him to question her vitriol for the Fedayeen. Even so, he was uncertain how far her loyalty to his teams went.

"You can trust her, sir," Porter said when he saw his captain hesitating. "If she says she knows the way, she knows the way."

After the brief pause, Short replied, "What choice do we have?

Staying here's not an option. Take the girl and lead the way, Sergeant Porter. Find a secure spot to camp by the lake while we wait to find out where we're heading next."

"On it, sir," Porter replied.

With Porter and Fareeda in the lead, the remnants of the three teams moved out.

58

9:34 A.M., NOVEMBER 18

C COMPANY (BLUE MAX), 3RD BATTALION, 10TH AVIATION REGIMENT,

10TH COMBAT AVIATION BRIGADE,

10TH MOUNTAIN DIVISION (LIGHT INFANTRY)

NEARING THE JAHAR NUCLEAR LAUNCH FACILITY

CENTRAL PAKISTAN

While the Green Berets headed toward the lake, three hundred miles away the 10th Mountain Division was beginning to use their massive array of helicopters to move into place. In an endless stream, the skies were filled with whirling rotor blades. Bea Washington's Black Hawk was right behind the leader. Her entire helicopter company was with them, with the remainder of the battalion close behind. They were hundreds of miles into enemy-held territory. Next to her, Shaun White scanned the area around them for signs of a threat from any source. So far, the hostile terrain had yielded nothing. Behind them in the cabin, their crewmen, Jesus Mercado and Thomas Vinson, did the same, manning their machine guns and searching the passing ground. Eleven anxious infantrymen, the maximum the Black Hawk could hold, filled the remainder of the space.

With the Black Hawks capable of handling the frigid environment they were heading toward, the only modification had been to replace their tires with skis. In a few hours, they'd reach Camp

Nowhere. Yet, before they did, there was a stop they needed to make. Their Black Hawk's limited fuel supply dictated how far they could travel. In a combat situation the maximum distance was 370 miles. And with Camp Nowhere over seven hundred miles from Karachi, they'd no choice but to figure out how to land and refuel deep within the unfavorable landscape.

It hadn't taken long for the Americans to identify a solution. They'd set up a refueling point at one of the nuclear sites being held by the Green Berets. Jahar had met the criteria in both distance and the confidence the Special Forces Group had that they could secure it.

An hour earlier, the first 10th Mountain unit had arrived. It'd consisted of a company of infantry sent to reinforce the Americans' hold on the vital location. Once their defenses were in place, Chinook cargo helicopters, immense fuel pods dangling beneath their bellies, followed. Refueling stations were rapidly established.

Washington's company would be the next to arrive.

"How far to the target?" she asked.

White glanced at their instruments. "Ten miles, maybe a little less, ma'am."

"Once we get there, there'll be no time to waste. We need to refuel as quickly as we can to make room for the ones behind us. So no excuses and no delays. Gas up, get back in the air, and head for Camp Nowhere."

"Don't worry, ma'am. The entire company knows what to do. They're ready to spring into action the moment we arrive." White pointed. "Looks like that might be Jahar up ahead."

The place they were looking for was coming into view.

59

The embassy remained under bombardment, an unending siege that could doom it. With little warning, another shattering shell slammed into the earth twenty yards north of the command bunker. As its lethal shrapnel reached out to destroy, Erickson could hear death's fragmenting messengers whistling past. The blast created another smoking fissure deep within the nightmarish landscape. It was one of hundreds of exploding rounds that had arrived in the past five days. The devastating onslaught had been a toxic mixture of airbursts and land strikes.

The relentless artillery attacks, violent and unpredictable, had taken their toll. The ravaged landscape looked nothing like it had on the night the Marines arrived. Broken and bloodied, it was unrecognizable. With each passing hour, the areas around the embassy grounds appeared more and more like the macabre no-man's-lands of World War I.

A shallow breath after the ordnance exploded, two more screaming rounds assailed the embassy's defenses in the east.

Both had been airbursts. Erickson couldn't tell if they'd detonated inside the embassy proper or at some distance beyond. He waited, listening for more of the cultist's fiends to find them. But as it turned out, these were the last of a dozen shells unleashed in this barrage.

While the hours passed, the death and destruction the howitzers had wrought was beyond imagination. One hundred and fifty of the innocents within the embassy grounds had been killed by Satan's wrath. More than three times that had been wounded. An unfortunate Lauren Wells had been among them, with a red-hot piece of shrapnel shredding her right calf two days earlier. The haggard doctors had done what they could for her, sewing up her hideous wound and applying sterile dressings. Even so, her limp was as pronounced as Erickson's.

To make matters worse, two dozen defenders had succumbed during the numerous small-scale attacks by Fedayeen riflemen. The Marines were down to sixty men. Only half that number were unharmed. Nearly two-thirds of those who had arrived on the King Stallions were no longer in the fight. The supporting foreign defenders and their civilian counterparts were doing little better. Their lines had grown perilously thin.

The walls of the American compound were little more than a remembrance. There were gaping holes everywhere. Two major buildings had burned to the ground along with a number of smaller ones. Not a single structure had survived unharmed. Nowhere was safe. The landing shells had seen to that. And the desperate survivors knew it.

With the unpredictability of the artillery attacks, the fear of those sheltering inside was palpable. Each startling strike added to the terror. Occasionally, the insurgents fired a single round from the thundering howitzers. Sometimes, when they were certain Apaches weren't lurking, thirty or more would be unleashed in rapid succession. Only the arriving night was any protection from the roving bands attacking on the ground and the hidden crews firing the deadly howitzers. With each dreaded sunrise, their pestilence returned.

Bila Chachar had done a magnificent job of concealing the heavy guns. Try as they might, the Apaches hadn't been able to locate the well-hidden artillery. They'd combed the disjointed hellscape untold times but come up short.

After waiting to verify the latest barrage had ended, Erickson spoke into his headset. "Looks like it's stopped for the moment. Keep your heads down and hold your positions. If it's like it has been, the next artillery assault will occur soon. There's a good chance of a ground attack in the interim, so stay on your toes. XO, what's the damage on your side?"

"Not sure yet, sir," Tomlin, his recent head wound bandaged, answered. "Eastern parts of the embassy grounds took the brunt of it this time." He turned to look through the disintegrating wall behind him. "Looks like it might be significant. I can see Ambassador Ingram and Steven Gray trying to get things under control. But so far they're not having much luck. One of the smaller buildings is on fire. Lots of people running around. Others are lying on the ground. Some are screaming and writhing about. Others aren't moving at all. So we've got wounded and possibly additional dead. Medical folks are leaving the hospital and heading toward the worst of it."

Erickson let out a deep sigh. "Any signs of a ground attack building in the north or east?"

"Not that I can see, sir."

"Probably means the shelling isn't over. Tell your defenders to expect more soon."

"Yes, sir."

Erickson paused. The helplessness of the situation overwhelmed him. "I'll call for Apaches. Ask them to send every last one they can spare. Maybe we'll get lucky and they'll finally locate the Fedayeen artillery. Other than that, I don't know what to do."

"I thought you said, sir, with most of the Apaches supporting the arrival of the 10th Mountain Division, they told you their ability to support us today would be limited."

"They did. But what choice do we have? We've got to try. Maybe they can free up a few and send them this way."

"Hasn't worked so far. But you're right, we've got to do something. Bastards have obviously got those guns well hidden. With the pounding they've given us, there are no safe places left inside the embassy grounds. And our dead and wounded are mounting. Another week of this and we'll be so defenseless that even a modest attack will succeed."

"So tell me what to do, XO," the exhausted Erickson said.

"I wish I knew. But we can't sit here day after day while these people are slaughtered."

"Like I said, tell me how to solve it. We don't have many options here."

"Well, there's one. Late tonight, when the majority of the enemy is asleep, I should do what I proposed the other day: lead some of our men out to find those guns and silence them."

Erickson let out a sigh. "Scott, we talked about this. Only thing you'll do is get yourselves killed. Those guns are miles from here. And we've no idea where to even look. All we're certain of is they're south of us. If by some miracle you evade the Fedayeen, the chances of stumbling upon those guns is essentially zero."

Erickson understood his executive officer's assessment of how much longer they could hold out was correct. He was aware that tomorrow the Army divisions were going to unleash a massive assault. Still, he recognized that while the lightly armed 10th Infantry would likely succeed in tying down hundreds of thousands of insurgents, they didn't have the firepower to reach the embassy. That mission would fall upon the immensely powerful 3rd Infantry. Yet, with seven hundred miles to cross to reach Islamabad, even if their campaign was successful, all they'd find by the time they arrived were corpses inside what remained of the compound. Still, he understood what Tomlin had in mind was hopeless. All that any such effort would do was kill more Marines.

He turned to Corporal Genovese. "Put another call out. We need to make sure the higher-ups understand how tenuous our situation has become. Let them know they've got to silence those howitzers and they've got to do so soon if we're going to have any chance."

"On it, sir," Genovese responded. He began putting out the distress call.

As he did so, Erickson mumbled, "Somebody better get us some help here real soon."

"What was that, sir?" Genovese said.

"Nothing. Just do as I directed and let the outside world know the insurmountable odds we're facing. Then contact Camp Nowhere and get every Apache they can provide headed our way."

Two hours remained until the coming night and a modicum of safety would arrive.

But tomorrow a betraying sun would rise.

60

The dawn was approaching. The beauty the lake's vivid blue waters held was settling in. A few miles distant were a series of high, jagged hills. The Special Forces began emerging from the concealing bulrushes near the water's edge. Preoccupied with what the day might bring, the soldiers barely noticed the magnificent world around them.

"Grab your gear and get ready to move out," Captain Short said in a low voice.

In minutes they were heading toward the village. When they reached the northern edge of the lake, the first of what remained of the modest houses was right in front of them. The scorched structure showed every sign of being heavily damaged. The Green Berets slipped into the undergrowth along the lapping waters to wait and watch. Even if Fareeda was correct and everyone who had lived here was dead, they couldn't be certain who or what they might encounter. For all they knew, a thousand Fedayeen might be waiting.

The unimposing hamlet was silent and still. Even so, they waited still more. It didn't take long for an unmistakable stench to reach them. It was one they'd encountered on more than one occasion during their violence-filled careers. Decaying flesh. Moments later, in the half-light, Porter spotted a body lying in the mud near the closest building. Ten feet beyond was another, with a third, likely a child, by its side. Other than that, they saw and heard nothing.

Satisfied, Short motioned for them to spread out and move forward. As they did, the A Team commander reached out to keep Charlie Sanders from joining in. "Not you, Sanders. Stay here to protect the girl while we're securing the village."

A dawning sun shined down upon their fragile world. Aaron Porter was standing in the middle of the meager settlement's main street. The battle-hardened soldier couldn't believe what he was seeing. Despite his callousness, his eyes were filled with sadness. The village had been destroyed and he was surrounded by lifeless bodies. Many had their hands bound behind them. The majority had been beheaded. There was significant evidence of perversion and torture. Men, women, children, even babies—none had been spared.

"Do you believe this shit?" he said to Michael Noll. "These people didn't deserve this. No one deserved this. Fareeda said they did this to them because the men refused to join Basra's army."

"Bastards," was Noll's reply.

"The more of those sonsabitches we kill, the better I'm going to feel."

Captain Short approached.

"Did we find anyone alive?" Porter asked.

Short shook his head no.

"How soon till we move out, sir?" Noll asked.

"Just spoke with the battalion commander and relayed what we found. He wasn't able to provide a lot of details but said they've got something special planned for us. So we're to remain in place until told otherwise."

"After seeing this, let's hope that 'something special' involves killing lots and lots of these assholes," Porter said.

"Don't think you'll need to worry about that, Sergeant Porter. From the little he told me, we're going to get plenty of opportunities to fulfill your wish." Short turned to Sergeant Noll. "Tell everyone to return to our hiding place by the lake."

"Will do, sir." Noll turned and walked away.

The operational plan came through at shortly after two. But they stayed concealed where they were. Given the nature of the mission, the Green Berets would be far too vulnerable traveling during daylight hours. Unless the enemy forced their hand, they'd wait here, licking their wounds from the previous battle and preparing for what was to come. No fires, no talking, minimum movement.

Sanders had been tasked with shielding the girl from the perversion a few hundred yards distant. They had expected her to demand to see what had transpired. Yet she never asked to do so. Although the soldiers were careful not to mention what they'd discovered, she knew what they'd found. Despite her age, she recognized what it would do to her if she viewed the ghastly scene. She was much too young to approach the harsh reality of the death of those she loved. She understood what remained of her family was there. And she would have liked to say her goodbyes. But even if the Americans had let her, she wouldn't have viewed the horrors that had befallen the only place she had ever known in her short life. The horrors that haunted her every waking moment were already too much to bear.

Throughout the day, the soldiers took turns grabbing a few hours' sleep. Late in the afternoon, the three team leaders brought them together to plan their next move. They unfolded the crude maps they had of the area and with their GPS identified their precise position, but it wasn't of much help. The place where they found themselves was sparsely populated and not well defined.

"Doesn't seem to be any roads around here other than the one we blew up," Captain Henry said in a hushed tone. He looked to the northeast toward the craggy hills. The harsh terrain seemed quite foreboding. There didn't appear to be an obvious way to traverse the boulder-strewn landscape in front of them.

"Well, one thing's for certain," Short said. "We can't go back the way we came."

He took a look at the steep, unwelcoming landscape that greeted them. "Guess we'll have to figure out how to climb these hills if we're going to do what Group has in mind."

Henry's brow furrowed. "What concerns me most is not knowing anything about the area we're heading into or what we're going to find. We've got thirty miles to cover, all deep within enemy-held territory. Last thing we need is to be spotted and boxed in some dead-end canyon with no way of escape. And with every mile we travel, we'll be drawing closer to more fanatics than we can handle. Who knows what we might stumble upon as we move toward Islamabad? Did Group have an estimate of how many are in or around the capital?"

"At least a hundred thousand," Short said. "Possibly more. Nevertheless, we've got to get there and take out the target. If not, thousands of people are going to die."

"But we only have the vaguest idea where our objective is," Noll said.

"Does it matter?" Short responded. "One way or another, we'll find it. It's exactly the kind of thing we've been trained to do. And given the desperateness of the situation, no matter how difficult this becomes, we've got to try. We've got to reach Islamabad. We've got to succeed."

"Agreed," Henry said as he looked at the imposing peaks. "Anyone got the slightest idea which direction will give us the best chance of getting there without being detected?"

No one had an answer. Silence took hold. It refused to release its grip.

At the edge of the gathering, Fareeda decided the moment was right for her to speak up a second time. She was more than reluctant to do so but once again recognized they needed her help. "I know how we can get most of the way there without being seen," she said.

All faces turned toward her, anxious to hear what she had to say.

"Every Saturday, I used to help my father tie our donkey to the cart we owned. We'd then go over these mountains to Islamabad in order to sell the pottery the people in our village made. Sometimes, when the jingle trucks failed to arrive, we'd pick up things for those who lived here. I even know some shortcuts nobody but my father and a few of our villagers knew. It's not much more than a small trail, barely wide enough for our cart, but it will get us there. And it will cut the distance to Islamabad by more than half. Twenty kilometers, no more, and we'll reach the edge of the city. I can show you the way if you wish."

61

6:54 A.M., NOVEMBER 19
CHARLIE COMPANY (BLUE MAX), 3RD BATTALION,
10TH AVIATION REGIMENT, 10TH COMBAT AVIATION BRIGADE,
10TH MOUNTAIN DIVISION (LIGHT INFANTRY)
CAMP NOWHERE
THE SPĪN GHAR MOUNTAINS OF NORTH-CENTRAL PAKISTAN

If the Green Berets thought Camp Nowhere was a busy place when they arrived, they would have been astonished to see it now. With the addition of an entire American division, there wasn't an inch of space remaining on the icy plateau.

The time had come to unleash a massive attack in both the north and south. In the predawn darkness, head down to shield herself from the flesh-tearing winds, Bea Washington headed for her company's designated takeoff and landing zone. Behind her was her copilot, Shaun White. Their crewmen were already there. They'd removed the heavy tarp shielding the Black Hawk from the elements and inspected the craft's exterior. They spotted nothing out of place. Thirty yards to Washington's rear, eleven assault-ready foot soldiers struggled through the deep snow. Each was carrying a heavy pack and his individual weapon. Nearby, the crews and soldiers her company would ferry into battle did the same. Everywhere Washington looked, people were on the move. With the first assaults scheduled to begin within the hour, the secluded mountaintop was astir with activity. It would stay that way for the remainder of the war.

Once inside her UH-60, Washington settled into the pilot's seat and put on her headset. The moment she did, she performed the ritual she always did prior to taking off. She touched her fingertips to her lips and reached out to give the picture of her girls taped to the windshield a symbolic kiss. Having sat on the hilltop for fifteen hours, the inside of the Black Hawk was bitterly cold. Still, it did provide a buffer against the stinging elements. White joined her. In the rear of the helicopter, one by one the somber soldiers took their places.

She started the noisy engines. The blades whirled. She and White checked their instruments. Nothing seemed out of place.

Wanting her copilot to verify what she was seeing, she asked, "Everything look okay?"

"Just fine, ma'am," White answered. "Deicing of windshield, engine, and rotors is working properly. And there are no indications of our systems having issues. We should be good to go."

"We set back there?" she asked her senior crewman, Jesus Mercado.

"Yes, ma'am. Last of our load's on board."

Everything was ready. They sat waiting for the deicing to be completed and word to arrive for them to take off. In the coming minutes, theirs would be the first of many Black Hawks to depart the hillside. With 150 miles to travel to reach their designated drop zone, it would take most of the coming hour.

It was time. The moment the Americans had spent untold hours preparing for had found them. Washington lifted the buffeted Black Hawk into the air. Once it was stable, she turned the craft about and headed west. The remainder of her helicopter company joined them. Their goal was a location the satellites had identified as a major Fedayeen rallying point in that portion of the country.

62

7:10 A.M., NOVEMBER 19

4TH PLATOON, BRAVO COMPANY, 2ND BATTALION, 69TH ARMOR REGIMENT,

2ND ARMORED BRIGADE COMBAT TEAM (SPARTANS),

3RD INFANTRY DIVISION

ON THE FRONTLINES

NORTHERN OUTSKIRTS OF KARACHI, PAKISTAN

After two days of defending against one brutal attack after another, the Americans were eager to go on the offensive. So far, all four Bradley crews had survived. But others hadn't been so lucky. Seven of the infantrymen the platoon had ferried into battle were dead or wounded. At midnight, replacements for those they'd lost had arrived. So each Bradley would be carrying a full load of six foot soldiers.

Fedayeen losses were immense. But with two million fighters on the battlefront, it seemed to matter little.

Bravo Company would spearhead the attack. Fourth Platoon, Darren Walton's, would take the point. They'd lead the way toward an uncertain destiny. Behind them, spreading out for miles, were fifteen thousand soldiers serving in various roles. Their numbers included over three hundred top-of-the-line Abrams tanks and an equal number of Bradley fighting vehicles.

It was an imposing force. And its immense power was about to be unleashed upon an unsuspecting enemy. The prelude to the

American assault, an artillery bombardment by the division's arrayed guns, had begun three hours earlier. Its intent was to soften up the jihadist lines. The thousand-round onslaught had been unrelenting, with shell after shell smashing into the unprepared peasant army. The dead and wounded from the onslaught had been significant. Disarray had followed. To those being assailed, it felt like the dark night would never end. But end it did. At 7:00 a.m., as the sun's initial rays touched the horizon, the thundering guns went silent.

Ten minutes passed. The perplexed extremists hadn't a clue what was about to hit them. At 7:10, it was time for the thunder and lightning to begin. Without warning, six fearsome Apaches passed over the lead Bradley platoon. The moment they reached the first of the enemy, their Gatling guns raged at their struggling foe. Behind them, wave after wave of Reaper drones roared across the skies.

It was the signal for which the platoon had been waiting. "All right, 4th Platoon, let's move out," Lieutenant Cramer said.

"On it, sir," Walton replied. He spoke into the Bradley's intercom. "Okay, Aiden, you heard the man. Put it in gear and let's go."

As they freed themselves from their firing hole and moved forward, the platoon sergeant gripped his Bushmaster cannon's controls. He was ready to fire the 25mm gun at a moment's notice.

The four Bradleys churned through the soft clay. Behind them, four M1 tanks followed the Bradley platoon's lead. The Fedayeen lines were little more than a quarter of a mile distant.

63

3:00 A.M., NOVEMBER 20
OPERATIONAL DETACHMENT ALPHA 6333, CHARLIE COMPANY,
3RD BATTALION, 6TH SPECIAL FORCES GROUP (AIRBORNE)
IN THE RUBBLE
TWELVE MILES SOUTH OF THE UNITED STATES EMBASSY
ISLAMABAD, PAKISTAN

Fareeda had been right. The insulated mountain trail had taken the Special Forces soldiers to the edge of Islamabad. Along the way, they hadn't seen anyone. No one had appeared as they covered the twelve miles to the periphery of the sprawling city. Until the girl had stepped in, they'd believed it would take two exceptionally dangerous nights to make their way through the teeming enemy lines. Yet they'd completed the arduous journey in eight hours.

At 3:00 a.m., they'd found themselves staring through their night vision at the capital's endless ruins. The suffocating night was black and omnipresent. A light wind's whisper rose to greet them. They were four miles from where they needed to be. If they were going to traverse such a ponderous distance, they recognized they'd need a great deal of good fortune.

With this moment being the lowest ebb of the night, the majority of the Fedayeen would be hidden in the rubble, deep within their dreams. There would undoubtedly be sentries, but within their own lines few would be concerned with the world around them. Still, a single mistake, a miscalculated step, and everything could devolve in an instant.

Aaron Porter would be out front. They had three hours, no more, to cover the four miles. Any longer and the approaching day would betray them. They needed to hurry. But to do so in such a way that they didn't blunder.

"All right, Sergeant Porter, lead the away," Captain Short whispered.

Without responding, Porter started into the pitch-black maze. Climbing over, sliding under, moving around and through the unpredictable obstacles, he headed toward the southern portion of the city. One by one the others followed. All were highly skilled in escape and evasion. Each had spent countless hours polishing those immense abilities. In the center of the stretching incursion, Charlie Sanders kept the wide-eyed girl close to him.

They hadn't gone fifty yards when Porter spotted the heat emanating from three human forms. He signaled the others. He waited, trying to determine the threat they posed. It didn't take long to realize the enemy was asleep. Even so, the teams couldn't risk them awakening as they attempted to pass. They'd need to deal with all three before moving on. He motioned for the pair of Green Berets behind him to move forward.

After confirming no additional jihadists were nearby, they joined him. Each realized the slightest sound, the smallest mishap, could change everything. They were, however, far too adept to make such a mistake. Placing every foot precisely, the deadly soldiers soon reached their targets. They selected their victims and drew their knives. When Porter signaled, they edged forward and each ended a life. Task completed, the Americans froze, waiting to see if their actions had given them away. But nothing untoward appeared.

With the initial obstacle overcome, they headed through the masking night. Each understood countless challenges would be waiting. The first quarter mile was conquered. It felt much longer. There were many more to come. Taking cover whenever necessary while pressing forward when they could, they moved toward their objective. An hour passed. And then another. Every tentative step brought them closer to their goal. The number of Fedayeen lives forfeited along the way was rising. They were getting nearer, but they weren't there yet. Little more than an hour remained. And the closer they got to the center of the city, the more of the enemy they encountered. Their knives dripping red, they continued the fraught journey.

To the relief of all, somehow, someway, their luck had held, even if they'd left more than two dozen bodies in their wake. By 5:51 a.m. they'd reached the area for which they'd been searching. In front of them, they found the eerie shell of a mangled building with its lower walls partially intact. It was the perfect spot to hide while they watched and waited throughout the coming day. They slipped inside the ghoulish structure.

As soon as they'd set up their defenses, Captain Short turned to Fareeda. "How many times have you been to Islamabad?" he asked.

"Many times with my father."

"Do you know where the American embassy is? It's supposed to be near the Kashmir Highway."

"I know the Kashmir Highway. But with the way the city looks, I'm not sure where anything is right now."

"Once we finish with what we're here to do, we're going to try to reach the embassy. Was hoping you could lead us there."

"I'm sorry. I've been to some of the marketplaces within the city, but my father never said anything about where the American embassy was."

"Well, no matter. We've got the GPS coordinates. After we've completed our assignment, we'll use those to find our way."

With the sunrise, it was time for the well-concealed Green Berets to begin their observations. They had to pinpoint where the Fedayeen had hidden the howitzers.

"Which direction do you want us to search, sir," Michael Noll asked.

"That's the problem. All we know is the firing's coming from somewhere south of the embassy. GPS says we're eight miles from it. The cannons could be on either side of us, behind us, or in front of us. Until they unleash them, we've no way of knowing where to focus our attention. For now, we'll have to position ourselves so we can search the entire perimeter. Hopefully, it won't take too many rounds to narrow things down."

64

3:27 P.M., NOVEMBER 20
C COMPANY (BLUE MAX), 3RD BATTALION,
10TH AVIATION REGIMENT, 10TH COMBAT AVIATION BRIGADE,
10TH MOUNTAIN DIVISION (LIGHT INFANTRY)
CAMP NOWHERE
THE SPĪN GHAR MOUNTAINS OF NORTH-CENTRAL PAKISTAN

For a fourth time, Bea Washington was returning from placing 10th Mountain soldiers on the widespread battlefields. The Black Hawk hovered above Camp Nowhere's challenging setting. The howling winds and crowded conditions made the landing far from routine. Still, she handled the effort magnificently. The Black Hawk's skis gently touched the snow. Once her helicopter settled into the deep powder, she shut down the engines.

The moment she did, she hurried out to take a look at her aircraft. It didn't take long to find what she'd no doubt was there. Her battered craft had at least fifteen bullet holes in it. Their random pattern spread across its frame. Fortunately, none had hit a critical component. Her Black Hawk's armor had held. On her first distant foray they'd caught their unsuspecting opponent unaware. Without opposition, she'd dropped her soldiers and returned to the high mountains. Yet each subsequent trip for the eight helicopters she was leading had been far different. The rallying enemy, its numbers growing to immense proportions, was ready. Armed and angry, they'd been waiting.

On her most recent excursion, the fighting had been beyond intense, with the landing zone swarming with hostiles. With bullets flying and her crewmen releasing a torrent of .30-caliber rounds to suppress the jihadists, they'd attempted to land. She'd settled her Black Hawk near a protective outcropping just long enough for the eleven soldiers she carried to leap from the hold. The instant the final one did, she took off, frantically attempting to get some air beneath her craft. And to find a way out. In seconds, they were gone. Somehow they'd survived. They'd made it back to their icy home. Others, however, hadn't been so lucky.

She knew the answer but asked her copilot anyway. "How many did we lose?"

White looked as the battered force landed around them. Smoke was billowing from the final craft's right engine. Another had a significant hole in its side.

"Two for sure went down," he said. "Lieutenant Howsen's and Captain Meadows's. Howsen's was hit by an RPG and exploded in midair before he was able to get his soldiers out. Meadows's crashed. It slammed into that rock face to the west of us." White hesitated. "I guess there's a chance someone on it survived. But from what I saw, it's not likely. No idea what losses the other crews suffered." He looked at those landing around them. From the tents in the center of the hilltop he could see medics running their way. "We'll know in a minute."

The reality of losing two of the crews she commanded was etched across her features. It wasn't the first time she'd experienced such events, but that mattered little. Each instance affected her deeply. She recognized that it always would. She knew at some point, likely when she least expected it, this perverse afternoon would hit her. Its accusatory image would settle deep within her soul. She'd made no mistakes out there today. If anything, her skillful commands had saved lives. Still, it didn't matter.

"Get the maintenance crews to check her over real good," she said. "Don't think anything vital was hit, but we need to make sure. Then get our .30-calibers reloaded. Gotta be ready for whatever the next mission might be. It probably won't be long until we're in the air again. If we were wondering if the Fedayeen would put up a fight, there's no doubt now. Those bastards mean business. A lot of blood's going to be spilled before this one's over."

65

They had seven hundred miles to cover to reach Islamabad. So far, as darkness arrived on the second day of the 3rd Infantry's attack, they'd covered nine. And in the previous hours, as the enemy staged a massive counterattack, the division had seized almost nothing. To make matters worse, the fierce fighting had cost over one hundred American lives. Both were discouraging numbers. Still, it wasn't much of a surprise. They were hardly consoled by the British and French doing no better. With two million jihadists on the front lines, the Americans recognized the going would be slow in the assault's initial stages.

It had taken until the second morning for Basra's stunned force to recognize they were no longer the aggressors. Once they had, they'd dug in. Reinforcements had been sent, with multitudes racing toward the evolving scene. Even Salim Basra understood the threat of the foreign divisions to his chances of ruling this land. Despite his distrust for his second-in-command, he understood Bila Chachar was the only one capable of saving him.

He sent him south to take charge of the Fedayeen defenses while he addressed the attacks in the north.

Once Chachar arrived, he would spring into action. Still hundreds of miles away, he had a good idea of what he'd need to do. With his appearance later that night, he would order thousands of men to dig tank traps behind the front lines. The creation of huge minefields would follow. Immense numbers of IEDs would be buried. It wouldn't be long before these improvised explosive devices would line every roadway and field.

The Americans had anticipated three to four days of slow going until they broke through. As night fell on the second day, such an estimate was giving every appearance of being wildly optimistic. While they watched the jihadists' mounting response, it was impossible to predict the actual amount of time it would take before they'd breach the enemy's defenses. Yet the division commander was certain it would happen. Once the 3rd Infantry had, they'd rush toward Islamabad.

A hundred yards apart, the lead platoon's stalemated Bradleys battled the massive force in front of them. "Walton, just got word from Battalion," Lieutenant Cramer said. "Given our night-fighting capabilities, we're going to keep the pressure on."

"Makes sense, sir," the platoon sergeant replied as he fired his Bradley's machine gun at a well-concealed nest of fighters on his right. "Just be advised, we're low on gasoline and ammunition. At some point we're going to need a resupply if they expect us to attack until morning."

Three of the flailing defenders went down beneath Walton's highly accurate fire. But the others were not dissuaded. A lone figure rose, lifted an RPG onto his shoulder, and fired. The rocket-propelled grenade was a blur as it raced across the blood-tinged field. It smashed headlong into Walton's Bradley. The nasty ordnance exploded. A brilliant flash lit up the horrific scene. But the effort was of little importance. The Bradley's twelve-inch armor brushed it aside.

In the rear of the armored vehicle, an infantryman fired a lengthy burst from his M4 through his firing port. Two hundred yards away, the figure who'd fired the RPG fell.

"Same here, sir," said Sergeant Vigo, commanding the Bradley to the right of the lieutenant. "Used up lots of ammunition and our fuel's getting iffy."

"What about you, Sergeant Devine?" Cramer asked the final Bradley commander.

"Same as the others, sir."

"All right, I'll let Battalion know."

"Sir, did Battalion say anything about the Al-Khalid tanks the scout drones spotted?" Walton asked.

"Negative. Nothing new since sundown. Last report was they were twenty miles away and headed in this direction."

"Comforting to know we've got M1s behind us," Walton said. "Al-Khalids are good tanks, but there's no way they'll stand up to our Abrams. M1s will tear them to pieces."

"Don't forget what the Apaches will do to them," Cramer said.

"And what the M1s and Apaches don't get, the TOWs on our Bradleys will," Walton's gunner, Evan Minter, added.

Walton unleashed his machine gun at a half dozen peasants sneaking forward with satchel charges. The veteran sergeant tore them apart. Moments later, there was a massive explosion somewhere on the left. The Americans instinctively reacted to the reverberating sounds and the fireball that followed. They had no idea what had been hit or even which side had been caught by the mighty blow. The early evening fighting went on without letup. Death's grisly hand seized the unfortunate on both sides. What exactly was occurring, the Bradley platoon had little way of knowing. All they understood was it was going to be a long, painful night.

66

9:43 P.M., NOVEMBER 20
OPERATIONAL DETACHMENT ALPHA 6333,
CHARLIE COMPANY, 3RD BATTALION,
6TH SPECIAL FORCES GROUP (AIRBORNE)
IN THE REMAINS OF A DESTROYED OFFICE BUILDING
EIGHT MILES SOUTH OF THE UNITED STATES EMBASSY
ISLAMABAD, PAKISTAN

They had anticipated the trail of dead they'd created would cause the Fedayeen to conduct an intense search to locate its source. But it didn't happen. Instead, the fanatics had mistakenly believed the killings were caused by some sort of dispute between rival factions. So, with little thought and no investigation, they dismissed the carnage out of hand.

To the Americans' surprise, in the long hours hidden behind their well-chosen facade, they hadn't been stumbled upon by anyone. Hiding deep inside the destroyed building's devolving structure, they'd watched throughout the day. They'd seen what they needed to see.

The howitzers had fired enough rounds by midday to verify the general direction of the big guns and to make an accurate determination of their location by early afternoon. The place they were looking for was a mile north and quarter mile east of their position. The target was so well hidden that even with the Green Berets providing its general placement, their command element wasn't convinced the Apaches could find and destroy it. And should a helicopter attack fail, it would tip off the jihadists. They would no doubt move the artillery, foiling any chance the Americans had of destroying it. At dawn the next day, they'd begin firing once more. And the embassy's death toll would mount.

Facing such a reality, the decision was made to send in Short's men to eliminate them. Knowing they were going to have to take out the objective, there was little they could do but wait and watch as the life-seizing weapons fired one shattering round after another at the defenseless target. They knew people were dying. Nonetheless, they had no option but to let it happen. They couldn't eliminate their prize until the sheltering darkness of night. To attempt to do so in broad daylight would lead to abject failure and the swift forfeiture of their lives. None would get halfway to the guns before being identified and killed. And the mission's purpose would go unresolved. Still, such knowledge didn't please them in the slightest. They were men of action. Even so, they could do nothing but remain hidden as the endless hours passed.

Finally, the time had come for the anguished Green Berets. They had passed the day planning the attack and readying themselves for what lay ahead.

The time had come. If they were going to destroy the artillery pieces and traverse the seven miles to the embassy, they needed to move now. Otherwise, they would be unable to cross such an imposing distance before the next sunrise.

Short was reasonably satisfied with the approach they were going to take. It certainly wasn't perfect, but it gave the Green Berets a chance of getting in and extinguishing those guns. Still, he had to admit getting out and making their escape across such a stretch of enemy-controlled soil was going to be another story.

"So we're all on board, correct?" Short said. "Everyone knows what's expected of them?"

"Find some way to reach those guns," Porter said matter-of-factly. "Once we arrive, suppress any enemy fire. Create a path for Sanders and Davidson to reach the targets. Keep the bastards pinned down while they destroy those howitzers. If for some reason they fail to get there, render the guns useless by shoving hand grenades down the barrels. Then get the hell out of there any way we can."

"Head toward the embassy," Noll added. "If we don't reach it by sunrise, find a place to wait out the day. When night comes, attempt to make it. No matter what, we're not to allow ourselves to be taken captive. The Fedayeen don't take prisoners. They only take heads. So we're to fight until the end even when left with little to fight with. If possible, kill another of those soulless sonsabitches before they take us out."

"Good. Until we reach the target, you're to hang back with the girl, Sergeant Sanders," Short said. "Once we're close, turn her over to Sergeant Porter and you and Sergeant Davidson move in to finish the job."

"Yes, sir. We know what's expected of us."

"No mistakes out there tonight. Rallying point after we destroy the objective is the small grove of trees we identified earlier. Understood?"

"Understood," each responded.

"Then let's get to it."

Without a word, they put on their gear. Each recognized how dangerous the assignment would be. With every movement, they'd be edging deeper into a roaring lion's mouth that threatened to devour them. In the middle of a hundred thousand hostiles they'd attempt to do the impossible. Not only did they need to wipe out the howitzers; they needed to find a way out of a whirling vortex of death and destruction. To a man, they understood the majority probably wouldn't make it. It was possible none would. Still, it no longer mattered. They were the best there was for a mission like this. And those guns had to be silenced.

In twos and threes, like a passing breath they slipped out of the wreckage and edged across the disordered landscape. Each was an apparition, little more than a searing night's phantom.

They had no choice but to take Fareeda with them. While they didn't want to expose her to the danger they'd be facing, the moment they hit the target, the Fedayeen would be alerted to their presence. There would be no way of returning to retrieve her. And they couldn't leave her here.

67

10:32 P.M., NOVEMBER 20
OPERATIONAL DETACHMENT ALPHA 6333,
CHARLIE COMPANY, 3RD BATTALION,
6TH SPECIAL FORCES GROUP (AIRBORNE)
HIDDEN IN THE RUBBLE
SEVEN MILES SOUTH OF THE UNITED STATES EMBASSY
ISLAMABAD, PAKISTAN

Despite the enemy presence, the undetected Americans had crossed the mile separating them from the target area. Two hundred yards away, the howitzers waited. As they neared, their night vision picked up the considerable force defending the weapons. Jihadists were in the crumbling rocks and twisted steel near the well-hidden cavern. Others patrolled the areas farther out.

"How many do you see?" Master Sergeant Noll, lying next to Porter, whispered.

"At least twenty. Given the time of night, there are probably three times as many sleeping nearby."

"Have you spotted the howitzers?"

"Yeah. Eleven o'clock a couple hundred yards away. I can just make out the tips of their muzzles. They're in a straight line near the big steel girder rising up in the center of the area. They're about twenty yards apart."

Noll looked in the direction Porter had indicated. "Oh, yeah,

I've got them." He spoke into his headset. "Captain, we've identified the target. Go ahead and move the teams forward."

"We're on the way," Short replied in a low voice. "Sanders, you and Davidson stay here with the girl. While you're waiting, get your charges ready so we can get in, do the job, and get the hell out."

"Yes, sir. We'll get right on it," Sanders said while taking off his rucksack to find the explosives he intended to use.

"Okay," Short said. "In ones and twos, the rest of you head up to Sergeant Porter's position."

Shielded by the darkness, the teams skirted from obstacle to obstacle. The murky forms moved with a preciseness born from years of practice. Not a sound was made. Not a single misstep occurred. They slipped in and out of the chaotic world with a skill few possessed. One hundred yards remained before they'd reach the forward pair.

While he waited for the others to reach them, Porter examined the apocalyptic scene. It took some time, but he finally spotted what he was hoping to find. There was a soft spot in the peasants' defenses.

Eventually all were there. "What're we up against?" Short asked in a murmur.

"Far more than we'd hoped, sir. Their defenses run about a hundred yards in each direction. Six machine guns ring the center. Two in the north, two to the south, and one each in the east and west. Eight sentries are prowling the perimeter with more dug in near the guns. But there's some good news."

"What's that, Sergeant Porter?"

"I've identified a weak point."

"Where?"

"Southeast corner. Sentry stationed there is leaning against a cement barrier. He hasn't moved in some time. Given what I've observed, I wouldn't be surprised if he's asleep. Good chance the machine-gun coverage in the area isn't as strong as elsewhere. And from what I can see, there's only one soldier dug in in that portion of their defenses. If we can take down the sentry and the second guard, we'll be twenty-five yards from the target, with little blocking our path. We'll have a decent chance of reaching the howitzers without being spotted."

"So you believe we should move to the far side, eliminate the sentry and the dug-in guard, then attempt to slip inside?"

"Exactly, sir. That looks like the most vulnerable point. Our best chance of getting in undetected is from the southeast. If we approach from that direction, we might be able to avoid getting sucked into a major firefight while attempting to reach them. There's no way they can be prepared for such a maneuver. Attack from within, seize control of the center, destroy the big guns, and fight our way out."

"Are you sure, Sergeant Porter?" Short asked. He recognized they were only going to get one shot at this.

"As sure as I can be, sir. It really is the best chance we've got. Hit the weakest point, then move fast from there."

"It'll mean swinging all the way around to the southeast."

"Yes, sir. But it'll be worth the risk involved. Skirt the enemy defenses and attack from there. Strike before the Fedayeen are able to initiate a response."

"Get in, get out. Sounds a hell of a lot better than hitting them head-on and having to take on six machine guns, sir," Noll said.

They could see the captain considering it.

"It's our best opportunity to destroy those guns," Porter said. "And if it works, it'll give us a chance to clear the area before reinforcements arrive."

Short hesitated, running through their options a final time. "Let's do it, then," he said.

They'd reached the southeast corner. There they lay, waiting and watching. At the back of the grouping, Sanders and Davidson did their best to protect Fareeda. Their initial target was directly in front of them, thirty yards away. Other than momentarily opening his eyes while he scratched himself, the sentry hadn't moved.

"Remember, once we complete the assignment, the rallying point will be the grove of trees a half mile north of here," Short whispered to those present. "Is that clear? From what we were able to see, there appears to be a shallow depression there we can use to mask our presence while we organize our escape. When we blow those guns, all hell's going to break loose. So we won't be able to wait for stragglers. One way or another, make sure you get there. If not, you'll be on your own. Is that understood?" When no one responded, he said, "All right, Sergeant Porter, let's get to it."

The plan called for the others to remain where they were while Porter eliminated the sleeping guard and the one dug in some distance behind him. It was now or never. Porter removed his pack and handed it to Noll. He repositioned his night vision to ensure it was secure. Ready to strike, the lethal American edged toward his initial prey. He needed to remain hidden. He needed to do this without the slightest noise. This wasn't going to be easy. But the moonless night would help.

68

11:24 P.M., NOVEMBER 20

OPERATIONAL DETACHMENT ALPHA 6333,

CHARLIE COMPANY, 3RD BATTALION,

6TH SPECIAL FORCES GROUP (AIRBORNE)

HIDDEN IN THE RUBBLE FIFTY YARDS FROM THE HOWITZERS

SEVEN MILES SOUTH OF THE UNITED STATES EMBASSY

ISLAMABAD, PAKISTAN

Blood dripping from his knife, Porter slid the body to the ground. The dozing peasant never knew what hit him. Not a sound was made while slaying the hapless soul. Not a telltale movement occurred.

Task completed, the deadly sergeant paused. He knelt to verify his efforts hadn't alerted his foe. While he waited, nothing seemed out of place. There was no sign that anyone was aware of his presence. Satisfied, he prepared for what was to come.

The second victim awaited. The able American understood this kill was going to be far more challenging. For despite the hour, the sentry was giving every appearance of being observant. Nonetheless, the deft sergeant knew he had to prevail. And to do so without alerting others in the area. The mission, and the Special Forces soldiers' lives, depended upon it.

His breathing shallow, Porter dropped to the ground. He had to find a way to get behind the circumspect guard without betraying his presence. While he examined the area, he spied a slender opening in the shattered rocks and distorted steel. It appeared to be wide enough for him to slide through undetected. Ever so gradually he started crawling with his nose pressed against the unyielding ground. Slithering through one confined opening after the next, he edged forward at a pace untraceable by even the most skilled of observers.

It felt as if his efforts were taking forever, but he finally was able to make his way around his target. Lying a few feet behind his quarry, he made another cursory examination to ensure no one was nearby. His search found nothing.

The crucial moment had arrived. If the lookout was able to cry out before he was eliminated, the Americans' plan would be foiled. With the enemy alerted, they'd have to fight their way through the heavy defenses to take out the offending weapons. Even with their immense skills, the chances for success would be greatly lessened. And their ability to make their escape gone.

Knife in hand, he crept forward. With the loose rock and crumbling remains around him, it was no easy task. Even so, without betraying his presence, he moved ever closer to his goal. It was time to end this. The sitting figure was within reach.

His threadbare opponent had heard nothing. Yet, as he stared out upon a surreal world, a creeping feeling came over him. Something was out of place. Still, he was unable to put his finger on it. While the isolated sentry searched the world in front of him, rather than disappearing, the troubling sensation grew. Without explanation, the hairs on his arms stood straight up. He was confused by what his senses were attempting to tell him. He peered into the void once again, straining to define the frightful emotions. Yet nothing untoward appeared. He couldn't figure out the cause of it, but whatever was occurring was out of place. And then it hit him: the thing creating the baffling impressions was behind him. And quite nearby. At the last possible instant, the perplexed peasant turned.

Poised to seize another life, Porter responded with lightning speed. He was little more than a blur as he pounced. A flailing contest sprang forth. The Green Beret outweighed his opponent by fifty pounds. And his fighting abilities were immensely superior. It wasn't long before he'd taken control of the situation. With his knees pinning his hapless victim's arms, he stabbed deep within the wide-eyed individual's chest. The fatally wounded jihadist, his indescribable pain surging, attempted to cry out. Before he was able to do so, Porter placed his free hand over his month. Nothing but muffled sounds passed from the dying Pakistani's lips. With a second swift blow, Porter stabbed again. There'd be no need to do so again. A final breath and his opponent succumbed.

After verifying that his prey was dead, Porter released his grip. He had no idea if the brief struggle had informed anyone nearby. Once more he froze, waiting for the telltale signs of others being aware of his presence. He was, however, relieved to find he was too far away from the other guards for the attenuated sounds to be heard. And the brutal event had ended so quickly that it hadn't given him away.

Satisfied, he whispered into his headset, "Both guards are down. Bring the teams forward."

"You heard the man: Let's go," Short said the moment he heard Porter's words. One at a time, his force edged toward Porter's position. "Sergeant Sanders, when I give the word, you and Davidson move forward to eliminate those guns."

"Yes, sir. Explosives are ready. As soon as you secure the target area, we'll join you. Shouldn't take long to get everything set to blow."

69

11:42 P.M., NOVEMBER 20
OPERATIONAL DETACHMENT ALPHA 6333,
CHARLIE COMPANY, 3RD BATTALION,
6TH SPECIAL FORCES GROUP (AIRBORNE)
TEN FEET FROM THE HOWITZERS
SEVEN MILES SOUTH OF THE UNITED STATES EMBASSY
ISLAMABAD, PAKISTAN

The Americans had breached the perimeter. The gun emplacements were directly in front of them. Everything was going as planned.

Yet in a flashing instant, that was about to change. As they neared the broad entrance, a half-asleep Fedayeen soldier was heading out of the deep bunker, intent on relieving himself. While he walked by the gun on the far left and emerged from the significant cavity, the sleepy jihadist spotted multiple figures a few yards away. He didn't think much of it. People were constantly coming and going in the area. Then he suddenly realized something was amiss. It didn't take long to recognize the approaching figures were not his countrymen. And only a heartbeat more to comprehend the heavily armed force was there to do great harm.

He hadn't brought his AK-47. Seven miles behind his lines, he had seen no reason to do so. So he did the only thing he could. He screamed an extended warning.

Halfway through his hurried words, the leading Green Beret

opened fire. His spewing rifle cut the figure in half. The jig was up. The dying soldier's alert and the sounds of rifle fire ended any chance they had of slipping in before anyone appreciated what was happening. The world around them came alive. The area surrounding the howitzers was suddenly filled with animated shouts. Those manning the machine guns attempted to react to the menacing phoenix rising in their midst. They'd been prepared to address a threat from outside the perimeter. They'd never contemplated it would appear from within. Each attempted to turn his weapon. It wouldn't be long before they'd succeed in doing so. Once they had, they'd open fire.

There was no time to waste. Before the stirring jihadists got organized, the Green Berets needed to act. "First six, set up a defensive perimeter!" Captain Short yelled. "Next grouping enter the bunker and take out those inside."

With absolute precision, his teams did as directed. The initial half dozen found solid defensive positions and opened fire. Focusing on the machine guns protecting the northern side of the bunker, they took the nearest one down without its gunner releasing a single round. They were soon targeting the second, now-firing .30-caliber. As the Americans' bullets struck him, its gunner slumped face forward. Multiple rounds to the center of his chest had eliminated him.

An equal number of Green Berets ran inside the gaping opening. Michael Noll was at their head. The space was as dark as the bleakest of January nights. Yet, with their night vision, the entering element had no trouble seeing in this sightless existence. The enemy, however, had no such ability. Everywhere the Green Berets looked, the cavern was filled with rousing jihadists. By the dozens they were feeling for their AK-47s and beginning to stand. Unable to see farther than a few feet, they remained unaware that those who'd come for them were already in their midst. Nonetheless, the Green Berets entering the bunker understood that in a matter of seconds the closest Fedayeen would realize someone was present and open fire. The Special Forces soldiers were determined to make sure that didn't happen. They leveled their M4s and opened fire. Burst after burst cut down the hapless forms.

The overwhelmed revolutionaries were dropping so fast it was impossible to keep track. Five . . . ten . . . twenty . . . thirty . . . at an astounding rate, their numbers swelled. In every corner the mortally wounded fell. As the last succumbed, Noll signaled for the others to cease firing.

"Sir, bunker's secure," Noll said into his headset.

"Sanders, get in there," Short said.

"On our way, sir. Let's go, Davidson."

The pair leaped to their feet and ran toward the opening. As they did, they could hear round after round ricocheting off the tumbled stones around them.

Those outside the bunker did all they could to protect the nearing duo. But with the machine guns in the east and west now erupting with devastating fire, and scores of Basra's devotees arriving, their efforts weren't nearly enough to pin the Fedayeen down. In a half crouch, with bullets flying around them, the engineers hurried toward the opening. Scrambling over the objects in their path, they soon arrived. Unharmed, they entered the significant space. They were little more than a few feet from the first of the howitzers.

Sanders took a quick look around, making a final judgment on what they faced. The artillery was in a straight line some distance apart. "We're inside, sir," he said.

"How's it look?" Short asked. "Are you going to be able to take them out?"

"Piece of cake, sir. Ninety seconds and they won't be of use to anyone. Davidson, run down to the far end to destroy the gun on the right. I'll handle this one and the one in the middle. We'll set the timers for forty-five seconds and get the hell away from here."

"On it, Sarge," Davidson said. The instant the words left his mouth he rushed toward the farthest of the hulking guns. Forty yards away, his prize awaited.

"Everyone else, get out of here," Sanders said. "The explosions won't be big ones, but when the ends of these guns are ripped apart, you're not going to want to be nearby."

"You heard the man. Let's go," Noll said.

They scrambled out of the hole. At a safe distance, they took up positions to support those attempting to hold off the gathering masses. While they were doing so, Davidson arrived at the most distant gun. He tore off his satchel and pulled out the explosives. At the same time, Sanders moved over to the first of his objectives and did the same.

"Sanders, we're out of harm's way. Go ahead and blow them," Noll said.

"Sergeant Porter, bring the girl and join us. We're getting out of here as fast as we can after those howitzers are taken out," Short said as he watched the situation deteriorating.

"On our way, sir," Porter responded. Fareeda was lying next to him. She was trembling uncontrollably. He looked into her eyes. "Listen, I'll get you out of here. I promise. But you've got to stick close to me and do what I tell you. Do you understand?"

She nodded her head in response.

"Okay. We're going to get up and go over to where the others are waiting. We're going to move fast. The sooner we get there, the better off we'll be." He got up and lifted the girl to her feet. "Now!" he said.

Half running on the rare occasions the landscape would allow it, climbing over and under when it wouldn't, they struggled to cross the final twenty-five yards to reach the others. Like Sanders and Davidson, they were met by a torrent of seeking rounds. Yet somehow they survived. Once inside the teams' defenses, with his own body Porter covered as much of Fareeda as he could. He fired his M4, taking out more than one of their foes.

Inside the fissure, Sanders was ready. "Davidson, you set down there?" he asked as he looked in his direction.

"Yep. Just waiting for you to give the word."

"Set the timer, plant the explosives, and make your escape."

Davidson did as he'd been directed. In a few rapid heartbeats he was shoving the charge down the immense barrel. Sanders did the same. While Davidson scrambled to safety, the senior engineer hurried over to the middle gun.

So the explosions would occur simultaneously this time, he set the timer for thirty seconds and rammed it into the barrel. A rapid check of his handiwork and he headed toward the frenetic world outside. He threw himself on the ground a few yards away from the opening.

"Charges are set, sir. Should blow any second."

"Roger," Short said. "Everyone, hold your position until we're certain the guns have been destroyed."

They could barely hear him over the fiercely expanding battle. Holding their positions was going to be easier said than done. Intense pressure was building in every direction. Muzzle flashes lit up the night. More and more jihadists appeared and joined the fight. To a man, the Green Berets recognized the situation wasn't going to get any better. Still they fired their rifles, doing all they could to respond to the approaching whirlwind.

From within the expansive hollow, three explosions sounded. Smoke rose from the opening. The moment the event ended, Short said, "Sanders, Davidson, get back in there and verify those guns have been destroyed."

"On it, sir," Sanders said. "Let's go, Davidson."

The pair rushed into the blackened space. In seconds Sanders reached the first of the howitzers. The final two feet of the barrel was twisted and shredded. The end of its smoking muzzle was mangled beyond recognition.

"Middle gun's been disabled, sir."

"Same with the one on this end," Davidson reported.

"Let me check the one in the far left," Sanders said.

He worked his way through the tangle of bodies until he reached the last howitzer. What he saw brought a smile to his face. The result was the same. The howitzers were no longer a threat.

"Last one's out of commission, sir. We're making our way out." Leaving the stilled space, he and Davidson reentered the firefight.

The situation was growing more desperate. With every tick of the clock, more enemy were arriving. The American commander understood there was no way they'd be able to withstand the pressure much longer. If they were going to survive, they needed to act.

"Anyone see a way out of this?" Short asked.

There was a pause before the answer came. "Nothing's going to be easy, sir," Noll said. "There are rifles firing from every direction. But it looks like the majority are in front of us. So the last thing we'll want is to attempt going forward. In the eastern part of the battle, with the exception of the enemy machine gun, the gunfire's not that intense. If we can take it out, maybe some of us could try to escape in that direction."

"Same in the west," Captain Henry said from his position on the far end of their defenses. "Maybe we should split up and attempt to fight our way through on both sides. Once we have, we might be able to skirt their lines."

"Anyone disagree with those assessments?" Short asked.

"No, sir," Porter said. "That looks like our best chance." He took a look around. "Maybe our only chance."

"Then let's do this. Sergeant Porter, can you get a clear shot at the machine gun in the east?"

"Not an easy one, sir. He's hidden in the rocks a hundred yards from here. Only a small part of his body's exposed. But when you give the word, I'll do what I can."

From two years of watching him in the direst of situations, Neil Short knew Porter would figure out a way to handle this. He had little doubt his senior weapons specialist would succeed. The exceptional sergeant had never failed in even the most perilous of assignments, and Short anticipated he wouldn't do so now.

Short turned his focus to the .30-caliber on the other side. "Is anybody in a position to take out the other one?"

At least initially, no one responded. Captain Henry finally spoke up. "There are four M4s on this side who might be able to reach him."

"Okay. Let's approach it that way, then. Sergeant Porter, take out the one in the east. The four of you closest to the one in the west will handle the other. Keep firing until you're certain they've been eliminated. The remainder of us will continue to engage the force in front of us. Once those machine guns are gone, we'll split into twos and threes and head out. We'll do our best to conduct an orderly withdrawal a group at a time." He paused ever so slightly. "Are we ready on the left and right?"

"Yes," Henry answered.

Porter raised his rifle. Round by round, he intended to zero in on the target until his bullets found a home. "Ready," he said.

"Do it!"

In the west, four rifles focused on the solitary target. They unloaded burst after burst at the machine-gun nest. In the east, Porter did the same. His first volley struck five yards from his objective. A minor adjustment and he fired again. Three yards closer . . .

Ten seconds passed, then fifteen. None would ever know who had taken out its gunner, but in the west the machine gun fell silent. Captain Henry brought his rifle down, waiting and watching, doing his best to verify their efforts had succeeded.

"West is down," he announced. "That direction appears to be somewhat open."

"What about yours, Sergeant Porter?" Short asked.

"Working on it, sir. So far no luck, but it shouldn't be much longer. I'm positive I've struck his position multiple times, but he's still firing."

He fired an additional three-shot burst. This time he saw the figure behind the spewing gun flinch, so he knew he'd hit him. But the relentless firing didn't cease. He fired again. The figure behind the machine gun went down. The menacing .30-caliber stopped.

Like Captain Henry, he ceased his efforts, waiting to see if the pause was permanent. To his relief, the cessation continued. "Weapon's down, sir," he announced. "And at least for the moment it looks like there might be a way out of here. But from what I can see, it's kind of now or never."

The time to disengage had arrived. The moment to run was upon them. With so many Fedayeen between there and the embassy grounds, they knew they'd suffer significant losses along the way. It was possible none would survive the fraught journey.

"Everybody ready?" Short asked. When no one replied, he said, "Okay, let's find a way out of here." He paused ever so briefly, taking in the situation a final time. "Now!" he yelled.

On both ends, the uneasy Green Berets got to their feet. In the east, Porter, Sanders, and the girl would be the first to attempt the desperate maneuver. In the west, it would be Captain Henry and two others. As Henry's group stood, an initial American was felled.

70

12:34 A.M., NOVEMBER 21

OPERATIONAL DETACHMENT ALPHA 6333, CHARLIE COMPANY,

3RD BATTALION, 6TH SPECIAL FORCES GROUP (AIRBORNE)

NEAR THE SMALL GROVE

SEVEN MILES SOUTH OF THE UNITED STATES EMBASSY

ISLAMABAD, PAKISTAN

The first had reached the handful of pitiful trees. His partner hadn't been so lucky. Unharmed, the survivor slipped into the depression west of the insignificant grove. He raised his M4 and waited. After what they'd endured, he had no idea how many others would reach his location. Or what kind of shape they'd be in if they did.

Behind him, the bursts of gunfire, sudden and unpredictable, continued. Some were quick. Others sounded for an extended period. A minute later, a second Green Beret appeared out of the night. Behind him were two more. All three hobbling figures appeared to be injured. He breathed a sigh of relief as they joined him. Wounded or not, with four now present they'd be in a position to have a rifle pointed in each direction. They settled in and searched the horrific night, waiting for who knew what.

Porter, Sanders, and Fareeda were the next to appear. Alone or in twos and threes, still more came into view. While the survivors anxiously waited, their numbers continued to grow. The tenth, eleven, and twelfth were Captain Short, Master Sergeant Noll, and Sergeant Davidson. Three were nowhere to be seen. Captain Henry was among those who had not yet reached the grove.

"Reinforce the perimeter," Short ordered the latest arrivals. "We'll give the others five minutes. After that, we've got to leave."

The others failed to appear. No one had a clue where they were or what had happened to them. The survivors, however, were out of time. And options.

"All right," Short said. "We can't stay any longer. If we do, the Fedayeen are bound to find us. Again, in twos and threes, split up and head north. Use your GPS to locate the Kashmir Highway. Then follow it northeast toward the embassy. If you get cut off, do your best to hunker down and wait out the day before heading out once again."

After verifying that no threat was lurking about, they got to their feet and started out. Seven miles through thousands of agitated individuals before they'd reach the embassy grounds.

71

While the Green Berets attempted to make their way through the teeming enemy, Corporal Genovese was responding to a lengthy call on the radio. "Yes, sir. I'll tell him."

Erickson and Joyce turned toward him with an inquisitive look. Given the tone of Genovese's voice, whatever it was had to be significant. Lauren was standing with them. Her look matched theirs. As she'd done on many a night, once she was certain MaKenna was asleep, she'd struggled out to check on Sam and spend a few hours by his side. Each time she departed, neither knew if this would be the last they'd see each other. While they held on tight in these stolen moments, the unspoken bond between them had grown even stronger.

An hour earlier, three explosions had flashed in the distance. They'd been followed by significant small-arms fire. The raging battle somewhere in the south was now scarcely more than occasional bursts from automatic weapons, followed by periods of haunting silence. The confusing events reaching their ears had been erratic and unpredictable. The last had occurred minutes earlier. It was almost too much to hope, but to a person, every individual in the ravaged compound held their breath and prayed the damning howitzers were no more. Yet no one knew for certain. They were aware that American Special Forces were attempting to infiltrate the area and take them out. But with no direct communication between the embassy and the A Teams involved, they didn't know when the saboteurs might attempt to do so.

"That was Camp Nowhere, sir," Genovese said. "As we hoped, the explosions we heard were the Green Berets. They reported in that they've successfully eliminated the howitzers. None will ever fire again." Even in the darkness, Genovese could see the relief on his company commander's face.

"Are they positive?" Erickson asked.

"Yes, sir. The howitzers are no more."

"Oh, Sam, that's wonderful," Wells said, a smile spreading across her features and settling in her eyes.

"Camp Nowhere said they're trying to make their way through the Fedayeen lines," Genovese added. "They've seven miles to cover, so under the circumstances they've no idea what their chances are. If they make it, it'll be at least a few hours before we can expect them. They wanted to make sure our defenders know not to open fire on any approaching figures until they're certain they're not our guys."

"Understood. Let's hope at least a few survive. With the way things are going, we can use every rifle we can get our hands on. Especially when it's being held by people with the skills these guys have. Notify the men and have them pass the word to those in their sectors to be alert, help's on the way. Make especially sure those protecting our southern perimeter know to be watching for their appearance. The moment they spot them, I want our guys to notify us they're here. I've every intention of being there to shake their hands and thank them personally."

"Yes, sir."

"Sam, when I return to the embassy, is it okay if I tell everyone the good news?" Lauren asked.

"Absolutely. Find Ambassador Ingram and Steven Gray first and let them know. Then tell anyone and everyone that those guns have been silenced. The jihadists may attempt to bring others forward, but for now there won't be any bombardments."

Little did they know that the architect of the artillery bombardment, Bila Chachar, was much too busy with the Allies' attack in the south to give a passing thought to bringing additional howitzers to Islamabad. And none of those he'd left to man them had the ability to do so.

72

4:42 A.M., NOVEMBER 21
OPERATIONAL DETACHMENT ALPHA 6333,
CHARLIE COMPANY, 3RD BATTALION,
6TH SPECIAL FORCES GROUP (AIRBORNE)
ON THE MOVE
THREE MILES SOUTH OF THE UNITED STATES EMBASSY
ISLAMABAD, PAKISTAN

The scurrying trio had been on the run for four hours. There'd been lots of twists and turns in their movements while they attempted to evade those who would do them harm. And more than one moment when they'd been forced to turn back in search of another way. Early on, as they tangled with yet another band of miscreants, Sanders had taken a bullet to his left forearm. The offending area had been chewed up by the striking round. With no time to stop and tend to the wound, they'd continued on.

So far, they'd covered four of the seven miles they needed to cross to reach the embassy. But the closer they'd come to their objective, the more the Fedayeen had grown. For the past half hour, the insurrectionists had been everywhere. Because of it, their calculated pace had slowed significantly. Each step of the desperate action had been a struggle. On three occasions, they'd had to fight their way through roving bands determined to seize their lives. However, they weren't the only ones whose weapons had been fired in the past few hours. At indiscriminate moments, the sounds of frantic firefights, some nearby, others at a distance, had reached their ears. While the night wore on, the profound noises were becoming more infrequent.

Porter stopped and dropped behind a sheltering pile of rocks. He signaled for Sanders and Fareeda to do likewise. There were unwelcome forces headed who knew where in front of them. And not too far away. Porter searched in every direction, yet nothing pleasing reached him. No matter where he spied, his night vision was filled with movement. A substantial number of figures were near. If they stayed where they were, the enemy was bound to stumble upon them.

He had little choice. It was time to retreat once again. Yet, as he looked to the rear, he realized the way was blocked by more passing shadows. He examined the world around them, hoping to find an opening. Nothing appeared. There was no way out. They were surrounded by their swarming foe. And the situation was growing more desperate with each passing second. He knew the truth. They were in deep trouble.

"How's your arm?" Porter whispered.

Sanders examined his sleeve just below the elbow. Blood was continuing to accumulate and stain his fatigues. "Hurts like a son of a bitch, but I'll live."

Porter peered out at the despairing scene. He didn't like what he was seeing. There were scores of scurrying forms moving in his direction.

"What're we going to do?" Sanders whispered.

"Give me a minute. I'm working on it," was the tense response.

"We don't have a minute."

"Well, whatever we do, we can't stay here." That was when

Porter, frantically searching, spotted it. Thirty yards to their right, the shell of a burned-out structure rose from the devastated landscape. It wasn't perfect, but it was the only chance they had. "There . . . over there . . . Head for what's left of that building," he said while motioning toward the spot he had in mind.

73

11:45 P.M., NOVEMBER 21
OPERATIONAL DETACHMENT ALPHA 6333, CHARLIE COMPANY,
3RD BATTALION, 6TH SPECIAL FORCES GROUP (AIRBORNE)
HIDDEN IN THE SCORCHED REMAINS OF A DETERIORATING BUILDING
THREE MILES SOUTH OF THE UNITED STATES EMBASSY
ISLAMABAD, PAKISTAN

Night was full upon them. They'd survived more than one close call as the day wore on. Using his secondary specialty as a combat medic, Sanders had done what he could for his own wounds. Nevertheless, his efforts had been temporary at best. He recognized if the oozing area got infected he could lose the arm. They'd had no food and water for over a day. They were miserable, but they were still alive. That, however, wasn't true for everyone within the fragile framework. A few feet from them, behind a pile of debris, the bodies of the two Fedayeen soldiers Porter had been forced to deal with lay. Their throats had been slit.

While the trio prepared to move out, a dozen of Basra's mindless followers stopped in front of the building. Without a word, the group lingered. The uneasiness in their movements and their furtive glances at the world around them were obvious. The jihadists were up to something. Even so, neither American had a clue what it was. The motley gathering's apparent leader said something in Urdu. After a final look around, they slipped inside the creaking structure. Each moved deeper into the battered shell of what had been a beautiful three-story office building. All intended to move far enough into the black world so as not to be seen from outside. They were determined to enjoy an American-made cigarette. This was the last of those they'd pillaged from the Pakistani soldiers they'd slain weeks earlier. They needed to be careful. While they smoked, they couldn't let the burning embers give their actions away. If they were caught smoking at night, it would mean the lash.

They made a cursory examination of their surroundings, and once they were satisfied their efforts wouldn't be seen by anyone outside, each took a cigarette. They lit them and talked in hushed tones as they enjoyed this final one. If they'd been half as concerned with what was inside the crippled edifice as they were with what was beyond its badly damaged walls, it was likely they would have discovered the secret within. What they failed to see was twenty feet away: two American soldiers and a Pakistani girl were hiding.

Porter's hand was covering the girl's month. Sanders was gripping his M4. But he wasn't in a position to fire it. Having been caught by surprise by the jihadists' appearance, he hadn't been able to chamber a round for fear the enemy soldiers would hear the telltale sound.

Their breathing shallow, the trapped individuals waited as the glowing tips burned. The emaciated peasants took in puff after puff of burning tobacco while chatting about anything and everything. One by one, the cigarettes reached their ends. They extinguished them. The leader walked up to the building's opening. He scanned the area to verify no one was nearby. Satisfied they wouldn't be seen exiting the space, he motioned to the others. Each headed toward the doorway.

When the last had disappeared, Porter let out a deep sigh.

They'd survived another brush with death. How many more they'd face this night, he had no way of knowing.

"That was close," Sanders whispered.

"Yeah. We may not be so lucky next time."

"Let's get out of here while we still can."

Porter got up and moved toward the opening. After examining their surroundings, he signaled for Sanders and Fareeda to join him. They were soon moving north toward where they hoped the embassy would be. Each understood they were heading straight into the heart of the dogmatists. Yet it couldn't be helped.

With three frightening miles to cover, they had no idea what the result would be. Around the next corner, behind a passing rock, a sudden end could find them. They understood the Angel of Death would be waiting upon the passing mist. A single mistake and the leering spirit would seize their souls. Yet it was now or never. There was nothing they could do but take the next step and face their destinies.

74

The first hints of yet another day were upon them.

"Sir," Corporal Genovese said, "southern sentries are reporting two more Green Berets along with a Pakistani girl have arrived."

"Where are they?"

"Directly south, sir. At the moment, French troops are providing them with water and a bit of food. They're apparently badly dehydrated and quite hungry."

"Have our guys tell the French we'll be right there."

Porter and Sanders saw two Marines coming toward them. Both were bandaged. One was limping. As the images drew close, to their great surprise they recognized who it was. And it didn't take long for Erickson and Joyce to do the same. It was a pair of men neither would ever forget. They were the Green Berets who had saved Lauren from a certain death three years earlier.

"Oh, my God, Sergeant Porter, Sergeant Sanders. What are you doing here?" Erickson asked.

"Same as you, sir," Sanders said. "Just trying to stay alive."

"I'd no idea you were part of the team sent to destroy those guns. Or that you were even in Pakistan."

"Yes, sir. We're what remains of three teams, actually. Howitzers are definitely gone. Took them out myself."

"Has anyone else made it, sir?" Porter asked.

"Three others came in before dawn yesterday. It was a Master Sergeant Noll and Sergeants Davidson and Hernandez."

"Three? Is that all, sir?" Porter said.

"So far. But we're hoping others will find their way."

Erickson's words held little conviction. As it was, he was astounded that, so long after the action, Sanders and Porter were standing before him. All understood it was unlikely anyone else was coming.

"Sergeant Sanders, it looks like you're wounded. Let's get you into the embassy so we can treat that wound."

"You don't look so good yourself, sir. Still, I can use some help if you've anyone available to treat it."

Erickson turned to Joyce. "Gunny, why don't show them the way to the hospital. Have the doctors check them over real good. Then find Lauren and let her know they're here."

75

4:51 P.M., NOVEMBER 23
C COMPANY (BLUE MAX), 3RD BATTALION,
10TH AVIATION REGIMENT, 10TH COMBAT AVIATION BRIGADE,
10TH MOUNTAIN DIVISION (LIGHT INFANTRY)
CAMP NOWHERE
THE SPĪN GHAR MOUNTAINS OF NORTH-CENTRAL PAKISTAN

The 10th Mountain was accomplishing what they'd been sent to Pakistan to do. It hadn't been easy. Yet their constant pressure was tying down a significant portion of the Fedayeen's northern force. And when opportunity found them, they were pushing their fanatical foe from the mountains and foothills and onto the open plains.

On this afternoon, a frozen Camp Nowhere was buzzing with activity. Apaches, Black Hawks, and Chinooks were taking off and landing. Heavily bundled support soldiers scurried in all directions upon the glacial landscape.

In the center of the intense activity, a Black Hawk's engines were running. Its blades were whirling. Sitting in the pilot's chair, Bea Washington brought her fingertips to her lips and reached out to touch the picture of her daughters.

It was time for another mission. She'd flown so many in the past four days that she couldn't count them all. At this point, most were a blur. With the losses her helicopter company had suffered, she had little choice.

This time there'd be no troops within the Black Hawk's hold. Instead, the rear compartment was filled with food, water, and ammunition for a unit they'd dropped deep behind enemy lines. Embroiled in heavy fighting, the 10th Mountain's soldiers were short of all three.

"Everything secured back there?" she asked her crew chiefs.

"Yes, ma'am. We're all set," Sergeant Mercado said.

She turned to look at her copilot. "What about up here?"

Next to her, Shaun White responded. "Instrumentation looks good, ma'am. All three engines are running smoothly. Deicing's complete and we should be ready to roll."

"Then let's get to it."

With the late afternoon winds rising to near gale force, she deftly lifted her straining craft into the air. In seconds they were heading southwest. Hugging every sheltering nook and treacherous crevice, the low-flying Black Hawk roared. In fifteen minutes they'd reach their objective. As they escaped the mountains and entered the wide foothills, the snows lessened. With the falling elevation, the blanket of white was being replaced by sporadic splotches of dirty gray.

The racing Black Hawk neared its destination. A pair of Apaches, heading in the opposite direction, flew past. Both had been involved in supporting the fray-weary American force Washington's crew was scheduled to resupply. After an extended assault upon the teeming jihadists, the attack helicopters were running low on both fuel and ordnance. They had little choice but to withdraw from the battle. Outnumbered thirty to one, the isolated infantry platoon would be on its own.

This high up, the few trees were severely stunted. The remote area, filled with steep hillsides, brittle bushes, large rock outcroppings, and endless crags, was as inhospitable as any the helicopter crew had encountered.

When they neared the bleak environment, Washington asked, "Have you spotted our guys?"

"Not yet," her copilot answered. "But they've got to be nearby. Wait . . . there they are. They're scattered among the jagged bluffs north of that wide valley."

Washington peered in the direction White had indicated. "I've got them."

The struggling Americans were sheltering in the harsh terrain near the edge of a sloping hilltop. The enemy was everywhere. From above, the Black Hawk crew could see endless muzzle flashes. Agitated figures were running across the disordered landscape. Scattered among them, bodies lay strewn as if tossed there by a wrathful deity. A few hundred yards beyond the melee, a gathering of small trucks sat in the scattered hints of fading snow. A number of militants were surrounding each of the pickups. Some distance away, those in the helicopter could see Fedayeen reinforcements heading toward the clash.

Since arriving at Camp Nowhere, the Black Hawk had flown into many a tumultuous onslaught. Yet this one looked as intense as any they'd encountered. In the earlier struggles, the result had almost always been the same. Even when they outnumbered the Americans, the jihadists put up little more than token resistance before giving up ground and vanishing. Such was especially true when the toxic Apaches had been involved. But on this afternoon, rather than disappearing, the enemy presence was growing. And they appeared determined to stay.

None of the Americans realized how invaluable the location upon which they'd stumbled really was. And those they faced were determined to keep it that way. They'd fight to the death before they'd relinquish a foot of ground and reveal who they were protecting.

What the 10th Mountain soldiers had no way of knowing was

the gathering of trucks was Salim Basra's command center. Having been forced from the secreting mountains, he'd ended up here. While the Fedayeen leader cowered behind a rusting fender, those he commanded continued to martyr themselves to protect him. They'd fight until the last man to keep him safe. Whatever the result, they couldn't allow Allah's ordained one to die. If he did, all would be lost. Their campaign would crumble. When word of his death spread, his ragtag army would throw down their weapons and walk away. Their sainted leader would be gone and their continuing to die would serve little purpose. They'd crawl back into the hovels from which they'd come. And deny they'd been a part of this. With the death of a single man, the war would reach its end.

Unfortunately, the Americans didn't have the slightest inkling he was there. If they had, Washington's crew would've pursued him with relishing fury. They wouldn't have stopped until they'd seized his life and put an end to the slaughter. But it wasn't meant to be. For at the moment, the Black Hawk crew's concerns were upon a more immediate problem.

While they stared at the stark world beneath them, a concerned Shaun White said, "How do you want to handle this, ma'am?"

It took no time for Washington to size up the situation and decide what they needed to do. "Above all else, we've got to accomplish the resupply. Without the stuff we're carrying, our guys will be dead before nightfall. But with as intense as the fighting is right now, the resupply's going to be damn near impossible. There's an excellent chance they'll blow us and our cargo out of the sky before our skis touch solid ground. So before attempting to land, let's see what we can do to suppress the enemy even if we're only able to do so for a brief period. That'll at least give us a chance. Once we've pushed their noses into the dirt, we'll do what we can to find a spot to touch down. As swiftly as possible, we'll hand off the supplies. When that's done, we'll get the hell out of here." She looked at the rock-cluttered hillside. What she saw didn't please her. "I'm not seeing much. Have you had any luck identifying a place to land?" The first beads of sweat were appearing on her forehead. The scene was growing more desperate with every passing second.

"Nothing great," White responded. "This landscape's not exactly conducive for a helicopter landing. Setting her down in this place looks next to impossible. From what I can see, our only choice would be to put her down in the narrow opening between those two big boulders near the center of our defenses."

She spotted the space he was describing. The modest aperture didn't appear at all welcoming. Attempting a landing in combat this intense would be tenuous at best. With bullets and RPGs ripping at them, this was going to be beyond difficult. Without a clearly defined landing zone, it would be close to unattainable. Yet, if anyone could do it, Bea Washington could.

"That area's awfully narrow. Are you sure it's going to be wide enough?" she asked.

"No, ma'am. But unless you've identified someplace better, it looks like all we've got."

"I'm not seeing anything," she admitted as she searched the ground below.

Her Black Hawk was outfitted as a transport. It didn't carry significant attack weapons. Still with the .30-caliber machine guns her crewmen were manning, they were far from helpless.

"Why don't we make some passes with our machine guns blazing? Wreak as much havoc as we can. Hopefully, we can pin them down long enough for us to land. You guys ready back there?"

The pair stood on opposite sides of the rear compartment,

staring out the open doorways. Each pointed his machine gun toward the Fedayeen-held areas.

Mercado glanced over at Vinson. "Ready as we'll ever be, ma'am," he said. "Just let us know when you want us to open fire."

"We're heading in now. Focus everything you've got on pinning down the ones closest to our guys."

She pushed the throttle forward and roared into the heart of the caustic encounter. They couldn't inflict the damage an Apache or Black Hawk armed for an assault could, but their .30-calibers were capable of seizing many a life.

Flying east to west along the low hillside, both machine guns soon raged. Each spit out a certain death to the unprepared. Washington kept her low-flying craft steady as they rushed over the jihadist lines. She had every intention of assaulting the offending force from one end to the other. As the incursion began in earnest, they could see more than one fall beneath the Black Hawk. The American captain continued her lengthy run. To her crew's good fortune, there wasn't any indication of Stingers being present. Still, the Fedayeen were far from helpless. In response, a handful of rocket-propelled grenades and dozens of AK-47s were pointed skyward. Lengthy bursts rose to greet the rampaging Americans. More than one bullet struck its exposed fuselage. But they didn't come close to taking the Black Hawk down.

When they reached the end of the extended defenses, they whirled about to undertake another attack. Once more, they thundered forward. And the results were the same. When the second pass reached its conclusion, a dozen additional souls had endured their final, agonizing moments. Twice that number were injured. But even with numbers so great, it wasn't enough to inflict serious harm upon the force they faced.

At its end Washington said, "There's still lots of them firing.

Let's make one more attempt to suppress the opposition before we land." She turned and headed for the destitute forms.

A third round of malice and mayhem ended with a similar result. More of the enemy had succumbed. And the damage to the racing American craft had grown. Yet the crew remained unharmed and the assailed Black Hawk was still flying.

"Let's bring her down and get this over with," Washington said.

They rushed up the hillside toward the spot White had located. Once they reached it, Washington hovered the craft a hundred feet above the narrow chasm. She knew by holding her helicopter steady she was making the survival of the Black Hawk and its much-needed cargo tenuous. Still, if she was going to complete a landing in this challenging location, she had no choice.

There was adequate distance to land in front of and behind them. It was the limited area on each side that was her greatest concern. With only the tiniest of openings to slip the cumbersome helicopter into, she needed to line the landing up precisely. She recognized that if she made the smallest mistake, there'd be no reprieve. They'd forfeit their lives on the unforgiving rocks.

A cordon of bullets was flying around them. In the middle of a fierce engagement, she'd have to find a way to do this. No matter how precarious the situation became, no matter how many rounds struck her craft, her sole focus would be on executing the delicate maneuver. With an unrelenting tempest swirling, she could let nothing distract her. Foot by foot, moment by moment, she'd attempt to drop into the modest fissure. She couldn't rush this. She couldn't falter. The Black Hawk initiated its tedious decent. Seventy-five feet . . . sixty . . .

The peasants saw their opening. Many crawled from their hiding places and added to the lethal curtain of rifle fire. The world erupted, coming at the perilous crew from three sides at one.

Rounds were striking up and down the length of the Black Hawk. Yet not one had struck a critical component. None the worse for wear, the helicopter's highly vulnerable rotor blades continued to whirl. How much longer they'd do so, none could know. Yet its fixated pilot faltered not at all. "Fifty feet . . . forty . . ."

With a potential death striking everywhere, her crew members continued to fire their .30-calibers in response. The scattered Americans on the ground also answered, doing all they could to pin the enemy down. Even so, it wasn't nearly enough.

A hundred yards from the forwardmost Americans, three Fedayeen leaped to their feet. Each was cradling an RPG. As one, they raised the rocket-propelled grenade launchers and fired. The hurried shots rushed toward their target. None of the jihadists would ever see the results of their handiwork. A frantic blink after releasing their rockets, an American rifle cut the exposed figures down.

The RPGs soared across the tumbled terrain. Little more than inches from the Black Hawk's nose, the first screamed past the settling aircraft. It smashed into the hillside. The second rocket was high, racing overhead and doing likewise. The third rushed attempt came nowhere close. It chewed a hole in the steep slope fifty feet below them.

Washington continued the cautious descent. Thirty feet . . . twenty . . . The massive rocks were growing near. And the opening appeared to be as tight as ever.

"How we doing on your side?" she asked her copilot.

"Uh . . . not much room at all. It looks like we've got no more than a foot or two to spare. And we might not have that. If you could slide her your way, I'd feel a whole lot better."

"Not a chance. It's much too close over here as it is. I need to set her down exactly where she is or I won't be able to land at all."

Ten feet . . . eight . . . They dropped between the rising granite on each side. She had no time for even the slightest glance to the right to see how things were going over there. If she attempted to do so, the result could be catastrophic.

"How are we?" she asked, her angst obvious.

"We're in but not by much. We're maybe two feet from the rock."

"Same over here. But we're almost there. Five feet, no more, and we'll touch down." Holding her breath, she controlled the downward descent.

"Let's hope the rotor blade doesn't make contact with the rocks," White said. "If it does, it'll rip us apart."

"Yeah, let's. But we should be okay. Boulders looked like they were maybe eight to ten feet tall. This helicopter's height is nearly twice that."

The skis touched. They were on firm ground. She shut down the engines. Washington could do nothing but close her eyes and attempt to calm her nerves. There was a great deal to do. They had to remove the critical cargo and find a way to lift the helicopter straight up.

When she opened her eyes she saw a lieutenant and three soldiers running toward them. The quartet quickly reached the craft. The lieutenant directed his men to the side doors. Within seconds, they were assisting Washington's crew in freeing the desperately needed supplies. There was little room between the rocks, but each was soon carrying as many boxes as humanly possible and depositing them a short distant away. They returned for a second load.

"I've got four dead and seven severely wounded," the lieutenant yelled over the sounds of the ongoing firefight. "Once we've grabbed our stuff, I'd like to load them on your Black Hawk so you can ferry them out of here. My men are getting them ready, so it shouldn't take long to get them on board."

Even though the additional time on the ground would increase the risk to her crew, there was no way she was going to tell the lieutenant no. She'd never deserted a fellow American. And she wasn't going to start now. "We're not equipped as a medevac, but we'll do what we can," she responded. "As you can see, my Black Hawk's presence is attracting far more attention than we'd like. So we don't want to hang around any longer than we have to. Once the hold's empty, load the wounded and dead as fast you can and we'll attempt to get them back to Camp Nowhere."

They had been on the ground for seven minutes. It was far longer than they'd intended. But it couldn't be helped. They had had no choice but to wait as their countrymen were loaded. While Washington started the engines, the fighting hadn't slowed in the slightest. Lifting the aggrieved bird out of the confined space wasn't going to be easy. Even if successful, they'd be far from safe with so many determined to take them down.

"Instruments looking okay?" she asked White.

"From what I can see."

"Okay, it's now or never. Let's get out of here. Keep a watch on your side until we've breached these rocks. I'll do the same over here."

As had been the case while landing, for the initial ten feet the takeoff was painfully slow. It wasn't easy, but Washington lifted the craft with a skill few could command. It felt like forever, but they were finally free. The higher they rose, the more the jihadists focused on destroying them. Rifle fire and RPGs flew. Yet once more Providence was with them. When they whirled about to head back into the high mountains, they could see the pickups scurrying toward the valley below.

"We've still got a decent amount of ammunition. Want to turn about and go after those trucks?" White asked.

She hesitated. "Negative. We've pressed our luck as far as we dare. With the hits we've taken, I don't know how this thing's still flying. And every second we delay will cost our wounded. Let's get as far from here as we can. If we somehow make it to Camp Nowhere, we'll evacuate the dead and wounded and turn this bullet-ridden carcass over to the maintenance folks."

The crippled Black Hawk limped toward the northeast. In a minute, maybe two, it disappeared over a white-tipped peak. Despite the precarious situation, if Washington had had the slightest notion of who was in the leading pickup, she would have changed her answer in a heartbeat.

While they limped home, they had no idea what they had accomplished. They'd flushed Salim Basra onto open ground. For the remainder of the war, the Fedayeen leader would never return to the secretive mountains.

76

6:17 P.M., NOVEMBER 23
4TH PLATOON, BRAVO COMPANY, 2ND BATTALION,
69TH ARMOR REGIMENT, 2ND ARMORED BRIGADE
COMBAT TEAM (SPARTANS), 3RD INFANTRY DIVISION
ON A WIDE PLAIN
SIXTY MILES FROM DOWNTOWN KARACHI, PAKISTAN

With the sun sliding toward the horizon, the four Bradley fighting vehicles continued their battle-scarred slog to the northeast. They'd been the spearhead. They'd found themselves at the forefront of every action. Their pockmarks showed it. All around them, an unending line of armored vehicles joined the relentless push. Numerous Humvees were with them. In a continuous stream, screaming Apaches passed overhead.

It was the end of the fourth day of their assault. After leaving the outskirts of Karachi, they'd been able to cover forty-two struggling miles. Facing the multitudes blocking their path, the going had been painful. They'd crossed barely 5 percent of the distance needed to reach their far-off objective. Every tenuous foot had been purchased with sinew and blood. Yet they were in no way discouraged. For on this day they'd doubled the distance gained in the previous three.

The division's death toll was rising. So far, the precious ground they'd seized had cost them four hundred killed or wounded. Nonetheless, enemy losses were estimated to be hundreds of times larger. Every mile of the appalling milieu was strewn with corpses. Even with two million in the southern fight, the first fractures in the peasants' defenses were showing.

With over six hundred armored vehicles, the 3rd Infantry Division's commanding general was certain they were poised for a breakthrough. All it would take was one good push to smash the jihadists' defenses and reach open country. He was ready to initiate the decisive actions to make such an event possible. In the past hour, he'd brought every artillery piece he had to within a couple miles of the front lines.

With gunfire all around them, Lieutenant Cramer's voice came over the radio. "Vehicle commanders, word just came. We're to stop here for the night. They're about to unleash a massive artillery barrage against the Fedayeen to clear a path for the division. British and French are doing the same along the fifty-mile front. We're going to pound them throughout the night. Once the big guns have softened them up, we're to launch a full-scale assault the moment the sun rises. It's time to make our move. If we don't, all will be lost for those we've come to rescue. The embassy folks are holding on, but they won't be able to do so for much longer. We need to get there. We need to do so quickly."

"Understood, sir," Walton said. "I know my crew's eager to reach Islamabad and put an end to this. And I'm certain we're not the only ones who feel that way." He scanned the uneasy terrain. "That little rise in front of us looks like as good a spot as any, sir. Why don't we set up our defenses there?"

A careful examination of the area confirmed that Walton's judgment was, as always, sound. "Thanks, Platoon Sergeant.

Bradley commanders, you heard the man: Edge up and discharge your infantry. Once you have, position yourselves for the night."

"Aiden," Walton said to his driver, "head toward that rise. Stop about ten yards from the top. When we reach it, I'll dismount and guide you into place." He needed to ensure his armored vehicle wouldn't be overly exposed to enemy fire while placing it in a position where they could engage any threat that appeared.

"On it, Sarge," was Lester's response.

The hulking Bradley lurched forward. To their left, the platoon's other three did likewise. Scores of Bradleys and M1s were locating defensive positions and doing the same.

"Here . . . stop right here," Walton said as they edged up the modest slope.

The moment the tracked vehicle stilled, Walton turned to Evan Minter. "While I'm out there, make sure you're ready to lay down suppressing fire at the first sign of trouble."

"Already on it, Sarge," his gunner said. "I'll be ready to fire the machine gun or Bushmaster at a moment's notice."

Walton opened the commander's hatch and lifted himself clear of the compartment. He was soon standing on the ground in front of it. He walked up to the spot where he wanted to position the Bradley. At the same time, the doors on the idling beast's rear opened and the six infantrymen within its hold scurried out to take up supporting positions. Walton motioned for Lester to ease the ponderous load forward.

"Here . . . stop right here," he said as he motioned for Lester to stop.

After a look around, the platoon sergeant lifted himself onto the armored vehicle and disappeared into the command compartment. He'd scarcely returned when the first artillery salvo roared into the heavens. The 155mm shells exploded two miles beyond the American lines. More followed.

"Okay, let's settle in," he directed his crew. "We'll switch on and off keeping watch and sleeping. From what the lieutenant said, it might be the last we get for quite some time."

Even with the relentless rounds hurtling overhead and exploding in the distance, they had every intention of sleeping through it. While they started to relax for the first time in days, little did they know they wouldn't close their eyes for the briefest moment this night. For the ominous world was about to change in a manner none could have anticipated.

77

Bila Chachar had performed magnificently. He'd fended off the foreign armies while relinquishing little of the ground he held. They'd been pushed back by the Allies' advance. But they were holding on. Nonetheless, even with their massive numbers, his untrained, poorly equipped army couldn't do so forever. Those who opposed them were too strong for them to withstand much longer.

With every passing hour his defenses were growing weaker. Unless drastic action was taken, the unmistakable signs of collapse would become much too visible. And once his lines crumbled, the result would be irretrievable. There'd be no way to reconstruct his shattered forces. Their downfall would be complete.

The marginal supply system he'd created had never been designed to support so many fighters assembled in such a confined area. The majority of the jingle trucks were still arriving, even if the ferocious American attack helicopters were making such attempts beyond hazardous. Still, those that got through weren't nearly enough to resupply such a considerable army. Most of his men were hungry and were running low on ammunition. They still believed in their reverent cause. Yet, with so many dying and the conditions growing worse, morale was ebbing.

As daylight faded on the struggle's fourth day, Chachar recognized he needed to act. To have any hope, he needed to do the unpredictable. He had to risk it all, no matter how many lives it would cost.

He was going to attack. He was going to unleash his entire army. His only chance would be to inflict an obscene number of casualties upon the daunting force in front of him. With so many dead, he was certain the outcry by the British, American, and French citizenry would grow from a quiet murmur to a roaring din. Facing such a reality, their leaders would have little choice but to withdraw from the fighting. And the Fedayeen would be free to claim their rightful place as the rulers of this land.

"How many working Al-Khalids do we have?" he asked those gathered around him in his command tent.

"Sixty, more or less," was the reply of his second-in-command, Faisan Baqri.

"What about armored personnel carriers?"

"Nearly double that."

"Okay, it's time to act. The moment's come to commit the remainder of our armored vehicles to the battle. Once darkness arrives, order them to move forward and engage the enemy. Under no circumstances are they to withdraw. They're to continue fighting no matter how hopeless the situation becomes."

"It will be done," Baqri said.

"The enemy won't be expecting such a bold move. I know our ground forces are at a great disadvantage in night fighting, but send word to our commanders. They're to prepare them to accompany our tanks."

"How great a number do you want to send?" Baqri asked.

"Every last one. Send all two million. Not a man's to be held back."

"But to do so might mean our end," a stunned Baqri said. "If we lose this battle, we'll be defenseless. It will take little effort for those we face to break through. Once they do, they'll end our chances of conquering the remainder of our homeland."

"I'm aware what the consequences will be. Still, it no longer matters. The time for drastic action has arrived. Without it, all we'll be doing is delaying the inevitable. The enemy will wear us down, and we won't prevail. Our only chance is to change the course of this conflict. And to do so now. Within the hour, we're going to launch our entire army against those who stand against us. You're to unleash wave after wave to battle alongside our Al-Khalids. Like our armored force, no matter what happens, they're to continue fighting even when facing overwhelming firepower. They're not to stop until they've routed the heretics and driven them into the sea." He looked around the tent. Few were pleased with his edict. Even so, all nodded in understanding. "Is our martyrs' brigade ready?"

"Yes," Baqri answered. "Each has been issued a vest with twenty kilos of explosives that, when detonated, will puncture the bellies of even the stoutest tanks. They're eager to prove their worthiness to Allah and our sacred quest."

"They're to accompany the initial wave of attackers."

As the words left his mouth, the foremost of the Allies' artillery shells struck somewhere on the right. One after another, the shrapnel-laden ordnance continued without pause. A terrifying thunder poured down upon his fragile defenses. A dreadful lightning, filled with animus and suffering, lit up the coming night as it ripped his men apart. Anguished screams, emanating far and wide, pierced the awe-inspiring clamor. For the jihadists, the first of many had perished. Chachar paused and waited while round after round exploded. The alarming refrain appeared to be hitting everywhere.

The others looked at him. There was fear in every pair of eyes as they listened to the ravaging guns. Quite unexpectedly, the situation had changed. With the Allies' stark refrain, each assumed Chachar would postpone the attack. Yet, to their amazement, their commander didn't do so.

"You have your orders," he said. "Have our men begin the assault within the hour."

He understood attacking in the middle of so fearsome an offensive was going to lead to a nightmarish result. By doing so he was sending hundreds of thousands to their deaths. Most would never come close to the nonbelievers' lines before a gripping mortality devoured them. However, it no longer mattered. It was this moment or nothing if they were going to prevail.

78

7:31 P.M., NOVEMBER 23

4TH PLATOON, BRAVO COMPANY, 2ND BATTALION,

69TH ARMOR REGIMENT,

2ND ARMORED BRIGADE COMBAT TEAM (SPARTANS),

3RD INFANTRY DIVISION

SIXTY MILES FROM DOWNTOWN KARACHI, PAKISTAN

The brunt of the jihadists' tidal wave would be directed at the lead platoon. Darren Walton and those with him were sitting at ground zero.

The first of the enemy were drawing near. Cradling weapons or carrying hand grenades and Molotov cocktails, each was running as fast as his legs would carry him. When they crested a modest knoll a half mile away, the Americans spotted the approaching peril.

"What the hell?" Lieutenant Cramer said as he peered into the frightening world around them. "Platoon Sergeant, do you see what I'm seeing?"

Walton looked out upon the field through his thermal night vision. A writhing sea of human forms were headed toward them. It appeared to be without end. Yet what he spied to the right of the massive gathering was equally troubling. A significant number of tanks and armored vehicles were with the boundless images.

"Along with the infantry, I've got Al-Khalids on my right, sir. Personal carriers too. They're headed this way."

Cramer adjusted his view to locate what Walton was describing. It took little time for the lieutenant to identify the looming threat. With death coming for them, he recognized how much trouble they were in.

The 3rd Infantry tank unit a few hundred yards behind his platoon spotted the threat. Its four M1s churned forward to support their position.

"Looks like the M1s are moving up, sir," Sergeant Vigo said.

"Good. Bradley commanders," Cramer said, "have your gunner prepare their TOWs to support the M1s and address the approaching armor. While they're doing so, get your machine guns ready to confront the thousands upon thousands of foot soldiers headed this way." He switched to the radio. He had to shout to be hear over the horrendous sounds of the artillery bombardment. "Two-Six, this is Delta Four-Six. Two-Six, this is Delta Four-Six."

"Go ahead, Delta Four-Six," the battalion radio operator responded.

"Two-Six, be advised. We've identified a significant number of tanks along with other armored support heading this way at a high rate of speed. They're being accompanied by massive amounts of heavily armed infantry. They appear to be without end. From what we can see, the entire Fedayeen army's approaching."

"What, Delta Four-Six? Are you sure? In the middle of the pounding we're giving them, doing so would be suicide."

"Tell that to them. Because they're seven hundred yards from us and showing no signs of slowing down."

"Wait one, Delta Four-Six."

A mile behind the platoon's position, the radio operator turned to the battalion commander. "Did you get that, sir?"

"Every word."

"How do you want to respond?"

"Send four platoons of Bradleys forward to support the battalion's lead elements along with two additional M1 platoons. Then gather as many Strykers and Humvees as we can lay our hands on and move them forward. Finish by notifying Brigade of the tactical situation. Tell them we're going to need all the help they can provide. And we're going to need it soon."

"On it, sir."

The radio operator contacted the supporting units the battalion commander had identified. Once the radioman had reached the final one he said, "Delta Four-Six, be advised. Help's on the way."

"Roger, Two-Six," the lieutenant said. "We'll do what we can to hold on until they get here."

As the final syllable escaped his lips, the Al-Khalid farthest from the right fired its main gun at a target the platoon couldn't identify. The amassing hordes surged toward the Americans.

Eight indomitable Abrams tanks and sixteen Bradleys with the ninety-six foot soldiers they were carrying were on the way. In five minutes, they'd arrive. It would be an eternity for those at the battle's forefront.

Walton opened up with his machine gun. The platoons' other Bradleys did the same. On the ground, the small numbers of American infantry also responded. A lethal stream of searching rounds went out to greet the onrushing multitudes. Many in the initial element went down beneath the virulent assault. It didn't slow them in the slightest. Still more appeared. Like a rushing waterfall, those who were approaching went on forever.

Each of the Bradleys' gunners released a TOW missile at the Al-Khalids. In a matter of seconds, four savage explosions filled the darkening night. The devastated tanks were turned into pillars of fire. The M1 platoon joined in, firing their main guns. An additional quarter of Basra's armored vehicles were ripped apart.

The Americans adjusted their artillery fire. Much of it began striking a few hundred yards away. With every ferocious round, a dozen or more mangled figures were tossed into the air. The exploding ordnance tore huge swaths in the onrushing elements. An unmerciful phoenix rose to feast upon them all. Still, the heaving humanity kept on coming.

The tumultuous battle burst upon them with a plundering fury even the wildest of imaginations couldn't have envisioned.

79

Quite unexpectedly, the unthinkable happened. And for the Fedayeen, it couldn't have been more consequential.

Thirty minutes into the terrible contest, a screaming artillery shell struck dead center in their command tent. It tore the crowded scene apart. With only the slightest recognition of eternity's arrival, Bila Chachar perished.

His passing would seal the coming result. He wouldn't be there to command the attack. He'd no longer be in a position to call off his soldiers when the struggle turned senseless. With no one leading them, the peasants would continue fighting even when their falling and dying no longer served a purpose.

The British, French, and American response was taking form. For the Americans, the 2nd Brigade's five thousand soldiers were rushing toward the fighting. The remainder of the division was preparing to join them. At the front, their desperate units were doing all they could to hold on. Yet it was nearly impossible to do so. In places, the cultists had broken through.

"Jesus Christ, they're everywhere!" Walton screamed as he fired his machine gun at wave after wave of the approaching horde.

"Sergeant Devine, do what you can to take out that armored personnel carrier headed straight for us," Lieutenant Cramer screamed.

"On it, sir."

Devine switched to his 25mm Bushmaster cannon. Without hesitation, he poured round after round into the approaching armored vehicle. The personnel carrier ground to a stop. Smoke billowed from it. Its hatches popped open. Its crew attempted to make their escape. Devine changed to his machine gun. In two quick bursts he cut them down.

With every passing minute, 3rd Infantry soldiers were arriving. But through the unyielding artillery bursts, so were the enemy. The unceasing battle droned on. The whirlwind that consumed them wouldn't relent. The first of what would be many hours of carnage passed. Unimaginable chaos raged. Both sides' death tolls rose.

Despite being struck multiple times, the suicide bomber wouldn't relent. The wondrous paradise awaiting all martyrs would soon be his. It spurred his actions. Despite his crippling wounds, he was determined to prove he was worthy of the most exalted of places.

He was one of many in the whirling morass surging toward the Allies. When his lines momentarily parted, the running bomber spotted an opening he could exploit. His bloodied body heaving, he raced to the nearest American armored vehicle. The instant he reached it, he set off the explosives strapped to his chest. A startling detonation illuminated the night. A feral blast ripped the fighting vehicle apart. Engulfed in flames, Lieutenant Cramer's Bradley joined the endless fires. Massive pieces of vanquished metal soared skyward.

On the platoon's right, while Walton fired his machine gun at the rampaging jihadists, he heard the sudden result and saw the vivid display out of the corner of his eye. "What the hell was that?" he exclaimed.

In the Bradley closest to Cramer's, Vigo said, "Suicide bomber hit the lieutenant's Bradley! At the last second, I turned my machine gun to take him out. But it was too late."

"Did anyone in the lieutenant's Bradley get out?"

"Negative."

"Are you in a position to go to their aid?"

"Negative. I wouldn't get ten feet before an enemy rifle cut me down. And even if I was able to reach them, it'd serve no purpose. With the size of the blast, that bastard had to have been carrying a huge amount of explosives. There's no chance anyone on the lieutenant's team survived."

80

Yet another day of wading through one nasty skirmish after another for those protecting the embassy. The lists of those who no longer lived had grown. The defending countries were desperately short of fighters. Their lines were razor-thin. The Marines were down to thirty-five men. Sixty-one had perished. Seventy-three were too seriously wounded to continue. With Lieutenant Bates's death early in the afternoon, only the company commander, executive officer, and Lieutenant Ambrose remained.

The five Green Berets had done their best to provide assistance. Even so, those shielding the embassy were depending more and more upon the volunteers they'd trained. Along with them, the fifteen survivors of Steven Gray's men had moved to the front lines.

As always, the hospital was flooded with those in need of medical care. After twenty-four endless days, the overwhelmed medical staff was on the edge of collapse.

Of the six thousand who'd once been here, less than half remained. None knew how much more those who lingered could take. One strong push and, Apaches or no Apaches, the jihadists would likely gain their prize. Owing to the defenders' good fortune, the peasants hadn't realized how brittle the battlements had become. What those protecting the faltering bastion didn't know was that the cultists were as exhausted as they were.

Those in the compound had been told help was on the way. And such hope had kept them going. Despite the struggles those attempting to come to their aid had gone through, the estimates of the 3rd Infantry arriving within the week hadn't changed. The enduring question was whether any sheltering in this hellish place would be breathing when they reached them.

With the arrival of another night, the attacks had dissipated. In the previous two hours, only a rare shot had been fired by either side. Deep within a sandbagged bunker on the western edge of the American defenses, Aaron Porter turned to his partner. "It's pretty quiet. You think you can handle things for a while? I haven't seen Fareeda in three days. I'd like to check on how she's doing."

Since shortly after their arrival, the pair had been defending an area west of the embassy. It was a spanning section that once had contained ten Marines. "Sure, no problem," Sanders responded. Even with one good arm he was still better than any five of the interlopers.

"I'll be back at the first sign of trouble."

"Don't sweat it. Go check on her. Just don't get yourself shot while out in the open. Oh . . . and bring me back a hot meal if you can find one."

Porter crawled out of the hole and edged across the fragmented landscape toward what remained of the embassy's walls. He soon found himself inside the disordered grounds. The moment he entered, he began searching for Lauren Wells and the girls he knew would be with her. It took a while, but finally he saw her cameraman heading toward one of the more intact buildings.

"Chuck . . . Chuck Mendes," he called out while waving his arm.

Mendes spotted him and came to a stop.

"Been looking all over for you guys," Porter said. "Do you know where Ms. Wells and the girls are?"

"Yeah, they're right inside."

"I wanted to check on Fareeda. Any idea if she's still awake?"

"Was last time I saw her. I'm sure she'll be thrilled to see you. Asks about you and Sergeant Sanders all the time."

Porter was standing over Wells and the girls as they sat on the floor in the first room inside the doorway. With them were scores of other people. The girls seemed to be playing some kind of game he didn't recognize. He suspected it was one Fareeda had taught MaKenna.

He hardly recognized the young Pakistani. Given all she'd done to aid their cause, the ambassador had okayed the use of a little of their precious water to clean her up and wash her face. And it had taken no effort to locate a suitcase left by one of the evacuees holding girl's clothing her size. With immense pleasure, Fareeda had picked out a floral shirt and blue jeans. Although the girl didn't say so, Wells suspected it was probably the nicest thing she'd ever worn.

"Fareeda!" he said. For the first time in forever the grizzled Green Beret smiled.

The moment she heard his voice, she looked up and smiled a radiating smile in return. Because of what she'd been taught, even though she was extremely fond of Aaron Porter, she didn't say a word.

"How's she doing?" he asked Wells.

"Considering the things she's gone through, she's doing quite well."

"I hope she hasn't been too much of an imposition."

"Imposition? Not at all. Quite the opposite, actually. I've been happy to have her. She volunteers to do things even when I haven't asked. She's also been a tremendous help with MaKenna. The two of them bonded immediately. For the first time since we arrived here, I no longer have to carry MaKenna wherever we go. Now she takes Fareeda's hand and walks along with us. To my surprise, this morning she said her first words since that horrible night at the Marriott. We can thank Fareeda for that too."

He looked at the Pakistani girl and smiled again. "All that sounds wonderful. I was so relieved you were willing to watch over her. Glad to hear she hasn't been a burden."

"Like I said, I've been pleased to have her. How could I not be? She's an incredibly sweet child." Wells turned and looked at the two of them as they continued playing. She looked back at Porter. "Why don't we step outside? There's something I need to speak with you about."

"Sure, no problem. Fareeda, I'll be right back, okay?" he said. It was clear to the filth-caked Green Beret that something was troubling Wells.

"Girls, do you mind if I go outside to speak with Sergeant Porter? Mr. Mendes is here if you need anything."

"Okay," MaKenna answered in that sweet little voice of hers while never looking up from the game.

Once they were outside, Porter turned to her. "What's on your mind?"

"Have you thought about what's going to happen to Fareeda when we leave here?"

"Not really. There hasn't been time."

"Well, I've reflected on it more than a bit. And none of the answers I've come up with are good ones. If what they're saying's true, we're not going to be here much longer. A week, no more, and, God willing, we'll leave this vile place. Once we're gone, who knows what might happen to her."

Without a second thought, Porter blurted out, "Nothing's going to happen to her. I'll see to that. After all she's been through, there's no way I'm leaving her here. She has no one. Her friends and family are dead. Her village has been destroyed. Even if we defeat Salim Basra, Pakistan's going to be in horrible shape, with thousands upon thousands of issues needing to be resolved. There'll be no time and no one who's going to care about one little girl. But I do. So I'm taking Fareeda with me back to the States. If I don't, she'll be dead within the year."

"Look, I agree with you on what her fate will be. But my question is: How're you possibly going to bring her with you? Even if it's possible, who's going to care for her when you're away for a year or more on some far-flung assignment? What'll happen to her if you don't come back? You're still single, right?"

"Yes."

"And if I remember correctly, you told me once you have no brothers or sisters. You also said you haven't spoken with your mother or father in years. Has any of that changed?"

"Not really."

"So even if they let you take her, there'll be no one to care for her when you're not around."

He paused, thinking over his response. "I guess not," he admitted. He looked into Wells's eyes. His jaw tightened. "I guess if that's what it takes, I'll request a discharge."

"Quit the Army? You?"

"Yes, ma'am."

"Tell me again: How long have you been in?"

"Fifteen years."

"So you've got five more before you'd be eligible to retire. You're really not going to throw that away, are you?"

"Until now, I hadn't given it much thought. But if it'll save her life, what choice do I have?"

"Sergeant Porter, you and I both know there's no way you'd give up being a Green Beret. It's who you are. I doubt you've the slightest idea what you'd do without it. I can't picture you being happy as a security guard at some backwater mall. Can you?"

"I guess not. But I don't see how my situation's that different from the one you have with MaKenna. Didn't you tell me on the morning we arrived that if you couldn't find a relative who was willing to take her, you were going to do everything possible to keep her and raise her as your own?"

"I did."

"Well, then you need to be honest too. The demands of your job aren't all that different from mine. You're always headed to who knows where to cover the latest breaking story. So you can't guarantee you'll be able to provide a stable environment for MaKenna, either. And I don't see you giving up the job you love in order to care for that little girl."

"True. But you're really comparing apples and oranges here. What I have are a number of friends who'd take care of her if I have to be gone for a few days. And if I need to be away for a lengthy period, my mother would be eager to fly in from Chicago to stay with her. I can't tell you how many times she's told me she's dying to have a granddaughter. So I have a backup system. You have none."

His head dropped. "But it's going to be so hard to face this—turning my back and walking away."

"I know. But you've got to be realistic. If we survive the next few days, it won't be long before helicopters arrive to whisk us out of here. And it's not like you can bring Fareeda along and that will be that. Even if you decide you're going to give up everything for her, there's going to be tons of red tape involved in getting her out of here. It's not like we can drag a Pakistani child along with us with no questions asked. It might take months, even years, to work through the mountain of paperwork involved in such an action. You said yourself, Fareeda doesn't have that kind of time. So tell me again what you're going to do when the time comes to get on those helicopters?"

She hadn't intentionally set out to crush him. But someone had to ensure he understood where things stood. If not, when the time came, she suspected Porter and the girl would both be devastated. From the expression on his face, it was clear he was beginning to understand the reality of the situation. Dejected, he looked at Wells. A deep pain inched across his brow. He wasn't, however, ready to give up.

"There's got to be something we can do. Someone who can help," he said.

Even though she suspected it was futile, she didn't want to leave him without a glimmer of hope. "Before you return to your foxhole, why don't you speak with Ambassador Ingram? He knows Pakistan better than anyone. When he's not on the front lines carrying stretchers, he's been trying to determine if Kari McCaffrey had a sister. And how we'll handle things if she doesn't. He's doing all he can for me. Maybe he can come up with a way to help you too."

81

It was over. The horrific endeavor had ended in the dark of night thirty-six hours earlier. The battle's results were appalling. Over one million jihadists had perished. More than 70 percent of those who'd endured were wounded. With no medical care, many would perish in the coming days. Their leadership was gone. No one remained to guide their efforts. The stunned peasants were disoriented and confused. For the disheartened masses, only a token few were interested in continuing to resist. The majority had lost their taste for war. Most had thrown down their weapons and walked away.

As the smoke cleared, the Allies' numbers weren't exactly encouraging. The Americans had experienced three thousand casualties, the French and British even more. After the abhorrent onslaught, it had taken the division a day to gather its dead and wounded, resupply its units, and lick its gaping wounds. Finally the orders had come: "Leave your defensive positions and attack the enemy wherever you find him."

The breakout had occurred two hours earlier. It had taken little effort to brush aside the scattered cultists who stood in their way. With Walton in the lead and the platoon's other fighting vehicles flanking him, they rushed across the landscape. Two hundred yards behind them, the M1 platoon kept pace. To their rear, the division's unyielding caravan stretched for miles. Above, Apaches and Black Hawks kept watch. Reaper drones buzzed in every direction.

There were bodies and burned-out armored vehicles across the Allied front. They stretched far and wide. Yet finally the Americans broke free and reached a major highway running alongside the Indus River. For the first few hundred miles their intentions were to never stray far from the wide river. Through heavy agricultural areas and mangrove swamps, they'd work their way toward the northeast.

At a cautious fifteen miles per hour, the point element continued on. With Walton in command of the platoon, their broad tracks churned across the countryside. Every so often they'd hear smatterings of gunfire, but nothing overly significant. Always on alert, the veteran sergeant moved forward.

What lay ahead, they didn't know. At this point, they had no concept of how complete their victory had been. Each assumed the fanatics were re-forming. They suspected somewhere ahead the enemy had prepared a sturdy defensive network. Over the next hill, around the coming corner, Walton was certain a lethal engagement would be waiting.

None realized that the southern Fedayeen were in disarray. Only when cornered were they putting up the slightest resistance.

Inside the Bradleys, a sullen stillness consumed their worlds. After the death of the lieutenant and his crew, and the battering they'd taken, few words had passed between them since the attack ended. After inflicting so much suffering and receiving their share in return, an ominous black cloud consumed their battered psyches. An open wound, deep and painful, was crusting on their souls. From his intense combat in far too many wars, Walton understood no matter how long he lived, his anguish would never heal. And the vivid images of what had happened some hours earlier would forever live within him.

82

8:47 A.M., NOVEMBER 28
C COMPANY (BLUE MAX), 3RD BATTALION,
10TH AVIATION REGIMENT, 10TH COMBAT AVIATION BRIGADE,
10TH MOUNTAIN DIVISION (LIGHT INFANTRY)
CAMP NOWHERE
THE SPĪN GHAR MOUNTAINS OF NORTH-CENTRAL PAKISTAN

Their Black Hawk's repairs had been completed not a moment too soon. Scant minutes later, the urgent call came in. Near an isolated ridgetop, a half dozen men were trapped by an overwhelming insurgent force. They'd gotten separated from their unit and were trapped in a box canyon. One American was dead, with the remainder suffering wounds running the gamut from minor to severe.

There was no time to spare. Washington's crew rushed to their helicopter. It took some time, but finally all was ready. "Deicing's complete, ma'am," White said. "Engines and instrumentation looks fine."

Washington brought her fingertips to her lips and touched her daughters' picture. She lifted the straining craft into the air. As she did, a fifty-mile-per-hour gust came out of nowhere. It blew them sideways with her holding on with everything she had. Nonetheless, the sudden squall was little more than a momentary distraction. As quickly as it had appeared, the wind returned to manageable levels. She steadied the Black Hawk and raced skyward.

It would take eighteen minutes to reach the canyon. They had no idea what they'd find when they arrived. They would have loved to have had Apaches in support, but none of the far-flung attack helicopters were close enough to be able to do so. For this mission, they were on their own.

Rushing in from the north, they soared over the lip of the confining ravine. "There they are!" White exclaimed. "They're pressed up against the canyon wall on the southern side. At least a few are alive; I can see them firing. And hundreds of rifles are firing back."

The moment the Black Hawk pilot located the spot, a frown seized her. With where those she'd been sent to rescue were located, it was going to be nearly impossible to reach them. "How the hell are we going to extract them from there?" she said as they buzzed overhead with scores of AK-47 rounds trailing their shadow.

Her copilot paused, searching the scene for an answer. Yet nothing came to him. "Haven't a clue, ma'am. But we can't leave 'em there. We've got to do something."

They turned and rushed toward the menacing conflict in progress. As they did so, she seized upon an approach. It would be beyond precarious, but it was all they had. "With them pressed against the wall, the only chance we've got is to land between our guys and the enemy. With the edge of the canyon so near, it appears the best we can do is to set down about twenty feet north of them."

"Are you sure, ma'am?" White understood the extreme danger such an attempt would create. "I don't see how we'd possibly survive such a move."

"Well, if you've got a better idea, Shaun, let me hear it." Her comment was met with silence. "Risky or not, the one thing I'm not doing is turning and running away." She directed her next comment to her crew chiefs. "Not sure whether it's going to be better to land with our nose pointing east or west. But whichever way it is, the machine gun on that side will need to attempt suppressing fire while the other heads out to help get our guys on board. Don't know how many trips it'll take, but you're not to leave even one behind. Is that clear?"

Both responded with, "Yes, ma'am."

"Now let's do this."

She headed the Black Hawk toward the swirling chaos. Machine guns firing, they landed a short distance from the besieged Americans. The moment the skis touched, Sergeant Mercado leaped out and raced toward the wayward force. White rushed out to join him. Vinson and those on the ground unleashed everything they had against the jihadists. Yet their efforts had little effect. Scores of rounds slammed into the stationary Black Hawk. Its left engine sputtered. Moments later, with black smoke pouring from it, it died. They were down to two engines. But the remaining pair were more than enough to get them home.

Mercado grabbed one of the severely wounded and carried him toward the waiting craft. With bullets striking everywhere, he placed the American in the hold.

"How we doing out there?" Washington turned and asked.

Out of the corner of his eye, Mercado could see White approaching with yet another. "Need another trip for the last of the wounded and dead." His words were rushed. "Once we've got them, the two with lesser wounds will try to make it over on their own. The moment they do, we can get the hell out of here." He turned and raced back for another. White showed up with a second injured soldier. Dropping him in the rear compartment, he ran toward the one who lived no more.

In seconds, Mercado was heading toward the Black Hawk with another wounded soldier. Behind him, White picked up the lifeless form and carried it toward the helicopter. The final pair hobbled along with him. It wouldn't be long before they'd make their escape. Fifteen seconds and they'd be in a position to do so.

Suddenly, the Black Hawk's machine gun stopped firing. A puzzled Washington turned to look behind her. Inside the hold, Vinson was lying in a pool of blood. She glanced to her right. Her concluding human cargo was almost there. But so was something else.

Scarcely a blur, it ripped across the landscape toward the helicopter. Mercado, White, and the struggling pair had just reached the Black Hawk when the RPG hit. It struck dead center. In a tremendous blast, the wavering Black Hawk exploded. In less than a passing instant, the craft was engulfed in a ferocious blaze. The Americans were trapped. There'd be no escape. Its feral flames would soon overwhelm them.

Still alive, even if only barely, Bea Washington brought her fingertip to her bloodied lips. With her final breath, she reached out to touch her daughters' picture.

83

A single vehicle roared toward the encampment and came to a stop. Its screeching brakes announced its sudden appearance. Basra's oldest son, Muhsin, was behind the wheel. The moment he emerged from the vehicle, he said to the first person he saw, "Where's my father? I need to speak with him immediately."

The sentry pointed. Muhsin ran in the direction indicated. It didn't take long to reach his father. Out of breath, he yelled, "Father, I must speak with you. I've spent the night trying to locate your encampment. Thank the one true God I was able to do so. I didn't expect to find you in this place. What has caused you to leave the mountains and move so near Islamabad?"

"The foreign dogs have forced me from the safety of the snow-covered hills. I've had no choice than to take refuge here. What is it you want, my son?"

"I have come from the south. With me, I carry terrible news. An overpowering American force is on its way. They're being led by hundreds of armored vehicles and are moving fast. They're no more than two hundred kilometers from here. With every passing minute they shorten the distance between us. There's nothing to slow them. Our remaining southern units have been smashed. We're essentially defeated. What holy warriors remain will be brushed aside in the coming hours. It's my belief that in less than a day the Americans will reach Islamabad. If we wish to live, we must leave this place and hide deep within the tribal territories."

Despite what Muhsin had told him, Basra wasn't ready to accept his impending defeat. "I don't understand. Bila Chachar promised he'd lead us to victory. Why has he failed me?"

"Bila's dead, Father. Has been for a number of days."

Rather than responding to his son's horrific words, Basra turned to his followers. The intense fixation he carried hadn't waned. "Before we consider withdrawing, I must know: Does the American embassy still stand?" Fearing what the repercussions might be, none said a word. The highly volatile Basra's patience was at its end. "Does it?" he screamed.

"It stands," one quietly said.

To their surprise, such information appeared to calm him. It gave him something to focus upon other than Muhsin's unsettling news. "Such may be true. But it won't be standing much longer. Before we make our escape, I promise you we'll kill everyone cowering within it." He paused ever so slightly. "There can be no delay. We'll strike in the next few hours. We'll destroy all we find inside its walls. By nightfall, our swords will run red. I'll join you and lead you to a rapturous victory. With me at its head, our army will prevail in this final battle."

It was another of his false assertions. Basra would accompany them and give every appearance of being involved in the fray. He had every intention, however, of remaining safe. Rather than leading his followers as they stormed the walls, he'd secrete himself out of harm's way while others perished in his service.

"But, Father," Muhsin said, "you heard what the American attack helicopters did to those who attempted to do as you describe. Such an assault will cost thousands of lives."

"Such losses are of no consequence. All that matters is for those whose presence makes a mockery of Islam's holy lands to pay for their insolence."

"Father, please reconsider. I beg you not to do this. We're out of time. We need to flee before it's too late."

But Basra's mind was made up. "Gather our men. Under my direction, the American embassy will fall."

84

They hadn't been prepared for this. With the war all but over, the last thing those guarding the assailed compound had expected was another enormous attack. Nevertheless, when the threat appeared, they had responded quickly.

In the past ten minutes, a handful of Camp Nowhere's fearsome Apaches had arrived. With a mighty thrust, they'd roared into the formidable battle. Guns blazing, rockets firing, they swarmed over every inch of the contested field. A thousand fresh bodies had been added to the accursed landscape. And the attack helicopters scarcely had begun.

Even with the toll the Apaches were taking, the swarming peasants were nearing. With so massive an onslaught, it wouldn't be long before the weakened outpost would be overrun.

On the western edge of their fraying lines, Sanders and Porter fired their rifles at one inviting target after the next. Yet, screaming at the top of their lungs, the unceasing fanatics continued to scramble across the chaotic landscape.

When he paused to catch his breath, Porter spotted something strange in the distance. Numerous figures were crowded around a single individual. With each outlandish movement his animated gestures were causing one or more to scramble away.

"You see what I'm seeing?" Porter asked. He fired a lightning burst at a group of insurgents working their way through the shattered concrete two hundred yards away. A pair went down.

"What's that?" Sanders replied.

"Out there at ten o'clock—the crazy bastard jumping around and waving his arms? He's inside what's left of that big building. Most of the time he's hidden by the steel pillars. But every once in a while I get a glimpse of him."

It took Sanders a moment to find the location his partner was describing. The instant he identified the spot he stopped, examining the scene. The antics of whoever it was were beyond normal. "Oh, yeah," Sanders said. "What's with him? That guy's got to be nuts."

"Maybe. But do you see how those around him are responding? They look like they're terrified." Perplexed, he studied the situation further. "Hold them off for a minute," Porter said. "There's something I need to do."

The senior Green Beret spoke into his headset. "Sir, this is Sergeant Porter. Charlie and I have spotted a figure who appears to be giving orders. The way those around him are acting, he must be somebody important. I think we should take him out. Unfortunately, he's at least a mile from here. He's too far away for me to attempt to nail with my M4. Any chance you can lay your hands on a sniper rifle?"

"Not a problem. We've got one here," Erickson responded. "Gunny Joyce has been using it when a target appears to be of significant interest. Any chance we can eliminate him from where we are?"

"Negative. It looks like our only shot would be from here. If you can get me that rifle, I'll do what I can to take him down."

Erickson looked at the gunnery sergeant.

"I'll bring it to him, sir," Joyce said.

With bullets striking the area around the bunker, Erickson paused. "Do you think you can reach him?"

"Who the hell knows? But if Aaron Porter says the target's worth the effort, I'm sure going to try." Before Erickson could reply, Joyce grabbed the rifle and rushed out of the bunker.

"Gunny's on the way. Do what you can to provide suppressing fire," Erickson told the pair.

In a semi-crouch, Joyce rushed toward them. He had two hundred yards to cover in the middle of an extreme firefight.

Joyce dove into the foxhole. He squeezed in between Porter and Sanders. The stalwart Marine had been lucky. A single grazing shot had nicked his left arm. The superficial wound hadn't slowed him in the slightest. Out of breath, he handed the sniper rifle to Porter.

In halting words he said, "The target still there?"

"Yep," Porter said as he lifted the rifle and started zeroing it in. He adjusted the scope. The winds appeared relatively calm. Yet, at so great a distance, even if they were mild, they could affect the shot's trajectory. While he pointed the rifle and brought the target into view he asked, "What do ya think, Charlie?"

"Two clicks to the left."

"Sounds about right."

Porter made the minor correction. He was only going to get one shot. And the distance alone was making this an immense challenge. If he missed, the person he was targeting would drop behind the protective steel and stay there. The opportunity would be gone.

His victim continued moving about. But by all appearances he seemed to be making a concerted effort not to expose himself. With the girders shielding him, it was going to take a great deal of patience. The figure seldom stilled. Because of it, it was going to be exceptionally difficult to find the precise moment to release the round.

A minute passed. Using Porter's M4, Joyce joined Sanders in the fraught attempt to hold off the surging enemy. Porter, his breathing shallow, held the sniper's rifle perfectly still. But his shot didn't appear. With the agitated figure remaining hidden, his chance of taking him out might never come. Still, as he considered relaxing the rifle, he saw a portion of a head appear from behind the distorted metal beam on the right. It remained there momentarily. Even so, it wasn't enough for the talented Green Beret to have confidence in his actions.

"Come on, just a little more," he whispered. Much to his surprise, his objective complied. The figure stepped out from behind the restrictive barriers and waved his arms once again.

Porter fired. The bullet raced toward its victim.

Salim Basra had opened his mouth to berate his son and those around him. But before the first syllable escaped his lips, the racing projectile struck him in the center of his forehead. The back of his head exploded. Without a sound, he slumped into Muhsin's arms. The perverse Fedayeen leader was dead.

Unaware of what had happened, his followers continued to fight and die. But as word of Basra's death spread, each ceased his efforts and slunk away. Without their revered leader, God's exalted messenger, their grand purpose couldn't endure. It took little more than fifteen minutes for the final shot to be fired. And as scores of messengers went out, it did not take long for the jihadists to vanish from every battlefield. Each would drift away, heading to the place from which they'd come. The Fedayeen Islam was no more. Even if the Americans didn't yet know it, the conflict had reached its end.

85

10:19 P.M., NOVEMBER 29
4TH PLATOON, BRAVO COMPANY, 2ND BATTALION,
69TH ARMOR REGIMENT, 2ND ARMORED BRIGADE COMBAT
TEAM (SPARTANS), 3RD INFANTRY DIVISION
FIFTEEN MILES FROM THE UNITED STATES EMBASSY
ISLAMABAD, PAKISTAN

The trio of fighting vehicles rumbled down the Kashmir Highway. Behind them, an endless formation of armored units and heavily armed soldiers continued toward the city. Walton searched the anxious night for signs of the enemy. None, however, appeared.

The once-vibrant city came into view. As they saw the immense damage, to a man the Americans were at a loss to explain the insanity through which they were moving. None could comprehend the depravity it would take to do such things.

Where the Fedayeen were, Walton had no clue. The Allies had destroyed the jihadists' southern army. Yet, to the best of his knowledge, in the north a million or more remained. While they'd moved across the country, chewing up the miles, they'd been told to expect another fierce fight when they neared Islamabad. It hadn't happened. None in the division had faced a single shot in the past six hours.

Acting as the division's trigger, Walton continued to search far and wide. The unanticipated situation he was wading through was almost as frightening as the fiercest of battles had been. He understood around the bend untold multitudes could be waiting to take their lives.

As they moved deeper into the city, Walton said, "Aiden, based on the GPS, the American embassy should only be a short distance away."

"On the left or right?" his driver asked.

"Left. Slow a bit. Looks like it's safe enough for Evan and me to pop our hatches and help you locate it."

The gunner's and commander's hatches on the Bradley's turret opened. Two heads appeared. They continued on, each searching their accursed surroundings. That was when Evan Minter saw it. It was one of the few places where some semblance of buildings still stood. "Wait . . . could that be it?" He pointed to an area a few hundred yards away.

Walton looked in the direction Minter had indicated. The longer he surveyed the scene, the more his confidence grew.

"Got to be," Walton said. He took a look at the highway ahead. "Aiden, there doesn't appear to be an off-ramp nearby. Take her forward another hundred yards. When you find a decent spot, ease down the embankment and take us on in. I'll let Battalion know what we've found. When we reach the compound, give me a second to speak with whoever's in command to see where they want us to set up our defenses."

86

The scorched, bomb-cratered field south of the embassy held a half dozen large helicopters. Stretcher by stretcher, the first three had taken on the worst of the wounded. The weary doctors and nurses had joined them for the lengthy journey. The trio took to the skies.

The fourth Chinook's hold was filling with relieved souls. Inside the embassy grounds, Steven Gray was holding the manifests and calling out one name after another to the anxious gathering. Once he had identified those who would be in the next grouping, they were turned over to Eric Joyce to direct onto a particular craft. They were queueing outside the main gate in groups of fifty or more. The taxed pair had done their best to identify the survivors and their countries of origin. It had been no small undertaking. Based on when their flights would depart Karachi, they had grouped them in ways that made a great deal of sense.

The first of the remaining Chinooks would be carrying the Swedes, Norwegians, and Germans. The second, those headed for

Asian destinations, and the third, the English, French, Dutch, and Spanish. An additional half dozen craft were scheduled to arrive within the hour. More would follow. The lengthy process, which would continue well into the night, was underway.

Bone-tired individuals were walking across the bloodied grounds. All were elated to have heard their names called. Yet none was overly joyful. They were still in this perverse place and there'd been too many surprises in the past weeks for any to relax. While they struggled toward the helicopters, few looked up to take in the dreadful scene extending in every direction. With thousands upon thousands of Fedayeen corpses remaining on the disordered landscape, they had no need to relive what the endless days had wrought. They'd seen too much of killing. And none wanted to be reminded of it.

They were eager to leave this horrid place. As they struggled toward the Chinooks, with every step they grew nearer to their transport and the freedom it represented. When they crossed the roadway south of the embassy, their haggard but genuine relief grew. Their time in the darkest corners of Dante's imagination was complete. Despite the incredible odds, they'd somehow survived. In minutes, they'd take to the air and leave this accursed vista.

With the processions continuing, the ambassador walked up to where Sam and Lauren stood watching the helicopters loading. "How many have loaded so far?" the ambassador asked.

"First three, holding wounded, are gone. These are numbers four, five, and six," Erickson responded. "Four's about ready to leave. Won't be long until the other two do likewise. Which manifest are you and your folks on, Mr. Ambassador?"

"I'm not leaving until all these folks have departed. So, like you, I'll be on the final one. With so many people waiting, it looks like it'll be a number of hours until it'll be our turn."

"Then what? What comes next for you?" Lauren asked.

"Going to take a lengthy vacation. Planning on visiting my son, his wife, and the grandchildren. I'll stay until they've had enough of me. Which, to tell you the truth, may not be all that long. Maybe visit my brother and do a little fishing. Suspect some time on a quiet riverbank might do me some good. Then I'm coming back."

"Back here?" she said.

"Yes. It's going to take a great deal of effort to rebuild. Probably years. Even so, the Pakistanis have decided to keep Islamabad as their capital. So the United States embassy will remain where it is."

"Don't you think you've seen enough of this place?" Erickson asked.

"More than enough. But the president asked me to return. Said he couldn't think of a better person for the job. So what was I going to do? I guess I could've said no. And to tell you the truth, I came close to doing so. But in the end I just couldn't."

The lines of evacuees continued. Number six was filling.

"Were Mr. Gray and Gunny Joyce able to get an accurate count of how many survived?" Erickson asked.

"Twenty-seven hundred and fifty-three, from what we can see."

Erickson didn't say a word as he took in the implications of the number he'd been given. Counting the twelve hundred women and children who'd escaped in the first couple of days, they'd been able to save nearly four thousand people. Yet a third had succumbed, including many of his men. He'd silently suffered every loss. Even so, as he watched the loading, he also understood he'd been able to save the majority of those he'd been sent to protect. At the moment, he had no clue how to feel. He had no idea when the implications, both good and bad, would hit him.

"Next helicopter's taking off," an elated Wells said.

They turned to watch the Chinook rise and rush toward the southwest. With a refueling stop at Jahar, it was going to be an uncomfortable four hours locked in the belly of the helicopter. Still it mattered not to any.

On the perimeter, Porter and Walton stood talking. They paused to watch the departing Chinook. "So you promise to watch the girl until your unit departs in a couple of weeks?" Porter asked.

"Sure. No problem. Was hoping to be with my family for Christmas, but it looks like that's not going to happen. Tenth Mountain got lucky. They're returning home first. We're staying to ensure things stay like they are and to protect the graves registration folks while they work. They've got tons of enemy bodies to deal with and two thousand or so buried on the embassy grounds to dig up and return to their countries of origin. They're estimating that's going to take two to three weeks, possibly longer. Then we'll be on our way. I've got a couple of daughters of my own, so I'd be happy to watch Fareeda until we pull out."

"Can't tell you how much I appreciate it. That little girl means the world to me. I'll let her know whenever she needs something she's to look for you." He stuck out his hand to shake Walton's. Without another word Porter walked away. His head drooped as he moved toward the embassy. It would be a temporary solution at best, but at least he'd found a way to keep her safe for a little while longer. Still, he understood it wasn't going to be nearly enough.

And the worst was yet to come. In a few hours, he was going to have to do the most difficult thing he'd ever envisioned. He was going to depart on the final helicopter and leave Fareeda behind.

11:39 P.M., NOVEMBER 30
ALPHA COMPANY, 3RD BATTALION,
6TH MARINE REGIMENT, 2ND MARINE DIVISION
UNITED STATES EMBASSY
ISLAMABAD, PAKISTAN

The scene had been worse than Wells had feared. Fareeda was in tears, MaKenna hysterical, and Porter crushed. A similarly dejected Charlie Sanders had been forced to drag him away.

Along with Ambassador Ingram, the five enduring Green Berets were at the front of those approaching the helicopter. Erickson's remaining Marines weren't far behind. As they trudged through the darkness toward the Chinook, not one said a word. Each disappeared into its hold.

Lauren and Sam were right behind, with MaKenna between them. Erickson stopped at the end of the ramp, unwilling to enter. Lauren and MaKenna continued on. Even with the company's survivors waiting inside, he stood his ground. He'd vowed to be the last to leave this place. It was a promise he was going to keep. "Everyone on board?" he asked.

"Waiting on Sergeant Joyce and Steven Gray," the ambassador

said. "They were double-checking the compound to make sure we didn't miss anyone. Should be joining us shortly."

"You heard the ambassador," Lauren said. "We're about to go. Why don't you come on in and sit down, Sam?"

"I'm fine where I am." As the words left his mouth, he saw Joyce running toward them. The moment he reached Erickson he asked, "Sir, where's the ambassador?"

"Inside." Erickson gestured toward the open hold.

Joyce hurried past. Even in the darkened compartment, it didn't take long to spot Ingram. "Sorry to bother you, Mr. Ambassador. But Mr. Gray sent me to find you. Having checked all the other buildings and found no one, we entered the main one to make sure it was empty. As we were leaving, the phone in your office rang. It was the State Department. Said they need to speak with you about something important. Something that couldn't wait."

Ingram got up and headed with Joyce toward the ramp. While passing Erickson, he said, "Sorry for the inconvenience. I know none of us wants to stay here even a moment longer than we have to. But when the boss calls, you've got to answer. Hopefully, whatever it is won't take long."

The pair hurried across the field and entered the compound. When he reached what remained of his office, Steven Gray was standing there holding the phone.

"What is it?" the out-of-breath ambassador mouthed.

Gray shrugged. He handed him the phone.

"Alan Ingram."

Ten minutes passed . . . then fifteen. Those in the Chinook were growing uneasy. Finally, Erickson saw four figures approaching. As they grew closer, he realized it was Eric Joyce, Steven Gray,

Alan Ingram, and to his surprise, Fareeda. The group stopped in front of him.

Inside the hold, Porter looked out to see the girl standing little more than ten feet away. He leaped from his seat and rushed to join her.

"What's she doing here?" Erickson asked.

"She's going with us," Ingram responded, trying to sound as nonchalant as possible.

"What?" Porter said.

"I said she's going with us."

"I . . . I don't understand," a stammering Porter answered.

"It's kind of a long story. After you asked me to see if I could do anything to help Fareeda, I made a few calls. Didn't want to say anything at the time because I didn't think it'd amount to much. I was glad I didn't, because by all appearances my efforts had failed. I'd heard nothing back from the State Department, so I figured all hope was lost. But I was wrong."

"How so, Mr. Ambassador?"

"When the president found out about Fareeda's plight, he put everybody on the case: FBI, Homeland Security, Health and Human Services, you name it. At the last minute they struck pay dirt. It turns out some of her family's closest friends had left Fareeda's village and immigrated to the United States some years ago. They ended up settling outside Kansas City. Both have good jobs and are extremely happy with their decision to do so. In fact, both became American citizens some months back. When they were informed of Fareeda's plight, neither the man nor the woman hesitated. Both said they'd never forgive themselves if they didn't help. So they've agreed to take her in. From what I was told, their children were quite close to her when they were little and the entire family's quite excited by her joining them."

Porter looked down at her and asked, "Fareeda, are you okay

with this? Do you want to go to the United States and live with these people?"

"Oh, yes. Very much," the delighted girl said.

"The reason it took me so long to return was I knew even that wouldn't be enough to allow her to leave. So I placed an additional call, this time to General Bhatti. As the temporary head of the Pakistani government, I figured he'd be the one to speak with about her. After explaining the situation, it didn't take much for him to say yes. So Fareeda's going to America."

"Oh, my God, that's wonderful!" Lauren said.

"But that wasn't the only information I received from the State Department. This news, however, involves MaKenna. It turns out Kari McCaffrey did have a sister—one who's more than willing to take her in. She and her husband will be waiting in New York when you arrive."

"Got to admit, everyone out here was growing more than a bit frustrated by having to wait," Erickson said. "But as it turned out, it looks like every second of it was time well spent. Anything else we need to know?"

Ingram, Gray, and Joyce looked at each other. "Not that I can think of," the ambassador said.

"So is everyone who needs to leave present?" Erickson asked.

"Yes, sir," Joyce said.

"Then let's get as far away from here as we can."

They scrambled on board. A beaming Fareeda settled into a stiff seat on the left side of the helicopter between MaKenna and Aaron Porter.

Erickson sat down next to the woman he loved. In the seat nearest the rear entrance, he turned to take a final look outside. The ramp started closing behind him. He let out a deep sigh.

Lauren wrapped her arms around him. Tears began to flow.

As the Chinook rose, the clock reached 12:01. It was December's first moment. In the darkened compartment, Erickson searched each haggard, filth-streaked face.

It had been a long November for them all.

EPILOGUE

On the busy docks, the loading and unloading at the country's major port went on without pause. With the war over, the location was busier than ever. On the harbor's westernmost dock, two huge cranes, serving separate ships, reached down to snatch heavily loaded pallets filled with wooden crates of every sort, size, and description.

The cargo soon dangled in the air as it was swung over the side of each vessel and edged toward its forward hold. Each load was positioned aboard the massive commercial ships.

In the middle of each pallet, a nondescript box was hidden among the endless containers. Like those around it, both crates were identified on the bill of lading as "textiles." Yet they were anything but. The missing tactical nuclear weapons from Mishira were on the way to their final destinations.

Shortly before noon, each ship slipped its mooring to begin its long journey. The first was headed to the Port of Baltimore. When it arrived, the lethal box's ultimate destination would be the center of Washington, D.C. The second would tender at the Port of New York on a cold December morning. Times Square awaited.

Each would land in time for the Christmas holiday, when the Americans' defenses would be at their most vulnerable. Both would slip unnoticed through customs. Within days, they'd reach their final objectives.

Even after his death, the malevolent Salim Basra's surprise for an unsuspecting world would reach America's doorstep.

Photo by Charles Quinn Photography

Walt Gragg lives in the Austin, Texas, area with his wife, children, and grandchildren. He is a retired attorney and former Texas state prosecutor. Prior to law school, he spent a number of years in the military. His time with the Army involved many interesting assignments, including three years in the middle of the Cold War serving at United States European Command headquarters in Germany. His first novel, the critically acclaimed *The Red Line*, was named the 2017 Best Book Award winner for best thriller/adventure novel and was a 2018 International Thriller Writers best first novel finalist.

VISIT WALT GRAGG ONLINE

WaltGraggBooks.com

 WaltGraggBooks

Ready to find
your next great read?

Let us help.

Visit prh.com/nextread

Penguin
Random
House